AS IF LOVE WERE ENOUGH

Also by Anne Taylor Fleming

MARRIAGE: A DUET
MOTHERHOOD DEFERRED

AS IF LOVE WERE ENOUGH

A Novel

Anne Taylor Fleming

New York

Library of Congress Cataloging-in-Publication Data

Fleming, Anne Taylor.
As if love were enough : a novel / Anne Taylor Fleming.
p.   cm.
ISBN 1-4013-0105-3
1. Single mothers—Fiction.   2. Domestic fiction.   I. Title.

PS3606.L458A9   2006
813'.54—dc22
2005045619

Hyperion books are available for special promotions
and premiums. For details contact Michael Rentas,
Assistant Director, Inventory Operations, Hyperion,
77 West 66th Street, 12th floor, New York,
New York 10023, or call 212-456-0133.

FIRST EDITION

1   3   5   7   9   10   8   6   4   2

Book design by Jennifer Ann Daddio

To my stepsons:
Charles, David, Russell, and Mark

AS IF LOVE WERE ENOUGH

BOOK ONE

. 1 .

I never meant to fall in love with a married man. Who in their right mind—or right heart—would do such a thing? It is the route of sure pain, of melodrama, of comings and goings, of clutchings and leavings, the stuff of grand opera and soap opera. And if you are single, as I was and am, it is to settle for a half-life— only he is doing the coming and going while you wait, by the phone, the door, the bed, always part of you alert for his reappearance and disappearance, as I have done again this weekend. Coming into them, I always anticipate the voluptuous loneliness these weekends bring, pajamas all day, the special provender I lay in: a bottle of Cabernet, cartons of takeout, a video or two, and, yes, sometimes a tabloid or two as well. They are trashy and distracting when the hours go on and sleep won't come and the Ambien isn't working and you've watched the world's woes scroll by ad nauseum on the cable channels, flicking the remote, trolling for tragedy. The national pastime. A kid in a well, a bomb at an embassy, a hurricane battering a coastline, the drenched reporters still managing to do disaster play-by-play in their stentorian voices. Whatever did we do—we social pariahs, we shut-ins—without all-news, all-the-time. I have nicknamed myself: the CNN mistress. When I tell my lover this, he laughs with a flicker of guilty commiseration, but he doesn't say anything, no "I'm sorry"s, and I don't say anything. Never ever.

There are rules and we follow them. It is the only way to survive in this clandestine nest. And we have survived, six years and counting. I am forty-one. The math is easy. I have been a mistress right through the waning of my fertility. The joke is on me.

I go to the kitchen to get a glass of wine. It's only 6:43. Too early to eat. There's a long night ahead, but I've made it almost all the way through the weekend. That's an achievement. I've counted. Five years, 52 weekends, a total of 260 Sunday nights like this one. Sitting back down in my tastefully muted living room (the occasional maroon pillow, yellow sunflower, blue vase to give that little dash of color), I glance at the TV, hoping for just one of those distracting dramas somewhere on the planet, but alas, no, just more pompous pundits giving their inside-the-beltway spiels. I am, as usual, cradling the telephone, but jump anyway when it rings in my lap. A computer voice offering a line of credit. Damn, damn. He will call when he has a chance. Always has, always will. Always will, always has. He will, won't he? I wander toward the bedroom, thinking I might try one of my videos, but am drawn to the bathroom window, which has the best view in the apartment. I spend a lot of time here, standing on the toilet, craning out the small window above it. This is my perch, my view of the city. It is wet-warm after the afternoon rain and smells good. I love New York at night. It is still so strange, so dazzling to my Southern California eyes, even though I've been here now for nearly nine years. On a rooftop nearby, people in fancy clothes are moving about, like pretend figures on a stage. The sky is navy with streaks of black, and lights are coming on in faraway squares in tall buildings. Bling, bling. I'm home, I'm here—the anonymous urban greeting. I never tire of watching this nighttime ritual. Many nights, different seasons, swaddled sometimes against the winter cold, muffler around my ears, my head propped on mittened hands, or summer-sweaty in bra and underpants (my lover, Michael, surprising me one night, tiptoeing into the apartment—

must have sensed I was in there, he knows my habits—coming up behind me: "Don't move," he said). It is now October. Autumn. Pretty words both, but freighted with elegy. Daylight saving ending this weekend. I dread it. Slash—nighttime pressing down earlier and earlier, cocktail hour dropping perilously into the late afternoon, especially if you work at home as I do. The cold imminent. The clanking of the radiator. I swear I can hear it already. *Clank, clank, clank.*

But it's the phone ringing in my hand.

"Baby, it's me."

He is whispering into the phone. I can hear people talking in the background. I whisper back, "You okay?"

"So far," he says. Then, laughing, "Why are you whispering?"

"Don't know," I say, smiling. "I guess 'cause you are."

"Shit," he says, "here comes somebody. Call you back."

And he is gone again. On their rooftop the partygoers are now carrying plates of food. Candles have been lighted and everything looks very flickery and festive. Some of the women have thrown on brightly colored shawls—make that pashminas. I strain to see more closely, even though hanging on the back of the bathroom door is a pair of binoculars that Michael gave me four Christmases ago and which I never use.

"I don't want to see anybody," I said. "I just want to imagine them."

"You're weird," he said, laughing. He takes no umbrage at spurned gifts, not that there have been many of either—spurnings or gifts. We don't do much of that. I can't, so he doesn't. "I'll take them," he said about the binoculars, "and give them to one of the kids."

But he has forgotten them and they still hang around the door, clattering when I shut it. Things left. I can count them on one hand, even six years later: two pairs of old sweatpants, a sweatshirt with Notre Dame on it, a pair of concertedly unchic and scratched sunglasses (no sleek shades for my aging lover), and a few CDs, including his guaranteed favorite tear-tugger, Dylan Thomas reading his own poetry. Irish whiskey in hand, my Irish lover (might be obvious given the above items), will shuffle the floor in his socks, reciting along in a stage whisper.

The phone rings again.

"Hi," I say, assuming it's him. I feel someone there, but there is no answer. Then a click. Damn it again. Come on Michael. Come on, come on, come on. Find a minute, find a closet, go to the bathroom, elude them. I'm here waiting. When he does call, I will be funny and receptive as I always am. I don't rebuke or cajole or whine or talk dirty in case there is someone around; he is easy-to-blush, despite his age and been-around-the-block aura. There are rules, the discipline of the mistress. These romances (I hate the word relationships) don't tolerate much drama, contrary to popular myth. Marriages can be full of that, pushes and pulls, tears and recriminations, and they endure because of the legal bonds and the children and the shared history and the who-wants-to-divide-up-the-spoils sentiment. But in this netherworld where we mistresses live, there must be delicacy. A few too many scenes and the thing just, *poof*, blows up, goes away. He goes away. This, after all, is the place of refuge, the hiding place from the real world. Make it too real and *whammo*, you're out of the game. We are invisible, we mistresses of long standing, shadows—and what we know and what the wives know, what we, in fact, collude in, we two women, is to tiptoe around each other's existence, rarely discussing each other with our shared male, scared to tip him one way or the other. Toward her, toward me. Home or out. We collude in sharing him. We manage our jealousies. We practice denial. She has to; she has to know about me—not me me, necessarily, but some me, some younger woman he is seeing— younger because it only makes sense that I—or whoever—would be younger, since he and she are the same age, sixty-one. High school sweethearts. Tethered to the bone. Catholic. Irish Catholic. Of course.

I don't think about him with her (talk about denial): family parties, vacations, sex. Do they still do it, how often, how well? I don't ask him because I only half want to know and because I also know he will try to josh me out of the question in that lopsided smile, chin-thrusting way he has or lie, and we are already living a lie, and if you're living this lie you don't want to court others because it hurts too much. That's another irony: These hidden romances don't tolerate many lies. If he starts lying too much, and you know it—and you will know it, because you are exquisitely attuned to his moods; you cannot help it; you cannot allow yourself the wifely blindness or you will be blindsided and left with nothing—it just means he's losing interest and about to move on, or that you, with whatever is left of your mistressy pride, will have to do that first: Move on.

One thing I do know about her is that she is still attractive, in a generationally earlier beauty parlor way. I have seen a picture of her only once; I wish I hadn't because I have to block the face sometimes on nights when he is not with me, sometimes on nights when he is, and my denial mechanism isn't in top working order, and I get hazy with too much wine and too much longing and then guilt (the death trap of the mistress) and then self-pity (the real death trap of the mistress) and then optimism (the death trap of all death traps, the thought that, yes, he will up and leave her, won't he; he has to, because look what we've got, look what we are). But I always manage to get it under control before going too far, before tumbling into acrimony—or auto-acrimony—and causing real ripples. You have to be realistic here—part of the discipline. Realistic enough to know that since we are living at a time of the frisky, we-still-deserve-ours, sexual entitlement touted by the ever-growing number of magazines for the aging female (I know, I read them, I write for them; sixty's the new forty, they all declaim. Whoopee!), that they probably still have sex. I bet they do. I can't bear to think about it.

Certainly not tonight in particular. That's because tonight, sitting here alone again, waiting for him to call back again, I know he is not at one of his kids' for one of their usual Sunday suppers, nor in a crisis confab with the mayor—for whom he works. That's how I met him, covering the mayor for the few seconds I worked for a Long Island newspaper. There I was, still shiny and relatively new to the city, sitting in a press conference, he standing to the side of the podium. As everything broke up he came down toward me, a little rumply, chin forward. "New?" he said. "Very," I said, feeling shy and flirted with, and I hadn't felt either, shy or flirted with, in a long time. Nobody in my crowd flirts much, maybe in the whole generation. A little circling around, some drinks, some smiles, and there you are in condom-land, in bed with someone you've just met and haven't even flirted with. Right away this was different. Michael was. Older, different training. Now he is in the hospital being prepped for surgery, tomorrow, seven A.M. sharp. First time for this. Though a little heavy, a little too fond of whiskey, and disdainful of gyms ("Who the hell needs a gym," he says to me, "when you've got the streets of New York?"), he is to all outward appearances (and inward, according to his doctor) a reasonably healthy, Lipitor-taking American male. Has been. Now the shot over the bow. The first surgery. If he makes it through, which he is expected to do, barring unforeseen complications (but isn't that, I say to Michael, precisely what life is: unforeseen complications; us, for example), there will be days of recuperation while his family flutters around him, plumping his pillows, bringing him soup, measuring his intake of fluids (and outgo, those little bedpans with the measuring marks inside, looking perversely culinary; I remember them from my father). I am enjoined from that. Once he had a terrible flu while his wife was away—his kids are grown and married and have kids of their own—

and he was mine all mine to nurse. He crawled into my apartment like an animal to its den, curling up in the bedroom with a febrile moan. It was so sweet, so unexpected, so new, the chance to nurse— to undress him, not for sex, but for caretaking. I took off his shoes and socks, his pants and shirt, and tucked him into my big bed— which takes up the whole bedroom—and then sailed forth into the city, giddy in my new ministering angel incarnation, to pick up the necessities: cough syrup and throat lozenges and dry-up pills. It was spring, one of those luminous New York spring days when every- thing is beginning anew. People unwrapped from the winter, in shirtsleeves, the sun teasing their newly exposed flesh, reborn daf- fodils poking up around trees, everything suddenly leafy and green, the slightest breeze. I walked so happily to the drugstore, not my lo- cal, because they know me there, but farther—Michael was asleep, I had time; better just for him to stay out cold, or out hot—away to one on the corner of Lex and Fifty-second so I could say to the pharmacist, with barely camouflaged delight, "Oh, my husband is so sick" and she could say, "Awful to be sick on such a beautiful day" and, after a moment, "Got your hands full, I'm sure." We smiled at each other, sharing the commiserative, eye-rolling tut-tuts about men being such babies, our men, about all the tending involved. With elixirs in hand, I stopped at the market and got a chicken and some leeks and carrots to make soup (what mistress worth her salt wouldn't make chicken soup from scratch; it isn't all about sex) and then, strolling, sun on my own bare arms, just smiling, smiling, till I got nervous it was all a dream and he wouldn't be there, or that his flu had flown and he after it, just a note, all better, bye-bye, call you later, or worse, that it had become pneumonia and he had died right there in my bed (then what; what would I do, right then, not to men- tion forever after?) and I started almost cantering—a half-walk half-run, and up the elevator (violating my rule to always walk the five flights; indeed, who needs a gym?) bolting in and finding him in

his fevered fetal curl. I sat for a moment on the end of the bed, studying him. He is not handsome, not in any orthodox way. He was very
flushed, his graying curls (they still have a little copper in them)
damp and matted against his forehead, smallish eyes, biggish nose,
uneven mouth, the upper lip thicker on one side than the other. I
made soup in my tiny kitchen with the window open, hearing the
city sounds, chopping leeks and carrots, toying with having a small
glass of wine, until he called and I went to him. I plumped the pillows (my turn, my turn) and held his heavy head while he sipped
juice and took his Tylenol and then, throwing back the covers, gave
him a cool rubdown with a cold cloth and a little Vicks (my hands
smelling like mentholated onions) and he groaned, achy with fever
and—oh no, oh yes—incipient pleasure. "You're impossible," I
said, gently pulling the covers back up over him, leaning to plant a
sisterly peck on his demi-erection through the sheets. I lied; it is
about sex. "Go back to sleep; I'll wake you for soup." I tiptoed out.
My aging, aching trophy was in my bed. I was so happy that day.

Now you see what I really do these weekends. I reminisce. I play
back every detail of our time together, like running a video through
an internal VCR. And wait for the phone. My friends sometimes call,
but they have stopped trying to pry me out, stopped trying to fix me
up. But I have never said a confirming word about Michael to anyone. Not one person. Not once. That's the number-one cardinal rule
and you have to play by the rules. Have to keep your mouth closed,
your lips sealed, your bliss under wraps. That's why dinner parties
are dangerous. You go, you might even flirt with a stranger because
it's safe, a little intoxicated teasing, and then you will say his name,
not this flirtee, but the lover's name, dropping it, just to hear it—
that's what Michael always says—to make him manifest there in the
room with you for just a minute, and someone will notice—another
woman, a friend, and she will press you for details, for a last name.
That's the guy that works for the mayor, right? I've seen his picture

in the paper. She will call the next day and restart the interrogation. Oh, no, this is the way of ruination. You just never know when a gal pal might metamorphose into a gossiping snitch. So you become increasingly careful, suspicious, isolated. I did. I have. And the dirty little secret is that it suits me. Just fine.

I realize that the TV is still thrumming along. I've been out in memory-land and now I see that they've got themselves a mudslide in El Salvador, hundreds of shacks buried in muck, casualties mounting. They are trying to blow life into it, the TV sorrow-mongers with their unctuous empathy, but it doesn't get lift-off. We like our tragedies American. Flag-draped coffins. Exploding space-ships escaping the surly bonds of earth, Kennedy scions crashing private planes into the sea. We'll go for the faraway catastrophes if there are Americans involved, either as casualties or do-gooders. This won't qualify tonight and in a nanosecond, they've already switched from the mudslide. It's after nine. Time to make myself eat. I make a quick detour through the bathroom to check on my rooftop, but the candles are out and the partyers all gone. Always makes me sad. Damn end of daylight saving. Too dark too early. Time to hole in for the winter. I toast the night with the empty wine-glass in my hand and go to refill it. There are rules for this, too: how much you can drink. Three glasses max, one and a half before dinner, one and a half with. I get out my containers of takeout and a china plate. You have to have your standards, your ceremonies, if you live alone. No eating out of or on plastic. Real china, real silverware, a cloth napkin. The cornflower blue one tonight. If you don't do this, you can lose any semblance of touch with decent life. I have been tempted, of course, to eat peanut butter out of a jar with a spoon some nights, but only succumbed twice. I fill my glass and go back to the living room. Shit—when did they start putting grapes in the chicken salad. I start to pluck them out one by one with my fingers when the phone rings. Please, I say, please please please.

It is him. He sounds sleepy.

"Sorry I couldn't get back sooner. Everybody's been in and out. They've already given me a sleeping pill . . . not to mention a shave."

"That must have been scary," I say. I am trying to be light. I hear myself trying.

"Yup. Never been shaved down there before. Wouldn't even let you do it."

"Never been tempted," I say with a forced half-giggle.

"You okay?" he says.

"Think so. You?"

He doesn't say anything for a while. I wonder if he's dozed off.

"Michael?"

"I'm here," he says. "Listen, I don't know how all this is going to come out. The surgeon was here again and he says there's every reason to think that . . ."

He trails off and I don't say anything. I just hold the phone.

"Aw, hell," he says. "You can always just sit on my face."

"Michael, don't," I say, and then I hear him inhale, a guttural uptake against tears and I know he's trying not to cry.

"Can't," is all he says and the phone goes dead.

I realize there are grapes in my hand and I am squishing some of them in an effort to avert my own tears. Prostate surgery—that's what we're dealing with here. Michael assures me everything will be fine, that he will be, and that we will luxuriate again in flagrante delicto (that corny old warhorse of a phrase). He has one of the best surgeons in New York, the man who pioneered the nerve-sparing technique that allows a man to still get it up. I have done my homework. I have visited all the prostate cancer sites. Results are mixed, even with the best of surgeons. Some impotence is to be expected. Perhaps some incontinence. We joked—a little—about diapers the day Michael told me. It was the last time we were together, nine days ago. He came, looking pale, furtive. In the kitchen, making a bouilla-baisse, the Montrachet chilling (we were getting a dinner; as always, I was thrilled, aproned, and anticipatorily adoring), I looked up at that face as it came around the corner and my heart stopped.

"What?" I said, putting down the knife.

"I have prostate cancer," he said.

"Okay," I said, relieved, just for that moment, because he hadn't announced that he had to go and couldn't come back ever again. "We'll get through it."

We never had dinner. We went and lay down in the bedroom, in the waning light. I brought the wine, but we didn't drink much. We didn't talk much, except for a few mirthless jokes about those dia-pers. We lay, fully clothed, spoons, he behind me, our faces toward the window, watching the night come, listening to the occasional siren. We had no real appetite for sex, but by mutual if unspoken agreement felt we ought to do it. We didn't even take our clothes off. It was just a perfunctory, pants-down quickie. Then he left. I went back and finished the bouillabaisse and then froze it in three Tupper-ware dishes. I poured more wine and got into bed, hoping there was some sense, some smell of Michael still in it, but the whole encounter had been so brief and almost antiseptic that there wasn't much. It was as if he hadn't even been here. I went to get his sweatshirt from the peg beside the front door, but remembered, not finding it, that I had washed and folded it the day before, thereby cleansing it of his odor. Damn my infernal tidiness. I thought about listening to his Dylan Thomas recording but resisted. There were few other me-mentos to be tempted by and I was, at that moment, both grateful and bereft. Truth to tell, I didn't live among mementos of my own, either. In another lifetime, on another coast, I had had to clean out a huge house when it was being sold, purge it of all its familial memo-rabilia, my familial memorabilia. It was hot. I worked in shorts and T-shirt, my hair pulled back in a clip, for the better part of two weeks and I had not cracked, not lingered, not savored. The rest I put in storage or gave away, carting clothes and dishes and figurines and such to the Salvation Army (I hate those suburban garage sales; they are unseemly, all your stuff spread out on the lawn for bargain-hunters to paw through). I came away with very little, a picture or two, my father's gold pocket watch, a pair of men's white loafers—never worn, good for a laugh—copies of some of the scripts he had written, annotated in his small, immaculate script, and one nude, scrawled-on Barbie doll, "Ken" on one plump plastic cheek of her ass, "Barbie" on the other, with a "+" right down the crack—and it can still, these years later, remembering the day she came to be so marked, make me smile.

The phone in my lap rings again and I jump. I answer, hoping it is Michael and hoping it isn't. I want him to be asleep now. There is no answer.

"Michael," I say, "that you?"

I hold the phone but nobody says anything and I punch it off. "Love you," I say, getting up, figuring it was probably him. I get my final allotment of wine and head toward the bedroom, stopping for one last visit to the bathroom window. A marked diminishment of lighted squares out there. Sleep has come, even to the obdurate. Their Ambien has kicked in. The baby has quieted. The lovemaking is over. The fighting. Night-night, New York. I wash my face and brush my teeth—without toothpaste because it will ruin the taste of the wine—and settle in for what I am sure will be a long and restless night. I will, of course, take my own Ambien. None of us, it seems, is able to sleep without help anymore. I climb into bed and turn on the set to revisit the deathly mud trap, but that's old news. Now it's just the talking heads again, so I mute the set. I often sleep like this—set on, sound off. The tricks we learn. The phone rings again. I glance at the illuminated clock. 11:32. Surely Michael will be out by now.

"Yes," I say.

Again no answer, but I sense someone on the other end. Great night for a pervert. "Come on. Who is this?" I hear breath. I am tempted to slam down the phone, but don't in case it is still my frightened lover who cannot talk, but who wants me to. I soften.

"Hey, is that you?"

I am getting nervous now. I stand up and start pacing, phone at my ear. "Please," I say, "I don't like this. I'm going to hang up if you don't say something."

I do hang up but the phone rings immediately again and I pick it up. I can't not. I don't say anything. I just keep holding. Finally someone says, "Clare?" almost inaudibly, a female someone. Not, after all this time, a wife or a daughter. Not tonight, no, no.

I sit back down on the bed. It is my turn to say nothing. Finally the same voice, a little louder this time: "Clare."

It feels impossible, dream-like, this voice, calling from somewhere, from nowhere, from memory.

"It's me," the voice says. "It's Louise."

"I can't . . ." I start to say and then fall silent.

"Sorry to be calling so late," this voice says, this Louise, this sister I haven't talked to or seen for, what, twenty-seven years (except for the faraway peek at her I got at Daddy's funeral, she creeping around the periphery, hoping I would notice, hoping I wouldn't. No way I was going to deal with her that day). And now, here she is, this night of all nights. Go away, I am about to say, when she says, "I'll just hang on till you can talk."

I take the phone into the bathroom and climb up on the toilet, looking out again at the sleeping city. Midnight. He is over there behind those tall buildings on the right, in the hospital, no doubt now drugged into pre-op Never-Never Land and my sister Louise, Weezie, is actually on this phone that I have at my ear but somehow can't talk into. Minutes go by. I can hear her breathing. What do you say in this circumstance? Is there decorum? Hi. How's it going? Long time, no talk. I try to imagine what she must look like now. She will be, what?—I'm forty-one; that makes her forty-four. I close my eyes. I think about going back into the bedroom and just hanging up. Or saying, gee, nice to hear from you, but this isn't exactly the right time. Or, go away. I try to talk, but still nothing will come out. I carry the phone to the kitchen, tucking it between ear and shoulder, and rummage in the cabinet for Michael's bottle of whiskey. I pour myself a few fingers—as he loved to say; a few fingers, please. I take a big, throat-searing swallow and sit down at the kitchen table. Finally I say: "What do you want?"

I hear a quick intake of breath. "I know this is . . ." Louise trails off and now she falls silent. Another stretch of time passes. I sip my drink in the dark, legs tucked up to my chin. I realize my heart is pounding.

"I need," Louise says, trailing off again and then rushing back, "to see you."

"You need to see me."

"Yes."

"Sure. Absolutely. When do you want to do this?" I hear the sarcasm in my own voice.

"I know this is abrupt, but I really need . . ."

"To see me. Can't you call back at a more sensible hour and we can arrange this monumental meeting. You can come to the big city and do a touristy . . ."

"I'm here."

"You're here. Here where?"

"In New York."

"New York. Louise, I remember you were always a little impulsive, but . . ."

"Clare. I'm in trouble. I need to see you."

I hear my sister's voice and those words, "I'm in trouble." They were always irresistible. I am trying to block them now. It has been a long time. Everybody is a grown-up now, has to take care of themselves. Not now, my long-lost sister. This won't work now. Call me back when you pull yourself together and we'll have a nice big chat about old times.

"Clare," Louise says. "I know it's out of the blue and I'm sorry, but I need you."

Irresistible? I hold the phone while memories have their way with me. I think about the Barbie afternoon, the two of us with our dolls. Finally I say—sarcasm tabled—"Okay, call me tomorrow afternoon and we'll arrange a time."

"No," Louise says. "I mean now."

"Now?" I say, guard back up, sarcasm attendant. "Right. Absolutely. I'll just barrel out of bed at midnight and run . . ."

"I'm sorry, but I don't know who else to . . ."

"This is crazy. I'm not going to dress and come out into the . . ."

"I'm just around the corner at the coffee shop at Lexington and Fifty-fifth, the one that stays open . . ."

"What are you doing here, Louise? You don't even know where I live."

"I found out. It's not that hard. Please. I'll wait here." She hangs up.

I take the phone back to the bedroom and lay down in the dark, willing myself to stay put, willing the Ambien to kick in hard. There are rules, after all. You don't just barge back into somebody's life and say you're around the corner and need to see them right away— at midnight, no less. It's selfish. It's laughable. It's Louise. No "How are you?" No "I know this is thoughtless." No nothing like that. Nice to know she's the same. I turn off the TV and lie in the dark. I snap it back on and start channel surfing, but it's no use. I can't even watch long enough to find out what's on. I turn it off and go into the bathroom and splash cold water on my face and brush my teeth—

with toothpaste this time—and, half-consciously, start to stroke on a little mascara and appraise my hair, tousling it up with my free hand, because if I actually go and meet this woman, this sister, I want to look good. Stunning that vanity can insist upon itself, even at moments like this, at midnight on a night already heavy with anxiety, that it can almost toss you a perverse lifeline. Here, freshen yourself up a little and face the world. It'll all be okay. You'll look okay. It's crazy. I am, to let myself be pulled out, pulled back. Go away, Louise. You can't do this again. Go away and leave me alone.

I dress, warmly—hat, mittens, parka—even though it's still post-rain warmish out. I have finally learned that the weather can change in an instant. Took me a while. If the sun was out in the morning, I would sail out without scarf or coat or umbrella. I have come home with wet head and chattering teeth more times than I can count. I am finally hip to the climatic drill. But it is actually still warm and I am out of my hat and coat within a block of leaving my apartment. There is almost no one out—Sunday night, midnight— but I am not scared, never have been on these streets. It is just not my locus of fear. My fear is suburban, not urban. And now, resurrected from that past: Louise, Weezie, the most beautiful sister a girl could have. Drop-dead stunning, her mother's daughter, our mother's daughter. Ice blue eyes, pale skin, thick, dark hair. Movie material, people always said. So long ago, though. Is she still that? Can she be? I am not sure what to want, Weezie as she was or a midlife woman, her face plump with fatigue and disappointment, her body soft from childbearing (two sons, my father told me, and I know from glancing at the pictures he left around for me to see), beside whom I can feel like the well-preserved, pretty one. "You're pretty, too," our mother always said to me after some stranger had ogled Louise. Louise couldn't have been more than—what, eight, nine, and was already creating that magnetic clamor of excitement that preternaturally pretty people do, very beautiful very young girls in a uniquely disturbing way.

She is over there in the corner, turned in profile to the door, hands around a cup of coffee, a scarf around her hair, dark glasses. Dark glasses? In the middle of the night? I watch her for a moment before crossing the restaurant. A little Jackie Kennedy effect. I stop before she sees me. I can still turn and walk away—I try to conjure up the old anger—but my heart has gotten out ahead of me and is moving over there because there sits the only sister I have. It is a siren call; she is. Years' worth of being MIA and then one phone call and I am here, summoned from my bed at midnight. And the sure instinct that I am about to be reentangled in something Louiseish, the strong tickle of foreboding is overcome, at least in this moment—as this sister turns and beams that big, beautiful, movie star smile at me, our mother's smile, mouthing my name "Clare" and then, "You came"—by years' worth of suppressed longing, which, sliding into the banquette, I tuck way away where she cannot see it.

"It's so bright in here," I say, looking away from her. "I feel like I'm in some Edward Hopper painting."

"Yes," Louise says, appending a quick, inauthentic-sounding laugh to try, I know, to break the tension.

Now what? The waitress comes and I order some decaf. Louise keeps her sunglasses on, for whatever reason, and I don't ask. This is her hand to play. I am trying to be cool.

"We're sure pale, aren't we?" Louise says, adding on that little laugh again. (Where has that come from? It sounds so apologetic, so un-Louise; does she use it all the time now, not just in a circumstance like this, if there ever was another quite like this.) "I mean, compared to the way we used to look."

Danger zone. Childhood looming. I steer us back to the present. "I thought you lived somewhere in Florida."

"I do," Louise says, "but you know how concerned everyone is about the sun now. I had a few little skin things and now I avoid it completely."

"Your hair's bigger, too," I say.

"I know," Louise says, adding her little laugh again, reaching up to rearrange the heavy piece that has fallen down across one eye. "And probably a little too black. It's easier for you with blond hair to take the gray out. You know, they have so many wonderful ways to do that—what do you call it—that weaving, but with us dark-haired types, you know they always get it too dark or too red or too something . . ." She is fiddling with her hair, patting it down but it is stiff, obviously with spray, and it can't be squashed, even a little and, taking pity for a moment, listening but not listening to her prattle nervously, I want to reach out and take her hand and put it down and say, no, it's okay, tuning in again to hear her say, "But Timmy likes it this way."

Timmy. That was the husband. So he is still around. I remember Daddy talking about him—solid citizen, owned a small construction company. I think he's good for her. If you say so, I said, cutting off the conversation. I know he visited them when they were still in California, but we didn't talk about it, about them, about her. Daddy knew how I felt. She'd walked out and not looked back, not at me anyway—no calls, no cards, no nothing—and now here she is again, as if conjured from the dead. Welcome back, Louise, swell to see you, how can I help?

"So Timmy is still in the picture, then?"

Louise puts her hand down, but doesn't say anything.

I watch her with her slightly bent head, slightly trembling lip. I have seen this before. I want to be back home in bed, with my thoughts of Michael.

"So," I say, "what did you do, run away from home again?"

"I suppose I deserve that," Louise says, barely audibly, pushing

her dark glasses finally up on top of her head. She has been crying.
Her eyes are red and swollen. Her trump card.

I don't want to do this, not tonight, but I find myself leaning forward and saying, "What is it? What's wrong?"

She is quiet for a stretch and then says "I'm scared," and I believe it. I can see it.

"Of what, Louise?"

She just shakes her head a little and I see tears starting. "Of Timmy? Is it Timmy?" I say, and she seems to nod her head in assent. "Oh, shit, Louise, you don't let him hit you, do you?" I say, with a tart, fatigue-abetted laugh. "Is that what this is . . . ?"

Louise starts to get up, but I say, "Hey, if anyone's walking out, it's me. I'm sorry, I just can't do this tonight. I just can't."

Louise slips the glasses back on without saying anything. I stand up and pull on my parka. "Call me in a couple of days," I say, "if you're still around."

I walk out of the coffee shop, forbidding myself to look back. No, no, no, no, no. My heart is racing and I am instantly hot again, even though the temperature has dropped maybe ten degrees, just like that. I was only in there maybe fifteen minutes. The streetlights cast a yellowish glow. I pass one young couple and then nobody as I turn the corner toward home. A cab passes and I have to fight the temptation to hail it and go sit in the hospital, anywhere in it, not in his room, of course, just somewhere near, in some lobby or waiting room, where nobody will notice me. But you can't do that. There are rules, still rules, always rules and you don't go violating them just because you want to or because you think, if you can't be there, near him, your heart will break. Rank sentimentality. Isn't that what I said to him one of those first nights? Don't like your rank sentimentality, about the songs it was, the pleased, post-coital humming of "Danny Boy." Or was it about the poems, the Yeats recited at odd moments, in fact, the first time we were in a bar together and I was reaching to clip my hair out of my face: "Fasten your hair with a golden pin, And bind up every wandering tress . . ." I grimaced then and said something tart about sentimentality and he shied back, though not for long. Not for long. He wooed me with all of it and it worked. I have lived entirely in the cocoon he has spun for us.

I am home. I let myself in and feel much more alone suddenly than I did on the cold, empty nighttime street. He will come back. He will. I make a last visit to my bathroom perch and look out; just a few stalwart insomniacs doing their own reckonings. I pop another sleeping pill (oh well, no cogent work tomorrow), and crawl into bed, flipping back on the TV—without sound. Yes, he will live, they say, cancer not spread, caught in time, etc., etc.

The sleeping pills finally begin to blunt the rush of thoughts and as I start to drift downward, only then does Louise reinsinuate herself. I have, with adamant determination, kept her at bay since walking out on her in that coffee shop. It has been relatively easy to do so because she has been gone so long, so out of mind. But now here she is again, like some strange apparition—almost unreal, with her pale skin and high, dark hair. Is she still sitting there in that coffee shop, hugging her mug? Or has she gone somewhere, anywhere, just away, a hotel, the airport to catch the next flight home to her menacing spouse? That is the assumption, isn't it; that is what she wanted me to assume. And why this night of all nights, reappearing like some dark omen—the red-eyed angel of retribution come to exact her due. She makes me nervous. She wants something and I don't want her to want anything from me; I don't want her to stick around and ask me for it, whatever it is, and then I see—because I can't help but see—Weezie the last time she left the house, standing on the dusty eastside shoulder of the Pacific Coast Highway at Topanga Canyon, her thumb stuck out, small cardboard sign in hand, saying "North," as my father and I drove past her on our way into town, me fourteen, fully turned in my seat, looking out the back window and

seeing her there with her racoon-like blackened eyes from the mascara that she still had on from the night before which was, I saw, as I
said "Daddy, stop, stop," running down Louise's face in her tears.

"We can't leave her. We can't."

"She's leaving us," my father said.

. 2 .

S he is sitting on the stairs of my building when I get home from
my interview with an octogenarian shrink, a tough little
silver-bunned crone who lives in a cluttered apartment in the
West Village and has achieved notoriety of late saying women have
demanded too much. I am writing a profile of her for one of the
magazines I work for and am arguing with her in my head so that I
almost don't recognize Louise sitting there. It has been three days
since our late-night encounter. I am sure I look startled.

"Sorry," she says. "I didn't mean to scare you. I was just afraid
you'd hang up on me if I called."

"No," I say. "I don't think I would."

That makes her smile a little. "Thanks for the honesty."

"No, I mean, I wouldn't have. I'm sorry about the other night. I
just had a lot on my mind."

"I'm sorry. It's hardly appropriate to barge in on someone like
that at midnight after . . ."

"Oh, a decade or two away."

She stands up and I see her mouth quiver a little.

"I'm sorry," I say again. "I'll try to do better. It's just a little
weird."

"I know," she says.

"How are you feeling?"

"Better," she says, but it's a bit tentative and I think that she might be thinking of bolting and at least half of me doesn't want that. I am lonesome enough without Michael.

"You know if you want some help with all this—whatever it is— I know a lot of people . . ."

"Why don't we not do this right now. Maybe we could just try to be friends a little and not talk about anything big. Does that make sense?" It is the sweet, from-the-heart Louise smile. That I could remember. Not the show-stopper, the man-dazzler. This is the little girl, slightly-lost, it's-gonna-be-okay-isn't-it? smile.

"Good idea," I say. We stand there for a minute, looking at each other, shyly, and then away and then back again and I finally say, "Hey, listen, I'm sorry I can't ask you up or ask you to stay or anything. My place is a mess. I work there, too, and it's small."

"Yeah," she says, "I read that piece of yours about working at home. I liked it."

"Thank you," I say.

"I've read all your stuff. You're really good."

I am touched. I can't help it. It never occurred to me that she would be reading me.

"Listen," I say, "I have a little while. Want to go get some lunch?"

"I'd like that," she says. We are talking, muscles unused in centuries. I note her coat, a little too long, a nowhere length between knee and ankle, and the paisley scarf knotted around her neck—the matron in from the suburbs for lunch—and something in me twitches protectively toward her. She seems to read it.

"I've only been here once before, to New York, I mean," she says, with a self-conscious pet of the scarf, eyeing—or at least I seem to feel her eyes on me from behind the dark glasses—my narrow dark pants and short leather jacket. She was always the chic one, with her embellished school clothes (skirt rolled up to here, collar of the white blouse rakishly atilt to frame her long neck) and her well-thumbed copies of *Seventeen* and then *Rolling Stone,* going from preppy to hippie in a hip heartbeat, leaving me in self-conscious thrall. Now here she is reborn as the quintessential suburban mall mom and I am the trendy one. We seem to acknowledge, without saying anything, the passing of the fashion baton. What sisters do: Read each other. Still.

"I'll take you to a real New York dive," I say.

It is twelve thirty and the sidewalks are dense with people. I automatically start my toreador moves through the crowds—twist, slither, lean—and lose her behind. I stop and let her catch up.

"Sorry," I say. "I've got native feet now."

"I see that," she says.

"Here," I say, hooking my arm through hers. There is an instant dermal zing. I haven't touched her for decades and yet, so instantly, her arm, her flesh feels known to me, remembered.

The place I've chosen is jammed, always is. It is famous for its tomato-colored wallpaper with zebras on it and "secret" spaghetti sauce. The bar is three-deep with smokers handing glasses of wine back to those behind them. We leave our coats and squiggle into a corner near the phone booth after giving our names. We have to shout to be heard. But we don't say much. We are just barely getting the hang of this thing: sisterhood redux. So much to say. So much not to say. And what about the husband, the damned husband? We will get to that in time. Not today. She has set the parameters. I am grateful for that. She keeps on her sunglasses and looks—I can see now, catching people looking at her—provocative, a little old-fashioned and out of place, but more arresting because of it. She is, I suddenly realize, looking at her sideways, more full-breasted than I remembered.

She is looking away from me and when she turns back I say, nodding chestward—not meaning to sound mean but I realize it does a little the minute I say it—"Did you always have those?"

She flushes and reaches again to pat down her hair.

"Not quite," she says, that giggle from the other night, an air-filling apologia in it. "You know, after the kids, they sort of, well, you know, drooped, so I had them fixed. Actually Timmy gave them to me as an anniversary present three years ago." Another soft little laugh almost like a throat clearing. "They don't look too big, do they?"

"No," I say, trying to sound reassuring, not judgmental, though in my head I'm already telling Michael, "You know, the big blue meanie husband actually gave her a pair of boobs," and he is laughing. I collect things for him, like I did for my father. Her hand is back up in her hair. Who is she? I don't really know a thing about her. A planetary divide seems to open up between us again, me the modest-chested, chicly dressed career woman (the unmarried career woman with a married lover), she the dutiful wife (the dutiful scared wife) with the swollen eyes and the silicone. What now? What do we do here? What is she doing here?

We are seated for lunch, on the side at a small table, and the melee of the restaurant washes over us. We don't have to talk much and that helps. We shout. I do at her, menu in hand, telling her what's good—stuffed artichoke, the spaghetti with the secret . . . and she says, "Just order for me," and I can see she has done it, with him, a hundred times: deferred. Maybe this will be it, a meal and we will go our separate ways again. We are too different, too far gone into our own lives. We will have lunch, I will give her some names of therapists (not the one I've just interviewed; Louise clearly needs to demand more, not less) and a hairdresser or two and she will fix both, her head and hair, and go home. Bye-bye, nice to see you again. Hope it all works out. I feel her eyes on me as I order, even from behind those damn glasses. I feel disadvantaged. She can study me at will.

"When are you going to take those off?" I say.

The little giggle. "No," she says, obviously mishearing me in all the noise.

I laugh. She thinks I am laughing at her. Hands go this way and that, a light brush of the new breasts, back up to the hair. Pat, pat. Put them down, Louise. It's all right.

"How about a glass of wine?"

"Yes," she says. "That would be nice."

"Red?"

"Yes," she says.

"You don't have to drink red."

"No," she says.

"No which?"

"Red is fine," she says.

"Chianti or Cabernet?" I'm baiting.

"Anything," she says.

"No, you choose . . ."

"Doesn't matter."

"Louise . . ." I start, but then the waiter is there and I order two Chiantis and the food comes and we eat. She eats with pleasure, with childlike intensity. Artichoke leaves and all the stuffing and the broth, forkfuls, then spoonfuls, looking up at me from over the bowl, the unworried sensual Louise stretching on her towel on the bluff as we lay baking in the sun, Coppertoned and lazy, her *Seventeen* open between us, all dog-eared and oil-stained, her transistor playing . . . "Under my thumb, the girl who once put me down . . . ," warmish cans of Coke tucked into the grass behind our heads.

"What?" she says.

"Nothing," I say. "Glad you like it."

The giggle. "It's so good. We don't get things like this at home."

She puts her spoon down. I've made her self-conscious again. Go ahead, I want to say, but I don't. When the pasta comes, she is subdued, doesn't go at it with the same relish. I try to josh her back into her appetite. I tell her the story of a famous New York writer who allegedly snuck some of the "secret" sauce out in a container and then had it sent to a lab in New Jersey to have it analyzed. Probably one of those urban myths, I tell her.

"Weezie," I say, using for the first time her childhood name, "I'm sorry. Please eat."

"No," she says. "I am really full and I've been trying to lose some weight."

"Shit," I say, putting down my own fork and spoon.

"No, really," she says and then the waiter is there asking if we want to take it home and do we want coffee. I ask Louise if she wants hers to go and realize I have no idea where she is staying—a hotel, apartment, where?

"Louise, do you want this? I don't know if you have a way to heat it up . . ."

"No, thanks," she says.

When he leaves, I say again that I'm sorry I have no extra room that she can stay in and she says, "I'm staying with some friends from the . . . from home. They're in Brooklyn, but I'm learning the subways. Their daughter comes in to work and I come with her."

Does she float around the city all day? Go to museums, plays, tourist sites, wait for me on my stoop? I am tired now. This is hard work, trying to be friends—lighthearted, midlife friends out for a gabby, New York lunch—trying not to get entangled. Nice enough woman, Louise. Still beautiful, yes. Too bad about that husband. Wonder what triggered it; wasn't always like that, was he? It's okay. She'll fix it. Up here staying with friends in Brooklyn. Doesn't seem to be scared—now. Guess he's not coming after her. She'll float around for a while, get herself together, and go face the music.

"I have to get back to work," I say, reaching for the check as the waiter puts it down. I hesitate for a second and she reaches out to take it. "No, no, it's not that," I say. "You are okay, aren't you? I mean, he won't come after you here . . ."

"No," she says. "No, but thank you for asking."

I feel like a shit for not asking sooner, but there is no edge in her "thank you." She seems in no hurry to elaborate. "I didn't mean to keep you," she says. "I enjoyed this."

"Yes," I say. "We'll do it again. I just have a few pieces to get out of the way this week . . ."

"I always admire people who can work at home," she says. "You have to have such discipline. But you always had that."

"It just takes practice," I say. "I've been doing it a long time, except for a little time out for gainful employment."

"I've been doing a little writing myself," she suddenly says. "I mean, it's not like yours, but I'm enjoying it."

"That's great," I say, watching her, imagining a journaling class at the local JC. Everyone's a writer these days.

"Listen," I say, "I really do have to go. I've got a deadline to meet."

We get our coats and head outside. There's a coldish wind, but the sun is shining. The city is brisk, autumnal, hyperpurposeful after a long hot summer that dragged well into late September.

"I smell like a cigarette," Louise says, standing there, the sun picking out the few gray strands in her dark mane.

"I always forget that," I say. "People still smoke a lot here, don't they?"

"Next time is on me," she says, leaning toward me. She kisses me lightly on the cheek and I smell her—yes, the cigarettes and a faint whisper of some florally perfume, might just be body lotion or even hair spray, and under, a nervous animal smell, female, glandular, and I realize what this is costing her, too, this sibling dance, and the effort it must have taken her to get here away from whatever, whomever, and I blurt out an offer to take her for a big city makeover, hair, eye-brows, the works, if she thinks that would be fun, and she smiles and says she'll think about it and turns and starts walking away. I watch her, the wind lifting her hair, not in strands, because it is too sprayed, too stiff for that, lifting a lot at once, and I walk fast to catch her and tell her I really do want to take her to my hotshot salon—if she wants, only if she wants—but she turns a corner and gets swallowed by a post-lunch surge of office returnees. I, too, get surrounded and carried along. I move to the outside and peer up over heads and think I see hers again and then we are under scaffolding, above and around, and are picking our way, all of us, over and through the mess. I haven't even asked about her children, asked to see pictures—nothing. My nephews. I have nephews, somewhere, after all. Is he abusive to them, too, or are they old enough to belt him back? Hope it's the latter. Don't think about them from year to year; haven't thought about them, ever, except in the vaguest way. I want to find her, but now I seem to have really lost her. The crowd thins and I turn the corner toward home, but suddenly I see her again en-tering someplace. I slow and as I get there, I realize it is a McDon-ald's. She is in line, back to me, ordering. She is still hungry. I stand outside watching her, a little to the side so that if she turns, she won't see me. She sits down and begins unwrapping her hamburger, squirting the little packets of ketchup onto her fries. She eats—again—with a childlike gusto that tugs at me, the aging beauty queen in the fast food joint. She is happy here, at home, no fluttering of the hands. I feel closer to her here, looking through the window, than sitting opposite her making small talk. She hasn't taken off her coat, but now she does, settling in, stirring cream in her coffee. She even pushes those dark glasses up on top of her hair. I wonder how many meals she has had in places like this, the kids after a game, rowdy, their cleats clattering on the hard floor, sliding noisily into their seats, Louise between them, the harried, happy mom with the

softening middle, trying not to eat her fair share but doing it anyway. Or after a dance, picking them up—she and Timmy—the boys
a little glassy-eyed from the clandestine gulp of booze out back behind the gymnasium or the quick shared joint, but okay, sweet
enough, good boys (I hope, I hope), the father tense, watching,
watching his beautiful wife, never not watching, while she, here in
the bright light of a Foster's Freeze or Burger King, surrounded by
these jocular, rassly boys, feels the safest of anywhere on the planet.
Let's not go home; let's never go home. A man brushes past me going in, bumping me slightly from my spot. All temptation to go in
myself is gone. I want to leave her alone with her Happy Meal. She
pushes the tray away and reaches for her purse and out comes a little
diary, one of those pink ones a girl might carry, and a matching
pen—oh Louise, Louise—and she begins, with a slight smile, to
write. The man, with a cup of coffee, interrupts her, leaning across
her table to get her attention. He is tallish, hair blond and short, almost a crew cut, in a Windbreaker. Smiling. He looks around for a
minute, furtively, even out my way. I flinch back, but keep watching.
He says something more to her and moves away while she lowers her
dark glasses. Yes, I want to say. Keep them on at all times. This is a
big, mean metropolis. Be careful here, beautiful sister of mine. Don't
talk to strangers. Don't let them see your gorgeous, sad eyes—like a
beacon, they will be, you will be, to the greedy and mean, the per-
verts and creeps. Go get on your subway and go back to your friends
in Brooklyn. There is the sharp impulse to march in there and take
her back to my place and tuck her in. But I will myself against it. I
cannot. There are deadlines, a life, a lover. A shiver of longing
comes over me as I walk away from that window. There will be no
visitor tonight. Not even a call, probably. I am tempted to go back
and ask Louise if she wants to go to a movie, maybe, but stop myself. We've had our lunch. She's had her two. Let her scribble away
in her little pink diary. I stop on impulse at the drugstore near my

building to get her these little soothing eye pads, good for crying eyes (yes, I've used them). I kneel down in a cluttered aisle and find them on a lower shelf under all the discount mascaras. They're a peace offering, a sign of my sympathy. I will give them to her at our next lunch, a little present, a token of friendship. Around me, I already hear it: the noise of winter, the coughers and snifflers at the pharmacy window getting their prescriptions. And feel it: the woefully overheated emporia of cold-weather Manhattan. Time to layer up and layer down, the seasonal striptease. Sexy if you've come from a warm coast where clothes were not an issue. Sexy if you're doing it to crawl in next to a warm body. The muffler and gloves, the coat and sweater, the shoes and stockings and skirt (skirts and heels always; with Michael I had—have—allowed myself to go girly again; the age of him, the bulk of him), the shirt and camisole, the panties. Sometimes left those on. Brown or navy or nude. Never black (too obvious) or pink (too lollipopish). Michael, stretched out on the bed, half-clothed, pants still on, shirt and shoes off, would sing a bawdy tune—bawdy, not vulgar, as he reminded me—or proffer a little husky-voiced poetry ("When my arms wrap around you I press . . . My heart upon the loveliness . . . That has long faded from the world . . .") or just lie there looking at me as I unbuttoned and unzipped and unhooked. I fell in love with him in the winter, a stretch of breathtakingly cold days, fell in love with New York, too, in those shimmery holiday days, dark and cold so early, everything Christmas-lit and festive, ducking off the bustly streets into a bar or pub or hotel, he there waiting. It was my third Christmas here. This will be my ninth. Pushing a decade. Can we do it again? Can we start over? Can you be waiting there, in that bar or that suite, for me to get out of my nubbly winter skirts and suede pumps?

"You all right?"

I have slunk down on the floor, little jar in hand, and a garishly made-up older woman with a small leashed dog is peering down at me.

"Yes, yes, thanks. Just dialed out for a minute."

She moves on by. I pay for the eye pads, pick up some cough drops—just in case—and head back out. Now it's good and cold. I hope Louise is on her subway by now. I realize I don't even have a phone number for her—not where she's staying, not a cell, nothing. I never asked. I've been wanting to leave this all to her, otherwise I'll start to be in it in ways I'm not. I'll be checking on her, worrying—a lot more than I've let myself do so far. She's a big girl, a mother. She got herself here. That takes some planning and some guts. She'll figure it out. "In her way, Louise is a survivor," my father said, the night after the day we left her standing on the highway, running eyes, tennis shoes, thumb jutted out. "She'll be okay." We were sitting in front of the fire, the family remnants, eating dinner off rickety side-by-side TV tables in the living room.

"Daddy," I said. "I don't want to sleep upstairs anymore."

He laughed—a small laugh, a little bitter, but tender. Always that. "No," he said. "I know just what you mean. You go ahead and stay down here with me. You take the little room off the kitchen."

That was that. Daddy had been sleeping downstairs for quite a few years and now I was joining him. Neither of us slept upstairs again. It was as if the whole second story of the house had been cordoned off. Up and down we went for clothes, but then, bit by bit, moved them down. The occasional guest stayed up there—not in the pastel-colored master, never that—in Louise's or my old room, and the serial cleaning ladies drifted up there to dust or vacuum, and if any of them thought it odd that we had relocated to the downstairs "maid's rooms," nobody ever said anything. No doubt behind our backs, yes. But not to us. Or maybe they did and we just didn't hear. It didn't matter. We were downstairsers now. That's what Daddy called us with an amused, sad-eyed wink through the thick lenses of his glasses: the downstairsers. You and me, kid. Now I am an upstairser, an apartment dweller, a cold-weather kitten in camisoles and camel hair. Sometimes it still seems like a dream—being here, ever being there. And now this Louise—floating back from that dream into this one, all grown up and yet still something schoolgirlish, something innocent about her, there with her greasy fries and little pink diary and fear-inflected eyes. How do women let it happen? Yes, I've read all the stuff about self-esteem—the lack thereof—and interviewed the women and written about them and railed against their abusers. But still. Louise didn't come from it. It makes me sad and it makes me mad. Welcome to the real world: Your long-lost sister is a battered wife. I will be nice to her if she calls back. I will take her in hand and get her some help and she will grow strong and grateful and we will be the best of friends and I will write a best-selling book about our reconciliation and we will work the talk shows together: Oprah fodder par excellence. How's that sound?

.3.

The room is, of course, overheated, and quietly but deter-
minedly pink with huge floral arrangements in a couple of
corners, multiply reflected in the gilded mirrors. A proper
ladies' tea salon in a proper hotel on the Upper East Side, relics and
matrons-in-training in Chanel, and there in a small seashell of a
booth, in his customary tweeds, clean-shaven, unruly hair slicked
down like a boy's, is my out-of-place lover. His choice. Odd, of
course, a little decorous to say the least. I've asked no questions, so
happy was I when he called, so happy now coming across the thick
floral carpet in my winter white skirt and jacket toward him—I have
dressed as always, with great care, though he doesn't notice often
(he does and doesn't, a kind of quick, loverly appraisal)—though it
does hit me now with full force what a strange locale for the ren-
dezvous of separated sweethearts.

I slide into the booth. I am grinning. Michael looks sideways at me.

"White?" he says.

"Winter white."

"Fetching."

"Bridal." A barely detectable flinch.

"You look . . . how do you look?" I say.

"Okay. Lost a little weight. They won't let me have a drink.
Hard on the plumbing, still."

"Thus the tea salon."

"I didn't know what else to do."

"Makes me feel ladylike."

"That was the plan."

"Fuck," I say.

He laughs. "Coulda gone to a movie, I suppose."

"I don't like this," I say.

"No," he says. "I know. I'm a little off-footed here." He reaches for my hand under the table.

The waitress comes and we order tea. Sandwiches, scones. Earl Grey okay? It feels surreal. Nice nice tea tea. I hold his hand hard and he winces. "IV," he says, detaching it and bringing it up on the table. The whole back of it is bruised and I, without thinking, lean to kiss it.

"Hussy," he says and then he laughs like pre-op Michael, a bawdy gruffness. It is half-real, half-effortful.

"I missed you," I say.

He puts his hand on my leg under the table.

"Everyone treat you well?"

"They fluttered over me," he says. "Even the daughters-in-law, even the mean, stringy vegetarian one."

"Do tell."

We laugh. I know the cast of characters. Inevitable after a stretch of years. I actually remember some of their birthdays. Some of the grandchildren have been born on my watch—on my something. Watch isn't exactly the right word. I know which of his kids are political, nice, funny, vegetarian, and which ones aren't. Then I lose them from time to time, thoughts of them, of their natures, of their married names. They float away. Right off the earth. But today they are around, attendees. I feel them all hovering. His tribe. What have I to put up against them? Who? One sister, one magically reappearing, battered sister. That's the extent of my tribe.

"My sister's back," I say.

"Your sister?"

"You knew I had one."

"Yeah, but long lost."

"Now found."

"Weird."

"You don't know the half of it," I say, and then I regale him, be-tween nibbles of crustless cucumber sandwiches, with all of it: her appearing in the city out of nowhere, calling me at midnight, her backcombed hair ("She'd fit right in here if she dressed a little bet-ter," I say, looking around. "You're so tough," he says, but he's laughing), leading up to my grand finale—the anniversary breasts from the apparently abusive mate.

"Jesus," he says, still laughing, "amazing what people put up with, isn't it?"

I let that go. I have to let that go. We are working on a reclama-tion here, on reclaiming our coupledom. I go flirty.

"What do men think of those things? When you get the clothes off, don't they feel weird?"

"You're asking the wrong guy," he says. "I don't like big breasts, as you well know. You know what I always say: Superfluous is any-thing more than you can get in your mouth."

"Corny," I say, "and a little vulgar in such refined circumstances as these."

"But true," he says, essaying a wink aimed at my chest.

"Speaking of corny," I say.

Our banter is thin. We don't know what to do with our longings.

The check comes and we leave. Is it my imagination or does he seem a little shorter? He is ever-so-slightly folded, pain-protective. I feel better up, walking beside him, out into the day, into our city. It is gray and cold, what Michael always calls bed weather. I pat his back, little circles, just for a moment, as we set out, then put my hands back in my pockets.

"Can we walk a little?" I say, hoping he won't jump into a cab.

"Sure, Miss," he says, putting on a brogue. "I'll see you home."

"I'd like that," I say, playing my part.

We start down Madison then cross over to Fifth, to the park side. The foot traffic is fairly light. It's cold enough that those who do pass have their heads down. It seems impossible—as it often does—that I cannot hook my arm through Michael's. I don't. I walk slightly carefully because of the uneven pavement stones. Taxis rush by and buses lurch, their doors like rubber lips smacking open and shut, people getting on and off. The cold begins to penetrate. But I am happy just to be walking with him. We walked, in our first months and years, every inch of the city. Michael loves it to the bone, the marrow, loves its immigrant pull, immigrant past. The Irish here, the Italians over here, the Jews, the Chinese. Where they landed, where they settled, how they shifted. He gave me the history as a present. We even did the boroughs on foot, the Puerto Ricans and Haitians and Guatemalans. We ate *pupusas* and boiled beef and cabbage and dim sum. Everywhere people knew him and made noise over him and he made noise back. Says when his kids left, he wanted to move right back in, but his wife likes the suburbs—safer, better for grand-children. His whole clan is out there now, which is why the city feels like ours.

"Helped clean the place up, you know," he'd say with pride whenever we walked around.

"Yeah, you and your posse of Republican prudes," I would josh.

"You don't know what it was like before. You got here at a great time. Anyway, I'm not a Republican or a prude."

"Around the edges," I'd say.

"Around which edges?" he'd say. But he wasn't listening. He was looking shiny-eyed, as we walked, at the city, eyes up and down and around. On a stolen summer weekend, when it was hot and soggy and the place was practically deserted, he might slip a hand into my pocket as he steered me into a cool, dark place for a beer. There didn't seem to be a bar or tavern or pub he didn't know, hadn't been in. "Just part of the job," he'd say, when I marveled at the breadth of his watering hole knowledge. I wish for that today, that we could duck into some warm, noisy place and have a Jack. A Jack for me and the lass, he would say. Foreplay.

"How long before you can drink?" I say.

He laughs. "I was just thinking about that. A week. You need to get out of this cold?"

"I'm fine."

"Bed weather," he says.

I don't say anything. I glance at him. He continues to look slightly stooped.

"You okay?" I say.

"I don't need Depends, if that's what you're asking."

It's tart. "Sorry," he says. We don't say anything for a stretch of blocks. A few flocks of schoolchildren spill into and out of the park, flush-faced, full of cold-weather energy. The city, as it sometimes does, seems decibels louder all of a sudden, every car horn or kid's voice magnified so that, for a minute, I don't hear Michael beside me.

> That is no country for old men. The young
> In one another's arms, birds in the trees
> —Those dying generations—at their song,
> The salmon-falls, the mackerel-crowded seas,
> Fish, flesh or fowl, commend all summer long
> Whatever is begotten, born, and dies.
> Caught in that sensual music all neglect
> Monuments of unageing intellect.

"Sailing to Byzantium," I say.

"Good," he says, starting again. "An aged man is but . . ."

"Michael, don't," I say, looking over his head into the thinning trees of the park.

But he goes on, very quietly, every soft-spoken word polished, unmistakable under the beginning rush hour din. ". . . unless Soul claps its hand and sing, and louder sing For every tatter in its mortal dress . . ." It's almost dark, lights coming on. It's actually a little less cold. I feel the sidewalk stones up through the soles of my shoes as we near Fifty-ninth Street, the Plaza, the tourist-snagging carriages lined up, smell the horse shit apparent even in the cold. ". . . To lord and ladies of Byzantium . . . Of what is past, or passing, or to come."

I have come to a stop. He turns and looks at me, that lopsided smile.

"Michael," I say. "I . . ."

"That was a long hike," he says. "I'm gonna grab a cab at the hotel. You want one?"

"No."

"I'll call you later. I'm staying in town 'cause I have a real early doctor's appointment."

My face betrays me. "I'm accompanied," he says. "Being watched like a hawk."

"Now?" I say.

"I know. Comic, isn't it?"

With a quick brush of my arm, he bolts away and disappears into a cab in front of the hotel. Gone. The city looks grimy all of a sudden, drained of color. I stand there looking at the hotel. It seems, for a moment, corny, touristy, a relic. The horse smell is oppressive, sad. I want to be home and I don't want to be home. Up the stairs, the solitary dinner, waiting for the phone. Why not a spoonful of peanut butter? Who have I been fooling with my small rituals? The china plate, the linen napkin. The line between mistress and spinster is finer than one knows. After all the fornicating and the fellatio, in the arid and solitary aftermath, they are sisters, we are sisters, plucky and alone. I start toward my apartment. The crowds are thick now, pushy, trying to get somewhere, get home. Everyone has a destination: a bar, a dinner, a train to the suburbs. I start to wander. I have no place to be, no one to meet. I think about it, about walking by the St. Regis, popping in to have a drink at the King Cole bar, because that's where Michael stays when he's in town and not with me—or says he stays when he is with me. What—to catch sight of him with his wife? No, Clare. It's just another night to be gotten through without breaking any rules. It's like emotional Lamaze; breathe, count, hold it, and the pain will pass. I do and my heart rate slows and I find myself walking up the steps of St. Patrick's Cathedral at Fiftieth and Fifth. I hesitate—surely this is blasphemy—but then go in. There's a pretty good crowd, some on their knees in the pews, some milling about with their digital cameras. On the little screens, I see the vaulted ceiling, the stained-glass windows, magnificence miniaturized. Somewhere up front a baby is wailing, but the cries seem small and faraway. I sit midway up on the left-hand side. All the candles, lit by tourists and supplicants, are flickering in their little amber glass containers and I, a secular humanist (how's that for a cumbersome phrase?), nonetheless succumb to a little sentimental awe. What am I doing here? Have I come to curse my lover and the faith that keeps him from me or have I come to pray for him and for his speedy recovery? Have I come to offer repentance for my own transgressions with one of their own or come to make bargains: If you grant him this, I will do this. If you let him be whole—how's that for delicacy, for chutzpah, the mistress praying for the erectile restoration of her adulterous Catholic lover?—then I will help Louise. I will be kind and sisterly, a shepherdess. Dangerous these bargains, even for a nonbeliever. They seem to contain their own code of ethics, especially if made in the House of the Lord. I don't belong here. This is tacky stuff, trying somehow to nestle up to Michael's faith in lieu of having him to nestle up to. Maybe I'm jealous. How comforting to have certainties, beliefs, axioms, even if you violate them. Then, of course, you have a ready-made path of repentance, confession. I cast around, looking for the confessional booths. What a marvelous little box; step in, shed your sin, step out, and go on your way. Does Michael do it, confess his adultery, furrow-browed and earnest and then buoyant and relieved, come out and call me as soon as he hits the sidewalk?

I get up and start to make my way down the center aisle. Halfway back, in a pew on the other side, I think I see that man from the other day, the one with the blond buzz cut and the Windbreaker who was talking to Louise. Can it be? This one's wearing a tweed overcoat and his head is bowed, but something in the color of the hair, the general look—I'm sure it's the same man. I retrace my steps up and then traverse over and walk down the other aisle past him to see if I'm wrong or being paranoid. I walk by quickly and then stop to see if he turns around. I am sure now that it is he. He seems to shift about there in the pew in the wake of my passing and half-turn, but then resumes his prayerful posture, camera around his neck. This is weird. Is he following me? A lot of people come to see this place. It's probably just a coincidence, but it sends an eerie chill, and when I reach the street, I move quickly, as quickly as I can, the pavement now slick from a light but steady rain. I don't have an umbrella. I never do. Michael chides me. You just don't think they're fashionable, he says. Agreed, I say. I usually have my big, floppy rain hat scrunched into whatever purse, but in my eagerness today, I forgot it. Home feels safe now, not lonesome as it did when I left Michael on the street. He will call later. I have to stop feeling freaked. Still, I feel a little clammy about that man in the cathedral. I should warn Louise. But what will I tell her? Anyway, if he's following any-one, apparently it's me. This is paranoia; happens in a big city. You catch sight of a stranger on serial days or outings and if you're not careful you begin to move in an urban noir film of your own imagining. I have, I realize, been somehow insulated by Michael's blustery love. If strangers have noticed and/or followed me, I have not noticed them. I have floated around freely, unseeing, safe.

When the phone does ring, I have a towel around my head and am in my pajamas peering out my bathroom window at the rain-misted city.

"Hi," I say, girlish.

"Clare?"

It's Louise. I am let down, but remember my bargain. Be nice. Help her and he will be all well. I tried not to make it, but I did, sitting there amid the stained-glass grandeur. I suppose these bargains are my form of faith. If I do this, will you grant me that? Placating the fates. That's how I think of it.

"I thought I would take you up on your offer of a makeover, if it's still . . ." She trails off in a giggle, a real one this time, not her nervous, half-baked new one.

"Louise," I say. "Where are you?"

I hear laughter in the background. Louise is with people. She is happy, drinking wine, I am sure. I have a twinge of jealousy.

"My friends are just having a little dinner party, but I thought I'd catch you."

"Yes, fine," I say. "I'll call and make an appointment, for, say, Thursday. You'd better give me a number where I can reach you."

"I'll call back tomorrow. I don't like to give out their number. Ta-ta."

"It'd be easier . . ."

But she has hung up, gone back to her party. Ta-ta. I was going to say something about the man in the Windbreaker—what, I'm not sure. Probably just as well. No need to spook her unnecessarily, not when she's having some fun. She deserves it. I wonder if her friends have big hair too. Well, we'll take care of that Thursday.

I make myself make an omelet. Back to the rituals. I turn on the TV, pour the wine, fold the napkin. Best to adhere to habits, what with the ground shifting a bit underneath. I am in bed typing up my interview notes on my laptop when the phone rings again.

"I'm in the men's room," he says, a bit slurry.

"You're cheating. You've had a drink."

"Aw, don't be a scold. I have a wife for that."

There is a pause. I don't say anything.

"Clare?"

"I'm here."

"Don't be cross."

"I don't like that kind of talk."

"Come on. I'm sorry. I just miss you and wanted to tell you how pretty you looked today in your—what did you call it—your winter white."

"But you shouldn't be drinking, right?"

"Okay, okay, you win. I've been a naughty boy."

"I don't like that, either."

"All right. Listen, I gotta go. People are beginning to rap on my stall."

I laugh in spite of myself. "They are not."

"The pissing hordes," he says.

"Michael," I say, "are we going to be all right? Are you going to be all right?"

"Fit as a fiddle in the blink of an eye, me lass. You'll see fer yerself."

"No more booze, please."

"Not another drop, I promise. Not till yer lyin' in me arms."

He hangs up. I don't much like the rogueish brogueish stuff. It always feels corny, sideways. He uses it (like the Yeats, but the Yeats is beautiful). But tonight I'll take the corny stuff, too, right along with my now habitual half Ambien. I wonder if he and Louise will ever meet, if she would like him, he her? Odd to think about—the lost half and secret half of my life meeting up. Would they flirt, tease, tease me? Best not to find out, I think. Best not. Back when, Louise got the attention of everybody's boyfriend without even trying. A spillage of young panters and drooling older men, the producers or directors Daddy brought home, even the ones with starlets on their arms. They wanted to put Louise in their movies but Daddy wouldn't let them. Easier not to be that beautiful.

"You are beautiful," Michael says.

"Pretty enough for all practical purposes," I say.

"The impractical ones, too," he says.

· 4 ·

"It's so odd being up here," Louise says.

"I know what you mean," I say. "It's one of the few things I haven't gotten used to."

We are sitting side by side on the second floor of a corner beauty parlor, windows onto Lexington. It does seem strange sitting up here looking down with a head full of tinfoil, something funny about second-story vanity, you up here getting gussied up in quasi-plain view while the life of the city surges around below.

"Florida's just like California," Louise says. "All the salons are on the ground and you're back in them so nobody can see you."

We are chatting, nursing our cappuccinos, leafing through magazines, Bronx-born Martin and his assistant, a slithery, ambisexual Puerto Rican, attending to both of us. They have talked me into more gold highlights, Louise into a few red streaks and a "hipper" cut. She is chatting, I know, because she is a little nervous, especially since her hands have nowhere to flutter, given that she is more or less shackled by a plastic apron.

"Timmy will be shocked," she says. "I mean if and when . . ."

She stops and we don't talk anymore while the men are still busy with us, painting and wrapping strands of our hair in the little silver squares. We fall back to showing each other pictures of stars in our respective tabloids. When they're finally done and take their rolling trays of goop and brushes away, I say, turning to look at her, "What are you going to do about all this?"

"I don't know," she says.

"Are you going to need help?"

"I don't really know. This is not usual. I mean, he's always been . . ."

"Sweet?" I say sourly.

"He really is, and he's such a good father."

"Meaning he's never hit them."

"Clare," she says, looking at me with tears in her eyes. "He really is a good man."

"Okay," I say. "I've heard it before. Something triggered it, right? You triggered it. You're still a beauty, Louise, and I am sure men pay attention to you . . ."

I see her flush, with pleasure this time, and she says, "Oh Clare, do you really think so? I've been feeling so sort of, I don't know."

"Nothing that a few red streaks won't help."

"Oh my, what do you think he'll say?"

She is smiling again, shy, pleased. She wants him to see it. She will go back.

"Will you promise me one thing?" I say, and when she turns, I see again that fear, and my entreaty takes on an edge. "Louise, you have to get some help here. You have to, before you go back. I can find you someone. You can't live like this."

"No, I know," she says. "I know you're right. But really Clare, this was an . . ."

"An accident? A fluke? That's just bullshit and you know it."

She flinches when I swear. "Clare, please don't use . . ." She stops. "I know you're only trying to help and I appreciate it so much." But she still has the residue of that pleasured smile and for a moment, I almost want to slap her myself, slap it away, slap some sense into her.

"He will do it again. You know that."

She shakes her head. "You don't know him."

"Oh, shit, Louise, why don't you just go back and get it over with?"

She is quiet for a while. The smile has gone. There is a tenseness around her mouth. She is looking out the window, not at me.

"You're so tough, Clare. Daddy said you'd gotten . . ."

"That's a taboo subject, Louise."

"He was my father too, Clare. You can't . . ."

Martin is back. He catches my eye in the mirror and cocks an eyebrow. He is asking whether he should go or stay, I can read that, and I pick up a foil, as if to say, please, stick around.

He starts to take my foils out and his assistant comes and de-foils Louise. We aren't talking so the men are chatting around us and occasionally at us. No doubt sibling feuds have been in these chairs before. We are ushered into seats to be shampooed and then back again to have our hair blown dry. There is a thaw as we all admire Louise's new streaks. She flushes. Odd how her beauty hasn't protected her from such self-consciousness. Maybe it has made it worse. Or maybe time has, the fear of losing it. I watch her. She is looking in the mirror, turning her head from side to side. "Wow," she says, "I guess it'll take time getting used to." I insist on paying for both of us and she impulsively leans to kiss my cheek there by the front desk.

She is a bit giddy as we walk the streets, turning to catch her reflection in the shop windows.

"I feel so different," she says. "I wonder what people will think."

"Your new friends up here or your old friends?"

"They're old friends too."

"I thought you said you'd only been here once before."

"They came up here last year to run the . . . oh never mind, I'm boring you," she says, hooking her arm through mine and turning again to a window, the sun now coming out behind us, to catch her hair. "Look, Clare, you can see the red streaks," she says, moving closer to the window.

There we are, midlife siblings, staring at our faces in a shop window and I suddenly realize that with her hair not all dark and poufed up, with the streaks and the layering, she looks much more contemporary, yes, but—I see now, have to admit it—less startling. Had I meant that to happen? She looks there, in the window—face shape, eye shape—more like me. I wonder if she sees it, if she knows.

"I'm sorry," she says to my face in the glass, "about what I said."

"I'm sorry too," I say, back to her face in the window. "I don't mean to ride you. It's none of my business really, but you did come here presumably for help."

"Yes," she says, "and you've been wonderful."

"I haven't done anything. You haven't let me."

"Letting us be friends—that's what I wanted."

We walk on, arm in arm, Louise turning often to the shop windows and then to me. "It's just so different," she says, shaking her head from side to side. "So . . ."

"Flat," I say, lightly touching the top of her head. We laugh together.

"This is so much fun," she says. "Let's go buy something for my new hair. Timmy gave me some money and told me to buy . . ." She catches herself. "I'm sorry," she says. "I won't mention him again. I know it upsets you."

"Listen, all I want to know is that he's not coming up here after you. I don't exactly know what I'd do if he did, but . . ."

"No, he's home with the kids. He wouldn't leave them."

"Aren't they old enough to look after themselves by now? They must be . . ."

"Fourteen and seventeen," she says and she is smiling. "Oh, wait, let me see if I can find a picture. I always sent Daddy some. Did you see them?"

"Not now," I say. I sound curt and she stops fumbling in her wallet for the pictures.

We walk along in silence.

"I'm kind of tired," I say. "And I need to get back to work."

"Don't go, Clarie," she says, using for the first time my childhood nickname. "Please don't go away mad."

We walk a bit more and, while trying to hold on to me, she still can't help herself from glancing in windows to see her new self, and I melt a bit.

"All right, just a little while," I say and she once again links her arm through mine and we are walking up Lexington Avenue, strolling sisters, something I would never have imagined possible just a few days earlier. It feels a bit surreal still, Louise beside me, Michael momentarily sidelined: a life reconfigured in a stretch of days. But he'll be fine. He'll be fine. Here I am meeting my side of the bargain, being nice to Louise, custodial. I will insist again—make that gently insist—that she get some help. Maybe she'll be able to leave the SOB. Maybe I'll go down there with her and meet my nephews and kick their father in the balls and tell him if he ever touches my sister—My Sister—again I will kill him. There she is again, stealing a glance at herself with childlike excitement and appetite, like the way she eats, and I tighten my own arm grip and steer her up the street toward Bloomingdale's. We run the gauntlet of all the aggressive perfume purveyors on the first floor, a phalanx of tall-limbed, black-suited, red-lipped models manqué with bottles cocked to spray. Louise is baring arms and wrists and laughing and tossing her new hair. They are drawn to her, as are the makeup artists beckoning from the inner aisles. I can see them as we pass, itching to get at her. A tall black woman finally just says, "Hey, sister, come with me," and takes her hand and Louise, laughing over her shoulder at me, says, "Is this okay? You have the time?"

"Sure," I say, following in their wake.

The woman, cooing and dabbing, goes to work. Twirling around Louise's upturned face, she applies foundation and eye makeup and lip liner, the whole works, and, as with the hair, Louise metamorphoses into this stunning, made-up, high-toned New York woman. But again, I feel a twinge of guilt. I have besmirched her real allure, toughened it and hipped it up. Now she will look like any number of those women, these women—in the store and out there on the urban streets. I watch her with the mirror, moving it to and from her face like a kid with a lollipop, and can barely remember the pale-faced, high-haired woman I first saw in the coffee shop a few days ago.

"Look what you have done to me," she says to me, smiling huge, eager, pulling out money from her purse to buy the pencils and jars the makeup "artiste" is pushing into her hands. I stop myself from stopping her. She's having fun. Let her buy, even though she will doubtless—like most of us—never use this stuff again. Who cares? Let her throw "his" money at this.

"You do it now," she says.

"No," I say, "it'll take too much time. Let's wander for a minute and case out the clothes."

Louise takes my arm again. I always forget till we are side by side that I turned out to be taller than she, especially now that her hair is down. Only by an inch or two, but I feel it beside her. I take her through the design floor and we *ooh* and *ah* over slinky dresses and diaphanous blouses.

"Who can wear this stuff?" she says. "You can see all the way through."

"Yes," I laugh. "That's the point."

"I guess I'm just an old prude," she says.

Who would have thought it, I start to say, but don't.

"Well, you don't look like one . . . anymore," I say, emphasizing that "anymore."

She winces ever so slightly.

"I didn't mean it meanly."

"It's okay," she says, but again I can see the light dim in her eyes.

"Let's get out of here," I say with determined cheerfulness. "It's too hot."

On the streets I ask her if she's been by Rockefeller Center yet to see the ice skaters, and she perks back up with girlish enthusiasm. "Oh, no," she says, "and I've been meaning to."

As we walk, she can't help but glance occasionally at a window—now there's not only that new hair but a new face full of new makeup. She is engaged, I can see, in an inner dialogue about who will like it, who won't: husband, sons, friends.

"They will think you've flipped, right," I say and she smiles because I've read her right. Her hands flutter around her face and hair. This time, I take them down. "You look fine," I say, "just great."

We stand at the rink watching the skaters do their thing. Louise, now looking like a native—save the clothes, which we have yet to hit—is acting like a delighted tourist.

"Oh, look at that one," she says pointing at a novice hacking his way around. "He's going to get hurt out there."

The flags around the rink are flapping and there are sharp, intermittent stabs of sunlight, like spotlights going on and off, and the good skaters seem to make for them with the instinct of a star for the limelight. It's getting cold and Louise and I instinctively move closer together at the railing. Once I saw the man I had been dating when I met Michael skating here. He was making easy, controlled loops, a small child by the hand, so young still and so bundled up I couldn't tell from up here whether it was a boy or girl. I knew he had married. I'd read the announcement in the *Times*. A match of Ivy League litigators. Mr. Keenan works at so and so and so and so. Mrs. Wylie-Keenan works at so and so and so and so and so. Could have been me, not the lawyer part obviously, but the bride part, and the mother part. He was my last chance for a "normal life," as he reminded me when we broke up. A normal life. Husband, kids. I feel Louise beside me. She has a normal life, right? I put my arm around her. She shifts toward me and I catch the edge of her smile as she stares intently at the rink.

"Oh, look, Clare," she says, as a tall skinny male skater with a red-and-white striped muffler lifts a small girl into the air over his head and the crowd around us makes appreciative noises as she arches her back, legs behind, arms out to the side. He removes a hand, holding her by just one; she's light as a feather. They spin through a shard of sunlight and then into a shadowed place and back into the sun. I feel the warmth on her small back and then the cold-ness and then the warmth and suddenly I realize it is me up there, that little girl, high, high in the air, face chafed, arms out, half scared, half exhilarated. I am eight and Weezie is eleven and it is the night of our annual Christmas party and the rink has been put down in our very own backyard, a bluff in Malibu overlooking the ocean, and a male skating instructor with tight red curls and slippery black pants has lifted me up and I am like a small bird, tummy down in the palm of his hands, the night rushing by my face and arms. I see Daddy, in his bow tie and shiny shoes, beaming back at me and Mommy over by the door in her long, white velvet dress (it's soft; I ran my face against it before she put it on) talking to someone, leaning, laughing, not looking at me. I am above the crowd, star-touching high, the red and white Christmas lights strung around the rink like blurry candy drops as I fly by, out toward the ocean and back toward the highway, the house off to the side like an all-lit-up ship.

"Weezie," I say, "do you remember our rink?"

"Vaguely," she says.

"Really. You don't remember it?"

"It was on the bluff beside the house, wasn't it? And we weren't bad, right? We should try it again." She is still looking down at the skaters and we are still standing close, though my arm is no longer around her.

Her memory is anemic, generic, distracted. Weren't bad, right? Who is this person beside me? She looks suddenly silly with her new hair and new face, an impostor, a sister-impostor in urban drag. For a flash, I have the feeling that is exactly what she is: someone who has inhabited the skin of my long-ago sister. That sister would remember our rink, that night.

"You really don't remember?" I press.

"We remember what we want to remember," she says, eyes still on the skaters.

We stand a while longer not saying anything. "Listen," I finally say, "I need to get back to work."

"That's okay," she says. "I'll just stay and watch a while longer. I don't have to meet my friends' daughter to catch the subway until five thirty."

"You're sure you're okay? I hate to just leave you here, but I have . . ."

Over her shoulder at a point just out of eye range, I see him again. I know it's him. This time he's back in the Windbreaker. He sees me see him and ducks out of view behind some rink-watchers down the way from us.

"Shit," I say.

"What?" Louise says, turning to me. "What is it?"

"I saw the man again."

"What man?"

"The man from the cathedral," I say and she looks perplexed. "The same man that was talking to you the other day at McDonald's. Then I saw him at St. Patrick's when . . ."

"What man at McDonald's?" she says, her face tightening.

"The one in the Windbreaker. I saw him talking to you."

"What were you doing—following me?"

"No. I mean yes, I was coming to try to catch you because I realized you hadn't given me a phone number."

This is closed Louise—I'd forgotten her—freeze-you-out Louise, and I hear the very beginning of an old childhood wheedle start up in me: Don't Louise, please don't, please talk to me, and impulsively, before I can stop myself, I say, "Why don't you stay with me a few days?"

"I can take care of myself," she says. It is hard, a rebuke.

I start to walk away, but I turn back. "Louise, who is this man? Did you come up here to see him? Why is he following you or us or whoever he's following?"

She has turned back to the skaters, but I can see in profile that her anger is dissolving toward tears that are beginning to dampen and distort all that expertly applied makeup. Those raccoon eyes again.

"What is it?" I say. "Tell me."

"I don't know what I'm doing," she says.

"Come and stay with me," I say. "We'll sort it out. If we have to call the cops, we will. I'll protect you."

"No, no," she says. "You don't understand. He loves me. He would never hurt me."

· 5 ·

L ouise comes in breathless, face flushed, gloved hands holding a big bag of groceries. It is five thirty. She has been really good, leaves the apartment every morning after breakfast and does not come back before this appointed time. She appointed it.

"You have to work during the day. I won't be any trouble," she said, hugging me, the day she moved in. I have cleared Michael's few things, his hooded sweatshirt and old pants from the hook by the front door and she has hung up her coat there and under it her pink chenille robe with multicolored flowers on it. The rest of her stuff she has left in her small black suitcase tucked under the coffee table in the living room. She is, I can see, trying to be neat, respectful, un-obtrusive. I try, when she is gone, not to look through her things. I try and I haven't done too much snooping. But some. I am not proud of this, but here she is, in my lair, my forty-four-year-old sister, and I am still trying to know her. The sturdy, 36-C bra and can of indus-trial strength hair spray—they are on the top of the suitcase. I just open and close it. I don't go poking around. And her books are on the coffee table in front of the sofa where she is sleeping: one on needlepoint and two romance novels. I wasn't sure at first. Gone are the full-cleavage damsels-in-the-arms-of-Lotharios. This new gen-eration has quiet, elegant covers—a sunset, a house on a hill. Don't want to embarrass the reader anymore. Louise herself clearly did not want to be embarrassed. She actually had these tucked into the outer flap of her suitcase where I found them and left them. But one night, when we were in our pajamas—actually, I was in sweats (I don't own pajamas and often sleep, on cold nights, in Michael's sweatshirt atop my own) while Louise had on her cuddly robe and matching slippers—and we were sipping some of Michael's brandy with our Sleepy-time tea (courtesy of Louise; she has, I've been interested to find out, a few Holistic sprinklings in her sturdy, suburban mom habits: the tea, zinc tablets for potential colds, soy powder for hot flashes) I asked her what she liked to read (that was sort of mean) and she flushed and said she wasn't much for the newspaper and she didn't, what with the kids, have a lot of time for serious stuff and then she actually leaned down and pulled out one of her paperbacks. The brandy made her voluble and girlish—alcohol always did, I remember—and she opened it and read a little: "She saw him across the room and she felt an electric jolt of desire start in her inner thighs and she couldn't wait for him to be deep . . ." She couldn't finish. She was giggling and blushing. Which made me giggle.

"At least she didn't use the word loins," I said.

"I know it's not up to your standards," she said, shutting the book and reaching down to tuck it back into the suitcase pocket and I realized I'd put her on the defensive again. I keep trying not to do that. I really don't mean to. The truth is I am growing used to her. I like when she comes home at night. I cannot imagine anyone else in my apartment—anyone but Michael, of course—but this Louise. Even though it's a little awkward, a little contested, there are these sweet places we bump into. We are still staying away from the Topics—her husband, our past—as if by mutual, unspoken agreement. We are doing what she said she wanted us to do: be friends. She is gone most of the day, doing what, I am not sure. When I ask, she says, "Oh, I went back to the rink." Or, "I just wandered." Or, "I sat in a coffee shop and did a little writing of my own." That last, talk of her writing, makes her hands flutter because she is self-conscious about it around me. Like with the romance novels. What I really think is that she is with him a lot, the man in the Windbreaker. She assured me he was not a danger, not a spy, not—in short—the culprit himself or a buddy thereof. I still worry, though I am amused: Louise, it seems, has a lover. As does her sister, though neither fesses up. But here in our cocoon, we are doing some bonding, in fits and starts, and I am beginning to worry about when she leaves for good. She has only been here six days, not even a full week, and I am beginning to worry. I look forward to her coming home with her groceries. These are the things she has brought home: Cocoa Puffs ("the kids got me hooked," she says); the makings of tamale pie (I've never made or eaten one—cornbread on top of hamburger and beans, calories off the charts); blush wine (goes great with the pie); baco bits for our salads; a sewing kit ("No need to take those things to the cleaners," she says, taking from my arms the pants where I've snagged the hem, sweaters with missing buttons). She is a sweet, retro miracle of homemaking—the real stuff, the old stuff, the stuff of our childhood. "Didn't Mrs. Palmer make tamale pie?" she says, referencing an old housekeeper of ours. "I don't think so," I say. "I'm sure I've never eaten it before."

In return, I am beginning to gather anecdotes for her—that's always my sign of affection, the bestowing of the anecdote; see what I've got for you—things one of my interviewees says, an editor, things overheard on the street. I like it when she shakes her head at me and says, "He didn't really say that, did he?" or "She really didn't say that, did she?" I like to make her laugh—that apologetic giggle is way down now that she feels safe (safer) with me, and I am glad. I try not to swear so much around her. I try not to outcook her. I made my roast chicken with chestnut stuffing, Michael's favorite. I'd forgotten the chestnuts, so Louise and I bundled up and went out to the street corner on Fifth to get them and it was so cold and we had such fun and then, eating it, Louise got that dreamy look she had eating that stuffed artichoke and I decided to cool it a little after that. I have got her walking up the five flights. Three at first, then four, now five. I didn't bolt ahead of her in my jock gear—bicycle pants and running shoes—that night after our emergency chestnut run, as she was in Michael's sweatpants (I washed them, claimed that some old boyfriend had left them) and some old scuffed tennis shoes (yes, his too; he has small feet, though they were big on her and caused her to shuffle). I looked back at her, down at her, coming up the stairs behind me, her red streaks, her heavy breathing, and slowed down to wait for her.

We are, for the closeness of our quarters in my seven-hundred-square-foot, one-bedroom apartment, strangely modest with each other. We don't wander around naked or even half-naked, in bra and panties. Always a robe (for her), and at least a T-shirt and panties (for me). And if there is a momentary sighting, out of the shower, or Louise dressing in the living room when I appear from the bedroom, we turn away. I wonder how easily she disrobes with her pursuing suitor, down to those big, firm breasts. It's that, isn't it—them? It isn't modesty, per se. She doesn't want me to see them. They're the focal point of her protective modesty, not her slightly soft, childbirth-crenellated middle. I saw them once, the breasts, in profile, and they are silly, jutty firm. They tug at me. I don't want to think about him, the battering breast buyer, the husband, because I know that sometime, not so very far away, there will be some sort of a showdown. She will go back to face him, he will come here to face her. Has to happen. There are boys, a whole other life. But I don't want to bring up the topic anymore, don't want to abash my so recently returned sister with reality, not while she is having her moment and I am sharing it.

Am I jealous? She seems so innocently flushed and pleased when she comes back some days. She says she has had a good day writing—hands flutter-fluttering. "How was yours?" But I think she was with him. I do. Maybe even in one of "our" hotels, the very room. Six twelve at the Plaza, five fortysomething at the Stanhope, or any number of those blond anonymous suites in those convention hotels, the Marriotts and Hiltons, where, in early blush, Michael and I would meet for a quickie (or two sometimes) between his mayoral rounds and my reportorial ones. I have not lain with Michael since his surgery. Days stretch out, weeks, a month. Lain with. Such a pretty phrase compared with all the explicit, grunt-ugly expressions for sex. He calls at odd times. He's back at work only part-time and he'll call, on impulse, at eleven A.M. or four P.M. and I will jump out of my writing attire, my sweats, and into something girl-flirty and rush out to meet him. He is drinking again, gingerly, and we will sit in a noisy bar, sipping our cabernet, eating peanuts, knees bumping under the low table in the corner. I have brought stories, anecdotes: tamale pie (have you ever, I say; sounds pretty good, Michael says) with blush wine (I'd have to draw the line there, he says), romance novels (recite me some, he says with a wink, taking my hand and placing it on his crotch; he smiles when there is a stirring; soon, he says), the lover in the Windbreaker. I have turned my sister into a heartland, baco bit–eating anecdote and I serve her up on a platter to Michael whenever he and I meet. A new installment, a new recipe, the hair reasserting itself against its trendy layered New York cut, rising—just a little each day. I have seen Louise in the bathroom slightly, slightly backcombing it again, teasing it, ratting it (that's the old expression, isn't it?), and spraying it because it's the habit of a lifetime, I see (did she go right from her adolescent braids to this?), and she finally cannot not do it, pouf it back up, though she is trying to do it just a little so as not to arouse my eye and/or tart remark. I am trying to be kind. I want to be. This whole thing will be over soon enough. Has to be, though sometimes I have this fantasy— wholly unusual for me; my fantasies, for years, have tended to be

sexual (and professional: prizewinning books, for example) not
familial—that she will go home and gather up her boys and come
back up here and live with me, all of us squished in and loving, in a
sophisticated, umbilical way. The one is old enough; he must be
about to go away to college. So just the little one, the gawky, sweet
still-fourteen-year-old who will just flip for his hip, ultra-urban aunt.
I will show him the city, as Michael showed me, every corner and
cranny—not just Ellis Island and Grand Central Station, but Brooklyn and Harlem, the dives, the fabric—and he will become a writer
and dedicate his first book to me. I have finally seen his face, seen
pictures of both the boys. I came home late from a long, teasy bar afternoon with Michael (hand on the crotch, under the overcoat across
his lap, him a bit misty-eyed and hopeful, me a little grumpy, wondering if he is dry-running his new—compromised?—libido at
home, trying to rev it up, see if it is in working order before bringing
it to me. I almost ask him a half dozen times, but don't) to find a
darkened apartment. It was after six and I sensed Louise there the
minute I walked in, but I didn't see her as I switched on the living
room light.

"Louise," I said. "You here?"

I found her in my bed, on top of it, the chenille throw up over her
legs. She seemed to be sleeping, but when I got close, I could see that
her eyes were open and she was looking out the window at the New
York night. I thought I saw, by the light of the window (I hadn't
turned a light on yet), a glistening in the eyes.

"Weezie," I said, "are you okay?" sitting down beside her, putting my hand on her back. Her hand was up by her face and in it, I
saw, were photographs, small ones, the kind that fit in a wallet. I gently took them from her and reached for the light. She closed her eyes
tight against the sudden brightness and more tears fell, a silent cas-
cade, as if they were being squeezed out.

"I miss them so," she said.

I looked at the pictures, clearly the boys, her sons, my nephews. First time I was seeing them. I always refused to look at the pictures she sent Daddy. Sometimes he actually left them lying around and I would just, without looking, gather them up, put them in an envelope and put them back on his desk. It was a very occasional little game and he never said anything. But here they were in my hand. I reached for their names. I'd heard them, but . . .

"Lawrence?" I said.

"Lucas," she said. "Luke."

"The older one?"

"Yes. Matthew—Matty's the baby."

I looked at him, my fourteen-year-old fantasy kid. Baseball cap on backward, clearly his father's coloring or someone's, not Louise's. He's freckly and reddish-haired. He looked a little goofy. It was Luke who stopped me. A grave smile, high cheekbones. Something less boy about him. Not that he's a man or that it's a man's face. Something thin, almost ethereal but not ungendered.

"About to go away to college, I would guess," I said.

"No," she said, "he's had some problems, lost at least a year. . . ." and then she was sobbing and I didn't say anything more or ask anything. I turned off the light and lay down beside her, our faces to the window, and pulled the throw over both of us and put my arms around her. Her body shook for a long time and then she finally relaxed and we both dozed off. I awoke before she did but I didn't move—the thing I do with Michael, only Michael, never done with anyone else, didn't care enough to keep vigil over their sleeping—because she was still making small, snoring breaths and I didn't want her to awaken to her sorrow. Maybe she would sleep it off. Maybe we would pass the night like this. I imagined, of course, the things the boy has done or that have happened to him: a car accident—him driving—where someone was maimed, drugs, AIDS (okay, yes, that face is so thin and beautiful, but that's such knee-jerk politically incorrect stuff to surmise gayness from just a photograph). As the night went on and we lay there, I tightened my arms around Louise, and in the silence, simply let myself offer solace, love even, no disruptive banter or bitterness, no recriminatory memories. Sleep, sleep, Weezie. We'll face your troubles tomorrow. You'll see. I'll help.

I awoke in the morning, under the throw, still fully clothed. I had slept all night. Louise had slipped away at some point. Now I heard her in the kitchen. I stopped to pee and brush my teeth and then went out, expecting that she, too, would be carrying the sweet residue of our nighttime closeness. Sure of it. A big smile on my face. But hers wore the sadness she had finally given way to. It was visible under an armor of distaste. Her hair was medium-teased back up; she had lipstick on and her coat and her blue-and-brown paisley scarf.

"Don't wait dinner for me," she said, as she put her coffee cup in the sink and got ready to leave.

"No tamale pie?" I said, trying to be light.

She didn't say anything. "I think it's time for me to go home," she said.

"Did something happen, I mean, with your friend?"

She laughed, but it was a laugh edged with bitterness. "Oh, Clare," she said. "You always think you know everything."

I sat down on the sofa, a "screw you" threatening to come out. Instead, after calming down a minute, I said, "But you can't."

"What?"

"Go home. Nothing's fixed."

"This isn't working," she said. "I feel cheap." And then she said, "You don't understand."

"Try me," I said.

"We shouldn't do this now," she said. "You have to work."

"So you're just going to disappear again?" I sounded angry.

"Really. Let's not do this. We'll talk tonight."

She walked out and left me sitting there. The old fury welled up, but it was all tangled up with sadness. I didn't want her to go again. She'd waltzed back in and laid some claim to something in me and now she was going to waltz back out. Maybe if Michael hadn't been missing in action, I wouldn't have been susceptible. And then the holidays were coming and they were always tough for a mistress, especially one with an observant lover. All those midnight masses and grandkid Christmas pageant plays at their Catholic schools. No, I didn't want her to go back there, to him, to them. Maybe I would go with her, get her settled, bond with the boys, put the husband on notice while being eminently, sororally discreet about her time with me in the big, bad city. I determined to woo her, keep her.

That was three days ago and we are back on track, sort of. Everything feels a little weird. She is restive. Her cell phone rings often now at night and she moves into the bathroom with it before answering. Sometimes I hear her laughing, a thin laugh. Sometimes she comes out with red eyes. I don't ask who it is. I simply say, looking up from my laptop or the newspaper or whatever is in my lap that I am pretending to be involved in while having an ear cocked to her bathroom conversations, "Okay?"

"Yep," she says. "For now."

We are cooking little meals again. I am. Her heart has gone out of it, though I encourage her. "No," she says, "Clare, you do it. You're the master chef around here."

I don't like it. I don't like her punctured like this. I don't make anything very fancy: an omelet, a broiled chicken. I try to get her to shop with me, to bundle up and go out into the shiny, cold winter streets, but she won't. "Too many stairs," she says.

"I'll give you dispensation," I say, with a smile. "You can use the elevator."

It works sometimes, but mostly now she is curled in on herself. I don't ask about Mr. Windbreaker, husband, kids, her writing, nothing close to the bone, for fear of arousing her, scaring her off, making her feel threatened or judged. Sometimes, when we have had dinner and enough wine, we loosen up again and chat. I ask her to read more of that romance novel—if she is in a good enough mood for me to do it—and she obliges and we both laugh.

"Pretty corny stuff," she says. "I am sure we could do it better."

"Absolutely," I say. "We could do alternate chapters and . . ."

Her phone rings and she gets up with it and disappears again and when she comes back the mood is broken. In fairness, when Michael calls, I, too, disappear into another room and, depending on the conversation, on whether we are going to be able to see each other the next day, come back a little giddy or a little deflated. She doesn't pry, either. We are, in a very small space, making circles around each other and then finding sweetness sometimes at the center. I show her my bathroom perch and sometimes I find her standing up there watching the night, her scarf wound around her neck above her fluffy pink robe. I bring in the stepstool from the kitchen so I can stand beside her.

"Sometimes they have parties over on that roof," I say, pointing.

"It's so big, isn't it—so anonymous?" she says.

"I know," I say, "but you get used to it. It's home to me now."

"You'll stay, then?"

"I wouldn't know where else to go."

"No," she says. "I can see that. This suits you."

"Why," I say, after a long pause, "did you turn up at Daddy's funeral?"

She tenses, but recovers. "To pay my respects."

"You saw me there. Why didn't you come say something?"

"Because I figured you'd be angry." She is standing on the toilet, as I've shown her, and I am standing next to her on the little chair I've brought in, close enough to smell her hair spray, both of us looking out the window. She leans toward me and rather playfully bumps me with her shoulder. "No," she says, "because I knew you'd be angry. At that point he was yours."

I buy her a new scarf: cashmere, pinks and soft purples, and present it to her at dinner. "To go with your robe," the little card says, and she smiles and tears up when she says thank you and it feels real and it feels fake, the whole scene of it, as if we are playacting at being sisters while being sisters.

What is clear here is this: We are both holding our breaths, waiting for some shoe to drop, for something out there to come get us or hurt us or disappoint us. Or what, make us happy? That's possible isn't it, a happy ending to all of this?

.6.

We are having breakfast together when our respective cell phones ring. Louise, in her pink robe and scarf, immediately abandons her Cocoa Puffs—I am eating them, too, in a show of solidarity; actually it's kind of fun and transgressive—and retreats to the bathroom, where she begins one of her usual hush-toned conversations. I take mine in the bedroom and scrunch back down under the covers. Michael, of course. With him in my ear, I pretend he is next to me, my head on his chest, his coppery hairs tickling my cheek. He has a short meeting at noon and then is free. Can I meet him?

"Which bar?" I say.

"Not what I had in mind," he says.

"Shit," I say, "not back to the tea salon?"

He laughs. "No, I was thinking of something a little more X-rated."

"A movie?"

There is a pause. "Ah," I say, getting it. "That."

He clears his throat. "You think you're up to it?"

"Isn't that my line?" I say. Kittenish, bantery. Is that a chuckle or more throat-clearing? "Michael?"

Nobody says anything. Maybe somebody in the room all of a sudden. I hold on. Finally I say, "We don't have to do this, you know."

"That's my line," he says.

We laugh. A little nervous. Starting over. "We can't be here," I say, "because of my sister."

"A hotel it is, then," he says. "I'll call back."

"On the cell," I say. "I have to go by the magazine."

When we hang up, I lie there, trying to invite a languorous optimism. I look out the window. Hard to tell the weather. Looks reasonably bright, but, of course, that doesn't mean anything. Louise and I were about to flip on the TV so we'd know how bundled up we had to be, but the phones rang before we could do it. I realize I don't hear her out there. Maybe she's slipped back into the chair and is finishing her puffs. I hope so. I would like a little idle chitchat. But I don't find her. She must have slipped out. Underneath my half-finished bowl, I find a little note. "Had to run. See you tonight. Might have a little surprise."

Are surprises ever good—even "little" ones? They're always, per se, an emotional ambush, even the so-called good ones. What will hers be? Surely not a new haircut or recipe. No, I fear she might be moving on, moving out, moving back. Lots of those late-night cell phone calls, red eyes, thin laughs. I am worried but don't press, we are so recently tethered again, somewhat retethered. I can't help myself now, though. What is this surprise? Can I de-surprise it? I look around the apartment for clues. She has continued to be scrupulously neat. Is her robe still on the door? It is. I lift the top of the suitcase to see if she is more packed than usual and find everything as before, folded, her little makeup kit tucked on the top, jammed with the Bloomingdale's possessions she no longer uses, or even tries to. Truth is, she doesn't really need any of it. Never did. I scan the bathroom. I gave her one little glass shelf next to the toilet for her stuff and it's still there, lined up, toothpaste—rolled from the bottom; we are bottom-up rollers, Louise and I (or did she just mimic my tidiness?)—toothbrush, travel-size Listerine, dime-store cold cream. All still there. Okay. I get up on the toilet and lift the window and stick my head out. Blue, blue sky. Sun. But cold, cold. I hear the city hum, imagine people bustling about, windows full of orangey nods toward Thanksgiving—napkins and paper turkeys and dried leaves. Is it already here? Next Thursday. Louise and I haven't talked about it. Will we be sitting here having our own little Thanksgiving, my turkey, her stuffing? We will scrap over the cranberry sauce, I am sure. I don't like it sweet or made with orange juice and I am betting she will. I won't think about that, won't think about how many years it's been since Louise and I had Thanksgiving together, won't let myself count (won't—as the calculator starts; what's forty-four minus twenty-seven?), won't think about her surprise. I will think about Michael, warm and furry and expectant under a thick quilt in a quiet, uptown hotel. I will sail toward that in my winter finery. I layer on—thinking all the while of the unlayering, that seasonal striptease—satiny underpants and camisole, brown stockings with diamond pattern, brown tweed, knee-length skirt, cashmere sweater set in off-white, city-smart brown suede heels, not too low, not too high, big-collared brown coat with a belt, beige and brown muffler, leather gloves. That's where they start, right?—the strippers—with the gloves, one finger at a time. *Da-dum, da-dum.* I'm almost out the door, my own briefcase-like purse over my arm, when I see Louise's, the strap of it, hanging on the door under the robe. Has it been here before? Did she mean to leave it? I've seen her coming and going with it every day. She must have left with something smaller this time. I take it down and peek in. Papers. Her writing. I can see that. Ruled legal-sized white notebooks lined with small handwriting. I mustn't. This is a real violation. I'd kill someone who read my work-in-progress clandestinely. It would make me crazy. But the temptation. It's got to be silly, right? I used to write Louise's papers for school those last couple of years, trying to help her get through when she barely made it to class. I didn't make them really good, not

A papers, because that would have aroused suspicion. B-plus, the occasional B-minus, even the occasional C-plus. I knew how to hit it right on the money. How many spelling or grammar mistakes, how many lapses in logic or run-on sentences you needed to get exactly what grade. Louise thought it was funny—I was—in my effort to keep her going. I wanted her to finish, to graduate at least from high school. I didn't want her to have no skills, to trade on her daunting beauty. I was going to protect her from herself, from those sniffing-around producers and directors (and wife-abusers; it is still a long way from there to here, isn't it? Or is it, was that the slippery slope?). Louise, lying in bed reading a movie or fashion magazine or just listening to her little record player, would look over to where I sat at her desk, writing her paper, and say, "Okay, read me something." And I would and she would say, "Whoa, that's way too goddamn good." She was the swearer then. And I'd say, "Do you really think so?" And she'd say, "Yeah" and laugh. And I would laugh. "Just can't help yourself, can you?" she'd say next. "I'll write it this way and then I'll make it worse," I'd say back.

It takes all my willpower not to read her pages. Tempting, but I just can't. I leave them there on the door and make my way out into the day. Stunning, as it appeared to be from the window, every skyscraper sharp against the blue sky, not a cloud anywhere. But very cold. I take my muffler off and wrap it around my head and ears, holding it with a hand at the throat. Everyone is moving fast, heads down, their exhaled breaths little puffs in the chilly sunlight. I have to stop and talk to my editor about the aged shrink piece. She wants me to do something, gave me the blah blah sweet talk, so much good stuff but a little more of this or that. A hint that I've been a little boldly acerbic in places. Up I go in a hushed elevator of skinny young women, newly post-college by the look of them, pullover sweaters over untucked shirts, tails out over low-slung pants, chunky shoes. I am an overdressed anachronism. I am, I realize with an inner laugh, Louise to their Clare. I sit in the outside office waiting for Miriam. This is her baby, this magazine for twenty- and thirtysomething women who want stuff: flat abs, designer jogging wear, good men with flat abs. Acquisitiveness masquerading as liberation. Oh well. I like Miriam. She is smart, a seventysomething divorcée who reinvented herself (thanks to her megamillion divorce settlement) through her own late-in-life hunger for what she'd missed. She gets her readers. A little health, a little spirituality, clothes, exercises, and sex—but not too X-rated, not even very R-rated. This is tame, capitalistic turf and it's working great. I do some of the "thinking" pieces for them—as Miriam calls them—about women and men, about adoption and infidelity and about how soon is too soon to have your first nip or tuck. Lets me use decent words, be a little writerly, pays well. I usually don't do profiles but she wanted me to do the psychiatrist. Now she is not overly pleased, I can see. We are sitting side by side, staring at my words on her computer screen. She is all energy, brushed-back silver hair and matching cream-colored cashmere pants and pullover, tapping the words with her discreetly polished fingernail. I am holding my phone. Michael hasn't called. I hope Louise doesn't leave. Not before Thanksgiving. I'll let her put the orange juice in the cranberry sauce, the marshmallows on top of the sweet potatoes. I promise. Okay now—Michael, call.

"Clare, sweetie. Can you just tone it down here a little? This woman is becoming a real heroine among my readers. They loved her book, *Making Peace with the Feminine*."

I start to say, "Come on, Miriam; she's all grandmotherly bromides about being true to your inner woman, gift-wrapped in a little Jung and twelve-step jargon." But I don't because, of course, that's what this magazine is and I am writing for it, so who am I to cast stones? Miriam knows exactly what she's doing, anyway. She would just smile at me. She does that when I grump a bit. Then I fix it (mostly) her way. She always lets me leave in a little sliver of something to salve my ego or pretensions or whatever it is (that's what I mean by smart). "Okay," I say, "I'll temper it. You have to admit, though, she talks in needlepoint. Happiness is reality divided by expectations. Can't you just see that on a pillow?"

"Good idea," Miriam says with a smile. "I'm sure they'd sell like . . ."

"Thongs," I finish.

Her tolerant motherly beam. She is about to pat me on top of the head. At least it feels that way. "You want to just sit here and do it now? I have to go talk to Max, anyway."

I look at my watch. 11:12. Where is he? "Sure, I'll stay for a little bit."

She leaves and I stare at the screen with no particular intentness. Words, my words. Funny to see them here. Disembodied. Pulsing slightly. Puny, somehow. That's what strikes me. I usually do the revisions at home. It feels more—what, important, controllable, mine? Here, it just feels like another product to be fed into this machine, where it will be tweaked and spit out, assembly-line fashion. I get up. I can't do this here. From Miriam's corner office here on Park and Thirty-fifth, I see the city in its late fall luminosity, from up here a pop-up book of a city, no street grunge, no homeless, no honking cabs or assaultive smells. Just bridges and skyscrapers, all shimmery from up here, steely and assertive. So much yearning to conquer. I loved that about the city when I first got here. I would join the throng of yearners and conquerors. I would write. I would start over. The cliché always went the other way: People went west to my home state to start over. Edge of the continent stuff. This was an edge, too, it just tipped the other way. I came here, got a New York apartment, a New York life, a New York lover. I was a cliché-bender. Who am I kidding: I don't bend clichés; I recycle them. All I have to do is glance at the screen, those hackneyed phrases from the latest media-anointed guruess that I am cheerfully quoting. I am nothing but a cliché pimp.

Where the hell is Michael?

I tell Miriam's cheerful male secretary, Gardner, that I will fix the piece at home and get it back to her tomorrow.

"Love the pumps," he says, pointing at my shoes.

"They work," I say.

"I'd say," he says.

Just then the phone rings—a momentary confusion, his or mine. We both answer. Michael, at last, on the other end.

"Running tight," he says. "Where are you?"

"Park and Thirty-fifth."

"Let me think for a sec." I hold. Gardner is watching me, eyebrow cocked. I turn away, toward the elevator. "The Waldorf then," he says. "At one."

"You sure that'll work?"

"Hey, 'member me? I've got pull."

Sure. I do remember. Not for the first time, certainly, I think again of the smoothness of all this, of my inevitable predecessors. Had to be some, huh? Michael will never tell. Even when I resort to a little postcoital prodding. Tell me about the others, their specialties? What others? he says. There haven't been any others. Do I say the obvious? There is at least one other. I do not.

The phone rings just as the elevator comes. It's empty and as the door closes and Garden mouths a "bye-bye" accompanied by a little wink, I hear Michael's voice. "Room eleven forty-three."

A room number dropped into the phone, into the cold, crystalline day. A destination. I walk slowly. The normal city smells are leached clean by the cold. I have time to kill. I try to let anticipation kick up through me, try to feel the silk against skin way down underneath all the layers, but there is a foreboding tickle down there too. How's this going to be, exactly? Someone opens the door from the inside and I walk through. I pause before the elevator, nervous, unwrapping my muffler, catching my own eye in the shiny door.

"Now that we know what you are, let's haggle about the price." The punch line of a joke I would like not to have remembered just now.

Michael lets me in when I knock. He has a cell phone tucked between ear and chin. Shoes and tie off, first shirt buttons undone, the curlicues of coppery hair. A place for my head—that chest. I will be happy. I will put my head there. He is frowning and, I realize now, angry.

"That's the goddamn stupidest idea. Who let him do that?"

A pause. The rebukee is trying to talk, but Michael interrupts . . . "So you guys managed to do it so it can make the news at five. Congratulations."

He takes a breath, remembers to smile at me, a chin-thrust, a semi-wink, tilts his head in a gesture at the champagne bottle on ice. I am touched. Haven't had that in a while. Of course, we haven't been anywhere, out of my apartment, for a long stretch—a year or two—then just a weekend night out on Long Island. But this, hotel city sex, is different, a throwback. I sit in the chair by the champagne. Michael, hands free, makes the uncorking motion. He taught me how, way in the beginning, to tuck the bottle under your arm, at an angle, and delicately twist the cork, calmly. I flinched the first few times it popped, spewing bubbly liquid onto the carpet, but now, no problem. I am an old pro. I sit there for a minute beside the window, still fully swaddled.

"Well fix it," he says into the phone. "Issue a correction immediately. Let me know." He puts his the phone down.

"What," he says, turning to me, "lost your nerve?" He is talking about the bottle of champagne—I think that's what he's talking about—which he is now opening, the bottle damp and dripping as he turns it. "Gorgeous out there, isn't it?" he says, looking over me out the window. "Speaking of . . . you look pretty gorgeous yourself."

Does it sound corny, tinny, or is it just me? I try to smile.

"Gonna stay?" he says, and I do smile. He hands me a glass of

champagne and starts unbuttoning the rest of his shirt. We're on a
tight schedule here. His phone rings again—and he mouths "last
call" at me as he answers. "Read it to me. Don't make it so groveling.
An honest mistake is all." He sits down on the edge of the bed, still
listening, reaching with a free hand to take off a sock. Then the
other. "That'll do. Run it by Jack if you change anything. I'll be out
of reach for an hour or so."

An hour or so. Let's get at it. I think of keeping everything on.
Me clothed, him naked, a nude pawn for me to work over with hands
and mouth, his mouth, in turn, on the layers: wool, cashmere, silk. I
think of the other, him finding me sometimes clothesless, nothing
on, when he comes in, the feel of his wool pants against my bare
skin. It is exciting, the disjunction. Should we try that?

"Aren't you," he says, clearly on a different fantasy page, "a little overdressed for this?"

"Guess so," I say, taking off my coat. Forgot: The gloves go first.
No time for that now. Michael is already under the covers. He is not
looking at me quite. I strip quickly and slide in beside him. This is a
thing to be done. A necessary reconsummation. We hold on, not
even kissing, just all arms. There is, I think, fear in this bed with us.
Michael kisses the top of my head and tucks it down on his chest. I
love it here, before and after the sex. My place in the world, the city.
You can always hear it, before and after, sometimes during even: not
just the obvious, the occasional siren, but the thrum of life down
there, the heartbeat of the place, all that yearning and striving. Even
if you can't really hear it, you imagine it, all going on, everybody
out and urgent, rushing to meetings or restaurants or shops, buying
and making deals and arguing and laughing while you, floors up,
slippery and incubated, partake of explicit joy in the broad daylight,
curtains open because you're high enough that no one can really see
in and, a kicker of an aphrodisiac, you don't care, now sitting on
your lover, a slinky sea creature in a high-rise aquarium in the sky, if

they can catch a glimpse from over there in their work cubicle in that sleek steel tower.

Today no. Today there is a hitch. Shall we talk? Or shall we just lie here in one another's arms? Or must we rustle ourselves to the task at hand? I do, I try, I will, I can. I minister, I administer. I am alternately salacious and tender. I keep thinking, for some inane reason, of Paul Revere: One if by land and two if by sea, and I on the opposite shore shall be. One if by hand and two if by mouth and I . . . over and over. Up and down, up and down. One if by land and two if by hand and I on the opposite shore shall be. I expected this; I'd read the literature about prostate cancer, knew this a good possibility. But I didn't expect it or allow myself to expect it. Not really. Not Michael. I fight, his penis in my mouth, tears.

"Guess we jumped the gun a bit," he says, lifting my head. "Come back up here."

He tucks me against his chest again, but there is no humming, no recitation of Yeats. After a while, as I am drifting—Paul Revere has galloped away—he says, "I can do you."

It sounds crude and mechanistic—so un-Michaelish. Do you. Not the language of lovers. Kids use it. Did he "do you"? I don't say anything. I just shake my head "no." He slips out of bed and disappears into the bathroom and comes back with a half a hard-on and I try not to think of him in there, like a boy masturbating picturing God knows what, as he climbs on top. We make the motions for a little, but it doesn't hold and he rolls off.

"It's not a big deal," I say. Women say that. That's what we say. And we mean it and we don't mean it. "Really," I say.

His phone rings and he swings over and out of bed and we are both relieved to have the distraction. He is himself again, hectoring a colleague and then laughing. "I told you, Jack, you can't trust these pikers. You gotta watch them better." His back is turned to me and love for that back just overwhelms me. I get up quietly and put my arms around him that way and my cheek against him as he continues to talk on the phone and he reaches back and puts a hand on my ass. We are fine. Just fine. It will be fine.

He puts down his phone but doesn't move. We stay standing tucked together until his phone rings again. I go to the bathroom with a grabbed handful of clothes and dress without, this time, catching my own eye in the mirror. He is dressed when I come out, sitting on the bed, leaning over to tie a shoe. I walk over and put my hands on his head and he leans into my stomach. I lean to kiss his curls then put on my coat and muffler. He walks me to the door. We never leave together. I go first. Ladies first, he always says, kissing me one last time at the door and he says it now just like always. "Run along," he says. "I'll call you later."

The door shuts and there I am, walking down the plushly carpeted corridor and into the elevator and through the lobby and out into the still bright day. It feels even colder and I take my muffler from around my neck and cover my head and ears. I don't want to go home, don't want to face the rewrite, don't want to face bed-thoughts of Michael there. If it weren't so cold, I would just keep walking. The thing to do in this city, let yourself be jostled and comforted by strangers. But it is now borderline bitter, if still radiant. A chilly wind has kicked in. I decide to hop a cab and head to the Metropolitan Museum. It is my place of refuge, huge, cavernous. You can wander a trail of beauty from Egypt to current days. This is my church, my synagogue, my mosque, my St. Patrick's. This is where I worship and genuflect, before the things made by human hands. By the time I get there, the wind is so strong people seem to be blowing up and down the wide stairs. Inside, it is the opposite, calm and overly warm, of course. I de-bundle and head toward the ancient coffins and the cases of gilded artifacts. I banish all thinking, all memory of the afternoon. Denial is a friend of the mistress in the best of times and, oh, now, in the darker. I hold his back again, my breasts squashed against him, our melded nude figures pressed against the glass behind which is a death mask of a beautiful young king.

I wander for a long time, sitting for stretches on a bench here or there, looking at this or that, seeing and not seeing a small carved, flying horse from some eons-ago Egyptian dynasty, a Jackson Pollock, manic and orderly disordered. I won't go home until it's dark. I will stop at the market. I will go home and eat and work, not on the piece but on the stories. Time to get serious about finishing them. Michael will call, slurry with whiskey or some other inebriant, a man full of reinflated blarney and bravado, a man restored. We will flirt on the phone, make a new date, new plans. He will croon in my ear. Come fly with me, come fly, come fly with me.

I feel better for my stay in the museum, especially when—as luck would have it on a cold, cold night—I manage to get a cab right out front when it drops someone off. I get off at the little corner grocer and buy a box of dried linguini and a couple of cans of clams, parsley, a lemon, and then I remember Louise's surprise. I kind of hope she isn't there to spring it on me, that I can have my little solo meal as usual— usual before her reappearance ten days ago already—and get to work. No wine. Promise yourself. No wine with the Linguini Vongole.

I trudge up the steps, cold to the bone from the outside, though again, it is hot in here, so much so that when I reach my apartment, I am actually sweating a bit in all my layers. That's what you get for wearing silk and cashmere. I unlock and open. It is dark, not a light anywhere, save from the window, but I sense someone there.

"That you?" a voice says, slurry—this one for sure.

"Louise?"

"Bingo," she says.

"Weezie, what are you doing here in the dark?" I say, switching on a light, knowing full well she is—or has been—drinking. She covers her eyes with the back of her arm and says, "Oh, no, Clare, turn it off, please."

For some reason I do. I go to the kitchen to leave the groceries and she calls after me, "Get yourself a glass, sister. I bought some good stuff from that place you took me to. They told me you like this."

I laugh at the "Get yourself a glass, sister"—it sounds like something out of an old Western—but the truth, is, once again, I am touched. She has bothered about me. In the bedroom I change out of my finery and get into my sweats and join her back in the living room. I hand her my wineglass and she fills it. I can't see the label well enough to read it. I sip and smell, heavy, red, California.

"Good, isn't it?" I say.

"It works," she says. There is—what, angst, sorrow, bitterness? I can't quite differentiate.

"Weezie?" I say. "You okay?"

"No," she says. "I don't think so."

"Is it the guy in the Windbreaker?"

"I wish it were that simple," she says.

"Is it Timmy? Is he after you to come home?"

She doesn't say anything for a long time. "It's so hard," she says. "The hardest."

I don't press. I wait for her. Sisters on the verge of confidences. But she doesn't say anything more and in the silence, my own sadness comes unglued. She says, "Oh, Clarie, Clarie, what is it?" And then I do what I promised I wouldn't do with anybody, anytime, anywhere. I tell her about Michael, not all of it, just some: the man I love, older, prostate cancer. I go funny about the afternoon, the antic efforts to arouse—she has been there, yes?—all of us have, haven't we? She laughs.

"You always knew how to tell a story," she says, reaching to pour me more wine. I embroider a bit, have myself doing X-rated back-flips, and she laughs and I swear I can see her blushing even in the dark. And I delete, a lot of that. She listens, punctuating the narrative with what I take to be commiserative chuckles. They egg me on. Then I conjure some earlier days, sweet, sweet city days. As if I were a virgin, I tell her, when I met him. When we were first together. The places we went, the things we saw and ate. How I got myself dressed up.

"Like today," she says.

"Like today," I say.

"Why didn't you guys marry?" she says.

And here I catch myself. "Not in the cards," I say. "Just fine the way it was. Is."

We sit a while longer in the dark. I encourage her to tell me about her boys, but all she will say is that she wants to keep them as a surprise, because I will love them. Wait and see. Especially the older, Luke, something magic about him. Everybody says so. She sounds not unlike me talking about Michael just now. I hear it: dreamy, enchanted. I see his thin face from that photo, but I don't ask anything about him. I don't want to scare her off. And in that moment in the dark, sister across from sister, I am jealous of her, her motherhood, and feel for the first time—really deeply for the first time—the loss of children, a child. The man I was engaged to when I met Michael wanted them (clearly has them now, as I saw that day at the rink). We would have had them, or one of them, or tried. I didn't know if I could get pregnant, had never been. But, of course, I had been very careful. All the way through, careful, careful, careful. Then I met Michael and the decision was made.

She says, as if reading my mind: "What about children? Didn't you want them?"

"I didn't think I could protect them," I say, realizing I have spoken the real truth.

"Nobody can," she says softly.

"Weezie, what is it?" I say. I see her shaking her head against whatever it is, shaking it firmly, side to side. "What?" I say.

But she doesn't answer, except finally to say, "Hey, what time is it? I have to call home." She turns the light on as she gets up and is gone just like that, into the bathroom, mumbling into her cell phone. When she comes back, I can see she is re-armored. She has splashed her face with cold water. It is still damp, and she has fluffed up her hair. Louise is back. Weezie is gone. I wonder if I have said too much. I feel a little tawdry, having resurrected the afternoon, given it away somehow, cheapened it. But wait, this is a woman with a couple of romance novels in her suitcase and a lover out there. I ask her if she would like some food and she says she stopped for something.

"McDonald's?" I start to ask, realizing though that it would have sounded snappish, realizing, too, that I am feeling a tiny bit that way. More confidences from my side than hers. I am usually way too careful for that with anybody, everybody. But a sister in the dark and a gut full of sorrow. That's a different matter. She says she is tired now and I say I'm just going to grab some tea and a sandwich. I hear her changing for bed. I get my snack and head off, tossing a "good night" over my shoulder. I stop for a minute.

"Hey, what happened to the surprise?" I say.

"I didn't have the energy for it," she says. "Maybe tomorrow night."

Michael has the flu. He didn't call last night. I was restless, the way I am when I don't hear from him. He called just now, full of aches and pain and self-pity. But a little relief. I deduce that or maybe it's me. I don't know. Postpone the next attempt. We will talk on the phone. He will give me his temperature readings, tell me when he last had his aspirin. His wife does charity work. He will be for long stretches unattended. He will hector me while I write.

"I will hector you," he said, through a hacking sneeze.

"Figured," I said.

"You'll call nine-one-one, won't you, if I can't breathe?"

"You can count on me."

"Makes sense," he said.

"What?"

"Yesterday. I wondered if I was coming down with something."

I leave it alone. "Hot tea with honey," I say.

"Wish you were here to . . ."

"Give you a rubdown."

"Anything wrong with that?" He is rousing himself to a flirt, but a cough gets him.

"Hang up now. I'll be here."

Normal life. Normal life, that is, for a couple like us. I go back to staring at my screen. I am sitting on my bed, pillows behind me, notebooks open, trying to find a quote from the shrink that will please both Miriam and me. I want to let her say something drippy and meaningful, something about young women reclaiming their feminine selves, but the truth is that stuff is great, goes over like gangbusters. Miriam will love it. I'd been sparing with those quotes and, in fact, it's exactly what she wants more of. I am sitting perusing my notes when Louise sticks her head in.

"I'm off," she says.

"You don't have to go," I say. It is the first time I've said this.

She smiles and when she smiles now, that's when I see the sorrow. Her face in repose or when she's talking, no. But when she smiles, her eyes are full of it, the contradiction between the content of those eyes and her upturned mouth startling. I start to say again, "Louise, let me help." Or, "Louise are you getting ready to leave?" Or, "Louise how do you like your cranberries? You will stay for Thanksgiving, right?" I am half tempted to pat the bed, say, sit down, sit with me, let me read you this, did I tell you about this hilarious shriveled shrink I interviewed? But I don't. I prattled on too much last night, gave away too much. Anyway, she is dressed, bundled, has a mission. Her daily mission, whatever it might be.

"Thanks," she says, "but I have things to do."

"You'll be home for dinner? I'll make something festive," I say.

"Yes. Okay," she says, but it's absentminded, absent-hearted. I am losing her. Not that I had her. Her hands are fluttering again.

"Fish or meat?" I try again.

"Doesn't matter," she says, turning away.

And she is gone and I remember about the surprise. Maybe she's forgotten, too. Maybe it was no big deal. Maybe, in fact, it was the bottle of wine and I missed it. Shit.

I try to work with some attentiveness and sly pleasure—digging for those damning quotes—but give up and give in and let Ms. Octoshrink have her way with the piece and the young female readers of America. They will learn soon enough the limits of "feminine" behavior, how tough you have to be.

Michael doesn't call for hours. I am relieved. He is sleeping, snoring, no doubt, his signature little *puff-puff*s of exhaled air. Wonder how long this will go on. I send in my piece and then log on to the Internet for Viagra stories. I've been to the library and photocopied stuff from magazines and medical journals. I haven't done this before. There wasn't exactly a need. Now—well. Does it work? In what cases? Side effects include potential heart attack, flushed face and limbs, and a hard-on that won't quit. Turns out, on close reading, it isn't the aging men of America who are lining up for it. Oh, no, it's the younger men scared of not living up to some media-mythic dream of sexual prowess. Fits right into my piece, the refeminizing of the American woman who can stop threatening the American male so he doesn't have to pop a pill. Forget it; Miriam will never let me go there, not in any honest way. Best just recycle the clichés.

As an antidote, I call up one of my short stories—they're linked—and I am okay with it as I read. It's the one I like the best. It's the only one I really like. It's about an overweight teenage boy who brings home a stray pit bull for Christmas and his family goes nuts, even though the dog never does anything. He is a fawning wimp of a pit bull, a real sweetheart, but everyone else gets vicious. It's funny and mean and feels pretty real. But the next one is lame. And the next. I stop reading and unconsciously/consciously start waiting for the phone to ring again. Been hours. It's darkening already. Only about three thirty. I've had my head down for a long time. I'll go out and get something to eat and then buy food. A fish stew, all warm and tomatoey—shrimp and clams, no mussels or scary things to alarm Louise. I grab a cookbook and head out. Over a grilled cheese and pint of beer at a dark little place Michael and I like, I plan dinner, as if for a lover, as if for him. The fish market that I really like is on the West Side, so I decide to walk through the park. It's gray again but warmer. There are a few people with dogs and an occasional hand-in-hand, rather glove-in-glove, couple, a rowdy bunch of black kids on the swings. I am never scared—I don't come in the dark. I love being down in this place, the city all around, love it especially on afternoons as the day becomes night and the lights go on. I am late today, probably will have to get a cab back. I buy my fish and decide to walk back, not through the park—it really is getting dark—but down to Fifty-ninth and across. I detour for fresh bread, whole wheat sourdough, at a new little bakery on Lexington and then home. Inside, what? A message from Miriam—no doubt. She'll be pleased—no doubt. And a message from Michael—no doubt. I miss him. He loves my fish stew. Louise—will she be there?

Juggling groceries, I find the key and open the door and she is there sitting on the sofa, a bottle of wine in front of her, three glasses. I somehow take them in at once and am confused and then I hear the bathroom door open and footsteps and it is the man in the Windbreaker, now in a brown-checked sport coat and slacks, cream-colored shirt. I look, I am sure, abashed. I look at Louise. She is smiling—the sorrow still in there, but a little less—and standing.

"This," she says to him "is my sister."

He comes toward me. "Here let me take that." I look at him as he takes the groceries. Crew cut, blond, deeply tan, high cheekbones. Attractive in a straightforward, aging quarterback, masculine way. Louise's type.

"Your surprise," I say with a cocked eyebrow and half-smile, turning to her as he goes into the kitchen with the groceries. Her hands are fluttering. She is nervous, reaching for a glass to pour me some wine.

"They said you loved this, too," she says, handing me the glass. And then as he reappears, her hands really fluttering, she says to me, as softly as she can say it and still be heard, "This is Timmy."

"Timmy?" I say, shaking my head a little, looking from one to the other. "Timmy," I repeat.

Softer still, she says, "My husband."

"Your husband." All along. The husband. Of course. The fucking husband. I look at him again. I had never really seen a picture, always refused Daddy's stash. A surge of anger starts in my belly and crawls up my neck.

"Your abusive husband." I am speaking quietly. I do when I am really angry for fear of exploding into pieces.

"No," Louise says. She has now moved to stand beside him and they are holding hands, both smiling at me, lightly smiling.

"I don't want him here," I say, looking only at her. "Get him out of here. Now."

"Clare, it's not what you think."

"I don't care what it is. I don't want him here."

"Please," he says. "Let your sister explain." In his eyes, there is a companionate sadness to hers that quiets me. I can't read it. Is it repentance? The batterer's refuge. I am looking hard at him, my anger tempered for a moment. His voice is higher and thinner than his body type implies. He doesn't seem threatening, at least to me, right now. But do they ever . . . at first take?

"Please," he says, bowing his head slightly—a posture of contrition—reenlisting my contempt.

I turn to Louise. "What do you want to say?"

I sit, perched on the edge of the armchair, still with all my outerwear on, gloves and muffler and coat. They sit opposite me on the sofa, still holding hands, knees touching. He looks at her, clearly encouraging her to talk.

"I'm sorry . . ." she says, looking at me and then at him and then at the floor, trailing off.

I don't say anything, not going to. Let her go now. Let's hear this. She starts again and stops. There is a long silence in the room. Nobody says anything or picks up a glass to sip. The radiator clanks and I realize how hot it is, but have no inclination now to stand up and take my coat off, no inclination to stir in any fashion. Just sit and stare at my stammering sister. Timmy says nothing. He seems to understand to say nothing. He finally undoes his hand from hers and pats her gently on the back. Encouragement. She starts again, looking at me and then the floor and then back at me as she starts to talk again, in a rush this time. Going to get it out now.

"I needed help," she says. "Need help. We need help. Luke is sick and we just thought that you could help us."

I am tempted to say, "You might have just asked me," but she's plowing on, a breathless narrative I hear acutely, I am registering it, but through a scrim of incredulity.

"I came here because I needed, we needed your help, but Daddy said you were still very angry or hurt and so I didn't think you would help us. So I thought if we were friends, if we could be friends—like we have been, we have been," she says, looking up at me with that little girl smile. "We've had fun, haven't we, I mean, the cooking and that trip for my makeover. I know it didn't last," her hands are fluttering now around her hair, "but Timmy likes me this way," smiling at him, then back at me. "You are such a good cook. You were always so good at everything you tried and you know so much, like about the wine and the only thing I've ever been good at, really good at, is being a mother. . . . Timmy will tell you, won't you?" (She looks at him again, but now with tears and he has them, too.) "And when he got sick . . ." She stops.

Again there is a long silence. Timmy starts to speak, but he can't do it at all, his voice now very high and choked and impossible to understand. We all sit. I watch them. Everything seems slow motion. She starts again.

"We thought it would be all right, that it wouldn't get serious, but he's crashing, that's what they call it, and we needed help. We got him on the list, but it's still taking forever. . . ."

I'm not exactly sure what she's talking about, but don't interrupt. I don't want to help. I don't want to be in this conversation. Friends. Thought we could be friends.

". . . and I just thought that since you're a writer you could help us. You could write about him . . . he is your nephew; and wait till you meet him, and somebody will see about him and they'll want to help him because you write so well and they'll see that, they'll understand. This is the way it gets done now. I mean, people take out billboards and use all the famous people they can to get someone farther up the list. There's thousands of people on it, waiting to get organs. Thousands. You don't know what it's like waiting, watching someone get sicker, and he never complains. Wait until you meet him. And I just thought, you know, there must be a way, and I thought of you and that maybe you could help us or would help us . . . if we could be friends again. And we have been, haven't we? We have had fun. I told Timmy all about it, about your cooking and taking me shopping and we did have fun. Talking and stuff in our pajamas. You don't know what it's like. You just don't know. You never had kids."

"Sweetheart," Timmy says. He's trying to calm her down.

"Well, she didn't. She didn't have kids," Louise says to him. "She has no idea what we're going through. You don't. You don't know what it's like," she says, turning back to me.

Her voice is rising. She wants me to respond and I won't. I'm afraid to because I don't know what's liable to come out.

"It's not a lot to ask, is it? You can write about him. You can make people see him. You are good at that. I've read all your stuff. You write these tearjerky things about other people's kids, like those foster kids who were killed in New Jersey. So why not my child? Is that so much to ask? Just because we haven't seen each other in a few years. I came here to ask for your help and I thought if we were friends . . ."

I flash a terse, inadvertent smile when she uses the word tear-jerky. She's done her homework, all right. I say that, almost without realizing I'm finally talking. "I see you've done your homework, Louise. That was never your strong suit."

"Go ahead and be smug. You were always good at that too. . . ."

"Sweetheart," Timmy says again, but he might as well be invisible.

"I know you've been laughing at me behind my back, my Cocoa Puffs and my teased hair. Trying to change me so I didn't look out of place up here with you. . . . Walking around with you. Don't you think I know?"

"Louise," her husband says, his voice lower now. "Stop. This isn't going to work."

"I don't care," she says, and she's crying now, big gulps with words coming out of them. "I knew it was a long shot, but I thought maybe you'd changed and that you'd help us, but I see now I was wrong."

She is standing up. Timmy is still sitting. Her face is puffed up now with animus. It looks almost silly, our mother's face in one of those TV movies she made at the end, a face that said, "See. I'm really angry." I smile.

"I hate you," she says, "and all your smugness. All the stuff you know to eat and drink. Who cares? It's all meaningless. You don't have kids and that's what matters and you'll never have them running around with that married man. You think I'm too stupid to figure that out?"

"Fuck you," I say.

"It's pathetic. Not to mention immoral."

"Who appointed you the moral arbiter around here?" I say. And

I'm smiling again, my quiet, superior little smile. I feel it on my face, pasted over my rage. "I'm not the one who took all the drugs and caused someone to lose his . . ."

I see her face, his face. He is looking at her. There is a collective breath being held. I am beginning to feel sick. I shake my head. "Get out, Louise. Just get out."

I get up and leave the room. I shut the door to my bedroom and sit on the bed. My heart is pounding. I don't turn on a light. I curl up finally, still in coat, shoes, muffler, and throw the quilt over my legs. I hear night sounds far away, or rather imagine them, people in restaurants, laughing, toasting each other, ordering another round, people cooking in their apartments, the people I nod to from my bathroom window and out there, in my living room, the intense whispering of my sister and her husband. Are they arguing? I didn't mean to say what I said. What did I mean to say? How could you, Louise? Worming your way into my home, my affections, conjuring memories. Just enough of those. Not too many. I rehearse conversations, all of them since she came, the deft charade of befriending. I had forgotten, or chosen to forget: In many ways, Louise is the clever one. A survivor. That's what Daddy said. He was right, of course. But the kid; what about the kid? Of course, that's even better, isn't it? She's holding the high moral cards. She's restacked the deck. I hear more whispering, moving about, around the living room, into the bathroom—packing, I assume. It goes on for a while and then finally a door opening and shutting and, lying there, I have to fight the temptation to call Michael, try to call him, hang up if a woman answers. But I can't call him, can I? Never can and tonight it riles. I think about the Ambien, now—why not? But it would probably take three to knock me out. My body feels like a fist, clenched, but a grief, way inside, begins to snake up through it and finally comes up out of my mouth in a wail. And then tears. I look at the New York night through them, what I can see from the window.

Never true night because of all the urban lights. Everyone far far away. She is gone now, Louise. Again. Back to her little nuclear family with its ailing prince and I am alone again in my apartment, my spot of the planet, dug in with my laptop and slim skirts and little meals. It's too late, way too late, the gap too big to navigate. But Michael will be back. He will. He is my family now, all that I need of one. But there is that whole other thing, isn't there? What if? What if he can never be inside me again, humming his giddy ballads? And I, in turn, cannot hold his cock and cradle it between my breasts and tease it with my "tresses"? I will become the silliest of things, a laughingstock: the mistress of an impotent lover. What will we do when he comes over? Sit and talk? Hold hands? Neck a little? He can still sing and recite and pace, but there will be a thing lost and, over time, slack and penitent, he will go home to his wife for good. I will be alone again—maybe forever—and grow old and walk the streets in my low-heeled, sensible shoes. I can see myself, one of those aging, well-kept-up girl-women I see all around the city, especially at cultural events—theater, museums, concerts—quiet hair, good coats and scarves, plucky and attractive but a little pallid from lives unlived, children unhad (yes, Louise, oh, yes), coming back to their one-bedroom apartments, just like this one.

I awake achy and coiled. Stretching, I see out the window that it is still night. The clock says 4:12. Maybe a hot shower. Something to eat. The semblance of normalcy. I get out of my clothes and into a robe. There are no lights on, no sounds, but when I peak into the living room, there on the sofa is a sleeping form. Startled, I yelp and the form stirs. It is a man, Timmy clearly. For a moment I am relieved. No Louise. No more. But then anger comes quickly.

"Please leave," I say. "I am going to take a shower and I would like you gone when I come back."

He is sitting up now, raking a hand through his hair. It is dark and we can see each other, but not eyes, or mouths, or expressions.

Just a body, a form. No, a brother-in-law, actually. First time I have thought of that word to describe him. My brother-in-law. I have one. Here he is and all I want is for him to go away forever. "Please," I say, "I have no stomach for any more drama."

When he doesn't say anything, I move into the room. "Come on, just go, go be with your wife."

And there they are again: the tears of men. I don't hear them. I just see his shoulders shaking. "Damn it, don't. It's not fair," I say. I sit again in the chair opposite the sofa and when he can't stop, I go get a glass of water from the kitchen and bring it to him. But I still don't turn on any lights. Better this scene in the dark. Maybe it can be hurried along if we don't actually look at each other.

"Thank you," he says, as I hand him the glass. "I know . . ."

"Are we going to have to do this again?" I say.

He stands up and for a second I feel menaced.

"What, are you going to hit me now?" I say.

He sits back down. His voice is very soft. "I never hit anybody. I would never hit anybody. That was her idea."

"What are you talking about?"

"Louise came up here intending to talk to you, to tell you about Luke, but you were . . . she didn't think you were . . . anyway, once you thought she was running away from me, she just let you think that. She was stalling for time, hoping you two could be friends again and then you would help her, help us. . . ."

"You're joking," I say, letting out a sharp, barking laugh. "That is the sickest thing I've ever heard."

He doesn't say anything. "I just can't believe it," I say again.

"I'm sorry," he says. I can barely hear him and I sense his tears coming on, even in the dark, the preliminary shake of the shoulders and I can't hear that again, so I soften, try to.

"You have to understand . . ." I start.

"I do," he says, voice thick. "But you have to understand your sister is not in her right mind. She's frantic about Luke and she got it in her head that somehow you were the one person who could save him."

"I haven't seen her in twenty-five years—more than, and not a call or a card—and then she waltzes in here pretending to be a runaway wife so I'll be sympathetic and we can be friends so I can save her son who I don't even know by writing some tearjerky story about him so someone somewhere will give him a . . ."

"Liver," he says. "A liver transplant. He's not very high up on the list and he's getting sicker and we're terrified that . . ."

"Couldn't she just have asked me? Or you. This whole thing is so . . ." My voice drops off.

"We didn't think we could. Your father said you'd gotten . . ." He stops himself.

"Gotten what?"

"Nothing," he says.

"What? Gotten what?" I say again, louder.

"A little hard."

My father. Said that. I don't say it out loud. He would hear too much in my voice, the blow struck. Daddy said that? When? To whom? These people are dangerous. I have to get them out of here. Not just her. Him, too. Now. Morning coming on, lightening up now out the window. New York coming awake, alive. I want him gone before I have to really see his face again, look at his eyes, this brother-in-law.

"I want you to go," I say, standing up.

"I didn't mean to hurt your feelings but you asked and you do seem . . . well, I don't know you, but I do know Louise and she's a good person. You have a lot in common. You're both writers . . ."

I snort. Both writers. My sister with her little pink diary and hand-scrawled pages.

"You have to go," I say and now he does stand up.

"And Luke," he says, and I hear those incipient tears again, "you should get to know him. He's . . ." his voice catches. "He's an amazing kid. It's not fair. . . ." He walks to the door and turns, hand on the knob. He starts to say something, but I cut him off.

"Who would have thought it," I say, with a derisive laugh. "Instead of being my sister's abuser you turn out to be her fucking apologist."

. 8 .

It has turned bitter out, not beautiful sunny cold, but gray and ice-slippery cold, sharp, wind-whipped rain slicking the sidewalks and streets, freezing overnight. People walk carefully, their heads tucked down. The city feels empty—people gone away for Thanksgiving, which is tomorrow. I can't make myself make that dinner. I have gone to the market twice and stood looking at the turkeys, pretending to be interested. Which kind: Kosher, therefore pre-brined (brining being all the rage, of course)? Organic? Or plain old reliable Butterball with one of those little red buttons that pops up, which I am always dubious about? I find myself standing for long minutes staring at big, raw pink-tinged turkeys. I chat with the butcher in a faux-interested way, but don't buy, and then delicately make my way home again, planting my rubber-heeled boots on the ice-crusted concrete, just a bag of cranberries to show for the outing, which I toss on the kitchen counter when I come in.

I hate coming home so I hate going out. The apartment feels empty, prissy, all tidied up after the visitation. Not a sign left of Louise. Not a leftover scrap of her. I threw away her cereal and cornmeal and dairy creamer before, I suspect, she and teary Timmy were even at the airport for their flight back to Florida. Right before I took my shower, right after he left, shutting the door so softly it was more of a rebuke than a slam would have been, I went through the place, erasing traces of her, bathroom shelves, kitchen shelves, her cotton balls and Cocoa Puffs. She seems like a figment who blew in here with some trumped-up claim on me and then vanished without a trace. And yet the air has been altered in here, tampered with. A sister has been here, playing with my heart. A middle-aged, puffy-haired sister. What a hoot. What a scheme. Got to hand it to her. She got me, didn't she? I relive it. I can't help it. Our lunches and dinners. We did have fun, didn't we? Thought we could be friends. That first night, that first sound of her voice on the phone. Come on out, sis, I need help. I need you. If Michael hadn't been in the hospital, if I hadn't been, what?—vulnerable, worried, looking for distraction—my sensors would have been better, sharper. She thought I was playing her for a fool while she was playing me for one.

I have a glass of wine in my hand at one P.M., a violation of the normal rules. But it's a holiday, almost. I think about going back on the turkey hunt, about trying to scare up a pal or two to dazzle with my Thanksgiving repertoire, but I have let so much go, so much lapse. There are a couple of couples I can think of, people who used to ask me, where I used to go, toting my slippery orange pumpkin flans and braised leeks, but no doubt they are all long since planned up. I remember a call from one of the wives, a writing colleague on the paper, three weeks ago, maybe, but we had never talked. I'd just left a message declining because, at that point, I could only think about Michael. Then Louise—I figured we would be making dinner together. I did, didn't I?—chump that I am. Right down to her (inevitable) marshmallows and my inevitable flan. So I have no plans, no one to cook for, nowhere to go. Michael has called from his sickbed to say he is better and will try to sneak by on Friday if he swings by the office. He tries to be good during the holidays, a mindful lover, calling to include me, telling me about the family squabbles, about the ghastly green casseroles provided by the vegan daughter-in-law (she's gone vegan now; you know what that means, don't you?—no cheese, no dairy products, nada).

"Why don't you join her," I say. "It'll be good for your cholesterol."

"I don't have a cholesterol problem," he says. "My ticker's just
fine."

"Then why do you take Lipitor?" I say.

"Makes the doctor happy," he says.

"The pharmaceutical companies, you mean."

"Same difference," he says. "Hey, what are you cooking?" and I
know he means for Thanksgiving.

"Not."

"No? Thought you and your sister were going to do it up."

"She's gone," is all I say. No details and he doesn't ask.

"Great," he says, "the place is ours again."

Ours again. No further questions.

I look around when I hang up. I have put his stuff back, the
sweatshirt on the hook where Louise's robe was. In the liquor cabinet, I know, there is a new bottle of whiskey, Jameson's, his favorite,
and the binoculars back on the bathroom door. The stage is reset.

The phone rings again. Miriam.

"I'm sure you have plans, but just figured I'd try you for tomorrow. Gardner's coming with his new daughter" (his new daughter?)
"and a couple of other . . ."

"Strays," I say.

She laughs her big, tingly editor's laugh. "Don't be defensive,
now. Or a bore. Just come if you have nothing to do."

I have nothing to do. Can she smell that? This is the first year
she's asked me. Then again, she's fond of me at the moment, as I
caved on the shrink piece. Didn't even arm wrestle much. I am
being tamed. Am tamed, almost. You have a lot in common,
Timmy said. You are both writers, he said. He was serious.
'Course he was serious. Then why doesn't she write the tearjerk-
ing piece?

"Can I take your silence as a yes?" Miriam says.

"Yes, okay, thanks," I say, "but let me bring something."

"No. Just dress up. The boys think you are so retro chic."

"I'll take that as a compliment," I say.

I drink more wine, slowly, right through the afternoon, TV on, muted, no other lights. It's okay, a holiday. I'm allowed. The apartment is dark, save for the flicker from the tube, which I occasionally glance at. I really don't want to go to Miriam's tomorrow in my "retro chic" and engage in the pro forma intra-gender food and fashion badinage with "the boys." But I will. Have to get out when the self-pity sets in. That's rule nine in the Mistress Survival Handbook. Get out. Get out. Get out. I drift off and the phone wakes me, tucked up here on the sofa.

"It's me," he says.

Come on over. I bought you a new bottle of Jameson's. You can hold me. I'm cold. She's gone again, my sister. Do you see? And tomorrow's Thanksgiving. I don't say any of that. I say, "Hey."

"You asleep?"

"Was."

"Sorry," he says. "Can you give me that recipe for cranberries? I lost it."

"No," I say, "that was a one-time thing." I hear my voice, coy and churlish at the same time. He doesn't engage when I'm like this. He's too smart for me. Let her vent a little and she'll be fine. I gave him the recipe last Christmas. He'd had a taste of my leftovers from Thanksgiving the month before and swooned over them.

"That's downright kinky," I said, "taking my recipe so your wife can make it, like smuggling forbidden fruit into the family feast." We laughed together.

Finally I say, "Port. It's port. Don't put in . . ."

"Thanks," he says quickly, cutting me off. "Gotta go."

"Wanna see my tits," I say into the dead phone.

I am at Miriam's downtown loft, seated at the elegantly laid glass dining-room table between Gardner and his longtime lover, Larry—looking like twins with their close-cropped, gray-flecked hair and dark turtlenecks—and across from Gardner's parents, a round, bespectacled pair who are the proud chairs of the PFLAG chapter—"Parents, Friends, and Family of Gays and Lesbians," he says. "Lesbians and Gays, dear," she amends—in their Midwestern hometown. They are in the city to meet Gardner and Jack's new daughter, Mindy, one of these round-faced absolutely adorable Chinese baby girls who are everywhere now, the adoptees du jour. The men have only recently gotten back from picking her up in China from some orphanage and they have dozens of pictures to hand around and stories to tell. How hard it was, how exhilarating, the other families who went with them, where they stayed, the reams of papers they had to sign. Everyone is talking over each other, adding their bit, embroidering. Gardner's parents are already taking Chinese cooking at their local kitchen store and intend to go to China themselves next year so they can be familiar with "our grandchild's roots." Miriam's bare loft with its concrete floors and uncomfortable midcentury furniture is awash in heartland family values, everyone beaming at Mindy as she, sleepy and a little sullen, is passed between her dads and grandparents.

"Why," Miriam says, looking at me, "don't you do this?"

"What?"

"Go get a Chinese baby."

"We can show you the ropes," Larry says.

"Can we ever," Gardner says.

Everyone is looking at me. Is this a setup? Is that why I'm here? I want to get up and go into the other room. Instead I just flash a forced smile. "Can't fit it in right now."

"You'd be a wonderful mother," Gardner says. "I can just tell."

"You can?" I say, a little archly, but the happy new family members are all still beaming at me.

"Come with us when we go," Gardner's mother says, turning to her husband, "wouldn't that be fun, Ben?" He smiles at me.

A reprieve. The living room door opens and in come Miriam's square-looking daughter and stockbroker husband (I've met them once before) and their two young boys. Noise, greetings, chairs dragged up, and dessert handed around and, of course, the stories all over again about the procurement of Mindy. Oh, she's so beautiful. Oh, let me hold her. Oh, our friends just got one and they're so happy. I recede from the evening's agenda and am able to slip out early, claiming a deadline.

"Who else are you working for?" Miriam says in mock horror, playing to the crowd as she sees me to the door.

"Our offer still stands, dear," Gardner's mother says. She has gotten up and followed Miriam and me to the door and now she is hugging me, squat and sturdy with all her good intentions.

"Thanks for the offer," I say. "I will think about it."

"Promise?" she says, eyes twinkling behind her wire-rimmed glasses.

I am through the door without another word and out on the street, walking. The streets are very empty and still slippery and I'm way downtown, but start toward home, oblivious to the cold, propelled by my rancorous internal monologue. This was no gathering of strays. This was a gathering of people basking in their familial tethers. I, it turns out, was the token stray. I had been set up on a blind date, not with a man but with a Chinese baby girl. They were all in it, a conspiracy of do-gooders. Now, they were up there, back there, talking about me. You can bet on it. No one in her life? Too bad. She's plenty attractive. Ben would say that. His wife would say, "Ben." But they would laugh. I reach for Michael, the idea of him.

Always, he is tucked in there and I reach for him when I'm at a long, boring party full of the seriously partnered and when I see those pity eyes beamed at me as I have tonight. He is my secret, my secret place. But he isn't in there tonight. He's sitting now, I imagine, before a fire in his big old drafty house (yes, I was there once and no, we certainly didn't do "it" there, just stopped to pick up some papers he'd forgotten; years ago now), sated, snifter in hand, his own grandchildren clamoring about. Content, snoozy, full of turkey and (my) cranberries. Lucky bastard. My love. My lover. My family. But he's not that, is he? Let's be honest here. I do have family though, don't I? Those Floridians. Those treacherous Floridians who came looking for me because they wanted something. That's what I have to show for family.

M ichael doesn't come the next day. Calls whispering from a family outing to some diner.

"Sorry, babe," he says.

"Me, too," I say, wondering if this is the beginning of the dance of avoidance. All weekend, I fight twinges of bereavement. He's not going to bail. What would he do? Where would he put all that blarney and passion? I'm perfect for him. I have been perfect. We'll manage the other: the sex. He checks in reassuringly and for the first hour or so after hearing from him, hale and hearty and flirty, I feel fine. I rustle in the kitchen, cobbling together a little meal, pretending all is as it was and will be again. But by the onset of darkness, I crash a bit. I am drinking a bit more, quite a bit more, sipping at the Jameson's—neat—after my wine, sitting in the dark in front of the TV set. I'm momentarily done with the news, satiated with it. Can't sit still through the cop dramas nor abide the sitcoms with their smirky innuendoes and laugh tracks. I'm now down to the infomercials, fiercely cheerful hucksters—and washed-up stars—hawking everything from wrinkle cream to Crock-Pots to fashions for "the plus-size woman." I gorge a bit on them and then they don't work and then I try to work. Back to my pit pull. I get stuck there again and then try to fix one of the other stories about a sex ring in a retirement home, all very jolly and coarse, but unfelt somehow and vulgar for it. The idea is good, comes from a squiblet I read in the paper about an orderly at one of those places bringing in undocumented "sex workers" (great euphemism, huh?) to service the geriatrics at extortionary fees. I wrestle a bit more, but my head and heart are not in it and it remains vulgar, not funny and tender and vulgar, just pure vulgar. I can't bump it out. I haven't the energy.

Finally I give up and get on the Internet, start checking e-mail, but that doesn't help either. The twinges of sorrow are getting closer and closer together, like labor pains. I am fighting them. Another swill of Jameson's. A check of the clock. No more calls tonight. I start surfing around. I check my favorite food sites, and then, without thinking about it, I am face-to-face with a liver, a big, gorgeous, browny-red liver. I realize I don't even know what it does, this liver of ours, which they say here is the body's biggest organ. Forget the brain, the heart; it's the liver. I start to scan and click and read. "The liver is located on the right side of the abdomen behind the lower ribs and below the lungs. It performs more than four hundred functions each day to keep the body healthy." I know people can't live without one or with seriously diseased ones, but I don't even know what he has, this boy of theirs, this nephew of mine. His face floats back up from memory, from that one cursory glance at that one photograph. So slender, so pretty, so sick, they say. There is something called UNOS, the United Network for Organ Sharing, and it operates the waiting list for every kind of organ. There are thousands on the list. Luke is on it somewhere. I want to see if I can find him, but I am now into a zone of privacy. No names. I don't know where he is on the list or how long he's been waiting or how sick he is or what he has. Some old disease. Some new disease. Liver cancer, congestive hepathic fibrosis, hepatitis? Could be any of these. I continue to click and read. "Each potential recipient has an equal chance of receiving a transplant," a Web site assures. "UNOS shows no favorites and is not swayed by publicity." Wait a minute. What are they saying here? "The media may help boost the general awareness of the need for organ donation, but they do not enhance a particular patient's chances of receiving an organ. Well-intentioned media coverage has no influence on the distribution of available organs. Preferential treatment does not exist."

Well, well, well. So they were flat-out wrong. All their song and dance up here was for naught. And anything I might do is for naught. I'm off the hook. Nothing I can do even if I wanted to. No tender, tearjerky piece by an aunt about a rediscovered—not rediscovered, discovered—nephew needing a transplant will do a thing. I have to admit that the seed had been planted, no matter my enmity toward the planter. But now, I am officially off the case. What a relief. I shut down the laptop and push it over to the other side of the bed and turn off the light. Can't wait to tell Michael about the super-evolved family I had Thanksgiving dinner with. He'll love it.

O n Monday afternoon, after a phone call from just outside my apartment, he bursts through the door, all lit up, flushed and tigerish, pawing and laughing.

"I missed you so," he says, bear-hugging me.

"Is this foreplay?" I say, laughing

"How did you know?" he says, gently head-butting my breasts. I lift up his head and look at him.

"You okay?" I say. "You look flushed."

"Never better. Been dreaming about you, is all," he says, placing my hand against the front of his pants. "See."

There is an unusual urgency to his moves. We don't stop for a drink, don't stop to chat, don't stop to flirt. We don't even get to the bedroom, ending up right there on the sofa. The sex is very anatomical, genital. He hands himself into me, not rough, just deliberate. He is mostly hard and I can feel his relief. I am trying to be relieved, too. Our cadence is a little off, a little arrhythmic. I want to laugh. That's what we do. We laugh and pause and start up again, falling back into sync. I squirm under him, try to follow. I don't want to laugh anymore. I want to float away, float backward into other times, other fucks, not with anyone else, only with him, the man on top of me now, this earnest rammer. I want him to stop and I want him to come and I don't care if I do, but it would be nice, but I don't care. I can't put my hand down there to help and I can't reach to put his hand there because he's pressing too hard and too close. I open my eyes and close them again and my body, remembering, starts tracking better, loosening, wider and wider so it will be fine, pushing up high against him so that when he says "Okay"—half statement, half question—we are close enough in sync to come together, an overrated phenomenon but sweet nonetheless, always unexpectedly so because it means nothing but somehow something. He collapses to the side of me, heavy, heart pounding. I stay still, eyes closed, feeling his heart ease off as I lightly stroke his back. Finally I say, "You should have told me."

He leans up next to me. It's pretty dark in here now, but I see his face. "What?" he says.

"The Viagra," I say.

He is quiet and then says, "I'm sorry. I just didn't want to bum you out."

"Bum me out. Since when do you talk like that? You've been spending too much time with the grandchildren."

"You're angry."

"I'd rather you'd said something."

"Apparently I didn't need to."

"Now you're angry."

He disengages from me now. "I'm trying to make this work," he says.

"I know," I say.

"Wasn't so bad, was it?" He's trying to go light, but it makes me sad, the undertone of frisky boastfulness. Not been a part of anything for a long time, not since the very beginning, when he used it as a lure for reassurance.

"Not so bad," I say, trying to go light back.

"Better living through chemistry," he says.

"Better loving," I say.

He kisses me and I reach for his neck, there where those grayish curls are. He moves over me and gets off the sofa. Pad, pad, I hear him go toward the bathroom, watch his back and broad buttocks. Animal, male. He is humming now as he pisses.

"Can a guy get something to eat or drink around here?" he says, coming back.

I am up quickly. I am happy. He will stay for a while. We will have a postcoital supper. I grab a robe from the bedroom closet, two robes, and throw him my extra bigger one, then hand him the Jameson's and two glasses. I scramble some eggs and, side by side on the sofa in our pastel chenille robes, we eat them and sip our drinks. It starts to go too fast—I feel it—and I try to slow it down, hold him with a vivid description of Larry and Gardner and their dark-banged baby girl and her grandparents. He is laughing and mopping up the last of his eggs with a piece of bread and swallowing the last of his drink and is about to get up. I know it. Wait. Did I tell you they want me to get one?

"One what?" he says, standing and picking up his clothes.

"A Chinese baby girl."

"You?" he says, putting on his pants.

"Yeah. Is that so strange?"

"I don't think of you as the maternal type," he says.

"What's that supposed to mean?" I say.

"Come on, Clare. You've always said you don't want kids. That's all."

"I don't. It's just that sometimes . . ."

"Sometimes what?" he says, buttoning his shirt, looking down as he does it, not looking at me.

"Sometimes I get tired of this."

Now he does look up. "Just say the word," he says, "and I'll scram."

"You won't fight with every ounce of your soul to hold on to me?"

"That wouldn't be fair," he says.

"And this is?"

I am chagrined the minute the door closes—softly again; nobody will get mad and slam anything around here—and in the days after. Michael doesn't call, not the next day or the next, the longest we've ever gone without talking since the beginning. I am nervous, lonesome, can't get settled to work. I don't call, either. I don't know what to do. I don't know what I've done. I don't know why I did it. It was sweet, he was, barging in here with his hard-on. I knew almost immediately he'd taken something—he was right about that—the telltale Viagra flush. I'd done my homework. And it worked. Wasn't that the point? We were fine. A little odd, a little abrupt and purposeful, the sex was, but fine. And then staying for supper. A gift that was, normally, my idea of heaven, the two of us side by side in our robes, sipping our drinks and eating our eggs, my feet in his lap. But, sitting there, I kept seeing on the other side to when he would be gone, kept slipping out of my well-practiced mistress decorum. I've done it before, poked at him, bemoaned my status, only a couple of

times, but not in a long while. I feel a little queasy as I walk around
the city, bundled up. Normally the streets themselves are solace,
bustly with strangers, their imagined lives, especially at this time of
year, the time when we fell in love, the time when, like now, it is getting all tarted up with fairy lights and Christmas finery. Maybe I
should have a Christmas party. Haven't done that for six years.
Proper printed invitations, a sumptuous buffet, champagne. I pop
into a stationery store and peruse the books. That's what I'll do. A
discreet gold-bordered card. Clare Layton invites you to a holiday
bacchanal. Writers, agents, a few pols. (So it will get back to
Michael; I'll tell him anyway, but I like the leakage. See, I have a
life.) I look through my little date book for the right day. I am ahead
of the curve, so people will still be available. Saturday, no Friday—
people are so jazzed, end of the work week. December 13. Will start
the season for everybody. I start planning menus in my head. I'll
decorate the place, a tree, swags with gold ribbons, the whole nine
yards. I order invitations so I can't retreat. Six to nine? Seven to ten?
That always looks so bleak. Get out at ten. No, seven on, no end
time. I order fifty invitations, give them a deposit, and head back out,
buoyed up. I have a plan, a way to get through the season. My own
party with elegant, embossed invitations.

But the apartment still feels a little bleak when I get there. Always my haven, it now feels emptyish. I switch on all the lights, the
TV, start imagining the seasonal frippery I will bedeck it with. I get
a glass of wine, a stack of cookbooks, and plop down on the sofa,
still feeling queasy, antsy. Michael finally calls. I try not to say, but I
do say, "Hey, stranger."

He doesn't answer right away. There is noise in the
background—he's obviously at some function—so I don't know if
he didn't quite hear me or if he's trying not to take umbrage.

"Michael," I say.

"Yeah, sorry," he says, "lots of drunken Irishmen in here."

"A redundancy," I say.

"Cultural stereotyping," he says. "Thought you were above that."

We've had this conversation before, haven't we? A few times, a few thousand times. I say my lines, he says his. I hear singing now, male and silly and spirited. Michael will be swept up in it, swept away. "I'll try to call back when they settle down in here," he says. "Miss you."

"Me too," I say, because that's my line.

I try to feel happy, relieved, and I do. We will go on as before. We will meet. We will take our Viagra. I try to read my cookbooks, start my lists, but it isn't taking. I go get the jar of peanut butter and a spoon and the bottle of wine—my self-imposed rules are crumbling right and left—and climb into bed with all of it and when the phone rings again I don't answer it. I just don't want to hear myself say my lines. Not again tonight.

The next day Miriam calls and says she has an offer I can't refuse. I cut her off before she says any more. No more pieces for a few months, I tell her. I have something I'm going to finish. That was my post–peanut butter resolution in the dead of night. I will finish the stories before I do any more magazine work. I can afford it. I will call and cancel my invitations. That's not going to work, either. No party this Christmas. Let's just get on into the new year. But Miriam comes back at me, her usual bright-voiced obdurateness.

"Sweetie, you can't turn this down. All expenses paid vacation to Jamaica. We want a quick travel piece on this new resort in Montego Bay."

"I don't do stuff like that," I say.

"Well, make an exception. It'll be warm and you can relax."

"Let me think about it," I say, beguiled for a moment by the thought of sun.

"No thinking. We need this ASAP. You need to be on a plane tomorrow. I'll get Gardner to make the arrangements. Stay on the line."

"Wait a minute," I say. "I haven't agreed yet."

"Clare, it'll be good for you. You've seemed a little tense lately."

"So this is therapy."

"This is a gift," she says brightly. "Just hang on."

Gardner comes on the line. "Oh, you lucky girl" he says, filling me in on the available flights, the hotel, the weather there. I feel I have to ask about Mindy and the folks and I do and he audibly beams, but I get off before he can proselytize again. I call Michael and leave a message, telling him I'm off for a few days. "Wanna come?" I say, conjuring warm sands and balmy nights and me in a bikini, knowing he can't, not in this lifetime. I rummage for warm-weather clothes, buried under the turtlenecks and socks, and the next day at noon I am at the airport waiting for my flight. I've got my laptop. Maybe I'll actually jump-start fixing a couple of the stories that are bugging me. Warm sun, different scene. I have an hour. I get a coffee and pace through the gift shops and long corridors. I look out at the dark, gray day. I am happy to be leaving it behind, I guess. I am still antsy inside. I am not a nervous flyer, never have been, but my tummy is kicking around. Nor am I nervous about leaving Michael. He will be here when I get back. There will be more time, more love, more Viagra-abetted sex. But I keep pacing, pacing, through the shops, the corridors, and, seemingly without thinking, find myself downstairs at the ticket counter inquiring about changing my ticket, then pacing some more, then going back and swapping it so that when my flight is finally called and I board and am strapped in, I am on a plane not to Montego Bay, Jamaica, but to Orlando, Florida.

· 9 ·

I have landed in Orlando in a driving rain, managed to rent a car and a room in one of those generic, airport-adjacent hotels. It is a dark, dark late afternoon and I am sitting on the bed, eating peanuts, sipping bad red wine from the minibar and staring out the window at a fierce storm, that kind of wind-whipped rain that splashes at the windows. From framed prints on the walls, Mickey and Minnie and Donald and Daffy smile down at me. I haven't even opened my suitcase or gotten anything out or hung anything up. I haven't called Miriam, either. Getting up my courage. I have to do it almost immediately so she can dispatch another scribbler to Paradise while I hang out here. Maybe I can promise her a substitute travel piece about Orlando. I haven't been here before so I picked up a few guidebooks at the airport which I now start flipping through, only to learn what I suspected: This is hard-core, family Americana theme park central. Not just the metastasizing Walt Disney World adventure parks and water parks, but Universal Studios now, too, and Sea-World and, for the adventurous, Cape Canaveral out there in one direction and Daytona Beach in the other. This is testosterone turf, hardly stuff for Miriam's youngish female readers (unless they're astro-groupies or racetrack babes), as she will no doubt be the first to point out.

"Shit," she says, when I finally get up the nerve to call, "couldn't you at least have landed in Miami?"

I have told her I have family here, a sister in trouble. She is a bit curt, even though I have told her it's an emergency. I don't think she believes me quite, says something about never hearing me mention a sister. I tell her I'll make it up to her and she should send Gardner and company to Jamaica in my stead.

"Very funny," she says.

"I mean it," I say. "You don't need a writer, just someone to soak up the sun and sling around the encomiums. That's what the travel pieces are."

"Clare," she says, and I can hear a rebuke coming, but she cuts herself off. "Hope all goes well," she says. "Call when you get back."

"I am sorry," I say, but she's already gone.

A sister in trouble. I have said it. But I realize I didn't come to see her, in fact, don't want to see her, if I can manage. It is Luke I want to see, if only from a distance. I'm not sure I even want to talk to him. I just want to put my eyes on him. I don't know quite how I'm going to do this. I don't have an address or phone number, just the name of their town. I think Louise said it's something like an hour south of here. I guess, in my unformed plans, I'm intending to slink into the town, find Luke, and slink out. But where will I find him? I remember something Timmy said. You should see him in his element. But what could that be? Hardly a football field. He looks frail, obviously, now. But he doesn't look like someone who was ever robust enough to mix it up with the big boys of Central Florida on the gridiron or basketball court. A yell leader, a pep-rallyer, or maybe a gymnast or, more likely still, an actor, a delicate-faced, Hollywood-bound Romeo in tights, declaiming love in lovelorn couplets. The stage is his element. That's the most logical and I know I'm still kicking around the gay theme, the suspicion that that's a piece of the story here, another little detail his parents neglected to include. I have been back on the Internet and there is a connection between AIDS and hepatitis C, what they call a coinfection, more likely to have the latter if you have the former. My heart, for an instant, twinges for Louise, her adored first-born felled by his lustful teenage longings (remember yours, Louise? I do). But would they give such a kid a liver? Wouldn't that rule him out, being HIV positive?

I open my laptop and get back on the Net for follow-up liver research. I find another piece from another transplant ethicist telling people not to "solicit for cadaveric donations"—never heard that sad and spooky adjective used: cadaveric—because it won't work. But I keep going and finally find some evidence to the contrary. There's a story out of the middle of the country, slugged "Media Campaign Leads to Transplant," a triumphal story about a guy who got a liver after his wife and siblings mounted a major PR blitz, getting stories planted in newspapers and local television, starting a Web site and setting up a toll-free telephone line. So am I back on the hook, here?

I think about dinner, but can't face going downstairs and eating in some wildly cheerful, brightly lit, palm tree–bedecked, souped-up coffee shop where Disney World–bound families are eating fajitas or coconut-crusted shrimp (I've already scanned the menu in the folder beside the bed) and the kid din is off the charts. A few more peanuts, another small bottle of wine—that's dinner enough. I think for a minute of the other single women out there in their hotel rooms doing what I'm doing, an intrepid, untethered phalanx of the unmarried sitting in their anonymous suites, eating their minibar meals, maybe on business trips or, like me, on family business, bringing to bear on a rainy night like this all their habits and gifts at stemming the aloneness that could, if you let it, break through and bring you to your knees. Do they have married lovers at home, too?

I turn back to my guidebooks. In addition to theme parks, Florida also abounds in alligators that "generally mind their own business," and preachers who don't. They're a live crop down here, my cheekiest book says (the same one that has a gay and lesbian section warning same that Florida has a history of discrimination against homosexuals) and can be found in churches of all kinds, big and small, in cities and rural hamlets, in swampland and minimall. I am, I remember, in the South. Florida always reads coastal to me, the ultimate resort state, not Southern. But Southern it is, certainly, according to my books. New York—and my apartment—feels a million miles away. Michael won't have called. He thinks I'm out of the country. I'll let him know tomorrow about my little detour. I flip on the TV to get anchored (is that why they're called anchormen?), finally opening my suitcase, changing into my sweats, brushing my teeth, the nighttime rituals, and drift off finally, rain still splashing, CNN on mute, the pictures flickering, thinking that tomorrow, for the first time in his life and mine, I will, if all goes as planned, see my nephew. In his element, I hope, hoping, too, that Timmy didn't mean the hospital. It just occurred to me: Could he already be there, working the corridors, a jaundiced and jaunty Peter Pan showing the younger patients how to be brave in the face of death? Or could I actually be too late?

I awake disoriented. It is late and the sun is bright. I didn't close the curtains last night because of the rain and darkness. But now here is the sun. I clean up, pack up, and pay up, with a detour through the now quiet restaurant—the families are long since in long lines out there in all those playlands—for a quick breakfast. I page through the book and find their town, the name I remember, about an hour or two straight south, it appears. My fear in the night, that something awful might already have happened to Luke, seems unfounded and melodramatic in the bright light of day. I haven't formulated a plan quite yet about how to find him and not find my sister. My stomach, at the thought of her, starts kicking around again. But she has no right to keep me away. After all, she did come barging into my world. Still, I'm apprehensive, but also a little giddy as I drive out of town. It's warm, soft-warm, winter-warm. I put the windows down to feel the air after the cold northern days. I always forget how much I love to drive, long, open stretches like these in particular, a pleasure left over from a coastal girlhood on the other side of the country. But this coast, this road, this state, feels unbelievably flat, barely a bump or undulation, orange groves on either side punctuated by the occasional hotel or clump of buildings. It feels more rural to me than suburban, as if a slight detour off this river of concrete and you'd be in some brackish backwoods full of mobile homes and strange creatures, human and otherwise. Sunshine aside, it doesn't feel the least bit like California. Feels like a strange other planet. It gives me a little bit of the jitters, I have to admit. I'll get to town, get a room, and get settled. Don't want to be looking for a room in the late of the day. Have some lunch, then, what—a stop by the high school? I know Timmy owns—or did own—his own construction firm. I can cold call, get a secretary, pretend to be a friend, and get the low-down on Luke's whereabouts. This all seems a little madcap. Just how do I expect to see him and not her? At a gas station just outside of town, I ask a young man in a dirty blue jumpsuit about places to stay. Bad luck, he tells me; the convention's here and I'll be hard put to find so much as a bed in an old shack. Best, he says, to go back to the town before; they might still have a room.

"Picked a fine time to come here without a reservation," he says. "This is one of the biggest things every year."

I remember now that there's a racetrack around here, too. But they don't have conventions, do they?

"What convention?" I say.

"The baby evangelists," he says. "Maybe you read about it."

"The baby evangelists?" I say, sitting on my smile while imagining a host of precocious, Bible-spouting tots with slicked-back hair and shiny little suits.

"That's how they're known around here," he says. "You can probably still get a ticket to some of the early rounds."

"The early rounds?"

"The finals are all sold out. But you can get into some of the early stuff. That'll start tomorrow. The place will be filling up."

I pull back onto the highway, debating whether to listen to him and go back to the previous town. But now I'm curious to see what's up ahead. No mistake: The main street is beginning to jump. There's a banner across it saying: "Welcome Young Competitors for Christ" and the sidewalks are full of heavyset families in shorts and tennis shoes, a fair number of the kids wearing their mouse ears. I throw my reporter's acumen at the crowd and see if I can pick out any of the contenders. Maybe that one, a chunky, earnest-looking five-year-old eating an ice cream cone. I park and decide to find some lunch, but first slip into a gift shop to buy a sweatshirt and cap. Sort of silly, but I'm thinking of disguising myself somewhat, so in a casual drive-by, Louise or Timmy can't or won't immediately pick me out of the sidewalk crowd. I need to see Luke before I see them (if I have to see them at all). I know that. I just know that. Or else I may never see him.

The woman tries to sell me—and I am, for a moment, tempted to buy—the sweatshirt of the moment emblazoned with the name and date of the convention. But that does seem a bit morally cheeky and I opt instead for a pink one with "Orlando" written across it in iridescent silver and a matching cap. I don both, after pulling my hair back in a ponytail. With my sunglasses, I have, I figure, a bit of cover. I rejoin the crowd and find a hamburger joint on a side street. It's pretty full but quite subdued, given all the kids. When their food is put in front of them, a large family next to me joins hands and, with bowed heads, says a unison grace, punctuated by an "Amen" and a "Pass the ketchup, please." For a New Yorker this is the Twilight Zone. I smile: Fodder for Michael.

I try to call him when I'm back in the car, but get his voice mail. Don't leave a message. Never leave a message in case someone else picks them up. More rules. I have asked directions to the high school and have been told there are actually two, a close one and one farther out. I somehow bet it's the farther out one because Timmy, Louise said at some point—I think she told me—was building tract housing out and around from the town. Doesn't mean they live out there, though. I first cruise by the nearest high school and park across from the playing field. There are kids out there, some running track, some tossing a football in the middle. It's getting cooler but the sun is still out and the sky is still blue and everything looks so clean and so flat. What am I thinking? That my ailing nephew might actually be out there among them? I think of Louise (because I can't not) coming by here and looking at the raucous, healthy boys doing their healthy boy thing with a lump—or is it a curse—in her throat because hers cannot be among them. I park and walk into the main building. It feels very new, rows of shiny green lockers, no graffiti. Obviously between classes because there are no kids wandering around. I find the administrative office. A plump woman in what looks like a housedress says, when I ask, that she cannot tell me whether there is a Luke Brown here or not because that's against the privacy rules.

"I'm his aunt," I say, realizing I have identified myself that way for the first time.

"Doesn't matter who you are," she says, not meanly. "I can't give out the information."

"Thanks for your help," I say, a bit archly, but she's already turned away.

Now what? Haunt the corridors and ask some kids when the classes change? I wander a bit, remarking on the startling cleanliness of the place, as opposed to the dense and dirty public schools I've been in in New York. The bell goes off and students start coming out of the classrooms. School's over for the day and they push past me to get out. As they pass, I scan the faces, look for a friendly-looking girl whose eye I can catch. When the crowd thins again, I intercept a trio of girls, books in their arms, open-looking faces. They don't know him. Have I tried the administration office? I ask another stray boy, tall, lean, acned—doesn't look like an athlete, ergo might know Luke, I'm thinking—but he's never heard of him, either.

This is beginning to feel like a fool's errand. Back in the car, I decide to drive by the hospital. I find it on my local map, which I got at the gas station. Nothing's very far, but not all that close, either. It's all so horizontal, long stretches of highway between outposts of civilization: the town center, the high school, and, now, the hospital, a pinkish square with two low-lying wings, standing all by itself surrounded by flat, closely mown fields, looking as if it had just been dropped down by helicopter or something—the way everything looks to me here, toy terrain with buildings just plunked here and there by the whimsy of a child's hand. I go to the front desk and ask if a Luke Brown is here and as I wait for the answer, I realize my heart is pounding. I don't want him to be here. And if, by some awful chance he is, they'll be here, too. When the man behind the desk says no, nobody registered by that name, I feel a surge of relief. There is time—for what? For something.

In the car, I look back through the guidebook for hotels or motels and start calling places. The ones in and near town are booked. The farther outlying Quality Inn and Inn on the Lake (What lake? I haven't seen a lake yet) are also full. There's a motor inn about twelve miles back up toward Orlando and they have a room. I take it, imagining a long, noisy night beside the highway, but better that than being tucked in some woodsy, isolated place in the outback. At the mini-mart in the same gas station I stopped in earlier, I stock up

on junk—a screw-top bottle of red wine, pretzels, even a little carton of animal crackers—because I figure I'll just settle in for the
night. No point in trying to have a decent meal.

The motel is, as I suspected, just a little off the highway, low-
slung, brown wood, perfectly fine, I'm figuring. The parking lot is
full of both cars and RVs and out behind I can hear pool splashings,
laughter. It's gotten warmer again with the sun almost gone, the air
thickening with dampness, maybe rain threatening. The little dark-
paneled check-in room is crowded. People are hugging and saying
"Hi" at high decibel. It feels as if I've walked into a reunion. More
Mickey Mouse ears and shorts and Southern accents, some thicker
than others. People are making plans for breakfast, where to meet, at
the lodge or one of the tents, and it becomes clear that they are all
bound for the convention, which I gather is at a campground about
ten miles from here. They have printed schedules in their hands and
are looking at them. When it comes my turn, finally, to check in, I
see that there is a stack of the schedules on the front desk and I pick
one up and stick it in my bag. Night comes and brings more laughter
and splashing noise from the pool, welcome since it actually fights
the highway noise. People are moving around, pounding on their
neighbors' doors. I am the odd woman out, the stray again, eating
my second straight junk snack dinner sitting in a bed in a motel far
from home. I call Michael's cell again and again get the voice mail. I
want to regale him with a point-by-point description of this alien
world I've stumbled into, but no. Nobody tonight to tell my stories
to. I try to sleep but can't; the noise from the highway is decisive and
I never sleep well away from home anyway—even with the pills. I
flip on the light and reach for my satchel. Got a paperback in there. I
pull it out and find that I stuck the convention schedule in it. This is
no small event. They have a full-fledged, dawn-to-dusk schedule of
sermon-offs—what else to call them?—by the aspirant preachers.
Not babies, really. That was too good to be true, but kids seven and

up. There are age categories: 7–11, 12–16, 17–21. Prelims tomorrow, survivors to go on to the next round, finals Saturday, winners of each age group to preach Sunday at the closing session. Meals and prayer sessions and entertainment—including, yes, a Christian rap group called Do Me Lord—interspersed with the business at hand. At the back is a list of the rules. Each contestant gets five minutes per speech or per preachment, not one second more, and there's a list of names and start times for tomorrow with the bold-faced reminder that "God Waits for No Man. If you miss your scheduled time, you will be disqualified." I've got to remember to take this thing home with me. Nobody will believe it.

I start to turn off the light, but flip the pages again just to see if there are any girls among the contestants. Doesn't look like it. This is God's country and he likes his sex roles clearly delineated. A quick eye scan turns up no Tiffanys or Scarletts among the sixty or so names. There are Chips and Jimmys and Carls and . . . Lukes. Wait, wait, wait, wait, wait. Five twenty-five P.M., Tent Seven, Luke Brown. There it is in print; there he is. Right there. How stupid can you feel? How sad and stupid and wrecked and furious and manipulated and stupid and furious and tricked and stupid and stupid and stupid. It's the good news, bad news joke: Congratulations, you've found your nephew. Bad news: He's a Jesus freak, a baby evangelical, cream of the Christian crop. I keep feeling like I'm missing all the signals. Here I am in preacher-land; the guidebook warned me, didn't it? And all this convention crap. Of course. Of course. She had to have more, Louise did, another card up her sleeve, something else to hide or lie about. That's why she went to the lengths she did in her runaway-wife-we-can-be-friends visit to the Big Apple. Just when was she planning to tell me this, I wonder. When Louise, when? Where's the honor among Christians, huh? Goddamn you. I'm now ranting out loud—I hear myself—stomping around, slugging back another plastic cup of wine. I start to pack, grabbing my resort wear and cramming it back into the suitcase. I'll bolt with the sun. At least five hours to go, five hours to kill. I keep pacing and throwing clothes in, stopping to stare again at Luke's name on the page. Five twenty-five P.M., Tent Seven, Luke Brown. No mistake. No misread. He's still there, every time I look down at it. Round and round the small room I pad, declaiming, swearing, shaking my head, finally coming to rest in the ugly little chair by the window. I peer through the curtains. There must be clouds because I don't see stars. The little pool, still lit, glows turquoise in the darkness, exhaling a vaporous layer into the night. I take my wine and quietly go through the gate surrounding it and sit on an edge, dangling my feet in the water. They look ghoulish in the pool light. I move them around and around, not breaking water, not making noise. The place is all asleep, the God-folk and their silver-tongued offspring getting ready for the big, oratorical showdown. I am so far from home. And yet, the only family I have is here. What a bad joke. Did Daddy know about all this Christian stuff (it certainly wasn't his cup of tea—or vodka) or is it new—a geographic conversion when they moved to Florida from San Diego. Was this Louise's idea, another impassioned lurch at something, another dramatic gesture (the actress manqué in her?) or a stab at penitence—for things I know about and things I don't? Just bet it was her idea. I don't remember ever hearing anything—not that I would have, I suppose—about Timmy being religious. And the boy. What about him: Who is he, what is he, is he all hers, a chip off the old maternal block? I think about Michael, snoozing in Westchester, my adulterous Catholic lover, another God-fearer, or at least, as he says, an observer of the forms. My life is encircled by it; America is knee deep in it. It always seems anomalous for such a swaggery, young country with a decided amount of antiauthoritarianism in its bones to be so religious. But it is. And now I am literally encircled by it, the snores of the prayerful being emitted into the warm night from the small, family-packed motel rooms that surround the pool.

I stay outside for a long time. I think about going in to call the airline, but it doesn't matter. I'll just get out of here at first light and head to the airport, before the conventioneers fire up their little plug-in coffeemakers. It looks now not too far away, the dawn. I'll just finish packing and be on my way. But I can't move, feet still twiddling in the pool. I feel a tremendous backward loneliness for Louise, way, way back before the damage was done, the familial equation forever altered, and then, on the heels of that, a gut-flash of rage at her for coming back at me all these years later. To hell with her. I'm not going to slink away. I'm going to stay right here in Bibleland. I'm going to go to the convention. I'm going to see my nephew "in his element." That's what I came for and that's exactly what I'm going to do.

.10.

I am in Tent Five, as it says on a big placard outside, listening to a pale-faced eight-year-old deliver what is clearly his stump sermonette. It has turned gray and muggy out and the people around me all have a slight sheen on their skin. We are packed in, about forty of us, sitting slick thigh to slick thigh on small folding chairs that are rickety on the uneven ground. Shorts and T-shirts are the preferred uniform for the audience—I'm in mine, too—even though the kids who have come before us, like the current contestant, are dressed and shod to the max: shiny little suits, ties, heavy Sunday School shoes, beads of perspiration on their foreheads, sometimes running down their cheeks. I'm listening to this one and wondering where he learned to do this. He's the male analog to those pre-pubescent beauty queens who learn to strut their coquettish stuff in nursery school. We've had some timid entrants who looked at the ground and forgot their scriptural passages, causing their parents to mutter stage-whisper prompts from the audience. "He that saith unto the wicked . . ." "The word of the Lord came unto me . . ." But this kid, Charles James Newell of Birmingham, Alabama, has got it down pat. Short with a blond buzz cut, he is channeling Martin Luther King, a full-on basso profundo, certain words elongated for emphasis.

"Do not fear," he says, voice rising and falling. "He will show you the way. When it's your time, God will bring it to pass. You must learn to trust him. Be at one with his will, his timing. As it says in Psalms Thirty-one, verses fifteen to sixteen: 'My times are in thy hand: deliver me from the hand of mine enemies, and from them that persecute me. Make thy face to shine' "—stretching the shine up to a crescendo—" 'upon thy servant: save me for thy mercies' sake,' " he concludes with a flourish, mopping his eight-year-old brow with a handkerchief.

He's a freak, a master, a big hit with the crowd. He'll clearly make it to the next round. Our next contestant, Andrew Mason, does not fare so well. String-beany and self-conscious, he gets stuck trying to cite Philippians something or other, but he can't get by the word. "Phil . . ." he starts and stops. "Phila . . . Phil . . . a . . . pee . . . nuns. Phili . . ."

"Just move on, Andy," a voice hisses from somewhere up near the front.

But he's flustered and when he starts, "Finally my brethren, rejoice in the Lord," he quavers through it near tears.

I leave the tent grumpy, convinced anew that all these contests for kids—from spelling bees on sideways—are tantamount to child abuse. How will even that little Biblical toastmaster turn out? He might crash and burn on the next round, or next year, or the next, when adolescence has its way with him. Or maybe he'll never lose his way, becoming prematurely ossified in a mantle of self-righteous self-assurance, destined to make the big bucks hawking God to the masses. No question, he's destined to take home one of the little bronze paperweight Bibles on Sunday. I stroll the grounds, a can of Coke in hand, hearing scriptural snatches drift out of one tent or another. I have some hours to kill before Luke is up. I am being mildly furtive, not looking to run into my sister and brother-in-law just yet. But I suspect they won't be around until later, suspect that they've made their way through these tents in previous years, as Luke made his up the age ladder. I gird myself for his appearance, a too blue suit, a tie, slicked back hair. And the voice, the slicker, more adult version of Charles James Newell's, a voice, in fact, reminiscent of my mother's, assertive and theatrical, a voice I last heard at about the age Luke is now. Is this some bizarre full circle? For a second, I am tempted to bolt again, leave these people, this family, to its own devices, but again, a wallop of anger and curiosity keeps me here.

I go sit by the lake, a flat, bluish disc in a flat swath of grass. It feels like it might rain. A couple of people are having picnics, one with a boom box belting out rock and roll. A relief, a jolt back to the civilian world. Having slept not at all the night before, I put my head down and doze right off, waking to the vibration of my cell phone. Michael. I'd forgotten to call.

"So," he says, "are you tan in new places?"

"I'm not there," I say. "I didn't make it to Jamaica. I'm in Florida."

"What's there?"

"My sister. I think I told you."

"I thought you were done with that."

Done with that. Can one be? I don't want to go into it all. I start telling him about the convention, just a little, but realize I don't want to turn my family, my nephew, into laughing fodder. Not just yet, anyway. It's darkish out and still clammy. Michael puts me on hold and I look at my watch. It's 5:05. I want to get up there and hear a few of Luke's competitors, see what shakes in the more adult leagues before listening to him. I walk with the phone at my ear, but Michael hasn't come back by the time I reach the outskirts of the tent city, so I shut it off. Bye-bye. For a minute, I can't see him, can't picture him or the Northern winter-chilled city I call home. My heart scans around trying to latch onto him, the bulk, the smell of him, my apartment, my bathroom perch, but everything remains fuzzy, distant, as if he were someone else's lover and that apartment someone else's home. I think about turning my cell phone back on for a second, giving him another shot at me, but don't. The crowds are thick in the various tents, standing room only, with some people hovering outside at the entrances. With luck, Louise and Timmy will already be tucked up front in Tent Seven. By the time I slither in around the loitering crowd at the entrance and find a spot at the very back, one of the competitors is in full, earnest car salesman mode. I recognize this version from flipping around the TV channels and catching some of the televangelists speaking to their gargantuan congregations. This is not old-school fire-and-brimstone, you're-going-to-burn-in-hell preachment, but the opposite. This is smiley-faced, self-help Christianity.

"God wants you to be happy," the young man says. Big smiles, easy, easy cadence, folksy and intimate, lots of eye contact. I wonder if Master Newell is here to pick up some pointers. No fancy rhetorical tricks, just a gentle wink in the voice. No mopping of the brow, no flagrant hand gestures. This is cooled-down, mass audience, TV-ready religion delivered by a twenty-year-old dressed for the part, dark suit, white shirt, quiet tie, thick, dark hair with, yes, probably a little product in it.

"He wants you to be successful, to be fulfilled, and when a door closes in your life, he will open another one for you. All you need to do each day is get up and look in the mirror and say, 'I will be successful. I will be positive. God won't let me down. He's on my side.'"

There seem to be pleased mumblings in the crowd as he finishes and then enthusiastic applause. This is a breed and a brand that plays well. Makes perfect sense since we are all TV-weaned now. The next one up is more old-school, a little more retro-Swaggart, boomy and hectoring, more hair, shinier suit, gold tie, thicker Southern accent. I glance at my program. Bobby Coggins. My ear gets a little sleepy through this one, heavy as it is with scriptural recitations and warnings of doom. I glance around, eyes skipping off heads, until I think I see—can't be sure because there is a fair amount of coifed hair in here—Louise. My heart starts pounding. I try to squiggle around and see if I'm right, if there is a tall, blondish man next to her. But we're packed in pretty tight so I can't get a good view. These tents are bigger. Maybe sixty to seventy-five of us, counting those just outside the door. It's dark out now, the tent lanterns casting their full glow. A kind of cozy, magical place, I suspect, if you're a true believer. A baby starts crying somewhere near the front and a youngish woman threads her way out of her row and down the aisle, some eyes following her. I instinctively tuck down, heart still pounding, until people turn back toward the stage in time to hear Mr. Coggins's apocalyptic close.

". . . the destruction of the transgressors and of the sinners shall be together, and they that forsake the Lord shall be consumed."

There is clapping, even a wolf whistle (is that kosher?), but I can't properly calibrate the applause against his predecessor's (lighter, I think; definitely lighter) because my heart now is beating so loud I can hear it in my own ears because he is there now, coming up on the stage, having been announced—"Our next contestant is a local, Luke Brown; please welcome him"—and I am so avid to see him finally after all the waiting that I almost don't see him. It takes him some seconds to come into clean focus and when he does the back of my hand comes to my mouth to keep a noise from getting out because I would know him anywhere. He is without any of the trappings of the trade. Not a suit or a tie. A white shirt and a black Windbreaker, longish, dark hair, a few pieces of which are stranded across his left eye. Clearly no product in there. I am still. Everyone is. He has infused the place with stillness. Or maybe it's just the visual oddity of him, so different from everyone who has gone before. He is not looking out at us. He seems to be looking down or sideways. The silence extends and I begin to fear it is another, different kind of oratorical trick, along with the anti-outfit. Just as the crowd is on the verge of stirring—you can feel the restlessness building like the tension in the air before a storm breaks—he begins to speak in a voice, soft but clearly audible even where I am in the back.

"I'm not sure God wants us to be happy," he says. "I think he wants us to be good."

I hear a kind of collective uptake of breath and realize I am holding mine, my hand still over my mouth. This is like nothing heard yet in these tents, certainly not in my hearing, certainly not tonight. Luke has gone into different territory, into risky rebuttal mode. I don't know what the rules are, the real rules and the unspoken ones. He looks up finally and out into the audience, a slight smile playing at the edges of his mouth.

"Isn't that the point really, to try to be good? We all ask ourselves—or maybe we don't ask ourselves enough—what that means, but I think we do know. We do know," he repeats, even more softly, as if to himself, "even if we're not always able to do it. There's an inner rubbing, if we allow ourselves to feel it, if we really look at ourselves when we look in that mirror. It is in us to know. God is in us to know."

He goes on talking, but I don't hear it because I am staring so hard at his slender face. It is my father's face. I could not see that so clearly in the photograph, but it is. The whole demeanor—soft-spoken, self-effacing—is he: Philip Layton. I feel a ruffle of pride right up the backbone: my nephew. Luke Brown is my nephew, my father's grandson. Our tribe. Of course, this is still God-speak, but in a different vernacular. I like his moxie. He's taking it to them. Louise was right. Timmy was right. This looks to be a boy apart. I watch him, half listening now. No voice tricks, no gestural tricks, just a little up and down with the eyes, that small smile. No reference to being sick. I wondered if he'd use that for sympathy, for gain, and wonder, for a second, why he doesn't. Wouldn't all these like-minded folks, his brethren, really love that? Wouldn't that help him win this contest, not to mention get a liver somewhere, somehow? But are they like-minded? I dial back into his words and am taken again with how quietly he speaks but how clearly. The tent, lanterns flickering, seems momentarily enchanted. The quiet is fierce, exacting. I am not sure if it is respect or something negative, a kind of silent judgment because he has stepped out of the expected script and because they actually prefer all the bells and whistles, the God-as-self-help-guru patter. Luke has upended all of that.

He is quoting some passage now. That is probably part of the requirement. Galatians something or other I hear him say while I am staring, staring still at that face, Daddy's face—has it been made even more slender, more meager through illness?—and then I think again about whether or not he might be gay. More than anything, he feels otherworldly and again, I don't know if that's who he is, who he has always been, or if it's part of being sick, one foot here, one foot there.

" '. . . let every man prove his own work, and then shall he have rejoicing in himself alone, and not in another.' " He is reciting and his voice is even softer, head slightly to the side, eyes closed, like a singer singing a lovely ballad. " 'For every man shall bear his own burden. Let him that is taught in the word communicate unto him that teacheth in all good things. Be not deceived; God is not mocked: for whatsover a man soweth, that shall he also reap.' "

I slip outside in case he's nearing the end. I don't want to be caught. I stand in the darkness, looking into the tent, just him up there in the light, the soft voice, narrow face (not yellowish, at least it doesn't seem so), my view actually better from out here. I am now feeling tethered to this boy, this young man, to his words.

" '. . . And let us not be weary in well doing: for in due season we shall reap, if we faint not.' "

As the applause starts, I turn and start walking toward the lake, half wanting to turn back because the clapping does sound a bit grudging, or at least not fulsome, and I want to storm into the tent and say, "You fools, don't you see; this is the real thing," and up to Louise and tell her, "Yes, yes, you were right about him." But I don't because I am scared she will still want me to help. How am I going to do that? How am I, an avowed in print secular humanist, going to throw myself on the public's mercy now in the name of my Christer nephew's ailing liver? What moral pivot am I going to make? Take a look in that mirror, Clare; you're sleeping with a married man, speaking of moral pivots. Maybe that's the new moral math: Erase one pivot with another. I am virtually cantering now down toward the lake because there is an intermission before the next three speakers and people are spilling out and over to where there's a refreshment table. I am not ready to face anybody. What I'm really scared of is that she won't want me to help anymore. That's what I'm really scared of. That she won't let me know this boy.

It's still humid. I sit and take off my shoes and dangle my feet in the water. It's not very cold. I am trying to come up with a plan of action. How do I do this? I feel my phone vibrate but don't answer it. Michael it will be, Michael whose phone calls I usually wait for, count the minutes for. It wouldn't be anybody else, not anyone I can think of. Certainly not Miriam. She'll forgive me after being a little gruffly sympathetic. But at the moment I'm off her radar and she wouldn't call at this hour, anyway. Who else? I'm not exactly thick with friends—let them lapse—or family. Family—what there is of it—is up there in that tent. Just up there. I sit for a long time. Should I just leave and go home? Wouldn't that be the easiest thing—for all of us, for them? How is this going to come out good? How? But I cannot stand this thought: that I will not know him, never know him, should the worst happen. Maybe if he didn't look so much like my father. Maybe if he weren't seriously ill. Maybe if he hadn't shown so much character in there? That was something, some quiet, call-your-Christian-bluff something. And they knew it. And he had to know it, doing it. Is it just my vanity kicking up, my wanting people to know I'm related to him, to this maverick? I feel that shiver of pride again. But what about back home in my secular humanist, liberal media world? There it will be the opposite. There I'll read as that sellout who's whining in print about her nephew's liver, knowing he's a Bible-thumper. I sit until it finally gets cold and I've heard more waves of applause and then the cars, in the distance, revving up and driving off and then the lanterns being turned out so the little tent city is quiet and dark and I'm alone under the stars. It's clear tonight, finally. Funny where you're not scared. Never on the streets of New York—no doubt very scary to many, even natives, certainly at night—and not here out in the Florida countryside, feet twirling in a lake, not another person in sight. Day before yesterday, yes, I would have been scared here. I wanted to be tucked into a little safe, highway-side motel (with a lot of Christian folk). But now, my indecision is like an armor. I am rooted to the spot. I have to figure out what to do: go, stay, barge into the finals on Saturday night, the worldly New York aunt come to save the day. But will he even make the finals? I don't know that. Should I just pick up the phone and call Louise and say, bygones be bygones, I'm here to help (not that I mean it, the bygones be bygones part; that's way too much too fast, but the helping part, yes). But if she hangs up, that's it. I lose my chance. Maybe forever. What about Timmy? Should I try to get to him? That's dicey, too, given my parting shot at him. And he's Louise's, heart, soul, teeth, and toes. That became obvious. Her abuser. Jesus, what a stunt. Luke. It's Luke. I have to go straight at him. If I have a chance, that'll be the way to do it. I remember that there is a bulletin board out front of the main lodge, the only building, and that we congregants can leave messages there for the contestants (and vice versa). I have a surge of excitement as I pull my little flashlight from my purse, then find my Post-it packet and pen.

But I don't know what to say. And I have no idea what his parents might have said to him about me, ever, pre–New York or post. I have a flicker of shame, a flicker of hope that they didn't tell him about Michael. I don't want him to think ill of me, this young man, and I don't know, underneath his soft demeanor, just how priggish and rectitudinous he might turn out to be. God wants us to be good, he said, gentle-seeming, but the words are strong—maybe the strongest religious exhortation of all, when you think about it, and provocative in all its unstated ambiguities, and who knows how tough on the rest of us errant mortals this ethereal-looking young evangelist might actually turn out to be.

"Dear Luke," I write and then sit staring at the paper. Come on, Clare, just get it over with. He'll see you or he won't. "I came down here to try to meet you after your mother came to see me in New York. She doesn't know I'm here and I don't know how she would react if she did. But I hope you can find it in your heart to talk with me sometime tomorrow. I probably won't be at the conference, but I am staying at a motor hotel up the road. My cell phone number is 212-555-8209. Your Aunt Clare. PS: I saw you tonight and you were wonderful."

Does that sound groveling, that bit about him being wonderful? In truth, it's less than I think. Magic. That's what I would say if I were being honest. You were magic tonight. But that seems a little much so I just leave it as is. Enough brooding. I get up, slip on my canvas shoes, and pick my way carefully in the dark, up toward the lodge. Luckily I have my little flashlight, but its faint, thin beam doesn't afford much illumination along the way. I walk slowly and only now, released from my head for a moment, do I have a premonition of menace. A rustle of leaves makes me jump and I pick up my pace. At the bulletin board, I fold my note, write "Luke Brown" on the outside, and stick a pin through it, then hurry to my car, heart beginning to pound. There is one other car left on the parking field, fairly close to mine, but I don't see anybody and it gives me the immediate jitters. I quickly unlock my rental and jump in and lock the doors behind me. Then I see, in the other car window, a bare leg come up, and another, and notice the fogged-up windows and my heart slows down with a laugh. Birds do it, bees do it, and even baby evangelicals do it. Does my Luke? (My Luke?) Has he? Is that where he got the liver disease? Will he tell me? Will he see me? What if we hate each other? I suppose that will make it easier. Just get on a plane and be out of this loop. But thinking about flying home to my empty apartment, the cold, Christmas, I am more determined—more hopeful—than ever that I can find a place in this boy's heart. It seems, in the dark of this muggy Florida night, imperative.

I am sitting in what is essentially a Chinese coffee shop in a strip mall just off the highway a few miles south of the conference grounds. On the walls there are pictures of the signature dishes, a slippery clump of noodles in one, in another, chunks of fried meat in some sticky-looking orangey-brown sauce. You can smell the grease just looking at them and, sipping my hot tea, I have to swallow hard against an incipient nausea because I am already queasy with anticipation. I look away from the food photos and out the window. It is pouring. I can't help but wonder whether Luke will use that as an excuse not to come. I am clutching my cell phone in case it rings. It is my conduit to him. We still haven't spoken in person. I had two messages on my phone this morning when I got out of the shower, first one from Michael.

"You ducking me, lassie?" he said and then quickly, "Call. I need to hear your voice," followed by a snippet of Yeats, something I haven't heard before, something about a white deer with no horns. "Do you not hear me calling, white deer with no horns! I have been changed to a hound with one red ear . . ." That was it. Presumably he would have gone on and it might have made sense, but I could hear someone else's voice and he hung up. Then Luke, with no self-introduction. The same voice from last night, soft but clean. Effeminate? Stop it, Clare.

"So we don't play phone tag, let's say noon at the Bamboo Wok. It's in a mall off the main highway a few miles below where we were last night. I'm sorry I don't have the address."

That was it. It might have sounded curt, very curt, but for the easy tone—or at least that's how I chose to interpret it. And now I'm sitting here, hands around a cup of tea, staring into a gray storm. I keep trying not to look at my watch. Would he, in familial solidarity—having heard the details of our recent contretemps—stand me up? No, no. He's a Christian, remember.

So intent am I in staring out the window that I miss him coming in. He is there, slipping into the booth before I even look up. His face is more rugged up close, still my father's but with a few more planes, sharper cheekbones, longer nose, over the bridge of which is a faint half-moon of acne. Come on, there's Louise, too, the blue eyes and that thick dark hair, the strands strafing those eyes like last night. Beautiful, I could say if I could say, which, of course, I don't.

"Sorry," I finally say. "I'm staring."

He doesn't say anything and I turn quickly to look out the window again because I can't stop staring and because I feel the premonition of tears. Luke, you're beautiful. You look like Daddy. And Louise. Luke, tell me, how do you feel?

I do say that. "How do you feel?"

"Today," he says, "I'm okay."

"And last night?"

"Yes," he says, a slight smile. "Two good days in a row. In fact, two good weeks now. But I don't like to talk about me."

"How am I going to help you, then?" I say.

"Is that why you came?" he says. The tone again seems direct, without coloration or judgment.

"I don't know," I say. And I realize I mean it. We sit for a while, both looking out the window, then I feel his eyes on me and I make, for probably the first time in my life (or certainly that I can remember), that nervous Louise gesture, hand fluttering up to my hair. Is this where it comes from, that habit, that gesture—not from fear, from having the eyes of a possessive husband on her (as I had wrongly assumed), but from having these eyes on her, the eyes of goodness looking out of a son's face. I cannot turn to meet them just yet. It's not judgment. What's in those eyes, so calm and so blue, is an exhortation for me, for any of us who come under its gaze, to be our better selves. He means what he said last night. His eyes do. I have one of my whispers of empathy for Louise. What a daunting gift to live with, those eyes. I wonder if he had them as a baby. I wonder if they are different since he got sick.

To break the spell of my nervousness, I take my fluttering hand and sweep it around to take in the pictures of the food on the wall.

"Want any of that?" I say, a laugh added (shit, it's that Louise laugh with the apology in it).

"No thanks," he says. "Nobody eats here. We just meet because it's an easy location."

"Can't imagine it's any good for anyone's liver," I say, trying for levity.

"No," he says. He is smiling and I like that and I want to make him smile more, so I find myself prattling about all the greasy Chinese spoons—no, no, I mean Chinese greasy spoons in New York with laminated pork buns and pink things in the windows. You'll have to come and let me show you around. I can find all kinds of restaurants we can't eat in. When you're well, obviously. When you've had the . . . I don't say the word. It hangs there: transplant.

He says it: "Transplant."

"Yes, that," I say. "Luke . . ."

"I understand now," he says. "You need to ask. It's okay."

"I don't even know what you have or where you are on the list or how you got it. Louise—your mother—and I never got there."

"Hepatitis," he says. "B."

"That's more unusual, isn't it? Isn't it the 'C' that's worse?"

"If you have it for a while, it can be as serious."

"And you've had it for a while."

"Forever, apparently," he says.

"What do you mean 'forever'?"

"I came with it."

"Came with it? It isn't a genetic disease."

"No, but it can be passed on."

The light is slow coming on. I'm not getting it quite and then I think I do.

"Your mom? Is that what you're saying?"

He doesn't answer. There is a quiver at the edge of his mouth.

"Luke, is that it? Did Louise have it and so you got it at birth?"

Again he doesn't say anything, but I can see it's a yes.

"Was she sick? Is she still? Where did she get it?" I'm leaning forward and I have a thousand questions backed up in me like airplanes lined up on the runway waiting to take off.

"You must understand," he says, very softly, "I won't talk about my mother with you. Or you with her."

I don't say anything, trying to let the questions subside. I breathe them down, feeling chastened and slightly irritated. He will leave, I am sure, if I ask again something about Louise.

"Tell me about the list, then, where you are on it and what we can do?"

"I don't think there is anything to do. The sickest people go first. That's as it should be."

"But publicity can help. I know they say it can't, but it can, I think, if it's done right and I think your parents" (I flash him a slightly wry smile; this is, okay, right: your parents. I'm not talking about Louise here) "said you'd had some really bad days and I'd like to . . . Truth to tell, I don't know what to do. I don't know how to help."

"You'll know," he says, sounding like the boy-man preacher from last night.

"Even if I wanted to write something, I don't know how I'd do it. I'd have to tell the truth, I mean, and say you were this major Christian and that's just not anything I believe in."

"What don't you believe in?"

"God, for example."

"What about redemption?" he says, my seventeen-year-old nephew with the goodness eyes and a failing liver. Redemption he wants me to consider, this acned adolescent, here in this Chinese cubbyhole off a Florida highway with the rain pelting down. For a moment, it feels like an out-of-body experience.

"What about redemption?" I say, slightly starchy—for the first time with him.

"That's all God is," he says.

I hear myself exhale. "That simple, huh?"

"You think that's simple?" he says.

"Oh, Luke, come on," I say, trying to stop there, but plunging on. "Are we talking original sin, here, all of us born in sin so that life is one long struggle to atone? And who gets to decide what redemption is? You and your Christian buddies? You make all the rules about how the rest of us can get redeemed. And you run around talking about having this 'deep reverence for life' "—I make quotation marks in the air with my hands while stretching out the deep— "which gives you license to be antiabortion nazis and antigay and . . ." I am running out of steam here and I feel it. Those eyes are looking at me and they are absolutely calm and there is no defensiveness in them. When I finally stop, Luke says, simply, "Is there a question in there?"

"Guess so," I say.

"I don't mix politics and religion," he says. "I don't think it serves God well."

There I am again, up against his purity and most of me believes it and some of me thinks, "Am I being conned?" And what does it mean to serve God (what does he mean?) and again, I can't believe I'm having this conversation. He's smiling at me now. "We don't need to do all this, you know. We could just have some more tea."

"Is yours cold?" I say, trying to downshift along with him. Yes, let's just have tea and hang out together. Let's just relax and eat some of this awful food and do a little bonding.

"Are you sure you don't want to eat something?" I gesture toward one of the off-putting photos and we both smile. I ask a little about school and his friends, wondering if they are all Christian Goody-Two-shoes as I try to tiptoe around the elephants: Louise, God, and his failing liver—and whether or not he's gay (I no longer think so because I think I'm picking up a little heterosexual vibe) or a virgin (I do think so), not necessarily in that order. He asks a little about my life (I am desperate to know what Louise told him and what she didn't), what it's like to live in New York, and whether writing is hard and I find myself telling him about my book of short stories and my uncertainty about it, about whether I'm any good and can pull it off—which normally I never talk about.

"You'll do it," he says.

"Will that count as redemption?" I say playfully.

He smiles but doesn't say anything. The rain is still pelting down. The wind must have picked up because it's coming down aslant and is quite fierce. Looking out the window, we make weather small-talk for a few minutes: New York winter versus Florida winter, rain versus snow. Still looking out and not at him, I say, "Luke, are you scared?"

"I don't think so," he says. "There are things I want to do. And I'm scared about what it would do to my mother . . ." He trails off.

"Luke, what can I do? How can I help? I just don't know what to do."

"It'll work out," he says.

"Why can't all your church friends help? They could mount a killer campaign, billboards, you and God and the whole nine yards. I don't mean it that way. You know what I mean: They could really help."

"They don't know, most of them."

"What?"

"I couldn't do it, using my faith to get higher up on some transplant list."

"Oh, shit," I say, and I am laughing because is he really this good? He seems to be. "Oops, sorry about the swearing."

"I've heard it before," he says, but I don't think he likes it and I make a mental note to try to curtail it around him in the future. We will have one, won't we? I want one.

"Luke," I say, "can I to talk to your doctor?"

"You don't need to write anything. I don't want that."

"Then why did you let me come?"

It is his turn to laugh and as he does one of those thick strands of his hair falls back over his right eye and I want so to reach over and push it back. My nephew. Look at him. Listen to him.

"I didn't," he says. "You came and found me."

"Guess that's right," I say, laughing back. "I want to help. I understand about no publicity. But there must be something."

"Heck," he says, looking at his watch. "I've got to get back to the grounds. I'm up again in a half hour."

"Do you do something new each time?" I ask and I realize I'm not in smart-tongued Clare-speak, no "Do you hit 'em with some new preachments each time?"

"What was that passage again from last night?" I say. "It was beautiful."

"Galatians Six, four through nine," he says. "It is beautiful, isn't it? A lot of the Bible is, if you really read it. It's like good poetry, like . . . like Yeats."

"You like Yeats?" I say.

"How could you not?" he says, starting to get up. We leave the restaurant but stand for a minute under the little front awning, staring at the rain, only slightly moderated from its previous fever pitch.

"Guess I'll have to run for it," he says. "I don't have an umbrella."

"Me, either," I say and I wonder if I can reach out and touch him or kiss the side of his face and just as I start to lean that way, a car pulls up and it's all so fast that I don't see what's happening or who is jumping out of the driver's side until Louise is there, right there in front of us, screaming through the rain and her own tears. At me. I can't even make out the words because she's almost incoherent and the rain is so heavy, the water flattening her hair in about a second. Luke moves out to take her in his arms, right out in the rain with her. Him I can hear, that soft yet penetrating voice, and very calm now, even more than usual.

"It's all right, Mama, it's all right."

She tries to flail out of his embrace, but he tightens it and continues talking softly to her. "It's all right, it's all right." I start to move around them, preparing to bolt toward my car, and I hear her now clearly as she turns her head toward me and see them again as they were on the side of the highway years ago: those rain-raccoon eyes made by her dripping mascara.

"Get away from us, Clare," she shouts through the downpour. "We don't want you. We don't need your help. Make her go away, Luke, make her go away. Please make her go."

BOOK TWO

. 12 .

L ouise wasn't the first to leave our house on the bluff. Mother went first, on January 10, 1967. She left two weeks after our annual Christmas party, on one of those sunny, windswept Southern California winter days when everything is sharp and tinged with warmth. Those two weeks after the party were hallucinatory, slow motion. I kept my eyes on her as she came and went, leaving early in the morning in her slender skirt and high heels, hair in big rollers under a silk scarf, getting ready for a day on the set. *Click click* around the kitchen and then onto the gravel driveway and into the car—going away sounds. Often she had an early call and everybody in the house was still asleep, Louise; our father; our maid, Mrs. Palmer, in her downstairs bedroom. Mother making a dawn getaway, while I—the other one awake—would trace her movements with ear and eye, slippering down the staircase in my socks and pajamas. Once she caught me there, mid-descent, and with a theatrical gesture toward the upstairs and a voice tolerant but firm said, "Clara, back to bed now. Don't be sneaking around."

It was Clara then after Clara Bow and Louise after Louise Brooks. Mother kept their pictures on her makeup table and would say, as we sat beside her, dabbing rouge on our cheeks while she adroitly enhanced her sapphire blue eyes and corner-upturned lips, "Girls, these are your namesakes." We'd look at her and look at them and preen into the mirror. We were on our way, in our imaginations, into that strange enchanted playland of beauties where mother made her living. It was thrilling when she was recognized when the three of us were out together, a stranger asking our mother for her autograph. Her picture hung in the stores we used: the dry cleaners and the little coffee/sandwich shop we always stopped at in Santa Monica when we drove in from Malibu. There she was on a wall of the famous, the signed publicity photos a glossy gallery tucked behind a lunch counter or next to a rack of dry cleaning. "For Mona and Curt: The Best Dry Cleaners in Town—Patricia Layton," she had signed in her big swirly handwriting. Clearly, we had a famous mother, not as famous, though, as the people who came to our Christmas parties. They were movie stars and our mother was on TV, in a Western, her dark hair styled high with a bun in the back, big, long skirts, and shawls around her shoulders. That's where she met him. He was in the sheriff's posse, a tall, tan athletic-looking man with beach-bleached hair, the antithesis of our short, black-haired father, the perennial East Coast transplant with his cashmere cardigans and dark-rimmed glasses and pale face that burned in the sun. Daddy. About to be heartbroken, shattered.

I watched as everyone else slept. She came and went, Mother, as always, looking beautiful—yes, even in the rollers and scarves—singing songs I seemed to know, not the names but some of the words and certainly the gist: love. "*I'll be seeing you . . . Walking my baby . . . Love me tender . . .* " Who noticed? Who knew? I did. I had seen him that day at Disneyland standing by the teacups, an accidental interloper to a mother-daughter outing. "Oh, Joe, nice to see you," our mother said. "Care if I tag along?" he said, going on the rides with Louise that I was scared to go on, my mother and I standing waiting, she distracted, singing her songs to herself, almost to herself but loud enough for me to hear. Then they bounded off the rides, Louise and the man, holding hands, because why not? Pals, they were now, breathless veterans of the Matterhorn, laughing and telling us about it. The twists and turns, the dark places, the plunges. A bond. He finally left and I exhaled and Mother returned to being our mother and not some smiling woman with a man around. I had seen her do it on screen, with him, in fact, flirting with the deputy even though she was married to the sheriff. It was just a TV conceit, I told myself, not in those words, of course, but something on the order of it. It was a game; we were just suddenly in the middle of her Western and when we got home, we would be our family again and he'd be back where he belonged, on the TV screen, and not in our real lives.

But he was there that night, on the other side of that wall in that motel. We were having a girls' slumber party. We'd left Disneyland at dusk and checked into a little log cabiny place, bringing in packages of usually forbidden junk food, potato chips and Hostess Twinkies ("We won't tell Mrs. Palmer," Mother said, winking at us), a—it came to seem to me afterward—sugary bribe. Louise and I in one of the double beds, mother in the other. A little TV and lights out, Louise sleeping beside me almost instantly. And then the noise from the other side of the wall. I woke and crept to it, pressing my ear against the grainy brown wood, and there was Mother's voice and then the man's voice, the same man, and then tears, not Mother's, something deeper, his tears. The tears of a man; the first time I'd heard them, but unmistakable. I was affixed to the wall, tempted to cry myself, tempted to wake Louise, but afraid. Better to keep quiet and maybe it won't be what it is, whatever that is. I heard mother's soothing voice—the one she used on Louise and me when we were upset—and the crying stopped and then she was humming her songs and there was a counterpunch of laughter, hers and his mixed together and the laughter was scarier somehow than the crying. I don't remember getting back into bed, but I was there in the morning, next to Louise, who was sleeping the sleep of the innocent.

I looked at her with pity and with envy. I wouldn't tell her. She was starting to be angry at me a lot, for tagging along after her, hanging around when her friends visited the house. It was my secret. She'd been keeping her own with those friends, whispering behind her bedroom door, behind my back, even in front of me, dropping her voice and leaning into a friend's ear to say something when she caught sight of me. Now I had a big one and I thought if I kept it from her, I would not only be catapulted past her into a more grown-up place—because my secret was clearly a grown-up one—but maybe it would go away. I went into the bathroom and, looking at myself in the mirror (always that shock: I was not of their ilk, the stunning dark-haired, blue-eyed feminine tribe of Mother and Louise, as I imagined myself to be) made a promise, making that zipper motion across my mouth with the thumb and forefinger of my right hand, that I would never ever tell anyone.

But he was there, back in our real lives, the night of the Christmas party. Not at first. I didn't see him right off when the four of us, Daddy in black tie, Mother, Louise, and I in white velvet dresses, hers long and strapless, ours short with cap sleeves—descended the central staircase of our big, mock-Tudor, Christmas-bedecked house, my hand brushing the prickly pine swag that wrapped the banister, and made a grand familial entrance into the living room, the party already under way, fire lit, tree shimmery with hundreds of small white lights (all Daddy's doing, the decor; he was a man ahead of his time, attentive to domestic details, the aesthetic ones, anyway, in the way the mothers of our friends were. Not the fathers then, never the fathers), a fair number of the guests already there, the silver trays of canapés being passed—little crab puffs and water chestnuts wrapped in bacon—by a circulating, soft-spoken black couple named Francis and Tucker who always came for parties. I saw it all as we came down the stairs to the smiling, upturned faces of the waiting guests. It was magical; we were magical. We wandered into the crowd, my father taking me by the hand and introducing me to a man named Cary Grant ("the most famous actor on the planet," my father said, smiling from him to me and back again) who was very tan and had silver hair and a funny way of talking, his mouth not quite open, as if the sides were stapled. He was with a woman who had a lot of unruly blond curls and a loud laugh and was wearing a short, tight silver dress, the kind that women were just beginning to wear. Suddenly Louise was there, grabbing my hand, pulling me away.

"Wait till you see what Daddy's done this time," she said, dragging me to the window. Every year he had a surprise. Every year we were kept from it—closeted upstairs in our rooms all day—until it was revealed. We were standing, pressing our noses to the cold glass behind the curtains. Our father was there suddenly, pulling open the curtains and clapping his hands to silence the guests. "Okay, Tucker," he said, "you can turn them on."

The lights in the living room went off, except for the tree, and then lights out on the bluff went on, all bright red and white and strung between poles, beneath which lay an icy white skating rink (so that's what it was; Louise and I, confined to our bedrooms, had heard all this heavy machinery coming down the driveway and then going back up), where a man in a white shirt and black pants was swooping backward and forward around the ice. Everyone gasped, even the adults. "Gotta hand it to you, Phil," I heard a man say to my father, "I mean, a goddamn skating rink in Malibu."

The lights in the living room went back on so people could get to the French doors, now open, and make their way outside, where there was a big basket of blankets for the adults to wrap up in and another basket full of skates for the kids. Tucker came and helped Louise and me put ours on and then helped us clack onto the ice, where the man who'd been skating came over and helped us around. Louise and I had skated a few times before and she peeled off and went with another, older girl, Kitty, whose father was a famous director, and then as the man and I went around, he suddenly lifted me up over his head and we whirled around, my face burny in the night air. I saw my father's face, there by the rink, beaming up at me and then, over there, my mother standing just inside the door to the living room with a man, some man, and it took me two more glide-arounds to make sure it was the man from Disneyland. I was lowered back to the ice and my skates stayed where they should and the crowd around the rink clapped. I was all body-alert now, tense, and when the instructor wanted to lift me again, saying, "Ready, here we go," I said "No, no, no" because I didn't want to be up there again where I could see them over there by the door, Mother with that man and her man-Mother smile. No, don't pick me up again.

I undid my hand from his and stood by the side of the rink, hoping to flag down Louise. When she went by I made a "come here" motion to her, but she didn't stop, so that the next time she went around with another girl I yelled at her. "Weezie, stop. Stop."

She did pull up the next time with an impatient older-sister look on her face. "What is it?" she said.

"Mother is over there," I said.

"Yeah," she said, starting to skate off again.

"She's with that man we met at Disneyland," I said.

"Big deal," she said. "He was obviously invited to the party."

That was all. I was relieved I hadn't told the secret, but there was still alarm on my face and Louise, seeing it, seemed to take pity on me. "Come on," she said, linking her arm in mine. "Come with Kitty and me. We're getting really good."

So off we went. We skated long and hard, round and round, and every time one of us was about to fall, the other two managed to shift and we all stayed up. Tucker called us to the side of the rink at one point with mugs of hot chocolate and we took big, throat-scorching gulps and glided on. Most everybody else had gone inside. Our father came out at one point and paid the red-haired instructor and he left and so did the last of the other skaters, so it was just the three of us. And then Kitty's parents came and got her so it was just the two of us. This is what I loved best of everything, when we were a unit. I didn't need anybody else. I didn't want anybody else. I didn't care that the man wasn't there to lift me into the sky, not if down here on the ground I had Weezie's hand in mine and we were skating in perfect tandem, sliding over the ice, sibling breaths emitted into the night, floating out over the ocean all the way to Catalina and China; I saw them go. We didn't talk; we didn't even look at each other. We just kept skating, the strings of lights fluttering in a cold breeze that had come up off the ocean. Inside, the Christmas carols had given way to Frank Sinatra and the adults were dancing, pressed together, and then, in the flip of a record, it was a whole new decade, and the couples separated and were gyrating solo to some loud rock-and-roll song. We stole looks into the room, trying not to let the other one know because then something might be said about who was dancing with whom and how silly they looked, mothers in short, spangly dresses "Twisting the Night Away," swiveling their bodies and tossing their hair and getting those posey looks on their faces, and dads, their jackets off, bow ties tucked into pockets, doing the same. And then somebody turned the lights lower and they put Sinatra back on and then neither of us peeked because we didn't like to see the adults all draped on each other in the semidarkness, a mother here, a father there, our mother all fluid now in her stocking feet, shoes long since abandoned, hair, though, still in place because she always sat out the fast dances.

Was he gone yet—that man from Disneyland?

We skated until Tucker and Francis, their arms full of packed-up leftovers, came to say good-bye, on the way to their car.

"Shouldn't you two be in bed by now?" Francis said.

"Nobody's come for us yet," Louise yelled over her shoulder as we sailed past.

"Let me stop and say good-bye," I said.

"No, let's not stop," Louise said, tightening her hands over mine and I understood that that was a good idea, not to stop, because then a night wouldn't end and a morning wouldn't come and we'd be gliding around this magical rink forever, everything frozen inside of Daddy's best surprise ever. So I just yelled a "ta-ta," and then the next time around, as Francis and Tucker started to walk away, I unhinged a hand from one of Louise's, pressed it against my lips, and flung it back out into the night at the departing backs of Tucker and Francis with such force that I unweighted us and we went down hard, skinning our chins on the ice, which, as we sat up, had little spots of blood on it.

"Now look what you've done," Louise shouted, as Tucker came toward us, planting his shoes gingerly on the slick surface.

It was over. The spell was broken. We were both crying. In a moment, Mother was there. Francis had gone to get her. She came barefoot across the ice—Tucker, Louise in his arms, saying, "I'll get her next, Mrs. Layton. Don't come out here like that," as she leaned down to me. I smelled her perfume and under it or around it or over it, alcohol, and as I turned away from her breath, I felt some big, strong arms lift me up off the ice and heard a voice, saying, "I've got her, Patricia," (Patricia? Nobody called our mother Patricia; it was always Pat) and it was him and he was really big and strong. He held me easily while he unlaced one skate and then the other and then we were walking toward the house. I had stopped crying immediately and now he said, "You're a very brave little girl." My chin was smarting and I was trying not to cry and not look up at him, either, but tilting my head back around so I could see the deserted rink, squinting so the lights blurred the way they did when you were skating by them, the music getting louder as we got close to the house ("through the good and lean years and in all the in-between years . . ."). And suddenly there was Daddy, just as we stepped into the living room, reaching up, saying, "Thanks, Joe, I'll take her from here."

I was handed down into my father's arms. He turned and carried me out of the room and up the stairs. I leaned into him. He smelled of the aftershave we always gave him at Christmas, the one that had the little basket around it; we'd done it again this year, he pretending to be surprised as always. "Daddy," I said. "You smell good." When he didn't say anything and we were almost at the top, I leaned up to kiss his cheek, bumping my nose against the thick rim of his glasses. "Oh Daddy," I said, "that was the best surprise ever."

"Wasn't it, princess?" he said. "Wasn't it just magical?"

. 13 .

We sat by the melting rink, trailing our Barbies' tipped-up feet across it. The sun was quite strong and we were both in shorts. The house, after the party, had gone dead quiet. Our father was sometimes there in his study—off-limits to us—and sometimes in town for meetings. Mother was gone all day and sometimes into the night. Mrs. Palmer was with her family and our cleaning lady, Norma, was staying. In her white uniform, she was slender and wordless; the only noise she made was when she used the vacuum, a mechanical hum matched by the noise of the lawn mower out on the bluff where the Japanese gardener and his teenage son, Tommy, were cutting the steeper part of the property where it pitched down toward the ocean. As we sat, I kept looking at the house and then at Louise and back again. When I was tempted to say something to her, I pinched my fingers together in my pocket, a reminder of how I had zipped the secret in. Her presence agitated me and I had to keep pinching those fingers together, but I didn't want her to leave me alone, either, so I kept thinking up ways and games to keep her when all she really wanted to do was go back up in her bedroom and listen to her records on her new little pink phonograph.

"Let's get our animals and make a real ice show."

"I don't want to do that," Louise said.

She started to get up, but just then Tommy came up from the bluff, his thick, black bangs tickling the top of his eyes, causing him to squint hard at us. I jumped up. "Tommy, you want to play with us?"

"Not with those," he said, gesturing with his head at our dolls.

"I know," Louise said, suddenly reanimated. "I'll go get some trays and we'll surfboard on the ice."

When she got back she was still restless and I had to go extra funny to hold her. I slid about on the tray on my belly, singing loud, off-key Christmas carols, then got on my back and shoved myself around, a bug with its legs kicking in the air. Even Tommy, reserved Tommy, laughed. I enticed her into tray races with our Barbies, shoving them from end to end—on your mark, get set, go. First in clothes, then in their bikinis, then naked, their hard, plastic bodies twisted into postures we knew were dirty but not really why. Ken and Barbie on top of each other, and then Barbie astride Ken's shoulders, an arm in the air to wave at the imaginary onlookers. It was then that Louise, a felt pen in her pocket, wrote the words on one of the bare-bottomed Barbies, "Ken" on one cheek, "Barbie" on the other, with that plus sign in the rear-end cleavage, causing Tommy to shake his head and leave. It was afternoon, the sun making its way toward touchdown in the ocean, and the ice was getting really slushy. "This isn't any fun anymore," Louise said. "I'm going in."

"No, don't go," I said. "Please don't go."

"Don't be a baby," she said.

We were fed and bathed and in our pajamas when we heard a car turn down the gravel driveway from the coast highway.

"I bet it's Mommy," Louise said, running to the door, with me following.

Every return was good, a cause of celebration, life going on. Louise had Mother in a bear hug around the waist and I stared at her face in the bright beam from the outside garage light. Scrubbed clean, no makeup, her hair in a ponytail. She looked so young that way, so unhard. This beautiful young mother wasn't going anywhere.

"How about a slumber party, girls?" she said. "Clara—that sound good?" She was looking at me looking at her.

"Yes," I said.

We bunked in front of the fire in sleeping bags. Mother, humming, made grilled cheese sandwiches and hot cocoa and brought it to the living room, and we told her about our day with the Barbies, not all of it, and she laughed, the firelight playing off that scrubbed skin and off the heavy whitewashed beams overhead. Our father loved the house. Its big, elemental bones, dark rafters, reminded him, he said, of the East, but Mother had insisted on whitening everything. Walls, ceilings, beams. Where was he?

"Your father's staying in town tonight, girls, so it's just us," Mother said, as if reading my mind. She put another log on the fire and put on some Christmas carols and we drifted off. I woke in the night with a start, sure she wasn't on the sofa where she had been. But she was there. Louise had crawled in behind her and there they lay, spooned together, backlit by moonlight coming from the high window over the French doors: a Breck ad of a mother and daughter.

D addy didn't come home for two more days and nights. It wasn't completely unusual, just a little. Mother said he was on a rewrite for a big movie with that nice, square-jawed man, Rock Hudson, who had been at one of our parties, and that he couldn't make it home, especially now with the fog. It had come in the day after our slumber party and hung on, a swaddling cocoon of damp gauze wrapped all around the house and the bluff. You couldn't see the ocean or the hills on the other side of the highway. Everything seemed fuzzy and faraway. Occasionally there was a misty break and I could see the light poles around what was left of the rink, a few glassy shards still intact. It was as if a small winter circus had come and decamped, leaving behind a puddly reminder. Mother seemed distracted, jittery.

"I hate this damn fog," she said. "I feel trapped out here." She disappeared for hours into her bedroom, closing the door, and, tiptoeing by, I would hear her on the phone, talking low in her actress voice. Then she would come out and we'd roast marshmallows or bundle up and walk to the edge of the bluff and look through the breaks in the fog at the gray, gray sea.

"I love having Mother all to ourselves," Louise said.

The third morning, we arrived downstairs for breakfast and there were our parents having breakfast. Daddy had slipped back into the picture late the night before, after we had gone to bed.

"Sleepyheads," he said, as we sat down on either side of him. He had nicked himself shaving and a spot of bloodied toilet paper clung to his upper lip where he'd been dabbing at the cut.

"Oh Daddy, does it hurt?" I said.

"Not as much as your chin, baby," he said. "Quite a thing, huh, our rink?"

"The best," I said.

"Weezie?"

"Yes, Daddy," she said, head over the comic papers.

Mother was reading, with the same attentiveness, the industry trade papers our father always brought home and both of them studied as we did our math books. "Jesus, Phil," she said, "did you see who got that part in Bill's movie? I couldn't even get in to read for it. Phil, are you listening?"

"Sorry, what?" he said.

"Your friend Bill . . ."

"Our friend . . ."

"Our friend couldn't even get me in the door. Maybe I should get rid of Wally and find a new agent."

"Sweetheart, give him a chance. You just got . . ."

"Next thing you know I'll be doing a goddamned soap opera."

"Mommy," Louise said, looking up from the comics, "you owe the pot a quarter for using a bad word."

"Oh, shit, then," she said, tossing the paper onto the table, "let's make it two."

She opened the door and went outside. Louise started to follow, but our father motioned her to stay just as the newly returned Mrs. Palmer in her squishy-soled shoes and apron arrived with oatmeal.

"Mrs. P, just redirect the oatmeal. The girls and I are going to make pancakes."

"You're going to spoil them," she said as she squished her way back into the kitchen and we listened to her muttering as she scraped the cereal into the trash bowl. Daddy, standing at the counter breaking an egg against the edge of the yellow mixing bowl, rolled his eyes and made us giggle but not out loud. The day kept trying to be fun. After we ate we went for a walk over the final droplets of the rink. Mother materialized in her tennis shoes, hair again up in rollers, floral scarf, mouth still tight but not as. Daddy smiled at her and winked at us.

"Whaddya think, should we do it again next year?" he said. "Maybe we should all take lessons so we can do a family act. How's that sound, Pat?" He reached for her hand and mimicked a skating move and she—finally smiling—twirled out and he reeled her back in while Louise and I clapped. Then the phone rang and Mother went in to answer it and didn't come back out and the wind went out of Daddy's chattiness and he said he had some work to do and there we were again, just the two of us. When we heard them arguing upstairs, we went up to the highway to count the passing cars that came fast around the bend from both ways, north and south. It was chilly, the fog still wisping around, but we stayed out a long time, inventing variations: Only count the cars with license plates beginning in A or B, F or G, plates with numbers that added up to ten, plates with zeros. An ambulance came screaming by, going north, and we wondered whether the sick person was already in it and as the sound receded, a honking horn behind us caused us both to jump. Turning, we saw our parents standing beside Daddy's convertible, both holding suitcases. Mother was in her camel hair coat and he was wearing his leather jacket and the cap he wore when he put the top down. What was this: Were they fleeing together?

We bolted toward them—Louise actually letting me hold her hand—and right into Mother's dazzling camera-ready smile. "Don't look so glum, sillies, you're coming with us. Run up and get your suitcases. Mrs. Palmer just finished packing them."

We ran up the stairs, Louise in the lead, screaming, "Mrs. Palmer, Mrs. Palmer." She was laying out our party dresses, Louise's pink one and my pale lilac one, across the clothes in our suitcases.

"No, no, I want the blue one," Louise said, rummaging in her closet and yanking it off a hanger. "This one, please. Can't you iron this one?"

"I don't have time to be doing . . ."

"I'll do it myself, then," Louise said, flouncing out of the room.

"Weezie, we don't have time," I said, following her. "And we're not allowed to use the iron, anyway."

Louise like this always made me nervous. She got so excited sometimes, like she was now, about our trip, that she did something to get into trouble and ended up getting sent to her room.

"Weezie, don't . . ."

The car horn went again. Louise gave up on the blue dress, abandoning it on the ironing board, and we bumped our suitcases down the stairs and out into the driveway. Mother had scarves for both of us and tied them under our chins because Daddy was going to put the top down on the big Ford Fairlane convertible. At the top of the driveway, he made a game and asked us which way he should turn, left or right. Should we go north or south, to the zoo in San Diego or that hotel we loved up the coast? Everybody yelled, even our mother. Left, right, the zoo, the hotel, no, not that way, that way, and Daddy, with his foot on the brake, wildly turned the wheel as we shouted out our preferences and then all at once lurched out into the fog across the highway and turned north. A horn sounded behind them.

"Jesus, Phil, be careful," Mother said. But in her voice I heard happiness, a kind of happiness. We were a postcard family off on an outing, man at the wheel, women in scarves. Take a snapshot for the album. The heat was on full blast, making our legs toasty, while the fog swirled around our scarved heads and the sun up there, trying to come out, looked like a flashlight under a bedsheet. The ocean smelled fishy, but good-fishy, we all agreed, while Daddy handed back sticks of peppermint chewing gum. "Hope you all used the little girls' room," he said, " 'cause there will be no stopping until we hit our destination point."

"Where are we going, Daddy?" Louise said, leaning forward and throwing her arms around him from the backseat. He jerked a little and the car did and our mother reached to unloosen Louise's grip.

"Not when he's driving," she said.

"Sorry, Daddy," she said. "I'm just so happy."

On cue, the car slid right out of fog and into sunshine, as if there had been a sharp line across the road and for the rest of the way up the highway the sky was clear and the water was sparkly blue. For long stretches, there was nothing but the ocean and the swooping gulls and occasionally a shack or two on stilts, hanging right on the ledge of the highway over the water, and on the right side of the car, the winter, green-furred mountains. Despite the sun, it was still dampish and Daddy kept the heat up high. We played our license plate game and even he joined in, until Mother started humming songs and then singing them and he joined her in that. We had to sing loud because of the top being down.

"Fly me to the moon and let me play among the stars," they sang, Daddy's voice underneath hers. "Let me see what spring is like on Jupiter or Mars." Then we sang round robins, Louise and Daddy making up one round, starting first—"Row, row, row your boat"— and Mother and I coming in behind. Then everyone fell into silence and Mother's head leaned back against her seat. We figured she was asleep, so we, too, kept quiet, while Daddy continued to hum. Finally we turned another curve of the coast and there he was on the right-hand side in his little pulpit, the big black chef with the tall white hat and apron, grinning and waving a napkin in the air, the afternoon sun glinting off his wire-rimmed glasses. Louise and I both screamed, "There he is, there he is," realizing that's what we'd been waiting for as our father turned the car into the low-slung white hotel with the blue shutters.

We checked in to adjoining rooms with a door between. Mother said she was going to take a nap and Daddy said he would take us for a walk on the beach. We went first by the bar so we could have a 7UP and some mixed nuts out of the little silver bowl while our father had a beer. The bar was romantic-gloomy with the waning afternoon sun and on the little square dance floor, the four-piece band was already setting up for the evening. I slid off my bar seat and did a mock waltz around the floor and the band laughed and Daddy laughed and even the sallow-faced young bartender laughed. "Come on, Daddy," I said, grabbing his hand. "You dance with me."

"Not now, sweetheart," he said, "let's take our walk before it gets dark."

We held our shoes, Louise and I, and scampered ahead in the sand toward the bed of anemones we knew were up ahead, toes ready to squish them. I turned back and looked: Daddy was sitting, staring out at the sea. I started to turn back, but Louise beckoned me.

By the time we got back to him, the sun was going down and we were soaked to the knees. There was a wispy, halfhearted sunset, pale gold slashes through the returning fog.

"I," Louise said, running ahead, "am going to get pretty tonight like Mommy. Wait till you see."

I started to run after her, but stayed with Daddy, my sandy hand in his.

"Knock on the door, Louise, before you go barging in," he shouted after her.

We found Louise slumped outside the connecting door between our room and our parents' room. She was still in her wet clothes, looking close to tears.

"She's locked the door and she can't hear me. I think she's in the bath."

"It's not the end of the world, sweetheart. Sometimes, your mother needs her privacy. You two get in the bath and I'll go around and unlock the door."

We got in the bath to wash off the sand. It was hot and steamy and we stayed until Daddy knocked on the bathroom door.

"Time to get out," he said. "You're going to turn into raisins." When we came out in our towels, Daddy was sitting on one of the twin beds. He had on a blue jacket—the one he called his blazer— and gray pants and a dark striped tie. He smelled like his Christmas cologne.

"Daddy," I said, "do you always remember your cologne?"

"Always," he said.

He helped us get into our dresses and tried to help us comb our wet hair, but the comb got stuck in Louise's and she yelped and said she wanted to wait for her mother to fix it.

"Where is she?" Louise said. "I want Mommy."

"She'll be here in a minute."

But she kept not coming and finally Daddy knocked on the connecting door.

"Pat," he said, "we're all waiting."

Still nothing, not a sound.

"Maybe she went ahead," he said. "Get your shoes on and we'll go down."

But Louise couldn't find her party shoes and she was refusing to put back on her tennis shoes with her dress, so Daddy finally went around and got a pair of Mother's heels and let her borrow those. It drove me mad, how slowly we had to go down to the bar because Louise was teetering along the hall in the heels.

"Can't you take them off until we get down there?" I said, anxious to set eyes on Mother.

"You're just jealous," Louise said, wobbling behind, Daddy holding her hand.

"Stop, you two," Daddy said.

She was sitting at the bar when we rounded the corner, wearing a shiny blue sleeveless dress and sipping a tall golden drink, in camera-ready makeup. "Oh, Mommy, where were you?" Louise said. "We couldn't fix our hair and I couldn't find my shoes."

"I can see that," she said. "Your father will need some lessons."

She slid off her seat and led the way to the table, the one in the corner where we always ate. There were small packages of crayons beside our menus. Louise pushed hers into the center of the table and said, "You can't use crayons when you're wearing high heels," and our parents laughed. Mother had another tall, gold cocktail and Daddy had a short, watery-looking one with an olive in it and they talked about whether to put in a swimming pool. The food came, fried shrimp with cocktail sauce, and while we ate, a large woman in a tent-like dress and short gray hair came up and asked Mother for her autograph. And this is your family. How wonderful. We all smiled. Then the music started and our parents got up to dance and when they came back to the table they were holding hands. They had another drink while we had sundaes and then, without prelude, Mother's mood shifted and she started talking again about the part that that woman had gotten and that she hadn't even gotten to read for.

"There will be others, Pat. She doesn't have your talent." Daddy was now using his soothing voice.

"I know that. But she has the part. Why didn't I get an audition? Damn that Wally."

A quarter, I wanted to say, but didn't because now it was escalating adult talk and you needed to stay out of that.

"I'm just being wasted," Mother said. "Why couldn't you have gotten me in to see them? You're a . . ."

"Let's not do this now, Pat. Please."

"Or at least write me something. Is that too much . . ."

The musicians, back from a break, started up again and I jumped up. "Daddy, Daddy, take me. I know I can do this. I've been practicing in front of the TV."

We hovered at the edge of a fairly packed floor of sharp elbows and show-offy moves and when I moved my starter hips from side to side with the music, Daddy imitated me. We got swept into the crowd and another song started right up and I convinced him to stay out for another try and we couldn't see the table anymore. When the song was over and we started back, we could see that our table was empty.

"You want to sit with your old dad while he has another drink or do you want to go on up?" he said.

"You're not old, Daddy."

"Figure of speech," he said.

"I'll stay with you," I said, "if you'll dance with me one more time."

"That's extortion," he said.

"What's that mean?"

"It means you won't stay with me unless I do what you want. Your mother's game, come to think of it."

"That's enough, Phil." Mother had reappeared out of nowhere. She sat down. She had on new makeup. More red lipstick, more black on her eyes. "Get me another drink, will you?"

"Where's Weezie?" I said.

But Mother wasn't listening or looking at me. She was staring at Daddy.

"Where's Weezie?" I said again.

"I'm married to a big-shot writer who can't get me an audition on his own goddamn movie," she said.

I had seen her like this. It was her angry-movie face. Her eyes were all blazing and her mouth was hard. For a minute I thought I might giggle. It couldn't be real. I tried to catch Daddy's eye, but I couldn't.

"Pat, not in front of Clara," Father said.

"I'm not leaving," I said, looking from one to the other, behavior normally not countenanced, but they weren't really paying attention to me. They were still looking at each other and I was sure they were about to start fighting again and it made me frantic, I needed to distract them, intervene somehow, and in the middle of my fear, the secret crawled right up out of my throat.

"It's that man, isn't it?" I said. "That man from Disneyland."

Both of them did look at me now. Nobody said anything. I looked at the band—they were back to playing slow music and there were a few couples still dancing, including that woman who had asked for Mother's autograph—and up at the fishnets with white, scratchy-looking starfish in them and at the silver cup with little rivers of water running down the outside of it that had held our sundaes and at the bar with all its pretty, sparkly glasses and neatly lined-up bottles full of gold and clear and even green liquid.

"What man from Disneyland?" Daddy said as quietly as you could and still be heard.

"Clara, go on up to bed," Mother said in that voice that had a "right now" in it.

"I want her to stay," Daddy said.

"I want her to go."

I stood by the table, looking again at the bottle with the green drink in it. I was outside my body. I wasn't a girl standing beside a table with her parents staring at her because she had told a secret. I was somewhere else, upstairs in bed with Weezie or at home with Mrs. Palmer or in the den listening to the TV with Norma.

"Go on, go to bed now," Mother said to me and then to Daddy, as I left, hearing her even with the music going, fast ahead, those adults with their elbows out looking silly and spastic, "You don't have to look like a whipped puppy, Phil. What did you expect?"

· 14 ·

We drove home in brilliant sunshine, one of those clean winter days where everything, the islands out off the coast, the mountains, the lifeguard stands, the seaside shacks, everything—even the other cars passing—seemed outlined in pencil, everything standing sharp against a blue, blue sky. The top was down and we had our scarves on and Daddy was wearing his jaunty motoring cap and the radio was softly playing, but everything seemed unnaturally still, as if the day itself was holding its breath. I had not looked at my parents that morning at breakfast, coloring furiously on the menu and playing hangman, with determined attention, with Louise. Pancakes and syrup and bacon. They slid under my nose, right onto the hangman game, and I still didn't look up, not even when Mother got up, saying she had to finish packing, leaving behind, in my range of vision, her lipsticked coffee cup.

In the car, Louise kept trying to get everyone to play the license game, but could find no takers.

"You're all boring," Louise said and then fell into her own sullen silence. After a while she poked me in the arm, causing me to yelp. "Stop it you two," Mother said, turning in her seat, and on her face, where I expected to see anger there was excitement, that look she got before going downstairs to a party. It was a look that did not leave her for the next stretch of days. Not that we saw her much.

When we got home we were more or less handed back to Mrs. Palmer's custody while our parents went back to work, leaving early, coming home late, usually in separate cars, usually after we were in bed. But I heard every coming and going, every tire on the gravel driveway. I padded around the big sleeping house at night, tiptoeing by my parents' room, tiptoeing into Louise's, patrolling the halls to monitor the disposition of the family members. The floor creaked, but I wore socks and slipped over it, like on that rink. Sometimes a window left unlatched would bang open and I'd jump, but I was never scared of intruders, bad guys or burglars or murderers. Night, in fact, began to feel like the safest time, the big old stand-up clock ticking in the downstairs hall, everyone in for the night, bedded down. Mommy, Daddy, Weezie, all accounted for. I'd crouch by her bed and watch her sleep.

Once, the yowl of a coyote wakened Louise with a start. "What are you doing?" she said to me, crouched there beside her bed.

"Just watching," I said.

"Go back to your room," Louise said, not angry, just matter-of-fact, through her matted tangle of dark hair.

And I did. I went back to my room and sat on the bed until I figured Louise had fallen asleep again and then I would glide back through the bathroom and into her room and take up my spot, making a detour sometimes by my parents' door. Just checking. Just checking. A toilet might flush. A faucet run. Someone up, someone back down. I got so I could hear it all, my ears now acute like an animal's. Daddy's feet, Mommy's feet, whose sigh, whose sneeze, whose muffled anger. On one of my prowls, I heard them talking softly and then laughing—yes, yes, laugh, don't stop. But they did stop and then Daddy, a quiet voice, the family, the girls, the house, and then Mother's voice, much bigger, not wanting the damn house, too big, too far from town, dying out here, must be more to life, and then Daddy, okay, go ahead and get it out of your system, and then

Mommy, a sharp laugh, is that what you think this is, and then a door opened and shut and footsteps went downstairs. After a few minutes I tiptoed down in their wake. Daddy was standing in the front window, looking out into the night. He had a robe on and a drink in his hand. After a while he wandered out into the night and down to the edge of the bluff. I padded behind him, quiet, quiet, my nighttime animal self. He sat down in the dirt. The grass wouldn't come down this far, even though Tommy's father had tried to make it grow here. I crouched behind him at a safe distance. It was chilly, the wind brisk off the ocean. It was clear enough and dark enough to still see some lights strung out around the bay. After a long time Daddy said, "Clarie, I know you're there. It's okay. Go get your old dad the bottle, the one with the clear stuff."

"The one you put the olives in?"

"Yep," he said.

I brought it back, my socks now clammy-wet from the dew on the grass. He filled his glass and we sat together looking out at the ocean. Was morning coming or was it my imagination that I could see out there?

"Daddy, I'm getting really cold," I said. He didn't answer. He poured himself more to drink.

There was nothing to do but sit with him. He kept drinking and kept not talking. The first pinkish light of dawn came, tickling the outline of the shore. As it warmed, I could smell things, the sea, the sage, bluff smells. Neither of us looked back at the house. I figured my father had had plenty to drink, but I didn't look over at him, either. The sun came up behind us, warming my back. Finally a door opened and then shut and we heard a car start, sitting there together, neither of us turning, and heard it go up the gravel driveway, heard someone get out and the old, metal gate being moved and then the car door shutting and then the car turning onto the highway—in the early morning, when it was quiet, before all the cars started going up and down, you could hear all this even from out on the bluff, if the ocean wasn't too loud like it wasn't this morning—and still neither of us moved or said anything, until Daddy, turning away from me, began to heave, his body shaking as he started to throw up over and over while I, sitting beside him, my hand on his back, stared out at the sun-spattered bay.

W e had dinner with Mrs. Palmer in the green-and-white breakfast room. She had told us keep it down during the day because Daddy was home and wasn't feeling well and needed to sleep. The breath that I had held waiting for Mother to go had now been let go but I was holding a new one waiting for Louise to find out she had gone. I had avoided her all day. I had kept too many secrets from her. It had gone too far. I felt sick to my stomach and kept pushing my pork chop bites around the plate and into the applesauce.

"Stop playing with your food, Clara," Mrs. Palmer said. "If you don't eat something, you can't have any ice cream." When she got up to go back to the kitchen, Louise stuck her tongue out at her back, an act of daring that always drew a giggle from me but not now. "What's wrong with you?" Louise said. "You haven't been any fun all day."

"Leave her alone, Louise," Mrs. Palmer said, sitting back down. Louise started to push her bites of food around and Mrs. Palmer said, "Louise, come on, finish a little and I'll get you both some ice cream."

"I don't want any ice cream," Louise said.

"Louise, don't be rude to Mrs. Palmer." It was Daddy coming into the room. He hadn't shaved and he was in his blue sweatshirt with "U of Penn" written across it in red. He sat down at the fourth place.

"I'll get you some food," Mrs. Palmer said.

"No, I'll pass," he said. "Maybe just a glass of milk."

"How was school?" he said.

"Daddy, are you just being silly?" Louise asked. "It hasn't started yet. We're still on vacation."

"Oh, yeah," he said.

"You don't look good, Daddy. Maybe you should go back to bed. We'll come and watch TV with you and wait for Mommy."

Nobody said anything. Nobody made a move, except for Mrs. Palmer, who got up and left the room without taking any plates. Louise started to say something—I saw her start and then saw her stop and then saw some fear start up in her.

"What is it?" she said. "What's wrong?" She was looking from Daddy to me and back, eyes picking up speed. "Where's Mommy? Where is she? What happened?"

"Sweetheart," Daddy began . . . and faltered. "Your mother . . ."

"Where is she, where is she?" Louise was screaming now.

"She is going to stay in town."

"Tonight? She won't be back tonight?"

"Not tonight and for a little while."

"What do you mean, what do you mean?"

"She just needs a little time. She's going to stay in town for a little bit until she figures out . . ."

"No, no, no." Louise was sobbing now. "Daddy, Daddy. Mommy."

"It's only temporary," he said. "I'm sure it's only temporary."

Louise looked at me. I had said nothing. Louise stopped crying. She looked back at Daddy.

"You're lying," she said.

"What did you say?" he said.

"You're lying," Louise said. "She's not coming back. She's never coming back."

"No, Louise," her father said. "You don't know what you're talking about."

"I do too," she said. "She's gone and it's all your fault. You lost her."

There was a flash of a hand, the sound of a slap, and a high-pitched scream, which I realized, as Louise jumped up and ran from the room, a pink mark on her cheek, had come from my own throat.

Daddy slumped forward in his chair. "My God," he said, putting his head down on his arms, now folded on the table. "My God," he said again. I sat with him for a while longer and then got up and went to the bar and got the bottle of vodka. I brought it back and put it in front of him. "Here," I said, and then went up the stairs and lay down on my bed. I didn't even try the door to Weezie's room, nor the door to the bathroom that connected our bedrooms. They would be locked. I knew that. There was no one to comfort or get comfort from. There was no reason to stay up and patrol. It had all happened. When I couldn't stand it any longer, I got up and went to Louise's door and tapped lightly.

"Do you want some ice cream?" I said.

There was no answer. I sat down beside the door and tapped again. "It'll be okay, Weezie," I said. Then I went and got the pillow and the cover off my bed and brought them back and lay down outside her door. "I'll be right out here if you want me," I said.

The house was like a ship, sick passengers quarantined in their rooms. That's how it felt. I would look out at the ocean, note the weather and imagine our ship afloat out there, sailing toward some faraway shore where our mother, the actress Patricia Layton, was making a film. Was it in Brazil or Paris or Africa? On they sailed toward their delightful family reunion. Daddy stayed downstairs in the second little maid's room with his bottles of vodka and his dark, thickening stubble. Mrs. Palmer tried to keep me away from him.

"Come on out of there," she said, gently tugging me away. She was still wearing her uniforms and squishy-soled shoes, but even she was letting down, as if her moral authority had more or less vanished along with Mother. Her normally tightly coiled, gray-flecked dark hair was a little breezy and unbrushed and she'd given up trying to maintain order. She didn't really need to, as I was her only upright charge left and I had become very efficient, very self-policing. I made the rounds of the rooms, checking on Daddy—down and out and snoring horribly, so loud sometimes Mrs. Palmer went in and gently rolled him over and he stopped for a while—and then on to Weezie, just tap-tapping on her door and announcing what food I was leaving. Louise was taking it in and leaving the empty tray behind but still gave no evidence of wanting to see anyone. Suddenly there were new kinds of days, new habits. I got up early and got downstairs even before Mrs. Palmer was in the kitchen. I had learned how to make the best hot chocolate with thick cream and cocoa and I made a big mug and took it up to Louise's room and set it outside. Sometimes I put a dusting of cinnamon on top because I remembered Louise loved cinnamon. I didn't bother to look in on Daddy until at least ten, Mrs. Palmer now forgoing any attempts to keep me from him. I pretended everyone had the flu and would be fine if I just kept up my ministrations. I came to think of Mrs. Palmer as my chief aide de camp and not vice versa and the odd thing was that she seemed to fall right into line. "We need some more cocoa from the market," I would say, going over my carefully penciled list, "and some of those baby marshmallows to put in it; I know Louise likes those. And more vodka."

"I don't think that's a very good idea," she said.

"If we run out," I said, "he might try to go away and get it himself."

"Okay," Mrs. Palmer said.

When the phone rang, I was the one who would answer.

"I'm sorry," I would say. "He can't come to the phone. He's not

well." And then, "Can you spell that, please," and I would, on my
lined notebook paper, pieces of which I had now cut into squares to
leave by the phone, print out the name. In my spare time I was practicing my writing because I wanted all the names clearly readable
when Daddy was ready to be well again. I didn't know how long
that would take. I didn't know how long it would take Louise. We
were supposed to start school again in a week, but if Daddy was
still down, I wasn't going to leave him and I didn't think Louise
would want to go alone. Some days I pretended not that Mother was
in some foreign port waiting for all of us but that she had been carried away by the flu, the first victim of the awful sickness that had
put Louise and Daddy in bed, and that after I nursed them back to
health, we would be a happy but sad threesome going on alone.
That would be okay. It would be awful. But it would be okay. I
would go on answering the phone and making lists for Mrs. Palmer
and Daddy would go back to work and Louise would stop feeling
slapped and the people who came to our parties would admire us for
being so brave. Maybe Daddy would get the ice rink back next year
or put in that swimming pool he and Mother had been talking about
before she was taken ill and died and we would have wonderful
summer parties with all of our friends. That would serve her right.

It was very quiet. I had asked Mrs. Palmer not to run the washing
machine because it was near where Daddy was staying now, or the
vacuum cleaner, and there weren't many dishes to do because no one
was really eating, except for what Mrs. Palmer and I ate and what I
took up for Louise. It was mostly sandwiches now: peanut butter and
jelly or that deviled ham that came in the little white cans with the
red devil on them. Mrs. Palmer was willing to play a lot of games of
hangman and at night she let me lie next to her on her single bed—
which she'd never done before—and we'd watch TV together in our
pajamas and robes. It was hard going upstairs at night with Daddy
not up there and Louise still locked in but I had continued to sleep

outside her door. I didn't want to be in my own room and, just in case Weezie came out for some reason, I wanted to be the first person to welcome her back from her sickness. I wanted her to know right out that I had been waiting for her every minute, even when she was sleeping.

I went once into our parents' bedroom. The curtains were drawn and the bed was mussed up where Daddy had gotten out of it. Even Mrs. Palmer and Norma had stayed out of the room, as if it was now forbidden territory, a shrine. Nobody quite knew what Daddy would want done, so they simply left the door closed. I went immediately to the dressing table to see if Mother had taken all her stuff, a clue that indeed she would not return. It was all gone, all the little utensils, the scissors and tweezers with which she made her eyebrows into perfect arches and the glass perfume bottles and the little round jar of cotton balls. She had left, or forgotten, a few things on the windowsill just behind the table, including the two little pictures of Clara Bow and Louise Brooks. I threw them in the trash and then went to Louise's door and tapped: "I will no longer be called Clara. When you come out, you must call me Clare. You can be whoever you want. I will be back with a snack after I practice my writing."

I informed Mrs. Palmer of my name change and, for the next couple of days, corrected her every time she forgot and called me Clara, and by the time Louise and Daddy came out of their rooms, Mrs. Palmer had effectively made the transition. It was Louise who emerged first, stumbling over me one morning. She was dressed and carrying a large carton and I immediately got up and followed her as she went downstairs with it and out toward the garage.

"Weezie, Weezie," I said, following her, "how are you feeling? How's your cheek?"

She didn't say anything. She walked down the stairs and out the back door with me trailing behind.

"What are you doing?" I said. "Wait for me."

But Louise didn't slow down and she didn't say anything. She walked around the garage where the garbage cans were and tilted up her carton and, as I watched, dumped her dolls into the can.

I heard the thuds and then she tossed the carton in on top and turned and walked back toward the house, leaving me alone there. I tilted over the garbage can. Everything spilled out, Barbies covered in old mown grass and Mrs. Palmer's coffee grounds and Daddy's empty vodka bottles, one of which shattered on the pavement. I sat down next to the mess and reached for the dolls. Everything smelled awful and putty-colored clumps of old deviled ham were in their hair. I wiped the dried food and grass off their poked-out breasts and then went and got a bowl from the kitchen and a bottle of detergent and pushed them down in it. A head came around the corner. Tommy in an old grass-stained T-shirt tight across his stomach.

"What are you doing?" he said.

"Washing these dolls."

He leaned over the pail and pulled one out.

"Leave them alone," I said.

He stood looking at me while I tried to get the gummy stuff out of their hair.

"It's no use," I finally said. "I'm going to throw them away."

"I'll take them to my sisters."

"No," I said, shaking my head. "They're bad. I want to throw them over the cliff."

Tommy helped. We took them down to the edge, the morning sun pallid and wintery, and heaved them over, one by one, counting how many bumps they made on the way down as they bounced off the craggy cliffs.

"I'm sorry," he said after the last one had been heaved over the cliff. "I'll bet your mom will come back."

How did he know? It was enough that Daddy and Weezie and

Mrs. Palmer and Norma knew. But now Tommy and his dad knew and then other people would know.

"She's off making a big movie," I said.

"That's not what my dad says."

"He doesn't know anything and neither do you," I said. "Plus, you're fat and your hair's too long."

I turned and fled up the bluff, understanding now that no matter how hard I tried or we tried, Weezie and I, we weren't going to be able to keep the whole wide world from knowing that our mother had left us.

· 15 ·

She was in the big, green leather booth when we got there, the corner one that was always ours. Beaming at us, the three of us. It was our first public meal as a recently-sundered-yet-still-affectionate family. Ahead of the curve we were, way ahead: Father in Malibu with the kids, Mother with her lover at the Beverly Hills Hotel, which is where we now were. It was a great part and Mother seemed to love it, dressed for it—the makeup was quieter, less theatrical, as if to say, I'm a grown-up now, elegant, on top, and this is my family coming in for Easter brunch. I married a good man, do you see, and he is a marvelous custodian of our two girls. It's all working out wonderfully. That's what her smile seemed to say to the other diners. The place was full of other families. We knew a lot of them. They'd been to our parties. Now we were having one, a coming out party, right smack in their faces. Daddy had told us to behave, walk don't bolt toward our booth where our mother waited, heads held high, manners apparent. Louise strained at our side. I could feel her as we walked across the thick green carpet led by Bertrand, the captain. My arm still ached from brushing her thick, dark hair—she'd paid me her allowance to do it when her own arm had gotten tired—and she was, while straining to get to Mother, also enjoying the room's eyes on us. Then, just as we got there, she flung herself into the booth.

"Oh, Mommy, Mommy, I missed you," she said.

Mother patted Louise's head and said, "Oh, you've been brushing just like I told you," and then leaned to kiss me.

"Clara—excuse me, Clare"—a look passed between parents, a slight smile like in the old days—"you too?"

"No," I said, "she paid me to brush hers." They both laughed, our parents. The civility was wondrous, public. If we were something before, the Laytons, we were something newer and better and even more sophisticated now. As long as you didn't look in Daddy's eyes. If you didn't do that, everything was hunky-dory, normal as pie.

"Lovely to see you *en famille*," Bertrand said as he brought back Shirley Temples for Louise and me and Bloody Marys for our parents. We had Eggs Benedict and chatted *"en famille,"* Daddy occasionally nodding to someone across the room, Mommy offering a little finger-waggling wave, someone occasionally stopping by the table to say hi, a big man with no hair and an unlit cigar in his mouth and Kitty in a black velvet dress and her parents, all of them *oohing* and *aahing* still over our skating rink. Mother asked about school and talked about a part in a movie she was up for.

"Keep your fingers crossed, girls," she said. "Might be my big break."

It all seemed so normal and so surreal at the same time that I, watching and listening, finally just blurted out, "When are you coming home?"

We've been over this, her warm smile said. "Not just now, sweetheart. Daddy's taking very good care of you and you'll have such fun when you stay over with me here."

"When can we do it, when can we do it?" Louise said. "I love it here."

"I don't want to stay," I said.

"That's enough Clara, Clare," my father said. "Let's get out and get some air."

He took my hand and more or less pulled me from the booth. We walked around the swimming pool. It was cool but sunny and there were a few people in sweaters in the lounge chairs with towels over their legs like blankets. The big balding man was sitting at a table smoking his cigar. I could still hear the piano music playing from inside.

"Phil, I'm gonna send over a script I want you to look at," the man with the cigar said.

"Okay," Daddy said, trying not to stop.

"Great to see you all," the man said as we passed.

We went into the bar and sat on stools. There was still plenty of noise from the dining room. Daddy ordered a vodka martini and let me have the olives. He didn't say anything for the longest time and neither did I. The black-suited bartender brought me a Coke and winked as he set it down then picked up Daddy's emptied glass and set another drink in front of him. A couple of loud men in leather jackets at the end of the bar got up to leave.

"Your mother has fallen out of love with me," Daddy finally said. "Isn't that silly?" He gave out a strange laugh. He took another swallow of his drink and slid off the bar stool. "Come on," he said, "let's go find your sister."

The Louise we found wasn't the one I expected. I expected her to be angry at me, sullen and cold the way she could often be now. But instead, sitting next to Mother on a low-slung sofa in the lobby, she was entirely the opposite. She was chatting along, all happy in the face. When we finally got close, I could see that she had been made up and her hair poufed like Mother's. Her eyelashes were all darkened and she had on lipstick and red on her cheeks. She jumped up when we got right in front of the sofa.

"Mother says I can come next weekend without her," she said, indicating me.

"Louise, that's not exactly what I said."

"It is too, and I'm coming."

"We'll settle that later," Daddy said, as we walked out to get our car.

We drove home down Sunset, big, lurching curves all the way from the hotel to the coast. I didn't like to watch the road when Daddy was like this, when he'd been drinking, so I was lying down in the backseat. The top was down now and I had taken my sweater off and wrapped it around my bare legs. In the front seat, Louise was keeping up a constant chatter, talking about next weekend and the hotel and some blond actress named Joanne who our mother had introduced her to.

"I can't wait to stay. It's so fun there," she said as I, lying on my back, counted the palm fronds overhead, big whiskers in the sky. By the time we turned onto the Coast Highway, Louise was all keyed up. She had filled all the silence in the car. Now she stood up in the front seat. Daddy didn't say anything but it made me nervous. I sat up as Louise, in the late afternoon light, pivoted toward the side of the road and started to wave, a funny, wrist-twisting wave like the beauty queens did in those parades. She was waving at the occasional person we passed on the side of the road. There were the surfers in their slippery black skins, boards on their heads or under their arms, but there was also a whole new breed, scraggly looking, often with cardboard signs held up, saying North on them or SF.

"What does SF mean, Daddy?" I said.

"San Francisco," he said.

"Why is it on their signs?"

"Because they want to go there. They're hitchhikers."

"What does that mean?"

"It means they're hoping to hitch a ride in a car."

When we passed another one, Louise blew him a kiss and shouted, "Hello, Mr. Hitchhiker Man." Daddy turned to look and the car swerved. I grabbed Louise's sweater and held on to her and

Daddy righted the car and we were back to flying along with Louise waving and blowing kisses, all giddy and made up, a baby doll Barbie doll, thick hair flying behind. Even Daddy was laughing, which he hadn't done for days and days and days and days, so I figured it was okay even though it felt scary and I kept a hold on Louise's sweater.

"Come on, Clara—excuse me, Clare—come on up here and be a Rose Parade Princess with me," Weezie said. She unhooked my hand from her back and pulled at me and I crawled into the front seat and stood up beside her, on the inside, nearest Daddy. She put her arm around my waist and I lost my nerves and put my arm around her and we stood, sister to sister, waving at the occasional hitchhiker or surfer on the side of the road, blowing kisses while our still somewhat inebriated father slowed down a bit and tried to flatten the curves of the road so as not to pitch us out of the car as we sped toward home.

The nighttime noises of a house where a man has been left: an ice tray being banged against the counter, the cubes clinking into the glass, the stereo playing love songs—Sinatra, always Sinatra, over and over, Sinatra, day or night, come rain or shine, in the wee small hours of the morning—socked feet shuffling across the floor to change the record or refill the glass, mutterings, pleadings, cursings, the sounds of sorrow and self-pity. I heard them all; I tried not to. I tried to stay in bed, but it was no use. I was a wanderer now. When my father finally bedded down, sometimes on the living room sofa in full clothes, sometimes in the downstairs back bedroom, sometimes on the stairs, as if, yes, he could and should sleep in the master bedroom and up he went only to lose resolve on the landing and simply collapse, I would cover him with a blanket where he fell and then go and watch Louise sleep. How strange to be related to someone who could sleep so. Deeply, easily. It seemed to me that we were having entirely different childhoods right there next door to each other. Louise liked the window open even on cold nights and the sea breeze would cause me, standing beside her bed in my light flannel pajamas, to shiver. Louise awoke refreshed, ruddy-cheeked. She had the beginnings of breasts. Sometimes she would fall back into the ways of childhood. Sometimes she would wander into my room and play dolls with me or go up to the fence and count the cars and play the license game. There were more and more of those hitchhikers now, not just single ones, but couples with dogs. They were going both ways; they had signs that said San Fran or San Diego or just North or South or sometimes just a sign with a big question mark on it. The girls were festive. They had feathers in their hair and ribbons in their braids and wore long, floaty skirts and carried sleeping bags. Sometimes they had a baby strapped on the back or front. It was weird seeing them, coming back in Daddy's convertible from our weekends at the Beverly Hills Hotel, where the women were still wearing pearls and perfume and fluffy lacquered hair. Louise lived for those weekends. She took long baths and used Mother's eyelash curler and on the rides home, instead of casting kisses at them, she now cast sharp looks at the hitchhikers.

"They're disgusting," she said.

Daddy and I never said much. Louise was always wound up on these drives, full of longing and disdain, both more marked the closer we got to our house on the bluff and the farther from that big pink place Mother called home. She now had a bungalow there and she and Daddy had started to fight about money. They were all still markedly civil, our public appearances, and he never said a bad word about her to us, but I heard, on my nighttime walkabouts, his phone conversations with her.

"Pat, I know that, but if you could just try to be a little more careful."

Pause.

"I understand that, but I've got the girls and . . ."

Pause.

"I know, but I'm between scripts right now. Things are getting a little tight."

Pause.

"No. Yes. Right. Please." Daddy was usually down to one syllable by the end of these conversations, the other side of which, in those pauses, I could only imagine Mother importuning, demanding, needing things. If he ever went tougher with her than that, I certainly never heard. He never raised his voice, never begged her to come back, at least not within my hearing. The Disneyland man, Joe, was now a more or less permanent addition to our weekends with her. Fit and ripply-muscled, he played with us in the pool, Louise, who had quite easily shifted her allegiance to him (Was it that slap? Daddy had sent her a dozen long-stemmed roses in apology, which she had, with a certain icy grace, accepted), riding around on his shoulders and doing her beauty queen wave like Barbie that day astride Ken. From her chaise, under her hat and sunglasses, Mother waved back, that same wrist-torquing movement, while onlookers smiled. How pretty do people get, how photogenic? A habitual nonparticipant, I watched from my own chaise, homework in my lap as a smoke screen.

"Go on, Clare," my mother would urge. "Have some fun. Go in the pool."

I knew that if I said I didn't want to, she would accuse me of being sulky and go sulky herself. So I figured out to bring my homework, a math book, a story book, even—clandestinely—something Louise needed me to work on for her. I was doing that already: her math pages, her spelling book. It was some kind of unarticulated arrangement, a way for me to try to hold on to Louise as she slipped farther and farther away into this picture-postcard weekend world.

Over the edges of my schoolbooks I now watched her hard as, waving and preening, she rode around the pool on the broad shoulders of our mother's new lover. Weezie, get down. Get down.

I started making excuses not to go for the weekends. A stomachache, too much homework. Daddy tried to push me; Mother called. But I was stubborn when I needed to be and while it was lonesome without Louise in the house, it was less lonesome than scowling at the edge of the pool while she cavorted with the Disneyland man. That's what I thought of him as, always, never made it to calling him Joe, even as both he and my mother cajoled me to.

"Sweetie, he's part of us now," she would say. "Daddy understands."

"Maybe she wants to use my full name," he said, trying to be light. "Clare, would you prefer Joseph?"

"No, thank you," I said. A look went between the adults like the ones that used to go between Mother and Daddy. Stubborn little thing, isn't she? Ha, ha. Increasingly they all just left me alone and let me stay home on many of the weekends. Louise certainly didn't care. I would watch her pack, holding clothes up to her just-budding body and twirling before the mirror.

"What do you think?" she would say. "Should I take the pink one or this one?"

Lying on her bed watching, I feigned interest. "That one," I would say.

"No, I don't think so," she would say. "I think it's too babyish."

Friday nights we would do this and Saturday morning Daddy and I would drive her in and drop her off, pulling up under the hotel driveway canopy, and out she would go with her small suitcase and rarely, if ever, a look back: A fairy-tale princess off for the weekend. Acres of hours stretched ahead between her sashaying up that carpet and into the hotel and when we went to get her on Sunday afternoons. Daddy tried to make it fun. He and I would stop somewhere on the way home and eat a hamburger and split a milkshake—if I had my way. He preferred to stop where he could get a drink. We often went to a place farther up Sunset called the Cock 'n Bull, a dark, tavern-like place where the bar was noisy and Daddy always knew a lot of people. We were there for hours sometimes, whole Saturday afternoons. We knew the waitresses by now and they'd bring me a small slab of roast beef without me asking and Daddy the Welsh rabbit and keep his cocktails coming. That's what he'd say. "Keep my cocktails coming, Rose."

Loud men stopped by the table, saying things to me like, "Hey, sweetheart, don't you think it's time we fix up your old man?" They'd slap him on the back when they said it and wink at me.

"You'll be the first to know, Irv, when I'm back on the market," Daddy would say, all trussed-up cheer, as he handed me an olive from his newest drink. "Right, Clarie," he'd say, "we'll let him know."

The men would move off and Daddy would order coffee and I'd eat dessert and then we'd drive home, top down, silent when we passed the Beverly Hills Hotel again. I tried to imagine what they might be doing, Mother and Louise, at that moment and I tried not to imagine it. We didn't say anything for a long while after we passed it, sometimes not until we were all the way to the coast and had turned north. The house, on those weekends, was tomblike. Daddy and I usually spent most of the weekend in his downstairs study, he napping off the cocktails on his old leather sofa, me watching TV or reading a book on the floor. I'd make bologna sandwiches for dinner and carry them in and gently wake him, bringing along a beer because I knew that's what he'd want.

"You think of everything," he'd say. "But where's the mustard?"

I'd pull it out from the back of my pants, where I'd tucked it in the waistband, and we'd both laugh. "Go get me a couple of aspirins, will you?" he'd say and I'd pull the bottle of pills out from where I'd tucked them next to the mustard jar and we'd laugh again.

We'd eat and watch television and I'd fight the temptation to call Louise. Sometimes we did call. I made Daddy talk to them, her and Mother, and report to me because I knew I'd be disappointed or confused if I did the talking. I was here and they were there. At least I had Louise's homework to hold hostage.

Once Louise called Daddy—it was late and I could hear his voice shift. "It's all right, sweetheart, I'm sure she'll be back soon. That's okay. You call again."

I went into the kitchen because I knew what he'd do and he did. He called her right back and talked to her. I knew he wouldn't do it in front of me because I'd get worried. He kept her on the line for a while and then I heard another voice shift and it was clear Mother had come in from wherever she'd been and Daddy was saying, "Jesus, Pat. Leave her with me if you can't . . ."

He was cut off. When I came back in, he didn't say anything, just, "Your sister called to say good night."

I felt bad for her but wasn't displeased at the same time, and I don't think Daddy was displeased, either, because for a moment she let him be her father again. But when we went to get her the next afternoon, she had a shiny new little suitcase and the drama, such as it was, had long been forgotten. She wanted us to put the top up so it didn't blow her hair and Daddy obliged. It seemed eons since we had stood together in the afternoon air, on the seat of the car, waving at the hitchhikers. Eons. Everything was moving very slowly—those weekends, for example—and somehow fast at the same time as this new divided life of ours consolidated itself. Around the holidays, Thanksgiving and Christmas—a year now—I had to go and spend more time at the hotel. Even Daddy insisted, saying he'd be just fine, saying he'd been invited to a lot of parties, saying didn't I know that he was highly desirable now, an eligible bachelor in a city of lonely, loveless women?

"You're not a bachelor," I said.

"Okay, then a divorcé."

"Not that, either," I said. "You're still married."

"A technicality, sweetheart," he said. "The papers are all filed."

I asked Louise if she thought Mother and Joe would marry. She said she figured they would and that then they'd get a house and she would miss the hotel and the room service and all the people in the lobby. Had they talked about it? She thought so. What do you mean thought so, I asked. Louise just went dreamy: I'll be a flower girl or a ring bearer or, better yet, the maid of honor, and wear the most beautiful dress in the world. At school she was increasingly hanging out with the faster girls and I was doing more of her homework, just beginning to perfect my not-so-perfect versions of her math sets or take-home spelling quizzes so no one would catch her or me or us. It was a bond, one for which she thanked me at home while tending to ignore me at school, not in a mean way, just in a Louise way. She had her birthday at the hotel, in a small private room full of pink and white balloons. Kitty and her parents came and Louise's friends from school, Pam and Barbie and Clarisse, the pretty girls, the ones who were beginning to have boyfriends. Mother, now in a short dress with a new short haircut, vivid and hip, the puffy hair gone, the lipstick almost neutral, seemed to me as giddy as Louise, Joe beside her in a blue sport shirt, unbuttoned at the top, curls of reddish-blondish chest hair visible in the opening. And in the corner, by the little makeshift bar, Daddy in a brown-and-white checked coat, maroon handkerchief in the pocket, dark tie. There was going to be a buffet and some music. The decibel level went up and more people came, a few more girls from Louise's class, and finally a boy or two. I lost Daddy for a while in all the people and noise, figured he'd still be there by the bar, his safety zone. When people started to get in line for food—Mother, radiant and bossy, steering people to their places—I went to find him. He was standing with a man I thought I recognized, someone he'd worked with, a big man with slicked-back hair and a booming voice. They were laughing, he was laughing, the man, and Daddy was sort of laughing.

"You're some kind of sport, Phil," I heard the man say.

"Whaddya going to do, Sandy?" my father said, a kind of slangy agreeableness that didn't sound like him.

"Don't know if I could do this if my wife started screwing someone else under my nose."

"You're not trying to tell me Sand, that"—I heard the tone, jocular but edgy, and I thought about stepping in because when they saw me, men talking like this with my father, they usually just smiled and went away after patting me on the head or saying something about how I'd grown. Now as I moved in to do it, to make myself visible, my father completed the sentence—"you haven't had a lot of practice at this?"

I felt the man tense. "What?"

"Nothing," Daddy said.

"Fuck you, Phil," he said.

"Hey, sport, not in front of my daughter."

"Daddy, it's okay, I . . ."

"Fuck you, again," this man Sandy said and started to turn away and my father laughed, a kind of snort. I screamed because I was afraid of what was coming and as people turned, the man slapped Daddy hard across the face—not a punch, a slap, because I remember that same slapping sound, and he fell against the bar and his glasses came off and skittered across the floor. I didn't know whether to go for them or stay right next to my father and then I heard a crunch as somebody, coming toward us, crushed them underfoot and then Mother was there, alarm in her eyes—real alarm, not wide-eyed actress alarm—and Joe behind her.

"What the hell happened?" she said.

"It's okay," I said. "It'll be okay." But no one was listening to me. There was a crowd now. The man who had slapped him had gone away but Daddy's cheek was cut, I saw now, and mother had a napkin to it. He was pushing her hand down and saying, "Leave it, Pat, I'm fine," and then through the crowd, at about my eye level, suddenly there was Louise's face and it was wild with a kaleidoscope of emotions.

"Daddy, what happened?" she said, screaming over the noise, the music and the crowd and Mother. "What happened?"

He started to say something, but Louise screamed again. "I hate you. You've ruined everything. You've ruined my party."

. 16 .

I was lucky. Louise needed me, but she didn't need Daddy. That's
certainly how she saw it. I tried to tell her what happened and
that it was the other man's fault but she remained unconvinced
and for a few weeks, despite the two dozen roses Daddy had sent this
time, she would only talk to me when the three of us were together
having dinner. I tried to go silent back at her to make her talk to him.
But it was hopeless, I was, at being silent.

"Did I tell you what Clarisse did today in English class?" she'd
say, only looking at me and pushing potatoes onto her fork with her
finger.

I wouldn't answer. "Oh, isn't Clare clever, giving me the silent
treatment?" she'd say, forcing Daddy to say, "Can't you stop it now?
You've made your point."

"She was reciting that silly poem about trees and when she
couldn't remember some line she made tree rhyme with knee."
Louise's eyes were mean-merry.

"That's stupid," I said. "Did she get into trouble?"

"Made you talk, made you talk," she said.

Daddy got up and went into the kitchen. The phone rang and,
sticking his head into the breakfast room—the only place we ate
anymore, the dining room, like the master bedroom, now completely unused (I had tiptoed into the former to find that Mrs.

Palmer and Norma had set it right, made the bed and cleaned up everything in the wake of Mother's departure and one or the other clearly went in there when we were in school, at least, to dust), the big, shiny dark table and breakfront full of china looking now like a display in a museum—he'd say, "Clare, tell your sister there's a phone call for her."

Louise would leave and Daddy would come back with a coffee cup. I knew there was vodka in it, but he'd gotten self-conscious even around me. I'd ask about work, the script he was rewriting, and he'd say it was going okay or they were making his life miserable. The desk in his den had gone very tidy, which made me nervous. When Daddy was working, really working, there were notes and papers everywhere. He'd pad around, looking at the snatches of dialogue, and then assemble them like a collage, muttering: "Jesus, Phil, you idiot, wheredya put that scene?" or, when he got his hands on something he wanted, "You're a genius, Phil, an absolute genius." But it was tidy in there now.

"Daddy," I said, "are you writing at that place you go to in town?"

"Checking on me, eh?" he'd say and we'd laugh and that would be the end of it.

Sometimes Louise would flounce back with a bowl of ice cream. Sometimes she actually brought me some, too, putting it down and standing there with a smile until I said, "Thank you." Sometimes she'd talk about Mother and Joe. They wanted to work together. They were looking at houses together. They say I can come live with them. They say this, they say that, they do this, they do that. I heard it all from far away, hearing and not hearing, scanning Daddy's face. When he'd get up, I'd glare at Louise with as much hatred as I could summon.

"I'm getting the Clare stare now, huh?"

"Louise," I'd say, and then no more. I'd get up and take the bowls to the kitchen.

It thawed after a while. Mother and Joe went away for a couple of weeks so Louise had to be home for the weekends. Daddy, handier than his small, somewhat professorial, East Coast looks implied, decided the three of us would strip the beams in the living room, put them back dark. He got tools and paint removers and ladders—rather, a ladder for him, which we were to anchor with our kid-weight, while he jabbed and scraped and muttered. Louise was willing to stay the course, to get white paint flakes in her hair, to bring sandwiches into the war zone of the living room, remembering even—without being asked—to bring Daddy a beer, a peace offering. We went out for dinner that first Saturday when she stayed with us to a little fish shack up the coast, all bundled up because it was cold, and she let Daddy put the top down and he let her put on her favorite rock-and-roll station and we all seemed to know the words to some of the Beatles' songs, even Daddy—"I should have known better with a girl like you"—and shouted them out in the cold night air whenever one of them came on the radio. There was an almost full moon, bouncing light off the ocean, and we all made wishes on it as we drove home with greasy fingers, the heat at full blast swirling around our legs, Louise and I packed in next to Daddy on the front seat. "Please, please me, oh yeah, like I please you."

Mother and Joe came back from Hawaii, tan and vivid, and they exerted their inexorable pull on Louise. Up went the convertible top, back she went to weekending with them. She had her hair cut, short and feathered—that's what she told me they called it: feathering—at some swanky place in Beverly Hills and started to wear shorter and shorter skirts, even to school. Daddy raised an eyebrow, actually talked to Mother about it, but she was now wearing them too. I was the pixie-cut, mouse-colored-hair holdout, still in jeans and T-shirts. One of the weekends I agreed to stay with

them—I was trying to be a better bridge, stay closer to Louise—
they took me to their salon, as a surprise (it was actually for my tenth
birthday—and the woman trimmed and fluffed and sprayed, my face
going tighter and smaller as I watched her ministrations). When we
got back to the hotel, I promptly got into the shower and washed it all
out and Louise and Mother didn't know whether to be angry or laugh
and they both did both.

"Do you know what that cost, that haircut?" my mother said.

"I told you I didn't want it," I said.

"Leave her alone," Louise said quietly to Mother.

"Oh," is all Mother said in response, cocking an eye at Louise.

Joe joined us for dinner in "our" booth. Any awkwardness now
seemed to be all gone. He just slid in as if it was his place in the world.

"How'd I get so lucky?" he said. "Three beautiful women."

When Bertrand came around, it was all chat and charm. We were
now an accepted unit, a team where someone had simply substituted
one of the main players. Joe was no longer on Mother's show; he'd
gotten a better part in another one, also a Western, more lines, less
horse time.

"I'm jealous," Mother said, pretending not to mean it.

Joe asked Louise and me about school, or rather he asked her
about her friends ("I bet that Clarisse has a boyfriend by now") and
he asked me about what I was reading. When I told him, he'd shake
his head and say, "Must have missed that one. Jeez, Patricia, you've
got yourself a real little thinker here."

When people came to the table now to ask for an autograph, it
was a toss-up as to whether they'd ask Mother or Joe. I'd sense a little tension when a stranger approached, both of them putting on
their meeting-the-public smiles. Louise, too, would sit up, brush her
feathered hair with her fingers, apply a smile. Everyone would relax
back down when the autograph-seeker had left, little joshings here
and there depending on which adult had been singled out.

"Clare," Mother would say, "you might be a little friendlier."

"Don't needle her, Pat," Joe would say. "She's got deeper things to think about. Right, kiddo?" he'd say to me.

Nights, Louise and I would make our way to the bungalow and get into the pull-out sofa in the living room, leaving the bedroom for the adults. Joe stayed over a lot during the week, but usually Mother was careful about him sleeping there on the weekends. Sometimes though, I would hear them slip in unnoticed, or try to, whispering by us there on our sofa—Louise, as always, in her enviable deep sleep—and into the bedroom, where there would be hushed giggles and purry moany noises and then, later, the door would open and he would tiptoe out in his socks, trailing a slight vapor of Mother.

Once I heard her crying in the bathroom after he left. Louise stirred beside me and I was grateful because I thought she might wake up and go in there and comfort her, but she just rolled over and I stayed put beside her, trying to cover my ears with a pillow. In the morning, Mother said she wasn't feeling well and told us to go have breakfast by the pool. As we left, Louise, having spent forever in front of the bathroom mirror, chatted about the upcoming day, the swimming—though she was doing less and less of this now because of her hair, the mascara—the shopping, lunch by the pool where there were sure to be some movie stars.

"What's wrong with you?" she suddenly said. "You haven't said anything."

"I'm not feeling well."

"You always say that."

"Maybe I should go home."

"You can't. Daddy isn't there, remember."

"He'll be home later."

"How are you going to get there?"

"I don't know. I'll take a cab."

"Clare, can't you be any fun?"

A fter that, Louise started taking one of her girlfriends for the hotel weekends and Daddy and I were back to batching it, as he called it. He was still trying to strip those beams and we spent hours together, radio playing, in the living room. Sometimes the Beatles, sometimes a baseball game, sometimes the news. There was a war in Vietnam. Daddy showed me on the globe in his study where it was and said that more and more Americans were going and that if it kept going, some of the boys Louise and I were in school with might end up there. At night we sometimes watched the news together in his study, me with hot cocoa, Daddy with his vodka—he was drinking a little less, it seemed, and was back to using a regular glass, not a coffee mug. There were grainy pictures of short-haired men in splotchy uniforms—camouflage suits, Daddy said—and then pictures of people called hippies who looked like the hitchhikers on the road, messy-looking girls and boys with long hair and beads around their necks and peace symbols painted on their foreheads. They'd be swaying somewhere, in some park or something, sometimes hundreds or thousands of them, it seemed, while music blared from somewhere. Looking at them, Daddy would say, "I don't think this is my era, sweetheart." But he didn't like the war, either, and he wept, one June night, sitting next to me on the sofa, when the news came on about Robert Kennedy being killed.

"Here, right here," he kept saying. "In this city. Terrible."

Mother actually called that night to commiserate because, as Daddy told me after hanging up, they had been so optimistic when his brother, John Kennedy, was elected and it had been such an exciting time.

"I remember, Daddy," I said.

"You were only four," he said, laughing a bit and wiping his eyes on the back of his writing cardigan.

When Louise came home that weekend, she was full of hotel news: Paul Newman was staying there and his eyes were like pools you could swim in, I mean, the color, and she and Clarisse had gotten his autograph and even Mother was pretty excited to meet him and he only sort of knew who she was, he didn't really, but was really, really nice when she said she was on TV and he asked which show and she told him and he seemed to know it and he was going to be there a whole week so maybe she could see him again next weekend, Louise told us in one breathless run-on sentence. She then said everyone there was really, really sad about Robert Kennedy being shot and that in the restaurant and coffee shop and bar, everywhere, the TVs were turned to the news of his funeral and Mother had cried a lot. But Clarisse's parents, phoning her there where she was staying with Louise, said they weren't very sad and that the Kennedys weren't nice people.

"Maybe," Daddy said, "you should get some new friends."

She didn't get new friends, just disappeared more and more with the ones she had, not just the weekends, but weeknights now, under the guise of studying with them even though I had shouldered more of her work. She would phone me from Clarisse's or Pam's to check on my progress on her report on Brazil or the brain and I would hear a TV in the background and giggling. Sometimes Daddy and I would go pick her up after dinner and she would, sitting next to me on the front seat, nudge me when he asked if she got all her homework done. There were no more strip-the-beam Saturdays for her, no languid Sundays in Daddy's study. She came back from the hotel with more and more plans, more and more news. They had looked at houses, Mother and Joe; they had looked at rings. She and Mother had looked at dresses.

"You don't wear white, not white white, when you get married a second time," she said as we drove home. "Off-white's okay or a pale color. And you don't wear a long dress; you wear a short one or a fancy suit.

"Hey," she said, whispering into my ear, "we got a B-plus on that Brazil paper."

I t might have gone on this way. We might have gotten through more or less as a family, a fractured family but a family, tethered in our way, spending birthdays and holidays together. Mother and Joe might have married and bought that house in town somewhere, even had another child—Louise and I displaced but amused to have a baby sibling, a little brother, Louise more displaced but somewhat okay about it all, since she was disappearing more and more into her own adolescence, thumbing those *Seventeens*, pinching those pubescent thighs to see if they were growing too much, putting less and less tissue in her bras because the breasts were beginning to be ample enough, talking about boys. Daddy, I suppose, might have remarried, himself. Some nights now, he stayed in town, leaving us with Mrs. Palmer. He always called, said he was working late, but sometimes I could hear laughter in the background and he finally confessed that one of the assistant casting directors on his last movie was "being kind to him." I asked to see a picture or meet her, but he said it wasn't a big thing and that his girls came first. I think her name was Penny; I think he told me that, but she never called the house and only once or twice, on my nightly rounds, did I hear him talking to her, or what I assumed was her—a bantering Daddy with a slightly false, ribald edge, trying to be a little hip, talking about peace demonstrations. ("They tell me that's where the girls who put out are; luckily you're saving me from that.") Still, as we grew, he might have found a way to love again. Might have. Instead, the equation shifted again, one night when Mother phoned to tell him that Joe had left her. Daddy left that night to be with her at the hotel, after telling us as calmly as possible not the whole truth, but close enough—for those of us listening, me (Louise, after he'd gone, saying it was probably just a lovers' quarrel)—and after, I noticed, sprucing himself up, switching from cardigan to sport jacket, putting on a little of his cologne, downing a cup of coffee to counteract the cocktails.

"I'll call if I'm staying the night," he said, a look of expectation in his eyes. I carry that face in my wallet, next to the one from the morning she left.

H e came home the next day. We were at school, but returned to find him in his study, moving papers around. I stuck my head in and he avoided my eyes.

"We'll talk at dinner," he said. "Go finish your homework."

It was hot, very hot for March, and windy—almost fire weather but not quite that hot. All the windows were open and you could smell the ocean. I saw Tommy and his father mowing out on the edge of the bluff, and Catalina in the distance. Tommy had gotten tall and lean, his dark hair in almost a butch, the opposite of the trends. Even Daddy's hair was longer, pieces in the back curling up over his shirt collars. He was also wearing jeans sometimes, but always with his cardigan or sport jacket. I wondered if some of that was Penny's doing (if that was her right name) and whether that meant she was younger or if it was all just the times. Everybody's father's hair was longer, even Clarisse's father, which made Daddy laugh.

At dinner he was not laughing. He wasn't even drinking. That was scary. He was choosing his words with extreme care, looking more at Louise than at me. I think he thought she was very attached to Joe. I thought so, too. There were tears in her big blue eyes, but they didn't fall. She held on to them. And she was unusually silent.

The thing is, Daddy said, things didn't work out between the two of them. Sometimes that happens. Your mother is upset. She'll probably take a weekend or two by herself. She loves you very much. Joe would love to still see you, take you for an occasional lunch or something. At this point Louise said something astonishing, a word she had never used and I don't even think we'd heard Mother say.

"Bullshit," she said.

"What?" Daddy said.

She saw the look in his eye and didn't repeat it. Then he said, "Yeah, that is bullshit, isn't it? You're never going to see him again." And then he started to laugh, and we did, too, and then Louise's tears fell right down into her open-mouthed laughter. Mrs. Palmer came out to see what was going on—we were laughing that hard— and suddenly Daddy got up and left the table. He walked out the French doors—it was dark but still warm out—and he went out on the bluff and sat down at the edge, looking out at the ocean. I followed a little and would probably have gone farther, but Louise came up behind me.

"Let's go do my homework," she said, putting her arm around me and steering me back into the house.

There were late night phone calls and sometimes Daddy stayed overnight in town, but he said nothing about it. Whether he was with Penny or Mother or with one one time and one another, who knew? He looked sort of happier than he had been, but his moods were mercurial. He might just have been consolation, a cardiganed shoulder to cry on. Louise and I didn't talk about it. She had gone back to being Louise. She wanted to know when she could go spend a weekend at the hotel again—she couldn't wait to go shopping for summer clothes with Mother—no real mention of the disappearing Joe.

"Mother's so beautiful," she said. "She'll have a new boyfriend soon."

We both finally went. Daddy said we should. Louise didn't even pack a swimsuit anymore, but I still took mine and both she and Mother came to sit on chaises beside the pool while I swam. They were looking more and more alike, the one face, though, young and buoyant, the other now a bit abashed, prettier in some ways for the sorrow in it. Mother tried to be jolly. She told us it was all for the best, she and Joe, that she wanted to concentrate more on her career again, what with the show ending. Her agent was promising to send her everywhere for the new season shows. She said Daddy had been wonderful to her. When he came to get us on Sunday he held Mother and kissed her on her forehead.

"You know . . ." he said, as we all stood under the canopy waiting for our car.

"I know," she said.

The next weekend Louise went alone because I had a paper due on *The Red Badge of Courage*. I told Daddy I was thinking about weaving Vietnam into it and he thought that was great but might be a grade risk.

"But," he said, "you might as well try it now. We writers tend to lose our courage as we go along." I had heard him talking to his agent about having to do TV work now, money going out, you know, Pat still in the hotel, girls still to get through school. We spent the weekend writing side by side and occasionally wandering in to stare at the half-stripped beams—project interruptus, Daddy called it. "Gonna have to get back at it after we finish our big assignments," he said, but he'd said that before and we hadn't gotten any more done. It was just another room now that we didn't use, didn't even really go in. It was as if, one by one, the rooms in our house were being cordoned off with some invisible velvet ropes, like in museums. The master bedroom, the dining room, the living room—and counting.

The Louise Daddy brought home that Sunday was a different sister. Mother had been off since Joe left, sadder, more distracted, but still roused herself with makeup and shopping plans, talk about auditions and diets.

"Got to stay in shape in this town, girls," she would say.

Almost in unison, we would say, "Oh, Mommy, you're still the most beautiful."

All I could figure is that Louise hadn't been able to say enough this time. Nobody would really tell me what happened. Daddy led her directly up the stairs. I could hear him talking to her and her crying, ragged, angry crying, trying to say something through it, but not making any sense. I was at the bottom of the stairs when he shut the door to her room. It was the first time in months and months, years, that he had taken her into her now adolescent girl's bedroom—Mick Jagger posters on the walls and clothes on the floor and her little phonograph with mistreated and scratched records stacked beside it—and put her to bed.

I finally went to bed myself. In the days after, all anyone would say was that Mother was having a hard time—that's all Daddy would say. Louise just shook her head at me and rolled back over in bed. Daddy let her stay home from school for a couple of days and I would come home and find them in his study watching TV together—not news like he watched with me, just old reruns. Sometimes, they would be sitting very close, Daddy's arm around her. Sometimes they would actually be laughing at something on the TV. If I had flashes of jealousy—and I did—I needn't have worried because Louise, soon enough, went back to her friends and her records and her now endless phone calls and her first boyfriend.

She was atwitter with him. He came to the house in jeans, his longish blond hair brushed behind his ears. Cute enough, a little surferish. He couldn't drive yet, so his father took him and Louise to a movie in the Palisades, left them off, and then brought her home. Daddy and I tried not to wait up, but we did, oh so casually looking up from the war news when she came into his study, flushed, blurry-mouthed. Clearly she'd been making out. That's what people did at movies. In cars, other more serious things. I overheard Daddy telling Louise about this, about sex, about when she needed some-thing protective, she could come to him or Mother. She cut him off.

"Daddy, we all know about all that already."

That night, she was Louise-high—not on anything, yet, but herself—so she let me flop on her bed while she changed out of her clothes and into her nightgown. Her body was rounding and I won-dered if this boy, Jake, had touched any of it and when I asked, she said, "No, no way, he's just my starter boyfriend."

I'm not sure either of us was surprised when Daddy told us that for the present there would be no more weekends at the hotel. Mother was going away for a little bit to rest and she would be in touch as soon as she got settled. He told us this over dinner, not drinking. He would do that later, I knew, but just then he wanted to be measured as he delivered the news.

"I know . . ." he started, and there was a quaver and then he pulled himself back under control. "I know this isn't easy, but you girls . . ."

"I don't care what she does," Louise said. "I'm sick of her and that stupid hotel." She got up and left the room.

Nothing more was said, not by Daddy or either of us. I went back to my homework, our homework, Daddy went back to his TV scripts—he didn't stay in town anymore and I wondered if Penny had gone away, just like Mother, or if she been an illusion all along—

and Louise went back to her friends and phone calls and Jake. She said she was already getting tired of him.

"I don't think he's a very good kisser, but how am I going to know if I don't try someone else? Clarisse says Mr. Jefferson kissed Carolyn. Maybe I should go after him."

"Louise, he's a teacher," I said, but she didn't even look at me.

The next Saturday, I awoke with a start, someone pushing at me. It was Louise. She never got up early, never before me, and certainly not on the weekend.

"What are you doing?" I said. I noticed she was already dressed, hair in a ponytail.

"Get up," she said. "We're going somewhere. I've already talked to Tommy and he'll take us."

"Where?" I said.

"It's a surprise. Just hurry up, will you? I'm not sure Daddy will want us driving with him."

I pulled on my clothes and followed her downstairs and out by the garage. Tommy was there already, sitting in his truck, his father's truck, but he was now old enough to drive it. There was an American flag decal on the back bumper and inside, as I climbed up next to Louise, who was next to Tommy, I smelled grass and oil. I could see that he was trying to start it as quietly as possible. Louise had no doubt told him Daddy might not want us to go. We went up the driveway and I slid down off the seat and went and opened the big gate, and then we turned left on the highway toward town. The morning sun was soft and there was practically nobody on the beaches as we went along, the truck lurching a little from side to side. Tommy kept both hands on the wheel and didn't look at either of us.

"Where are we going?" I said to Louise.

"I told you, it's a surprise."

"Can we turn on the radio?" Louise said.

"There isn't one," Tommy said.

"Well then, we'll just have to hum ourselves."

She started in on "Row, Row, Row Your Boat" and kept nudging me to try to make me join, but I was getting a little nervous.

"Louise, tell me where we're going."

"First stop, the coffee shop at Fifth," she said. She was smiling to herself. "Don't worry, this is going to be a lot of fun.

"Go up the ramp," she said to Tommy, "and then turn right and then left on Wilshire to Fifth. And then we'll go right. I think it's a few blocks."

After that, nobody said anything until we pulled up at the coffee shop.

"Are we having breakfast?" I said, as we walked in. Louise was first, then me. Tommy said he'd wait outside.

"Chicken," she said, and for the first time that morning, he smiled, with his eyes more than his mouth.

We sat at the counter. And when the waitress came for our order, Louise asked if she might see that picture, just there, the one of that actress, Patricia Layton, yes, that one, she said pointing, just near where the pies were, next to the one of Joey Bishop. We're her daughters and we just wanted to see it, right Clare, she said, nudging me again, like she'd been doing all morning.

"Yes," was all I could say.

The waitress came back with it and handed it to her. When the waitress turned her back to us to do something, Louise nudged me again and slipped off her chair and took off for the door. I flew after her. She had Tommy by the hand and the picture in the other and we jumped in the truck and he started it up and drove off, all of us a little breathless.

"One down," she said.

"Louise," I said. "We can't do this. It's stealing."

"It's not stealing," she said. "She's our mother."

Next we went to the dry cleaner's. That was easier. The man who was usually behind the counter had gone back to get someone's package of shirts—we'd heard the customer ask for them—so Louise just sidled up to the picture, which was on a wall near the door, and quietly took it. We were back in the truck in a minute, laughing now, even me, because we'd never done anything like it.

Louise had two more places in mind, one of them a yarn store inside a department store. She remembered seeing one there when she and Mother had gone to get yarn to knit Daddy a scarf for some birthday. But when we got there, the yarn store was gone and Louise was visibly deflated.

"What else?" I said, now a coconspirator.

"There's that fish restaurant, remember, we used to go to, near the pier? But I don't remember exactly where it was."

"I do, I do," I said and directed Tommy there, forgetting, of course, that it was morning and it wouldn't be open.

It wasn't, but there was actually a guy out back emptying garbage. Louise watched him for a minute and said let her out. She went up to him and we couldn't hear what she was saying, but he led her into the back door. She turned and winked at us as she disappeared and within minutes was back with another picture, this one different from the other two, a little more cleavage, her name, Patricia, right across it.

"What did you tell him?" I said.

"I told him she was dead and we needed the picture for her funeral."

"Louise," I said, but I was laughing and even Tommy, for what I could see of him, seemed to have a sort of smile.

I figured—I guess I figured—that Louise was going to make some kind of shrine or something or hang the pictures in her room, but when we got about halfway home, she asked Tommy to pull into one of the deserted beach parking lots.

"Come on," she said to me. "I was going to do this at home, but I don't want to run into Daddy."

She marched to the edge of the lot and I suddenly realized she meant to throw them off the small cliff that led down to the ocean, but I grabbed her hand.

"Louise, you can't, you can't. It's glass. You can't."

"Okay then, this will do," she said, walking up to the nearest big yellow metal garbage can. I was right behind her and I tried to grab the pictures out from under her arm, but she shook me off and, lifting one with her free hand, bashed it as hard as she could against the rim of the can, where it shattered into a million pieces. I stood there and watched her. She smashed the second one down, sunlight dancing off the shards where they lay at the base of the can.

"Here," she said, offering me the last picture. "Want one?"

I just shook my head and starting walking toward the truck, hearing the crash of the third one. I slid in next to Tommy. Neither of us said anything and then Louise, making the "all done" motion with her hands, brushing them against each other, walked back to the truck and slid in beside me. She was giddy on the rest of the ride home, chatting and laughing about everything, school and boys and Clarisse and the look on that guy's face when she told him our mother was dead and we needed the picture for her funeral, and all of a sudden she was sobbing. Tommy pulled over into the next parking lot and got out and walked around to Louise's door. He opened it and pulled her out and then, an arm around her, led her down the little rocky path to the beach, where they sat in the sun, backs to me, for a long time. Louise's shoulders kept shaking so I figured she was still crying. Tommy sat very still beside her, not touching her, their dark heads glimmery in the bright sunshine. I don't know who said what, if anything. Nobody said anything to me when they both came back to the truck. Tommy did say to me, hands on the wheel as he backed out, "Thank you for waiting," which struck me funny and actually struck Louise, too, because where was I going to go, and when she laughed, I laughed because it seemed there was still a sister in there, my sister, and we could laugh together, but she went quiet again on the way home and after that day she seemed to belong to Tommy.

. 17 .

It was a beautiful spring. There had been a lot of winter rain, mud slides periodically closing the highway, but now the hill-sides were covered in wild mustard. Even our own bluff had sprouted patches of sweet-smelling yellow flowers. Paul, Tommy's father, had pretty much retired and left our place to his son, but Tommy that spring was taken up with Louise, so things had gotten a little overgrown. I would find the two of them, heads bent together, talking or just sitting looking out at the ocean, Louise often holding a wild bouquet Tommy had picked for her. She wasn't mean when I'd come upon them, the way she had been when I barged into her bedroom and found her with Clarisse and Pam. She would simply smile up at me. Tommy was always very polite. He sometimes asked me to sit with them or offered to take me along when they went into the Palisades to buy something or get an ice cream and we'd racket our way up the highway in his truck, listening to music on an old transistor Louise brought along. She had tumbled back into our zone from Mother's—that's the way it felt. Her hair was long and free. She didn't set it anymore or have it cut or feathered. She didn't wear makeup, either. Most afternoons, as the days lengthened into early summer, I would find her, after school, in cut-off jean shorts and an old bikini top, lying on a towel, smelling of coconut oil, while Tommy knelt beside her or mowed around her prone body. I would

sit at my desk, doing our homework, and watch them. I didn't see
them kiss or touch much, a hand brush, a smile. Sometimes Tommy
would light a cigarette and, leaning down, let her take a puff. Sometimes he would bring her one of his bouquets, a foraged purple
flower stuck in the middle of all the yellow and when she'd come in,
as the sun went down, looking dreamy and sun-darkened, she'd stick
them in a glass and bring them in and set them on my desk, and I'd
smell them both, her, lightly sweaty and coconutty, slight cigarette
breath, and the flowers, the window open, Tommy gone, listening to
Mrs. Palmer make dinner, smell that, too, her leathery pork chops
and sometimes the ocean as well, depending on the wind. That's
when I'd read her one of her essays and she would say, "It's too
damn good," and we would laugh and I'd make it dumber and read it
to her again. "Perfect," she'd say.

I don't know what Daddy knew or thought about them, Louise
and Tommy. He was distracted with work, a rewrite, staying up
late. He'd thrown himself back into it after Mother took off the second time. That's how it seemed to me, anyway. He was also entertaining again, an odd turn. It wasn't so much that he was
entertaining as allowing the house to be used for weekend parties,
some of his Hollywood friends coming out and camping for the
weekend. Suddenly we were a hip destination, convertibles of pot-
bellied men in short-sleeved shirts with newly long hair and blond
starlets descending on us with cheap wine and deli platters of sandwiches and plastic tubs of potato salad and coleslaw (long, long
gone were Mother's delicate canapés), even sleeping bags. They
crashed—that was the new word—in the living room, the girls going in and out of the bathroom, occasionally straying upstairs to
use Weezie's and mine. Mrs. Palmer took that as her final cue to
leave; she'd never really regained her footing or authority after
Mother left, so her leave-taking was a bit of a formality. Daddy and
Louise and I stood in the driveway as her middle-aged son loaded

her small TV and suitcases into his VW bus and took her away, her curls back to being as tight and grumpy as they were the day we'd first seen her.

"Well, girls," Daddy said, "another era ends. We'll just have to look after ourselves. At least there'll be no more of those pork chops."

Daddy himself was looking a little hip-goofy, hair tickling up over the back of his polo shirts, jeans flared at the bottom. He was a genial if somewhat bewildered host, picking his way among the bodies and ashtrays and half-empty deli platters of a weekend morning. Tommy and I had taken over a lot of the upkeep. He was now more or less there all the time, still serious, still polite. He called Daddy Mr. Layton, and always to me, as he asked for another dish towel or mop, said "please" and "thank you." Louise was often nearby, grazing through a magazine, smiling up at us from time to time.

"You guys work too hard," she'd say. "Let's get out of here."

Tommy would excuse himself and they would disappear back upstairs. It was a foregone conclusion that they were sleeping together, at least for me, anyway; I assumed for Daddy, too. She was just fifteen. Tommy was seventeen, nearing draft age. His was the only hair anymore that was short, the only car of anyone we knew—except Clarisse's parents—that had an American flag decal on it. The war wasn't talked about, except once when Daddy asked him what his plans were while we were sitting around the breakfast table, Louise still asleep upstairs.

"I intend to go, Mr. Layton," is all he said.

"If it's school, college, I mean," Daddy said, "I'll figure out a way to help."

"No," he said, "I am proud to go."

Daddy registered nothing and I was sure he'd meant to ask precisely as he had, Louise upstairs. I didn't know what she knew about Tommy's intentions—maybe everything, maybe nothing. When he excused himself and went back upstairs, carrying her that same mug

of thick cocoa that I used to make her, Daddy said, "Poor son-of-
a . . ." He caught my eye. "I can't protect any of you, can I?"

As we moved among the partygoers, Tommy and I, picking up
plates and glasses, watching them smoke and listening to them talk
about the war, what a disaster, what a farce, what a this, what a that,
he didn't betray anything. He was there because of Louise; doing a
little clean-up (even among peaceniks) was his way of payback. He
did it without any attitude at all, no resentment, no obsequiousness,
just direct, the way he mowed the lawn. In the room, he made himself invisible, something I understood. I did it, too, moving in and
out without drawing attention. It was Louise, of course, slipping in,
who couldn't help but draw it. In a room full of other young women
and the older men who had brought them—having shed wives per-
manently or ducked them just for the weekend (I listened to their
coarse banter, less coarse when Daddy was around)—she was, with
her scrubbed face, shorts, and bikini top, the instant magnet. There
was a sweetness in her beauty that was never in our mother's, or
maybe it was an early sadness that sharpened it, made it seem more
adult, less pure beauty queen, of which there were archetypes—
slightly aging archetypes—right there in the room with their dyed
hair and trussed up breasts. But who noticed them when Louise came
in? The room tensed up and Tommy, used wineglasses in his hands,
tensed with it, eyes on everyone whose eyes were on her. She didn't
milk it, Louise, or not much; there was a little stretching out, cat-like
pleasure in her movements. But her eyes went to Tommy, causing
him to untense, a half-smile, their secret code in a living room of
leerers and swingers, as they—certainly the men—liked to think of
themselves. None of us seemed to be in control, in charge, certainly
not Daddy, who moved in and around his guests with the same sort
of gingerliness Tommy and I did. It was as if they came in and
camped and went away of their own volition after their pleasures
were had. We were a coastal way station, an oasis. There were rules,

though. Daddy had those: No smoking dope inside or in front of the "kids." No sex outside or in front of the "kids." And nobody upstairs doing anything (except for the occasional girls in our bathroom). And no really loud music, except maybe in the afternoons if it was hot and we could be outside. Tommy had fixed up some speakers so there could be music on the rustic patio outside the French doors. Sometimes, on long summer afternoons, while the Rolling Stones or Janis Joplin growled from the speakers, we all played poker, all of us, Tommy and Louise and Daddy and I and the three weekend stalwarts, an older guy named Marty, an agent with slippery black hair; his girlfriend, Marna, one of those blond starlet types; and her friend Jules, a quiet, dark-haired young woman with freckles across the bridge of her nose. Marty winked at us a lot, all of us, especially playing poker, and was around so often he took to calling himself "your old Uncle Marty." We were a family, there for that summer. The girls, as Marty called them, Marna and Jules, had washed up from some small town in Texas. They had a hopefulness to them that had already been deflated some and, of course, there were Louise and I, abandonees. And Daddy and Marty, an unlikely pair (Marty was always chiding him for being an old maid) who'd known each other back East and then gotten reacquainted out here after both had been divorced. And Tommy, the gardener's son, Louise's boyfriend. A family. It was 1970 and that's what people were doing, cobbling together families after the regular ones had come apart. We had "family" barbecues and "family" poker games and "family" spats, there on our summertime bluff. Louise and I let Marna put gold streaks in our hair. She even managed to get one into Tommy's crew cut, one night when he and Louise had shared a joint—I know because they didn't hide that from me and they hardly ever did it anyway because Tommy didn't think it was right. But this night there was a big moon and we could smell, from the upstairs bathroom, where Marna, in her shorts and bikini top (she'd taken to dressing like Louise, though she always wore these big gold hoops in her ears) was mixing the hair dye, the steaks that Marty was grilling even with the chemical odor of the hair goop. We could hear Janis wailing and Marty and Daddy—was that Daddy?—wailing along with her ("Freedom's just another word for nothing left to lose"), hear the ice in their glasses, hear Jules in the kitchen yelling over it all about when they wanted the potatoes ready and in a weak moment, full maybe of family-feeling himself and good will, his eyes relaxed for a minute, not trained on Louise because there were none of those leerers around, just us, just family, Tommy sat down on the toilet seat, a dope-grin on his face (he always grinned when he'd smoked, while Louise just got dreamier and dreamier), and said to Marna, "All right, give me one." She whooped and did it before he had a chance to rethink it and that night everyone called him "pretty boy" and Louise, usually shy about him, certainly in front of other people, sat on his lap and fingered the shiny gold streak. That was the best night, the best kind of night. It seemed as if you could smell, in the summer-night air, meat grilling on barbecues all up and down the coast and see, like fireflies in the darkness, the tips of joints that were being passed back and forth. Summertime family fun. We made it into early November, Louise and I coming home from school on Friday fall afternoons and finding Marty and the girls already there, cookbooks open, wine open, music on, Daddy still in his study. The house had taken on life again. We were even using the dining room and, with Tommy's help, the living room beams had finally all been stripped. Walking in from school, I would immediately go upstairs and case out my homework assignments and Louise's and make a chart for when I had to do what, while she hurried into her shorts and top to join the others.

We might have gone on, except for Marty. One late Saturday night, as I was in the kitchen cleaning, Tommy with me, the two of us handing dishes back and forth to dry and put away, we heard

Marty and Daddy talking. The girls were watching TV in the study, Louise, too, so it was just the men. They were in the breakfast room, a bottle of vodka out. Daddy never smoked dope and his drinking had tapered off, but this night, for some reason, he had started steady and hard and kept it up and Marty had chased his liquor with some marijuana. He went outside to smoke with Marna and when he came back in and sat back down in the breakfast room, he had that slightly slurry, looser-tongued sound. "Hey, old man," he said, "it's time. What are you waiting for?"

When Daddy didn't say anything—Tommy wasn't looking at me, nor I at him; we were sort of pretending we couldn't hear through the kitchen door—Marty said, "For chrissakes, the times they are changin' or didn't you hear? I've brought you this sweet, serious girl, just your type. She's been coming and coming and coming out here and you're too chickenshit to make a move."

I'd heard some of this before, a usually gentle baiting and poking. Mostly Daddy laughed it off or shrugged it off and Marty backed off. When there was a protracted silence, I figured that's what had happened. I figured Tommy figured that too. He'd been around long enough to know all the bantering rhythms of the household. We went on finishing the clean-up and then heard a fist bang on the table next door, causing us both to jump.

"Shit, man," Marty said, "you gotta forget that cunt that left you and move on. She was a fucking lousy actress, anyway."

A chair scraped backward across the wooden floor, someone getting up, someone, Daddy, saying so quietly we almost couldn't hear, "Get out, Marty. I don't want you here in the morning."

"Sorry old man, didn't mean to hit the soft spots . . ."

"I mean it," Daddy said, and we could hear him walk out of the room and into the living room and go outside.

Tommy put down his dish towel and went to get Louise. I knew that's what he was doing. He wanted to get to her before Marty

walked in and did whatever, made a scene, or just gathered up
Marna and Jules, who would then have to gather up their stuff from
all corners of the house. He didn't want Louise to have to watch
someone else leave. Up the stairs they went and I knew, without
looking, that he was talking quietly to her, his arm around her. Nobody cried that night. It wasn't that kind of thing, that kind of loss,
although the house started to feel emptied again, as soon as they'd
gone, as soon as we heard their car going up the driveway, knowing
they wouldn't be coming back the next weekend or the next, and
Louise invited me into her room to listen to records with her and
Tommy. I realized I had been hoping for the holidays, all of us
cooking turkey and decorating a tree. I'd even thought about us
maybe getting the ice rink back.

We fell back into our old quartet: Daddy writing, occasionally going into town, me doing the homework and housework, Tommy helping with the latter and keeping the land up again, mowing and raking
and pruning, Louise beside him most of the time. Just sitting and
watching him. He was teaching her to drive and they'd go up the driveway and turn onto the highway in the afternoons, Louise jerking the
already jerky truck and laughing—I'd hear her laughing and Tommy
telling her quietly to do this or that. Since Marna she'd been wearing a
little mascara again and taking more care with her hair. Sometimes I'd
see Tommy brushing it for her out on the bluff, stroke after stroke, sitting behind her, Louise leaning back into him. He braided it, too, with
great patience, weaving flowers into it sometimes. For Christmas they
gave each other kittens, a marmalade pair, brother and sister, and over
the roast beef and Yorkshire pudding Tommy and I made—we were
quite the cooks now, the two of us, he more sous-chef—we had a nam-
ing contest, Daddy the winner with Bacall and Bogie. That night we all
watched *Casablanca* on television again and Bacall almost got renamed
Bergman, but Daddy, vodka in hand, wouldn't hear of it. We made
noise, all of us—even Tommy—to fill the space where Marty and the

girls might have been and, before that, Mother and all of our other Christmas guests. The living room and dining room had fallen back into disuse and, of course, the master bedroom, which Daddy had never returned to. We had put our small tree in Daddy's study and we ate our Christmas dinner in the breakfast room. There was a huddling quality to us. Near ten, just as the movie ended and we were finishing our popcorn, the phone rang. Nobody moved at first, then Daddy got up and answered the one on his desk.

"And to you," he said. He turned away from us and Louise winked at Tommy and me, mouthing, "I hope it's Jules."

"Okay. Sounds good. No, I don't think so. Not right now. Yes, we did. Yes, roast beef and Yorkshire pudding. Quite the cook, she's become. I will. Okay. Yes, you too. Merry Christmas."

I knew the instant I saw Daddy's face and I think Tommy did, too, but Louise said, all kittenish, "So, Daddy, who was that?"

Before he could say anything, I said, "It's Mother."

"Is that right, Daddy?" she said, voice already rising.

"She'd like to visit, to bring you girls some presents in the next . . ."

"I won't be here," Louise said. She didn't jump up and flee. She was just matter-of-fact as she got up to leave. At the door, she turned again and said, "I mean it."

Tommy stayed behind. Daddy went and refilled his glass and came back. "Mr. Layton," Tommy finally said, "I know it's none of my business, but I don't think that's a good idea."

"Well, I guess that's that then. If you kids don't mind, I think I'll turn in." He sounded old and colloquial. "You kids." He never called us that anymore. We were a team, a foursome. Tommy didn't say any more as he and I did our usual cleaning up. He did finally say, "Clare, you know you have a vote too," and I realized I hadn't even thought about that, about whether I wanted to see her again, or whether we should let her visit. I hadn't talked to her—Louise and I hadn't—for almost three years. Presumably I could go with Daddy to wherever it was she was, not even tell Louise, but I didn't think that was a good idea. We had something here that felt sort of stable and I didn't want to jinx it.

"Yes," I said. "I mean no, I don't want her coming here."

"I'm glad," he said.

On Tommy's eighteenth birthday in May, Daddy took him and Louise and me to Trader Vic's on Wilshire at the beginning of Beverly Hills just across from the fountain that had the multicolored spray. He had asked Tommy to ask his parents but they declined. Tommy was dressed in a blue sport coat and tan pants, his dark hair bristly and shiny with a little something he'd put in it. Daddy had loaned him the striped purple-and-silver tie Louise and I had given him for Christmas. Louise was wearing a short pink skirt and sleeveless white sweater, hair in one of Tommy's braids. He'd even braided mine, though I didn't much like my hair all skinned back off my face. Daddy had brought a camera along and asked one of the waiters to take our picture, the last one, I think—I'm fairly sure—of our family foursome. Tommy was going to Vietnam. He had said it only that once, to Daddy and me—I don't know what he and Louise had talked about or whether she'd tried to stop him, but he'd gone and registered. It wouldn't be long. Daddy, who I knew thought the war was bad, never said a negative word to Tommy, never tried to talk him out of it. The other boys Louise and I knew from school who were, the first of them, heading off to college, were all talking about deferments. But it was something Louise and I just never talked about. What was there to say? It lay there on the table, his imminent departure, right beside the crab wontons and sticky-sweet spareribs. Everybody felt it, even as we toasted Tommy and ate coconut ice cream in coconut shells and surreptitiously sipped through a shared straw Daddy's Kamikaze drink, also in a coconut shell, when nobody was looking. As we were finishing, Clarisse and her parents materialized at our table. She had grown big breasts since I'd last seen her and looked much older and harder than Louise, I thought. It was, she told us, her sixteenth birthday, and she lured Louise out to see the new car her parents had bought her. We made small talk with them while the girls were gone: weather and traffic, with a war on and Tommy there. Rather, Daddy made it, and I knew he didn't like them much by his excessive politeness. Louise returned, flushed and giggling; the parking boy had flirted with them. He wasn't a boy, Clarisse said. It was the car, Louise said. The car. On the ride home, we put the top down and she and Tommy sat close together under the big, old lap blanket Daddy kept in the backseat for just such occasions.

"Nice evening," he said, as he let us all in the house. "Nice evening." His voice a little choked, he said, "Happy birthday, Tommy."

. 18 .

They floated down from the highway like brightly colored butterflies and lighted in our meadow. We came home from school to find them, a trio of hitchhiking hippies. They already had a tent up and were washing themselves with the backyard hose. Daddy, coming out of his study, told us it was okay, he'd told them they could stay for a couple of nights. Only sometimes, seeing him, old cardigan, cup of coffee or cup of vodka—he'd gone back to camouflaging the booze again—like at that moment then, did I realize how almost faraway he seemed, disconnected.

"People come, people go," he said, walking toward the kitchen. "But I told them: no fires, no loud music or drugs." Louise, eyes a little shiny with anticipation of the new arrivals, shot me a look that said, "Sure." She was up the stairs and into her summertime uniform, bikini top and shorts, hair in a ponytail, before I'd even unpacked our books and started the nighttime homework chart. I looked out the window: She was sitting cross-legged on one of their colorful rugs. There were two tall, blond men and a woman and a big caramel-colored dog. It was warm and the men were barechested, the taller one with a ponytail as long as Louise's. At dinner, she reported that the men were brothers, Jann and Carl, and the girl was Jann's girlfriend, Lisa, and the dog was named Jesus. Louise

thought that was funny. She said they were cool, that they were going north to join their friends in Humble County.

"Humboldt," Daddy said.

"Humboldt," Louise said, playfully repeating it after him. She
was clearly happy about the new arrivals, Louise-giddy. She'd been
in her room, solemn, listening to music, since Tommy had left for
basic training at Camp Pendleton down the coast. He'd be there a
couple of months and then be shipped out from Oakland. Daddy
said we might all actually drive up and see him off. I couldn't quite
imagine such a trip, how it could be fun, Louise all keyed up, going
up the highway, no doubt locked up with sorrow on the way down.
I hoped he'd forget the idea or that she would veto it. Now, for the
moment, she had a distraction.

"Let's go say good night to the new arrivals," she said.

It was a warm, starry night and as we neared the tent, we could
hear laughter and the beginning jingle of musical instruments.

"Hey, Mr. Tambourine man, play a song for me." It was the
girl's voice, Lisa, high and sweet.

"Hullo," Louise said, making a mock *knock-knock* on the side of
the tent. A large man stooped through the opening and introduced
himself to Daddy and me. It was Jann. He brought the others out,
Lisa and Carl draped in bright shawls, both with silver earrings in
their ears. The men looked alike, tall and lean with identical furry
blond mustaches; Lisa was small and dark, hair to her waist. They
smelled, all of them, of incense and beef jerky. No starlets or bikini
tops here. This was the new world that had floated down to us from
the coastal highway, which was now like a human river of people going up or down, signs up, thumbs stuck out. Jesus was roaming
around the edge of the bluff; I could see his tail going and hear him
snort and root. When he ran up, I could see he had only three legs,
which caused him to sort of hobble, but he still moved fast. Every-

one was very polite in a kind of spacey way. Louise wanted to know where they'd been and how the dog had lost a leg and how long they would stay. A few days, they said, and she said, "Oh Daddy, look, they have a hurt dog, can't they stay longer?"

He said, "The dog's been like that, Louise. I'm sure they'll want to move on."

Daddy said they could use the bathroom if they needed, just off the kitchen, through that door there. As we walked away, we could hear the music again, something reedy, and the clinky jangle of a tambourine, and hear Lisa's voice again and see candles flickering through the tent. Daddy sent Louise back to warn them about the candles, to make sure they were watching them and would put them out. When she didn't come back, he sent me after her. She was sitting among them, sweater over her bikini top, batting the tambourine against her hand, face lit by candlelight.

"Louise, come on," I said. "It's time."

She looked at me and laughed. "You go, silly."

"Daddy will come."

"He doesn't care," she said.

I reached to take her hand and she shook me off. "I'll be there in a minute," she said.

I stood outside the tent. Daddy had gone in. He'd come out, but it would be a while. She knew that and I knew that. He'd be filling his mug and watching the news, or fussing with papers. He'd been working on a new screenplay—"Just something for myself"—even as he was cranking out TV scripts now for a new family drama. "Who better, eh, girls?" he said. Sometimes, late at night, I'd find him reading books like *A Portait of the Artist as a Young Man* or *Buddenbrooks*, intent, a little drunk. Sometimes he'd be asleep with one open across his chest, and I'd cover him there and turn off the light. Sometimes he'd be talking to someone on the phone, and I'd wonder who, but he wasn't gone much—almost not at all—so I figured there was no Penny person anymore. He told me he was sad about Tommy going and had become obsessive about watching the war news, though he was always careful not to do it around Louise, which was fairly easy, since she was usually upstairs listening to music. Now she would have the tent people to visit. As long as they stayed. My stomach felt nervous standing there waiting for her.

"You do that well," one of the men said, presumably to her.

They sang for a while longer and then Louise came out, face flushed, hair down. "Come on," she said, grabbing my hand. "Let's go say good night to the ocean." She pulled me out onto the bluff, Jesus trotting behind us. "How does that thing go," she said, " 'member, that thing Mother used to say. . . . Good night stars and good night sun, good night to everyone. . . . that doesn't rhyme, does it? . . . Clarie, fix it, you can fix it, you can fix everything. . . ."

I knew she was high. It was the only time she ever mentioned Mother. "You're high, Louise," I said. "Daddy said no drugs and you know Tommy doesn't like them."

She dropped my hand. "Tommy isn't here," she said.

He was there that next weekend. So, too, were the hippies. In fact, there were now two more, two women in long skirts and a lot of turquoise jewelry—one called Eva and a virtual twin whose name I never quite got—and another dog, a small, furry white puppy named Elephant. Louise thought that was funny too. I watched Tommy, hair shorn to the scalp now, watch her. She took him over and introduced him to everyone, but by nightfall, she seemed to be his again, holding his hand, leaning against him on the chaise in the back, the two of them covered by the lap robe from the back of Daddy's car. She was crying and he was whispering to her while, around the other side of the house, the tambourine started up and then Lisa's voice. "Amazing grace, how sweet the sound . . ."

They were still making music while we in the house bedded down for the night. I heard Louise and Tommy talking next door and then silence. Daddy shut his TV off and we fell asleep—I did, anyway—to an a cappella version of "Blowin' in the Wind" from out on the bluff, where the campers had moved their sleeping bags for the night.

They were still there the next weekend. Tommy couldn't make it, Louise said, but in a rare move—one he hadn't made since Marty and the girls had left—Daddy had invited some people he was working with, a small, balding director named Fred something, a baby-faced young actor named Fred, too, and his blowzy mother, Tina, who was visiting from Palm Springs.

"Is that Fred too, as in Fred also, or Fred two, as in the number?" Carl said, when introduced by Louise. The house and bluff were now a kind of free-flowing zone, the tent people drifting in and out to use the bathroom or borrow some milk or eyeball the news. "Fuckin' Nixon," the sweet-voiced Lisa said, catching sight of him on TV from the doorway of Daddy's study. I started to make major meals: lasagnas—vegetarian lasagnas, because the newest arrivals didn't eat meat. Just the weekends we seemed to eat together. The weeks, we still lived separately, though Louise drifted back and forth. I didn't find her high again. Maybe she'd made a pledge to Tommy. She was alternately cheery, when just back from the tents (there were two, now), and cold and curled inward. Some days I tried so hard not to watch her.

The weekend of the Freds, as we all started to call them, was very hot. We were all up early, restless and sweaty. Short Fred, as opposed to young Fred, said over a breakfast buffet on the patio—I set out platters of fruit and bagels and juice—that he had a brilliant idea of how we, including "you hippies," should spend the day. We should put in a pool.

"What—dig a hole?" Jann said, sleepy-eyed, in his shorts, long hair slicked back with hose water.

"Yeah. A fuckin' big one."

"I think that's a great idea," Tina said.

"Mom, you're nuts," young Fred said.

"That's news?"

Everyone laughed. Teams were assigned. Young Fred would drive Louise and Carl to the local hardware to get shovels. Short Fred, Daddy, and Jann would outline the pool with string. Lisa and Eva and I would keep the food and drinks coming. Everyone else would dig.

Pictures were taken. Tempers frayed. We fought first over the design: kidney-shaped or rectangular, and agreed on the latter with allowance for digger sloppiness. Daddy measured and remeasured. Carl and Jann turned out to be mathematical whizzes—both had been headed toward graduate school, they now admitted—so they took that job over. It was agreed that the tent city had to be moved because it was on the flattest spot. That took an hour because everyone had nestled in with rugs and candles and dog bowls and musical instruments. The string was finally in place and the first shovel pushed into the unforgiving earth to camera clicks, from me, and general applause. Jesus and Elephant ran in dizzy loops, snagging the outline string at one point.

"Shit," short Fred said, "control those mutts."

"Don't be such a nazi," Jann said.

"Who you calling a nazi?" Fred said. "I don't like that shit."

"Easy everyone," Daddy said. "Easy."

The digging began. By lunchtime we had a small gaping wound where once the ice rink had stood. Louise got the hose and offered to wash anyone off and then started squirting everyone. Carl grabbed her from behind and they were laughing as he tried to wrestle the hose away, sort of, while holding her. We had tuna sandwiches under the patio arbor, wine and sodas, and then voted to suspend the digging until later in the day when it was cooler. People disappeared to nap, most of them in the house because the tents weren't back up yet. I lost Louise. I found Tina, though, in the back bedroom, the one next to the one Daddy slept in now, with short Fred's head in her lap, rubbing his temples. And Daddy—I found him in his study reading, the radio on so he could catch any news update. He looked, sitting there, older for the first time, a lot more gray than I had been seeing or letting myself see. I went and sat next to him.

"You okay, Daddy?" I said.

He didn't answer for a minute.

"Daddy?"

"Yeah, sweetheart?"

"Is this okay?"

He knew what I meant. The whole thing. "I don't think they'll stay much longer," he said.

"What about the pool?" I said. "Who'll finish it?"

"A harebrained idea," he said, then started to laugh, which always made me laugh, and we came a little unhinged with laugher until someone male, maybe Fred, from the other room, said, "Hey, keep it down in there."

"Shut up, yourself," Daddy yelled back, so unlike himself— yelling, the words—that we laughed even harder and when he said it again, louder and added a "fuck," as in "Shut the fuck up," we laughed even harder.

By dusk, the diggers had widened the hole and deepened it. Jann and Carl were standing, leaning on their shovels, their naked torsos smeared with dirt. "Let's call it a pond and call it a day," Jann said. They lay down their shovels and retreated to their reconstituted tents. I went into the kitchen to start making dinner and heard someone tiptoeing in and when I turned around, there was Tommy. I threw my arms around him. I'd never done that before. He blushed and I did. "Oh, Tommy," I said. "Just in time to help with dinner."

"Where's your sister?" he said.

My face flushed again. "Upstairs, I think. Did you look?"

He said he hadn't and when he left and I heard him going up, I prayed she was there and by herself. I went to the bottom of the stairs and heard her door open, still holding my breath, and then heard, "Oh, Tommy," and then heard the door shut. We had a convivial dinner, a lot of laughter about the pool, who'd done what, who'd wimped out. We had memories already, shorthand, insults. Everyone went to bed early; there wasn't even any late night music from the tents.

By the time I got up, Louise and Tommy were gone. I peeked in because the door was open. What if they'd taken off, were running away, like to Canada because he'd suddenly decided he couldn't go to Vietnam, or to Tijuana to get married (she couldn't get married; she was too young) or just anywhere? I went downstairs. Daddy was still asleep in the maid's room. There were bodies in the living room and no one was stirring out on the bluff. I went out to the driveway and saw that Tommy's truck wasn't there and went back and woke up Daddy.

"They're gone," I said.

"Who?" he said.

"Louise and Tommy."

"They probably just went to breakfast or to be by themselves."

"No," I said.

"Clare," he said quietly, "don't panic. I'm sure they'll be back."

"I'm going back to my room," I said. "Somebody else can make breakfast."

From my window, I watched the tent people rouse, wash themselves, play with their dogs, straggle over to the house. I heard people in the kitchen so I assumed someone had done something about
breakfast. Daddy came up at one point and knocked and said
through the closed door, "Clare, they'll be back. I know Tommy."

"But you don't know Louise," I said.

"That's where you're wrong," he said.

A t noon, the truck rattled down the driveway. I casually strolled
from my bedroom and down the stairs. People were lazing
around the patio—the pool project had apparently already been
abandoned—sipping coffee when Louise and Tommy came in, followed by Lisa. "Look, everybody," Louise said, pulling up her
sleeve and pointing at her upper arm. "Look." There was a little tattoo of a heart with "Tommy" in it.

"Show them yours," she said.

Tommy shyly pulled up the sleeve of his T-shirt and there, at the
top of his left arm, was a companion heart with "Louise" in it. I saw
Daddy grimace while the rest of the group whistled and clapped.

"Lisa knew exactly where to take us," Louise said.

"Young love," short Fred said, sipping a Bloody Mary, or what I
assumed was one.

"What would you know about that?" Tina said.

"Precious fucking little," he said, leaning to kiss her on the cheek.

T he day was slow and long and lazy, people drifting around from
tent to patio. Louise and Tommy were upstairs for most of it.
Reading on my bed, I could hear them laughing and then her crying.
Daddy found an old croquet set and the hippies started to whack
balls around, the dogs flying after them. That was the extent of the

day's activity. Someone went to the market to get hot dogs and cans of vegetarian chili for dinner and big half gallons of cheap wine. Louise and Tommy came down to eat. Her eyes were red. I watched the heart on her arm as she reached for the mustard, the onions, Tommy's name flashing back and forth. The Hollywood group left after dinner. I wondered, as they left, if we would see them again. It didn't feel like it, somehow. Carl and Lisa cleaned up and then suggested we all go sit at the edge of the bluff and watch the night take hold. Daddy and I declined, but Louise and Tommy agreed to go for a little while. I got into bed, my window wide open so I could hear the inevitable music. After a while Lisa's voice started and it was, I realized, a Frank Sinatra song and that she was perhaps singing a paean to her own memories of faraway parents, wherever they might be. Or perhaps it was simply a clever cross-generational endorsement of getting high. "Come fly with me, come fly, come fly with me . . ." I wondered if somewhere in the house, mug of vodka in hand, Daddy was smiling. Or being sad. There were other tunes and then silence and then I heard Louise and Tommy come up the stairs and her muffled giggles. He was hushing her and her giggles were ragged and coughy. It sounded like he had a light hand on her mouth and the giggles were coming through his fingers.

"Easy, easy," he said.

"I am easy," she said, "you know that." Her voice was slurry. She'd been smoking or drinking, probably the former. My nerves went up. But the two of them seemed to settle down. I could hear him clucking to her softly and then there was quiet. I drifted off and was jolted awake some time later by Louise's loud voice. "Come on, come on, I want to do it in my parents' bedroom." She was in the hall. I looked out and Tommy was trying to pull her back toward her own bedroom.

"Shh, Louise, come on. Let's go back now."

"Come on, let's do it in there in that shrine." She'd managed to pull away from him and went into our parents' bedroom. I came out of my room and started toward where she was, but Tommy was between us and I couldn't see what she was doing. "Come on, don't be a chicken. . . ."

"No, Louise," he said. "Just calm down. You've had something. . . ."

But she was screaming now. "Come on, Tommy, come on, come on. . . . You don't want to die without fucking me in here."

He moved into the room, I could see, and tried to pin her down now on the bed. But she was wild and screaming and somehow managed to get away from him. She flew out of the room and by me, topless, tearing down the stairs. "If you won't fuck me, I'll go get someone who will." She was out of the house. Tommy came out and went by me. "Go get your dad," he said over his shoulder.

I ran down to Daddy's room and shook him hard. I could smell the vodka in the cup beside the bed. I shook him harder and he came awake.

"Daddy, Daddy, Louise. We have to go. Come on."

I grabbed him by the hand and pulled and he was up. He had on boxer shorts and a T-shirt, but he didn't stop to get anything, just let me lead him. We went across the lawn where we heard voices and yelling. I couldn't hear whose; it was a tangle. Louise's still the loudest and craziest, then maybe Tommy's, then someone else's—male—and then a noise and then a scream, and then Lisa: "Oh my God, oh my God." We got there as Tommy stumbled back out of the tent clutching his face. Even in the dark, I could see blood or something dark coming through his hands. Louise was now sobbing. She was trying to put her arms around him, there where he sat on the ground, sobbing hysterically, her pale, plump breasts going up and down with the sobs. "Stop it, Louise," Daddy said, "stop it." And when she couldn't he turned around and slapped her, like all those years ago. "One of you go get a towel and a lot of ice. Clare, go get my pants and shoes and the car keys. And my wallet; it's on the dresser."

I took off and when I got back, Daddy had Tommy's head in his lap and was looking down at his face. Someone had a flashlight and I could see his right eye was almost out of the socket. Blood was everywhere. Louise was moaning now, but Lisa had taken her back inside the tent.

"You two lift him up and carry him to the car," Daddy said to Jann and Carl. "Keep him flat. Hold on a minute."

He leaned closer to Tommy's ear. "We're going to wrap a kind of ice bandage around your eye and then we'll drive to the closest fire station," he said. Someone had already rolled ice in a long thin towel and now Daddy tied it around Tommy's head. Tommy moaned and I could hear Louise stirring again, but Lisa talked her down from wherever she was and made her stay inside. We proceeded up the bluff to the car. Daddy had them lay Tommy in the backseat and made me get in next to him on the floor.

"Make sure that towel stays around his head," he said to me. Through the open window he said to Jann and Carl, "Stay with Louise till I get back. Don't let anything more happen." There seemed to be years' worth of anger in his voice.

We didn't talk on the way to the fire station. I knew it wasn't far. I kept one hand gently on the towel, at the side, and one on Tommy's folded hands. He moaned a little, but was mostly silent, too. At the station, Daddy jumped out and a fireman came out. I got out of the car and he delicately moved the bandage and then put it back. "I'm going to call an ambulance," he said. Daddy knelt down beside the open door next to Tommy's head and I heard him say things about it being okay and about him being so sorry. We heard the ambulance about ten minutes later. They lifted Tommy onto a stretcher and the paramedic in the back started ministering to Tommy even before they shut the door. The driver said they were taking him to St. John's, where both Louise and I had been born, and that we could follow them there. Go to the emergency entrance on Santa Monica, he said.

When we got there, Tommy was already in surgery, we were told, or about to be. Daddy was allowed to go through the swinging doors and talk to the nurse or doctor or maybe even see Tommy. I was told to wait outside in the waiting room. It was brightly lit and nearly empty. There was only one other man there, an old man, and a fish tank and a TV tuned to some station. Day after tomorrow, I remembered, was my fourteenth birthday.

A half hour later Daddy came out and sat down beside me. He had a paper cup of coffee and looked wrecked and sad. He said Tommy was in surgery and they weren't sure they could save the eye. Daddy didn't have to say anything: I knew what it meant. Tommy wouldn't be going to the war. I wanted to be happy about that. I tried, but it wouldn't work. Daddy and I were sitting, staring at the TV screen, neither of us really watching, when Tommy's parents came through the door. They were dressed as if for going out; he was in a coat and tie, she in a dress and sweater, lipstick. Daddy got up to greet them and I noticed, as if for the first time, the dirt and blood on his Penn State sweatshirt. We stood talking. Daddy introduced me and told them there had been some sort of fight—he wasn't there, didn't know what had happened; there had been some people camping with us, everybody friendly until this. I watched them listening, Tommy's parents, expressionless. Daddy said they were trying to save the eye, that he was fine otherwise. He tried to smile while saying that, but he couldn't manage. Daddy said he insisted on paying for all of this and anything that might follow, but Mr. Tanaka, Paul, said stiffly that that wouldn't be necessary and that we could go on home and they would wait for their son. Daddy said he would like to wait if they didn't mind, but Mr. Tanaka said, "Please, his mother and I would like to be alone."

We walked out into the brightly lit driveway in front of the emergency room. Daddy looked ashen in the white light, as if he were going to be sick. We didn't talk the whole way home and when we got there, Daddy asked me to go on up to bed. He would find Louise and make sure she was settled. I watched from my window as he walked out to the bluff and ducked into the bigger tent. He came out a moment later, Louise walking behind him, Elephant following. I'd noticed the puppy had become very attached to her. Carl came out of the tent and called the dog back. Louise didn't even turn her head. She just followed Daddy into the house. I don't know what was said, if anything. I don't know if Louise was done being high. I heard Daddy say something, but couldn't make it out and heard her come up and go into our bathroom and then go back to her own bedroom.

By noon the next day, when I got up, the bluff was scraped clean, tents and every trace of the occupants gone. I wandered the empty house, Louise and Daddy yet to appear. I wanted to call the hospital and find out about Tommy's eye, but figured nobody would talk to me and I'd have to wait for Daddy to be up and call. I half didn't want to know. I wondered if we'd see Tommy again, if he could just slip back and be with us like before but that didn't seem likely. I cleaned the kitchen and made some coffee. The silence was complete, reverberating from every room save the two where father and daughter lay sleeping.

He got up first at about two thirty. He got coffee and came outside where I was sitting with a book. I wasn't reading, just staring at the tidbit of a pool they'd managed to dig. Daddy looked awful, but not distracted, not that anymore. He told me to go get the vodka bottles and throw them all away, that there would be no more drinking, that there had been enough, and no more parties or overnight campers. I didn't know if he'd already called to check on Tommy and I didn't want to ask. We would all know everything soon enough.

Louise came down at four. She had been in the shower and was still slightly wet, hair a damp, uncombed tangle. She was in shorts and a T-shirt—not her usual bikini top. She sat down across from Daddy, tucking her legs up under her arms, folded up there. Nobody said anything. Finally Daddy said, without looking at either of us, "He won't see again out of that eye." Louise just crumpled more into a ball. She didn't cry, save a tiny yelp. I wondered if she felt even a twinge of relief about him obviously not going to Vietnam, not having to wait for him and fear for him and drive up there to see him off. That was all gone, the waiting—the letters and the longing and the frantic distracting behavior she would probably have engaged in. Had already engaged in.

"I want you to leave him alone, Louise," Daddy said.

Louise started to say something but couldn't.

And then he said one more thing, somewhat under his breath, as if he had to say it but almost didn't want her to hear it, but she did because she flinched slightly. "You're just like your mother," he said, as he got up and walked out on the bluff.

.19.

She didn't leave all at once, like mother. She drifted away and came back and drifted away and came back. She seemed to be trying out new selves. She moved in with Clarisse and her parents for a while. I would see her at school, a retro-teen in pleated skirt and Peter Pan collar blouse and makeup, hair curled, see the two of them with square-jawed fraternity boys in Clarisse's car. She was still going to school—at least then. When I saw her, she was nice, but she didn't look me in the eye. Daddy didn't much, either. And they didn't talk about what happened that night, but I never again saw her arm uncovered. Not once. Even after she came back after the Clarisse interlude, which lasted a couple of months, and took to lying out on the bluff again in the sun, letting me lie beside her, taking turns—the two of us—to oil each other's backs, I never saw that tattoo. She was now dressing in the reverse; instead of bikini top and shorts, it was now bikini bottom and a T-shirt. She was back to a scrubbed face and a ponytail, pronouncing Clarisse's parents to be "fascists." Like our mother, she was much more beautiful this way, clean-faced, unadorned, and now her beauty was flecked with a complicating sorrow that only deepened it. At least I thought so.

She stayed awhile and we had uncomplicated times, she and I, just lying there, not talking much. Dinners with Daddy were awful for the silence, me the little chatty go-between. How school was, how boring the new history teacher, what about the stew—noise to fill the space, until I felt stupid and shut up. He wasn't drinking still and I guess that was hard too. He was swilling Cokes; we had cases now in the garage. Finally we just took to eating dinner in front of the TV set, the three of us, often just the two of us, Louise taking hers upstairs. I kept up the homework, mine, but didn't bother anymore with Louise's. Somehow I knew she wouldn't be graduating, wouldn't be staying. She never said it, but every time we pulled out onto the highway—she had Clarisse's old learner car, a beat-up old Studebaker station wagon—I'd watch her eye the human tide, looking maybe for Jann and Carl or the pair of girls, Eva and the other one whose name I never did find out. Once I thought I saw Elephant and screamed out and Louise did a 180 on the coast highway, causing me to scream again. But when we pulled up, it wasn't him. It was just another small, scruffy white dog accompanied by a solo guy with long, dirty hair.

"Shit," Louise said.

"Maybe we should get our own dog," I said.

"Don't think so," she said. "We don't look after anything very well."

If she had been in touch with Tommy—or tried to be—I didn't know. I knew she wouldn't tell me since Daddy had told her to leave him alone. We had a new gardener, a Mexican whom Daddy had found, named José. It was weird looking out and seeing him mowing or clipping the bushes because it had always been Paul and Tommy and then just Tommy. Always. It was like looking out after Mother had gone, expecting to see her. I figured it would go away in time, the not seeing him—rather, the seeing him—as it had with Mother. She hadn't called again since Christmas, not so as I knew. Daddy never again said she wanted to visit and we didn't ask where she was or what she was doing. Louise and I seemed to be in accord about that. We didn't want to risk it again, seeing her. We never talked about her. Only once when Louise was looking in the mirror, she said, "Do you wonder what Mother looks like now?"

I said, "Sometimes."

"Maybe she's fat," Louise said. "I hope so."

We laughed. I loved it when Louise made me laugh because I spent so much time trying to make her laugh which, after Tommy, was usually so hard. Almost impossible.

Then one day she was gone again. She left me a note this time. "I'm fine. I'll call you and let you know where I am. Tell Daddy." That was it. She turned up at school a few days later—she rarely even bothered to go anymore—and asked me if I wanted to go "home" with her. I never ditched school. It was what I was holding on to, but I figured this might be my only chance to see where she was. We snaked up Topanga Canyon in the station wagon, steep gullies off to the right, past the big boulders that looked like prehistoric bones. If the coast highway was hippie highway, Topanga was their nesting ground. Louise, ever the sartorial chameleon, had gone a bit native. No more Clarisse-aping preppie wear, now she was in a long skirt and T-shirt and her hair was in braids. We passed a little market and she said she had to stop for some supplies. I'd never been in a market like that, small and homespun. There were huge vats of grains and rice. Louise scooped stuff into paper bags, then bought the biggest block of orange cheese I had ever seen.

"You can help me make dinner tonight," she said, "it's my turn."

"No, you have to take me home."

"Don't be a baby, Clare. Go call Daddy from the pay phone outside."

"No, Louise. I want to go home."

"Then you'll have to hitchhike," she said. "I have to go make dinner."

I was near tears, but angry, too. The market was dusty and smelled like one big vegetable, a little overripe, and the people who came and went were mostly scraggly, some vacant-eyed. They didn't look like Carl and Jann. They looked worse, dirtier and more absent. It made me nervous.

"Louise, can't you come home too?"

"I am home," she said, and only then did I realize that she was a little stoned on something. She'd had this sort of inward smile for a while and I thought it was because she had gotten me.

"I'm going," I said.

"Okay," she said.

"Louise," I said, but I saw that it was no use. I thought about trying to call Daddy and get him to come find us, but I didn't know where she lived and I knew she wasn't going to tell me now. I also wanted to know where she was staying. I didn't like not knowing. Just a little way from the market, past junky little stores, cheap dresses floating in the breeze, wind chimes dinging, we turned up a very steep driveway. Louise giggled.

"Hang on, sweetie pie," she said, making me realize—the sweetie pie—that she was getting more high, not less. Never once in all my life had she called me that.

We pulled under a pleated plastic awning that passed for a garage. There were two other old cars pulled off to the side. Three dogs came running, one big brown-and-black snarly one that made me stay in the car, not open the door, and two little ones. Louise simply hopped out and said, "Back off, Bone, and let my sweetie pie sister out."

A tall man came out. He was pale and paunchy and older—already had some gray in his long, curly black hair—and dressed all in white, gauzy pants and shirt. "Curt, this is my sister Clare-a," Louise said, hitting the "a." She giggled again. "Come get these, will you," she said gesturing at the groceries.

He nodded at me but had eyes clearly only for her. I saw her smile, not at him but about him. That's what she needed: She needed new eyes on her, our mother's malady, the malady of the beautiful. That was the salve: the new eyes. I knew that now. I think I had known it a long time. The man didn't seem to be stoned, just a little lovesick, which made me sick. I wanted to say, "Hey, did you see her tattoo? She's not yours, creep." But there was nothing to do now. I thought about leaving again, scurrying back down to the highway and doing my own hitchhiking home. But I wanted to make sure she was all right. Always that.

The house, shack really, was dark and had mattresses on the floor, no furniture except a round table and some chairs. "Where are the others?" Louise said.

"Out back," he said.

"Clare is a great cook," she said dreamily. "That's why I went and got her."

That hurt my feelings, but I didn't say anything. I stood frozen, watching this Curt move around and toward her, play with her braids, lifting them up and twirling her around with them, smelling the sweat of his underarms as he did it. That, and the always acridly sweet smell of incense tangled up with it and the same market-smell in here, from the kitchen, which I only peeked into and saw dishes everywhere, of overripe, slightly rotted food, which made me feel like I was going to be sick. I backed out into the driveway. They didn't even notice. I sat, listening to them in there, no doubt on one of those mattresses now. I didn't move. I made myself listen because, sitting there on a boulder in the sun, listening to her in there with a stranger, my sister having sex with a stranger, I was finally beginning to be able to hate her some, which I thought was going to be useful. But just as quickly I felt protective again, this older man preying on her. I sat them out—the sibling sighs and moans, the slicky sounds—until I couldn't stand it any longer. As I started down the driveway, Bone started up it, snarling again as he cantered up closer to me. I ran back through the front door, sort of backward, so I didn't have to see Louise and the man, and slammed it.

"What?" the man, Curt, said.

"I was going down the driveway and that dog came after me." I still had my back to them.

"Oh, he won't hurt you," he said.

Louise was up now, standing beside me, mussed and languorous, wrapped in the thin Indian bedspread. "Were you running away, Clarie? Don't do that. Not before dinner. I need your help. It'll be fun."

I stayed. We went back down to the market so I could use the pay phone. I never lied, but this time I did. I told Daddy I was studying with a friend. I never did that, but he'd been pushing me to get some friends, bring them around, so he left me alone. I told him I might be late. I didn't like lying. Not then. Not to him.

We bought other food. I told Louise I didn't know what to do with grains, so we got some macaroni and green peppers and onions. She promised she'd help clean up the kitchen and when we got back, we did that. She seemed more animated than she had been. She scraped plates into the trash bin and washed them and helped me chop the onions and green peppers. Curt had put some guitar music on and lit some candles. But he left us alone. I heard other people, but they didn't come into the kitchen, either, so it was just the two of us working side by side. Outside the window the afternoon sun was edging up off the steep canyonside. Louise had been humming with the music, but she had stopped and when she turned toward me, the last sun on her face, there were tears running down her cheeks.

"Come home with me Louise," I said.

"I can't," she said. "I can't stand it there without him. Anyway, Daddy hates me."

"He does not," I said.

"Have you seen the way he looks at me?"

"He doesn't look at you," I said.

"My point exactly," she said, wiping her eyes on the back of her sleeve.

We had dinner: Curt and Louise and me and some very skinny boy with thick glasses who seemed very out of it, and two girls with long, dark braids like Louise's. They looked like members of some cult: the three women. Curt said I should stick around because this was the best meal they'd had. Pretty soon I'd have braids. I wanted to get Louise away so I could ask her to drive me home, but when I came back from using the bathroom, a dirty, moldy-smelling room off the kitchen, she and Curt were gone. Nobody said anything. I heard noises from another room, but didn't want to listen this time, so I got up and started clearing the dishes. The boy helped without saying a word. Finally he said, "Hey, you want a brownie?"

He set a plate down in the middle of the table. The braided girls came back and started to eat them. I ate about half of one, but it tasted bitter, so I stopped. I didn't know where to put myself, the bedroom noises getting louder, everybody else just silent, so I went outside. The moon was huge. The air had swirls of cold and warm in it. It smelled like earth up here, not the ocean. I didn't know where the dogs were, so I tried to be very still. When Bone came around the corner, his face suddenly seemed huge, huger than before, fangs everywhere. I screamed, but didn't move. Then the other dogs came, too, the little ones, but they were also big now; they looked like dogs made out of multicolored balloons, when they twist and pinch them. Yellow and red and blue dogs. I heard Louise far away in the house, angry Louise. "Who the hell put these out?" she said or something like that. She was suddenly beside me, talking quietly but I didn't know what she was saying. I was watching her mouth and it was all wet inside.

"Louise," I screamed, "why don't you dry your mouth?"

Bone moved and I crouched down around Louise's ankles. "No, no, make him go away," I said. The moon was huge when I looked up again and crying, big splashes of water coming out of its eyes. I was getting wet. I curled up in a ball, but I was getting wetter and wetter. The man on the ice rink dropped me and I shattered into a million pieces, like mirrors, and the moon was in all of them, only now laughing, laughing moons in all the pieces of me. I felt Louise's hands on me. She was kneeling. She had my face in her hand. She was saying, "Look at me, look at me, Clare. You've taken something. It was in the brownies. You'll be fine. I'll stay with you. We'll stay here for a while."

A cold, icy panic went through my fingers, just the fingers, freezing. They were huge when I looked at them. "Cold," I said, "freezing, cold fingers."

Louise dragged me inside. I felt being dragged because my legs were wobbly. Somebody was licking my face, little balloon dogs, though they were now made of peppermint candies, all gluey together. Lick, lick, lick—everybody licking. "Don't," I screamed. "No licking." I heard someone laugh. It was the big, gauzy man. He seemed to be walking toward me, starting to crouch, big hairy arms coming out of his shirt, and I screamed again. "No."

"Leave her alone," someone said. Louise was here. That was Louise. We were in a dark room, just the two of us. We were holding hands. Louise was singing to me, the song about the moon. I see the moon, the moon sees me . . . over and over. I tried to say, "I'm going to be sick," but I couldn't get it out ahead of the vomit. I threw up over and over, there in the darkness. Pitty-pat, pitty-pat on my back went Louise, singing about the moon.

"You're all right, you're all right," she said. "You didn't get much. You're all right. You'll be fine."

I threw up again. "It won't stop," I said.

"It will. I'm here. I'll take you home in a little while. You'll see. It'll stop."

There was a knock at the door. I saw a huge hand coming in with a cup, a Disneyland cup where that man was, Mommy's man. We were all in the cup, laughing. Daddy and Weezie and Mommy and the man and me. Spinning around and around and around and it wouldn't stop and I wanted to say again, "I'm going to be sick," and then I was, or it sounded like I was. This awful smell came in. I had messed my pants. I was a child and Mrs. Palmer was there and I'd messed them. I was embarrassed and tried to curl up and the smell got bigger. I heard Louise again, "Take a deep breath Clare. See if you can have a sip of this."

She put a cup up to my lips and it smelled minty. I stuck my tongue in it. Peppermint dogs. It was the melted dogs they were making me drink. I shoved her hand away and hot liquid spilled on us both. We cried out so pretty together, *wanh, wanh, wanh,* and two nurses with long braids came in. They went away and came back with cold cloths and put them on us, where it was so hot on our skin. Someone was taking my clothes off. I folded my hands over my breasts. No peeky, no peeky, but someone was washing me with the cloth, a warmer one, the braided nurses, and then putting something over my head and I was pretty again and the bad smell had gone, but my hand hurt where the liquid had been. It was so hot. One of the nurses came back and put another cloth around my hand. For a minute things stopped in my head; everything went toward the cold cloth, the dogs and the moon sliding down out of my head onto the cloth. I wanted to sleep so my head would stop and my hand would stop. "Sleep," I said.

"Not here," Louise said. "I'll take you home in just a little while. You're coming down," she said. "You'll be okay."

I don't know how long we were in there. By the time we were in the car going down the steep driveway and then curving down through the canyon, I was more or less normal. But I felt sick and shivery. There was no heat in Louise's car and I only had on my thin sweater that I'd worn to school. I was back in my own clothes. They smelled awful. The moon was the moon at least, nothing else. We didn't talk on the way home. Louise did reach out at one point and pat my hand. When we got to our gate, she pulled up. I could see she had no intention of coming in. I got out and got my books from the back. I opened the gate and then turned back to latch it and she was still there behind the wheel, looking at me.

"Be sure to put some ice on your hand," she said. And then she drove off.

A week later, she came back. She'd cut her braids off, right at the ear, snipping them like branches, she said. Snip, snip. She now had a chewed head of short, dark hair and circles under her eyes and was a tiny bit plump for the first time in her life. But she was right: Daddy didn't look at her. If he was worried, if he stole a glance, if he was seeing her without really looking, he didn't let on. It was late. We both knew it. We all knew it, somehow. But I couldn't help myself. When she was in the room next to mine, sleeping, I liked it. She turned seventeen—with us, maybe an intentional nod to old times, earlier birthdays. I bought her a book of poetry, a small paperback of Yeats, and made a coconut cake, her favorite. We had dinner, the three of us, in the dining room, at one end of the long, cherry table. Louise had set it herself, polished the silver. She came down that night in one of Mother's left-behind dresses, a long-out-of-date pink sheath that came to her midcalf. She had washed her hair and pushed it off her face and put mascara on, gobs of it. She looked ghoulish and radiant, a seventeen-year-old hippie-matron with a heart-shaped tattoo on her upper arm. There it was again, though none of us made reference to it. We toasted. We tried to sing "Happy Birthday," Daddy and I, and when we were too faint, Louise herself joined in at high decibel. "Happy birthday to me, happy birthday to me . . ." Louder and louder. I looked to see if she was high on something, but she didn't seem to be. The song, in that big, never-used room, sounded like a dirge.

She was gone the next day. I got up and felt the absence in the next room. I knocked and went in and indeed, stuff was scattered everywhere. The pink dress was on the floor along with bunches of other clothes. I went downstairs and out the door to make sure the car was gone, but it wasn't. It was sitting there in the damp morning, windshields all fogged up. There was a white envelope tucked under a windshield, the "Clare" running a little in the heavy morning dew.

"Thought you might like this, the car, I mean. I won't need it. PS: Tell Daddy. PPS: I'm really sorry about the other night."

I didn't rush to wake Daddy and tell him. There was nothing he could do or would do. I knew that. There was no way to hold her anymore. I cleaned the birthday dishes and made coffee and went back upstairs to do my homework. Daddy and I had made plans to drive in and look at UCLA because my high school English teacher said I could take classes there while I was still in high school. It was around eleven then, that day, when we drove out the driveway and started down the highway toward the city. I figured Louise to be long gone by now, but suddenly there she was by the side of the road in her long skirt with her thumb stuck out and I tried to get Daddy to stop, begged him to, even though I knew it wouldn't make any difference if he did. But he didn't. He kept on driving and she got smaller and smaller through the window until her sign looked like a little postage stamp and then, with a curve of the highway, she was gone. That night I moved down and took the other small back bedroom next to the one Daddy had been sleeping in.

·2,O·

I graduated early from high school and by age sixteen I was at UCLA as a freshman. I drove in every day in Louise's station wagon. Daddy had had it fixed up and painted for me. It never occurred to me to live in a dorm or an apartment. I would stop at the market on the way home and get stuff for dinner, which we would eat in front of the TV. If I had had friends they might have found it weird but I didn't, really. I was young and my classes were large and I dressed for anonymity, jeans and sweaters. I sat in the middle, always on the left, taking, as I always had, copious notes in my clean hand. I walked between classes by myself, watching the other students. There were plenty of post-hippies, hair still long, clothes still costumey, but there were also preppy-looking kids and sorority girls who reminded me of Clarisse, canopy-bed girls who had been dreaming all their lives of coming to this campus and being cheerleaders and getting married, girls who had missed the guts of the sixties, slept through it, bounced through it unscathed and untouched, putting rollers in their hair and Clearasil on their faces. I wondered sometimes: What if it had all been different, if Mother had stayed? Would Louise and I have looked like this, all pretty and preserved and pettable?

Driving home, I couldn't help but scan the dwindling parade on the Coast Highway to see if she was out there. The human river had thinned, so it was easy to do. I still sometimes thought I saw Jann or Carl. But it was never them. I wondered if they were done roaming and had settled somewhere, the math whizzes, and become teachers and fathers and responsible citizens. Where was everybody? Where had they all gone? I turned sometimes, because I couldn't help it, up Topanga, taking the curves as we had that day and night. It could be foggy on the coast and you'd turn and within half a mile you'd be winding up into sunshine. In the winter it was beautiful, especially on a sunny day after it had rained and the craggy stone sides of the canyon were slick and clean. I sometimes ate at a sort of Zenlike place with a creek flowing through it. Brown rice and steamed vegetables and mint tea. I never, though, drove up to that house. I didn't want to know if anyone was still around. What if she were actually still there with that aging Svengali? What if the drugs had gotten harder and she was meager and wrecked-looking, giving lie to Daddy's theory that she was a survivor? I was also scared, wondering if my mind would be triggered back to the night of the crying moon. I saw it sometimes, that moon, not in a real flashback, but in my mind's eye, and it was still eerie. I had never touched drugs since then, not even marijuana when it was passed around at the very occasional school get-together I was invited and went to. It was the professors who liked me, not the boys. I started to know that at around seventeen, watching them watch me in one-on-one conferences. I was good on paper, logical and argumentative, but in person slight, blond, a little tense, which I began to understand read as sexy, somehow, as if I were coiled for pleasure—either or both, argument and pleasure. They liked that, to tussle about Cather (perfect, I said, the essence of the heartland) or Faulkner (sometimes self-consciously overwrought, I said) as foreplay. It didn't matter who I first slept with. I didn't for a long time, just because I didn't. I was pawed and petted. Then I decided, a week after my seventeenth birthday, in the office of a bespectacled, short, curly-headed Marxist-leaning political theorist with whom I had had a lively set-to about Hannah Arendt, to have sex. I checked his hand for a ring, his office for family photos. He locked his door, got a blanket out of his cupboard, causing me to raise an eyebrow.

"I work late," he said. "It gets cold in here."

"Sure," I said.

I didn't say anything about being a virgin. If there was to be pain or blood, I would just say I had my period. There was a bit of both, and only buried back there a body-thought of what pleasure might be had down the road from all of this. He was thick-trunked and I remember liking that, even then, the solidity, the stockiness, and was, at the same time, quite attuned and agile. He slipped down my body as if to engage in oral sex—which I had not had and did not want—and I made some excuse and pulled his head back up toward me. It seemed too intimate for this beginning.

"You sure?" he said.

"Yes," I said.

He wore, after, a kind of daffy postcoital smile and asked if he could see me again.

I said I didn't know, that maybe it wasn't the smartest thing as he was my professor. Oh, he said, he would never let the one interfere with the other. That made even me smile.

"Sure," I said.

We dressed as his smile ebbed. "You're a tough one," he said, the first time that was said to me.

I crossed campus to my car in a brisk wind, the hair and giggles of the coeds being buffeted about in the air. I felt neither happy nor unhappy. Mostly I felt disembodied, as if someone else had lain beneath that heavy-torsoed, curly-headed assistant professor, with his goofy, pleased smile. He had been nice, tender. I had not been. Yet he wanted to see me again. I wondered why, what it was supposed to feel like: liking someone. Forget loving. That I had seen enough of, the wreckage of it, and yet, sitting in my car, hands on the wheel, getting ready to make the drive home, I had a pang, sharp as hunger, for my sister. Weezie, I'm here, I made it across the Maginot Line. I'm no longer a virgin. I had nobody else to tell, no girlfriends, not one. I had never needed any.

I did see him again, my Marxist, as I came to call him, after an interlude of a couple of other men who had no idea where to put their hands or mouths, men with whom I felt awkward and embarrassed. I had seen him, of course, the rest of the quarter, a small figure behind a lectern way down on the stage of a drafty, auditorium-like classroom, with its tiers of hard wooden seats. (He was very popular, which is maybe why I chose him; I don't know. I think there was some of that, of looking around at all the other young women there and feeling a crotch-twinge of smugness.) Whether he saw me I don't know, but when, one spring afternoon months after our first coupling, I knocked on his door during office hours, he didn't seem to be surprised. He cocked an eyebrow when he saw my face, got out his blanket and, with his same agility, made love to me. He taught me things: about nipples and teeth, about pauses. I guess I liked him. I didn't even know. He took to bringing flowers, little white and yellow bunches, and sticking them in his coffee cup, clandestine bottles of wine and real wine glasses. Was I being wooed? I had no reciprocal vocabulary for it, for sweetness. One day, he said, "I can't see you anymore."

I laughed. It sounded brittle.

"Found someone else, eh?"

"No," he said. "This isn't fun anymore."

"It isn't?" I said.

"No," he said, turning away to zip up his pants and tuck in his shirt. "There's something missing."

"In me."

"I didn't say that."

"But that's what you meant."

That, too, I would hear again. There is something missing in you. I was sad somewhere, sort of, if only because I'd lost a destination and I didn't have many. School, home, home, school with a detour to a library or a market. I had become used to our sessions, our sex, the somewhat transgressive nature of it—office hours and all, when somebody could and sometimes did, knock on the door, "Professor Simon, are you there?" which served to intensify and quicken things, his hand on my mouth or mine on his to mute the grunts or groans. The sex was good, elastic, thorough. I knew that, even though I hadn't had much at that point. I wondered if he thought I would come back at him, turn supplicative, contrite, needy, knocking on his door, "Professor Simon, are you there?" But I never did. I never would have.

I stopped dating—that's hardly what you could call what we had done, my Marxist and I—for a while and reverted to my daughterly role. Not that I had ever really given it up. I was careful. I don't think Daddy even knew I had started to have sex. I don't think I showed signs. He kept encouraging me to go out, get out of the house.

"Sweetheart, why don't you date some? They must ask."

"No, Pop, too much trouble."

Daddy started to write a soap opera. It was what was left to him. The world, as he had been able to write it, the world he had wanted to live in, was long gone: Rock Hudson and Doris Day with their chipper conjugal badinage. Obliterated, to say the least. He had hung on, doing TV segments and now this: "The Doctors." He said he didn't care, really, did not harbor feelings of being the great American writer. He said, "I was a family man." And when he said that, there was a kind of mirthless little laugh. "Now it's just us, kiddo."

I helped him sometimes when I got home from school. We had all these medical books and dreamed up all these diabolical diseases for the hapless patients from beriberi to Munchausen by proxy. We watched the other soaps to pick up their language, the primary color emotions, and we got good at it. Daddy would sit at his typewriter and I would wander around his study and we would play the parts.

"It hurts here," I would say, palm spread on my lower abdomen.

"Yes, Miss Cody, I know."

"What is it?" I'd say, eyes wide, terror flitting through them. "What is it?"

"Miss Cody, just be calm. We might still be able to save that ovary."

"What do you mean, save my ovary? Does this mean . . ."

"Now, Miss Cody . . ."

"I'll never be able to have a baby." *Sob sob*.

It was fun, the switch from Marx and Faulkner to soap pap. "Don't get too good at this, sweetheart," Daddy said. "It'll ruin you."

"Ruin me for what?" I said.

"You're going to be a writer, aren't you?" he said. "I always kind of figured that."

"They're trying to talk me into graduate school."

"Not a bad idea. You can teach and write."

"I don't know."

"Go ahead, Clare. You don't have to stay here with your old dad."

"Why don't you date?" I said. "There are plenty of panting divorcées out there."

"Too much trouble," he said. We laughed.

He was lying to me. He was seeing someone. Acute as I am, I didn't pick it up for a while, mostly because he was there in the mornings and the evenings. He was slipping out midday. I was sick with the flu for a stretch, bed-bound. I heard him in the study talking on the phone. I knew it was a woman. Daddy was old-school still,

Daddy with his graying hair and slight paunch. He went courtly, so-licitous. Would you like to? Shall I pick you up? In my fevered state, I was amused and, as the days went on, and he kept slipping away—what? for nooners?—intrigued enough to follow him one beautiful Thursday, the ocean, as I drove stealthily behind him, one big mir-ror of sun, Catalina clearly visible, a few fleeting white clouds. Where did a courtly, aging father go for an assignation—to a good hotel, the Bel-Air, the Beverly Wilshire, or one of those sleazy mo-tels on Lincoln with water beds and X-rated videos? Did I misjudge him as he did me? He didn't exactly think, I don't think, that I was giving office hour blow jobs to my professors. We lived now in four rooms, he and I: our bedrooms, his study, the kitchen, the rest of the house uninhabited, unused, just occasionally dusted or vacuumed by the latest cleaning woman. And yet, I thought, smiling to myself, as I followed him, what did we know? He turned off the Coast High-way at Temescal Canyon and drove to a delicatessen in the little vil-lage of the Palisades. I watched him go in and come out with a paper bag. Ah—provisions. Did he have champagne in there along with the pastrami? He got back in his car and drove down a nearby resi-dential street that dead-ended in a bluff overlooking the ocean. There was no park, no real place to sit, just a dusty oceanside spit of land with big eucalyptus trees. No hotel or motel in sight. I pulled over and parked a fair distance away, but close enough to see him. He was wearing a tan Windbreaker and navy blue sneakers, my buoyantly smitten dad, and carried from the car a blanket and the sack of groceries. Someone was coming. He was laying out the stuff and, yes, there was a split of champagne and a bouquet, the small, sweet kind favored by the Marxist. I realized with a jolt: She could be my age. That was the going deal now. I caught a car in the rearview mirror, a woman's head, and slipped even farther down in the seat, so I didn't get a look as the car went past. Daddy was up, smiling, walking toward the now parked car, out of which stepped a dark-

haired woman, slightly plump, taking his proffered hand. I still
hadn't seen her face, but her body said not a girl. They sat and he
popped the cork and I heard a laugh, her laugh, and it went through
me like a bullet through the heart. Mother. A picnic with Mother. My
mother. All these years later. So this was it, his secret life, picnics
with his ex-wife. I never said anything to him, not that afternoon
when he peeked in the bedroom and checked on me, there tucked
back under the covers, or later. I played dumb. I made him keep her
as his secret. And after a while his outings tapered off—I knew because I was spending more time at home now that my classwork was
mostly done.

I did apply to grad school, but only to UCLA, and got in. I was
twenty, earmarked as an up-and-comer in the English department. It was easy for me. I learned the critical lingo, learned to use
words like paradigm and contextualize, learned to make simple
thoughts fancy. I picked out a new professor here or there, none in
my field, though. That was too close now. An anthropologist here, a
philosopher there. You could still do that, then; they could do it,
sleep with a student without thought of retribution or charges of ha-
rassment. I had my rules: I never touched a married man, not then,
not knowingly. I had my suspicions, about one in particular. He said
he was separated, which skated up to the line. I didn't believe him.
There were pictures on his desk: a pretty young wife and small son. I
only did it once. I saw my Marxist occasionally, walking with a co-
terie of groupies (not the preppies, certainly), and thought I saw,
one sparkly spring day, the sun glint off a shiny wedding band on his
left hand. I was close enough to see, but he was talking and gesticu-
lating to his acolytes so he didn't see me. Was he going to be faith-
ful? Did he have any intention of it? Would he have been to me? Was
anybody?

I started to hone my attractiveness, such as it was. I started to wear good clothes—Daddy's regular soap gig was making us flusher than we had been in a while and the house was paid off—fitted leather jackets, good pants, started to put the first blond streaks in my hair, since it had darkened with age, started to carry myself as the pretty one now that the others, the Layton beauties, were gone. I worked at my sexual proficiency as at my intellectual proficiency. I am good at this. This will serve me in good stead. It never occurred to me to move away, to move into town, to start a different kind of life, even though, from time to time, Daddy encouraged me—not full-heartedly, I ever thought—to do so.

He had his first heart attack. They called me at school from St. John's. They were reassuring, but it was serious. He was about to undergo bypass surgery. I raced to him, walking through that emergency waiting room with its fish tank and chairs, where I had sat that night when we followed Tommy here. He was already in surgery, so back I went to sit there with my cup of coffee. Who to call? His agent, Lawrence. He was all slick solicitude. Anything you need, we're here. Tell him to cool it, not to worry. I didn't actually tell Lawrence the whole truth, the surgery part. I said a mild heart attack, back to work in a week. Don't tell the soap people. I figured I could write the scripts until he was up again. There was no one else I could think to call. I walked around the streets waiting for Daddy to wake up. He would be fine, they said when I returned, had to cool it, exercise more, eat better.

"Shit," I said to him, sitting beside his hospital bed, "guess we're finally going to have to go vegetarian."

He smiled, but it was thin. "You know," he said, "my will is all in place. It's in the upper drawer of the filing cabinet in the closet. Take a look if you want."

"No need," I said. "We'll just mainline broccoli from now on."

"Clare, you don't always have to be so brave, you know," he said, and drifted off.

I got a raft of new cholesterol-conscious cookbooks and new medical books. We'd plowed through so many maladies already. I was now planting more sexually transmitted diseases in the scripts. We even managed to tease in a homoerotic subplot, ahead of the curve. Daddy would lie on his couch while I did the typing. Then he got a serious kidney infection and I had to measure the outgo in that little plastic toilet insert. It didn't bother me; it bothered him. It stretched on. He got pale and anemic. We got to go back to beef.

"At least there's that," he said with a weak laugh.

We had almost no visitors. Lawrence came, a groomed, fit young man in full suit and tie. To Malibu. It was the eighties. People were done up again, especially, it seemed to me, the young men, even when they came out to the beach. They'd gone preeny. Made one long for old debauched Uncle Marty with his button-down short-sleeved shirts, undone to reveal a furry gut. This new crop was tight. Daddy caught my eye when Lawrence came in, bearing some scripts, a box of chocolates. I thought: Should I try to seduce him just for the fun of it? But he didn't really even look at me. He was in and out in a heartbeat, after quaffing his bubbly water.

I finally decided to take a sabbatical from school, just an interlude, I figured, but in truth, the academic game was boring me. The language required to talk about a piece of literature was ludicrously arcane and, I thought, camouflaging its destructive envy in all that dense academese. I also knew I couldn't write soap scripts forever. I started trying to write short stories, but they felt forced. I tried a few opinion pieces, descriptive ones, about living on the coast, about the beauty of it, our bluff, and got them published in the newspaper. I did more. I started to do some interviews—with politicians, old hippies, schoolteachers. No actors, no Hollywood types: That was my one rule. I branched into magazine writing, leaving Daddy to his scripts. Within about six months, he got fired. The scripts weren't hip enough, they said.

"That's what happens," he said, "when you leave me to my own devices." But he wasn't upset. In fact, he felt quite free. There was enough money, he said. He'd been careful and there was the house "for you girls." I let that go: you girls. But he had started to scatter the photographs around where I could see them: pictures of Louise and Timmy, then of their baby, Luke. I glanced without looking, without really registering the faces—I knew it was she, the happy survivor with husband and kid—and Daddy didn't force them on me. He went to visit them. They were still in California, down south somewhere. He left the house in his convertible, top down, wearing that Windbreaker and his blue sneakers. I knew that's where he was going.

"Any message?" he said.

"Yeah," I said. "Tell her thanks for the car."

. 2 1 .

A widow finally got him, a small, pecan-brown, Republican Palm Springs widow in white Bermuda shorts. Her name was Mignon, but there wasn't anything French about her. She was pure desert widow. I never saw her in anything but those shorts, her arms and thighs tan and crinkly from the endless sunshine, a slight smear of blue eye shadow across the lids and frosted pink lipstick on her mouth. No face work. Not a stitch. That I liked. Actually I liked her okay. She was just so unexpected. Daddy had taken up golf and driven with an old friend down to the desert to watch a big tournament and five days later this Mignon brought him back in her big RV. They wheeled down the driveway, the first vehicle of its kind to turn down onto our bluff, shaking the windows of the house as it came, so that I was actually already outside when they stepped out, both in shorts. She said "gosh" right off as in "Gosh, it's nice to meet you. Your daddy sure does brag about you."

"Oh, I do not," he said and I could see that they already, in the forty-eight hours they'd known each other, had their banter, their shtick. I figured she was going to have him for a while.

That night they slept out in her big mobile home. I looked out and saw lights in it and heard Daddy slip out of his next-door bedroom and pad out. I went upstairs and sat on my old bed. I hadn't been in the room for years. I didn't turn on any lights. I just lay down. From up here, the house felt big and underused and sad for it. We had not, in forever, filled it with life, not since our earlier Hollywood and hippie infestations. Down in our warren of rooms it didn't seem so empty. But here on the bed, Daddy sleeping out in the driveway in an RV, it felt like an abandoned ship with me now as the lone sailor. I wondered if Daddy would now start touring around the countryside with his widow, pulling into this RV lot or that, the two of them sipping their drinks and grilling their hamburgers on their little portable hibachi among a compatible crowd of other itinerant geriatrics. I had a flash of longing for Louise because only she would have known how hard to laugh with me. Instead, lying there in my childhood bedroom, I found myself near tears.

They toured and I stayed. Their big vehicle lumbered down the driveway once or twice a month. They rattled into the house full of good cheer, bringing wine from the wineries they'd visited and handcrafted table mats and homemade jellies. Daddy almost caught my eye, never quite. He was happy and he was embarrassed for me to see that. We sat at night outside their "home" on folding chairs. They'd gotten me one and presented it with great humor and ceremony. And indeed we barbecued, not on our big old Weber but on their smaller model, watching the stars come out, listening, if we could hear them, to the waves.

"Wouldn't you guys be more comfortable in the house?" I said. "I could make you up a room."

"No," Mignon said, winking at my dad in the lantern light. "We like to do the old bouncy bouncy in our trailer, don't we, Phil?"

I left them and went inside for the night. Restless when they were out there, I paced and then often ended up on the sofa in Daddy's study, a book across my chest, a half-empty glass of wine, and he would find me in the morning, as I, back when, used to find him. I was almost thirty.

I t was quick and painless, happened in the night, she said, when she called from Palm Springs the next winter.

"We were in there, you know, doing . . ."

"Spare me the details, Mignon," I said, gently, I hoped.

She was crying. Daddy's body was at the mortuary in Cathedral City. She gave me the phone number and asked me if I wanted her to do anything. Her son was already with her. No, I said, I would drive down and take care of things. I would call her when I got there. We would have one last interaction and that would be that. I would not see her again. There would be no reason. I was fond enough of her as, I think, she was of me, but we would not keep track of each other, maybe a call on the first anniversary of his death, but that would be it. When I hung up I went and got his will. It was what I expected, everything divided in half between Louise and me. There were also notes hand-addressed to each of us and one to "My Grandson Luke." And one to Tommy Tanaka, that name out of the past. Good old Daddy. Maybe there was a check in it. I got a bottle of vodka, a cup, and took my note out to the edge of the bluff. I sat for a long time without reading it, laughing a little at myself because I didn't even like vodka. Daddy hadn't had much of it in later years, either. He and Mignon drank beer and Margaritas—made from the mix. I used to hear their blender whirring at five thirty promptly, rain or shine, summer or winter, when the RV was in the driveway. Between the sun and the alcohol I started to feel a little queasy and decided I'd hold the note and read it later. I had a lot to get through. I called Daddy's lawyer, a golfing partner of his, Mark Miller, and told him what had happened. He said he had a copy of the will and could send somebody, if I wanted, to pick up the other notes and make sure they got delivered. I asked him to call Lawrence the Stiff so they could, together, take care of the obituary. I would phone in a time and place for a memorial service. It was all so easy. There was nobody to notify, nobody to fight with, nobody to tangle with over any arrangements.

I made a thermos of coffee, packed an overnight bag, and locked up the house, something I never usually did. I'd never been scared there alone, even when Daddy was off on his RV wanderings. There'd been all that awful Manson stuff and other ugly stories, but the house—even as isolated as it was, there on its own bluff— always seemed safe to me, strangely inviolable, from the outside, anyway. I took the old convertible; it seemed fitting. The traffic getting out of town was awful—it was already early afternoon—but I wasn't in a hurry. If I just kept driving I wouldn't get there. It wouldn't be over. Even with the top down I was impervious to the belching of the trucks, the thick, exhaust-filled air. Finally things eased up and I got off in the last light of day at the Palm Springs exit, a loop off toward the mountains. I hadn't been here for years. We had come as children, every Easter, and stayed with our parents at the then-chic Racquet Club, with its tennis courts and grapefruit trees and movie stars, Louise and I falling asleep, still smelling of chlorine, our inevitably sunburned noses frosted with Noxzema, listening to the live band in the bar. Now Daddy had ended up on the other edge of town in an RV park.

I drove down the main street. Long abandoned by the Hollywood crowd, the little desert city felt as it had the last time we were here, throwback department stores and bathing suit shops with Hawaiian-print shifts for women and shirts for men. And, yes, there it was, the men's shoe store that Daddy had loved and made us visit every time we came. Its window was always full of white shoes for the suave desert male—white bucks and white loafers and white slippers in every imaginable style—and there was a sign that said, "More White Shoes Inside." Daddy actually bought a pair of the loafers as a joke, but never wore them. I wondered if I'd find them when I went through his closet. I would have to do them all: all the closets.

I arrived at the mortuary just before it closed. I cut through the practiced commiserative phrases of the pudgy, soft-spoken young man behind the desk and said my father wanted to be cremated and no, I didn't want to see him and could they please send the ashes to me in Los Angeles and here was my address and here was my credit card. I was pretty speedy and he couldn't get another word in. He just kept writing on his little pad and as I stood to go, he said again, "Are you sure, about not seeing him?" I blinked hard. It caused me to sit back down, the realization right then that there I was, Daddy in the other room, still tantalizingly there. He pushed the Kleenex box toward me, which sobered me right up. "No," I said. "Not." I was back up and nearly out the door, he just behind me, when he said, "I'm sorry, but I have to ask you one last question. He's in shorts. Do you have a change of clothes for him?"

"He's being cremated," I said, turning to look at him.

"I know," he said, "but sometimes people like their loved ones to be in their better clothes."

"Dress 'em up before you burn 'em up," I said.

He turned away. "Shorts are fine," I said to his back. "It is the desert, after all."

I had promised Mignon I'd come by for one last Margarita. There she was in her white shorts on her folding chair, the two others open beside her, in front of the big old tan-and-white RV in slot number thirty-six, just as she'd said. The place was full, peak season and it was cocktail hour. I could smell steaks cooking and hear laughter. People were milling around.

"I'm afraid I've already had a couple," she said, standing to embrace me, and indeed she was a bit slurry. I'd never seen her this way and tried to hug back, rather, tried to let myself be hugged. It was good enough. I felt her relax and heard her choke up in my ear and then pull back and say what she'd said the first time I met her.

"Your dad was so proud of you."

"And you," I said, "made him happy."

"I did, didn't I?" she said, teary. "We had a good thing, Philly and me."

I knew I wasn't going to be able to take too much of this. I started to sit and she said, "No, no, that's your dad's chair."

I took the next one over, leaving a space between us, and she handed me a sugary Margarita, which I gulped down. I realized how tired I was and tried to refuse a refill, but Mignon insisted.

"Don't let me drink by myself," she said. "Not tonight."

We'd never been alone, the two of us, and we didn't really have much to say to each other. She wanted to talk about "Philly" but I kept steering the conversation elsewhere. It was getting chilly out, a winter desert night with lots of stars. The park had quieted; the steaks had been eaten. The TVs were on now, hundreds, thousands, millions of them, I imagined, flickering in RV parks like these all over the country, the aging roamers getting ready—those that still had the appetite and energy for it—to do the old bouncy bouncy.

I looked at Mignon, eye shadow and lipstick gone, little Chicklet teeth shining out of her deeply tanned face. Now what? Another widower?

"Mignon," I said, "are you fine for money? Daddy had some and I know . . ."

"Just fine. Got all my ducks in a row."

"Will you stay here?"

"I don't know," she said. "I have friends in Arizona. Philly— your dad—and I used to visit them. It'll be so sad to go alone."

She teared up again and blew her nose. I should have left. I knew it. Too much tequila and too much unsharable sadness. I wasn't very interested in hers and I didn't want her near mine. I was now on my third Margarita.

"You're still very attractive," I said. "You'll find someone else."

It didn't come out right and she bristled. "You can't just go replacing people, you know. I loved . . ."

"I'm too tired for this. I'm sorry." Now I did get up to go. "I'll call you and let you know about the memorial service."

I stood there for a minute. Should I pat her, lean to kiss her on the cheek? I was frozen and a little drunk. She got up and walked up the little metal steps to the vehicle. "You know," she said, "your sister's a lot nicer than you are." The door swung shut behind her.

"Screw you, Mignon," I said under my breath and then louder, "Screw you."

I sat in my car a little while, trying to sober up, even swilling some of the cold coffee left in the thermos. My heart was pounding. She'd landed a deft parting shot. Points to you, Mignon. I knew on some level—how could I not?—that they had been to visit. Daddy was a grandfather, twice over. I knew there was a second baby, a second son. His big baby face was among the casually spread-around photographs of Louise and family that I noticed but didn't really look at. Christmas, I bet, when they had left early, saying they had friends to visit, the RV probably packed with clandestine tricycles and GI Joe crap. Other times too. Thanksgiving and birthdays, Mignon the surrogate grandma of the reconstituted family, me at home, the fool on the hill, the fool on the bluff. Well, it was finally my time to go.

But just then, that night, I could not go back there. Also, I was a little woozy to drive. I didn't want to check into an anonymous motel room either. I thought about finding a bar and just continuing drinking. But then I'd be a mess. Or maybe a coffee shop, have a few cups, eat something, and then drive back. But the thought of food was faintly nauseating. Instead I drove through the quiet residential streets of low-slung houses, lamplight bouncing off the white pebbles on many of the flat roofs, and found myself—by instinct—back at the funeral home. I parked and turned off the car and stared at the darkened building. This is where I would sleep. This is where, for tonight, I belonged, in my car, Daddy in there in his shorts. His legs were cold, stone cold. I wanted to cover them. I wanted to have brought long pants for him, like the man suggested. I got it now: the thinking about his bare legs. How that hurt.

"I'm here," I said. "I didn't leave. They all left. But I didn't."

She got the lead in his obit. I should have seen it coming, given the Hollywood pecking order (stars, even minor ones like Mother, first, writers last), but I hadn't even really thought about it. Suddenly there it was, without warning, in the morning L.A. *Times.* "Philip Layton, 64, ex-husband of sixties TV actress Patricia Layton, died of a heart attack Thursday in Palm Springs," the newspaper notice read. It went on to list his writing credits, from Doris Day–Rock Hudson movies right up through *The Doctors* (the perfect arc of the scriptwriting life) and his survivors: two daughters, Clara Layton of Malibu and Louise Brown of San Diego, and two grandchildren. Memorial Service to be held at the Westwood Mortuary, Saturday, January 24. Flowers came to the house and I didn't even bother to read the cards. I wasn't going to have the energy to answer them; I would just say an all-purpose "thank you" at the memorial service, figuring I'd hit many, if not most, of the senders. His study, where I was now living, sleeping, eating, everything, became oppressively sweet-smelling so I finally just moved all the floral arrangements outside. I had already started to do the packing, already listed the house with a local real estate broker. On the weekends, strangers came through, mumbling about this or that shortcoming, about it being a tear-down. The agent, a tough-looking middle-aged woman with a fairly new face-lift, had warned me of this.

"You might not want to be here for these open houses," she said. "People can be fairly brutal."

"It doesn't bother me," I said.

I packed methodically, one room at a time. Some stuff to storage—the better furniture, their original wedding china and silver (maybe Louise would want it; I would let Mark know where it was and tell him to tell her it was all hers)—a lot to the Salvation Army and Goodwill. I kept a few of Mother's dresses she'd left behind, including the pink one Louise had worn on her seventeenth birthday, and hung them in mothballs in plastic bags, and earmarked those for storage, as well. Who knew: She might yet have a daughter. I might. I searched high and low for the white shoes and finally found them at the very back of Mother's closet in a plastic bag, just as clean and brand new as the day they were bought. Day after warm winter day I worked, by myself, letting exhaustion tame the emotion, and then at sunset I would go sit on the bluff, wrapped in the old car blanket, taking a drink with me. Scotch, gin, vodka. I was just working through the bottles in the house and it all had the same effect, warming my insides and helping, as another night came, to still the tender-rancorous churn of memory—working in reverse sometimes if I miscalculated or got careless and had a little too much. Mostly I was disciplined, just filling boxes, making lists, calling people. My favorite dinner was just a hunk of cheese melted in a frying pan, eaten with a fork. I worked some nights, very late, sorting books and records. I actually took some of those for me, along with the Barbie with her print-emblazoned butt and some of Daddy's scripts, including a few of *The Doctors* we had written in tandem, laughing so hard sometimes (we did have fun, didn't we, Pop?) we couldn't continue. I marked those cartons with my name.

There were only a couple and I was going to leave them with Mark. He said he'd send them to me when I got settled somewhere. On a whim I went and got out that pink dress and stuck it in one of my cartons, on top of the white shoes.

The memorial service was at a small, country-feeling cemetery (a favorite among the Hollywood crowd) tucked in the heart of Westwood behind some movie theaters. It fell on an unusual gray day. We'd had nothing but winter-warmth and then this: a dark, drizzly day. The small, paneled chapel filled up about three-quarters, faces I recognized—hands to shake, cheeks to kiss, teary eyes to look into—and faces I didn't. Maybe some strangers who were just visiting Marilyn Monroe's tomb, over in one of the marble walls, and decided to wander in and see if another star was being sent on his or her way. No, sorry to disappoint. Just Daddy, in his urn up there beside the pulpit, a silly red-and-white horse-wreath of carnations around him. I spoke, as briefly as I thought I could get away with, knowing that the crowd wanted my tears, just as the gladiator crowds wanted blood. I bit down hard on my words, a spare string of them. A tender man, a good man, a man who loved words and his—easy Clare, easy—family. Over and out without a quaver and with just the right amount of laughs, now de rigueur in these new-fangled eulogies that were less like elegiac farewells and more like sappy, one-liner-ridden roasts (I had attended a few with Daddy for his fallen colleagues). That was it. I did not scan the crowd from the little elevated stage. I had had Mark call Mignon but I did not really want to know if she was there, nor did I want to see the other faces full of inquisitive pity for the steadfast spinster daughter who now, poor dear, at this late date, had to make her way in the world. Hear she's selling the house. Probably had to. Doubt there was much money. Wonder where she'll go. Maybe she'll marry and have some kids. Not too late. Unless something's wrong with her. Maybe she's a—*whisper, whisper*—lesbian. Nobody said any of this; they didn't need to. I heard it all coming right through their eyeballs as they looked up at me.

We had a little reception in an adjoining room, Sinatra singing in the background, and I ducked out early. A hand caught my arm as I made my exit and there, earnest eyes and curly hair: the Marxist.

"I wondered if this was your father," he said. "I'm sorry."

I stared at him for a minute. "I think I'm supposed to say, 'Thanks for coming,'" I said.

He smiled and I remembered the sex. "I like to come to this place," he said. "So many famous people buried here."

"I have to go," I said, removing my arm from under his hand, and then, because I couldn't resist, because the day had been long and now I had to drive to Malibu, snaking along the drizzly Coast Highway back to the empty house, I added, "What's the world coming to when even a Marxist professor genuflects before celebrities?"

I didn't look back. I found my car and drove carefully around the little circle. People were still dribbling out of the reception, saying their good-byes, and others were wandering around reading the little plaques in the ground and on the mausoleum walls. And then, in my rearview mirror, I caught sight of her, of Louise—I was sure it was she, even though she had a fedora-like hat pulled down on her head. She was standing alone. I couldn't see her face clearly at all because she was too far away and it was too dark and gray out. But, yes, oh, yes, it was she standing there that day while I drove away with Daddy's ashes beside me on the front seat of the car.

I spent the last night in the house bedded down in a sleeping bag in front of the fireplace in the living room, the urn beside me. I had lit a fire and opened all the doors and windows to let the sea air in and the ghosts out. I had bought a bottle of champagne for the occasion and as I sipped, everything creaked and rattled, an ungainly ship. It had sold fast for over the asking price. The real estate agent was surprised, doubly so because the new owners, she informed me, were going to keep the house, just renovate it, thought it was charming, had a lot of potential. She thought I'd be pleased. Most people liked the idea of their houses being preserved. But I was disappointed. I wanted to think of it as gone, torn down, erased. I didn't want it to pull at me. I had to content myself with the idea that they'd renovate it beyond recognition, put in the now requisite huge bathrooms and a kitchen with one of those impossible islands in the middle of it. It would no longer be our house. It would be some mansionized mongrel. I wondered if we'd moved into town, at any point, whether anything would have been different, whether I would have been. Maybe being out here, hunkered on this bluff, was malforming, made one antisocial, tough and timid at the same time. Maybe that's why everyone else had left, carried away by the highway with its promise of escape, a new life, even Daddy in the last inning. So was it me, something in me, that made me stay? Something in the house? I had been tethered so, to its bones, its solemnity and later, to its seaside shabbiness. Things flaked and got damp and you could, putting tongue to any outside wall, taste salt. The house struck me as an aging doyenne with a girl still in her, if you had the energy for the constant upkeep, which Daddy didn't much in the later years. In his note to me, which I finally read that night after the service, he said I could keep the house if I wanted, that there was a special codicil to the will saying as much and that Mark, should I decide that, would work out the financial arrangements with Louise. I had held off reading the note because I suspected this. By the time I read it, it was too late. Otherwise I might have weakened and stayed. I knew that. So did Daddy. "It's time for you to have your own life, Clare," he wrote. "Go do all the marvelous things you're capable of."

I left the house with the dawn, after walking down to the bluff edge one last time and noting the first rays being tossed about in the slightly choppy water. I looked at the curve of the bay and inhaled those smells, sea and sage, and remembered the morning twenty-five years earlier when Daddy and I sat there listening to Mother drive away, neither of us turning to look. He seemed so old to me then, that morning in particular, unshaven, his robe flopping open to reveal his pale, skinny legs. But he was still so young, only thirty-eight, so much of his life still ahead.

The next day, his ashes in a carry-on duffel bag under my seat, I flew east, first to Philadelphia, where, on a frigid winter day, on a little hill in a cemetery near the two-story white house he had grown up in about thirty miles from the city, I left Daddy with his parents and flew on to New York to see about beginning a new life.

BOOK THREE

. 2 2 .

Since I returned from Florida a few days ago, it has been blindingly cold—literally—an eye-stinging wind laced with rain and sometimes ice that makes you shut your eyes. I find myself resenting it for the first time. Maybe dipping a toe back into winter-warmth reminded me I hail from a place of mild seasons. I can't get warm. My apartment is overheated and I get sweaty, but it's external warmth, somehow. The clanking of the radiator annoys me and causes me to jump as I sit, hour after hour, laptop in front of me, in bed or at the table, learning about hepatitis B. It is, apparently, an inflammation of the liver which causes it not to function properly, too much bile in the blood, which is what causes the eyes and skin to turn yellow. I can't remember quite if Luke had a jaundiced flush. I was so intent on him there in that little Chinese restaurant by the side of the road, so intent on his features and his words and his presence that I don't have a clear sense of his skin color. It was as if I were staring through it, the skin, to see what was on the inside. If he had been really yellowed, I would have noticed. It all still seems surreal: being there, across from him, and now being back here.

I find myself ducking Michael for the first time in six years, sliding around him, claiming work, turning a deaf ear to his poetic entreaties. I think I'm being deft, kind, just slightly evasive. I don't really tell him about Luke, not in detail. I don't want to package my nephew as just another anecdote—for me, a big difference. Michael feels it. What about this kid? What's going on? What are you doing? I deflect him with small talk: How are the kids? Any Christmas pageants yet? There is a little gleeful malice in it, I have to admit. So many solo Christmases waiting for him to get free, to be done with the familial and religious rituals, and make his sneaky way to me, bearing some small token which I would, in turn, requite with something consumable, a new bottle of this or that, a roast goose or mince pie, so we could imbibe and/or eat the evidence. He could hardly go home with a new cashmere muffler or new boxer shorts. Now, in a way, I am flaunting my own family—well, one ailing nephew, anyway—and it feels perversely good, score-evening, though on nights when I don't miss him because my head is down and I am scrambling through the online medical archives, I miss missing him because it has been second nature to me, that longing. (Longing is what I do well; I was raised to do it well.) No question, I have been having flickers of guilt-flecked sorrow since coming face-to-face with Luke Brown and I think Michael suspects as much, even though we haven't really had a heart-to-heart or face-to-face—not to mention a lie-down—since I returned. We are scheduled to meet day after tomorrow. I have never come back here, since meeting him, without longing for him with every nerve ending and through him, for the city itself.

The only time I am happy is when I am surfing the Net for hepatitis information. I am by livers possessed. Transmission comes from unprotected sex with an infected person or the sharing of needles (so which was it, Louise?) and "can be passed from an infected mother to her baby during birth." It's awful, downright Biblical. I spend hours on the Internet, cup of coffee or glass of wine at hand. Miriam, like Michael, is also peeved at me and suspects I am avoiding her and the assignment I am clearly going to owe her for the one I ducked.

"What's all this newfound family feeling?" she says archly, when she finally gets me on the phone. "You owe me a piece, you know."

"It'll have to wait," I say. We are dancing a bit. She's not going to go tough on me, though I know she can and will, if pushed. She invites me to a Christmas party and I gracefully decline.

"I'm going back to Florida for the holidays," I say, realizing at that moment that that's exactly what I intend to do.

But how, but why, but what? Louise is poised. I don't imagine us having turkey together and presents under a tree. I still see her face. I carried it home with me on the plane, the puckered, distorting rage of it, but she came looking for me and now I am going to try to help, whether she wants me to or not. She can't just undo what she put in place. That's not fair. I just need to figure out how to help, who to turn to, what doors to knock on. I hatch schemes: Hook him up with a politician or a celebrity, but it all comes out the same way. A cheap hustle that the organ donor honchos—not to mention Luke himself—would never stand for.

Then at two A.M., as I am knee-deep into another obsessive search, there it is on the computer screen, pulsing out its hope. LDLT. Live donor liver transplant. I realize I must have passed by it before in my rush, but now here it is. I sit up, heart pounding. This is clearly the solution. "While most liver donations are cadaveric (there's that ghoulish word again), live donors can also be used. Unlike other kinds of organ transplants, the liver donor and the liver recipient do not have to be a perfect 'match.'" I hadn't a clue. I thought there always had to be a more or less perfect match for any organ donation, but the liver is apparently forgiving, regenerative. Give a piece, a lobe—livers have four—and it will grow back within six to eight weeks. Elegant, amazing. There are, however, certain qualifications. Donor and recipient must be approximately the same weight and body size. They must have the same blood type and the donor must be free—duh—of any serious disease, liver or otherwise. So why not? What's the problem? Obviously Timmy and Louise have thought of this. Just as obviously, Louise, the original donor of her son's failing liver, cannot be the donor here. I wonder if she was ever sick herself—Luke didn't say—or where she got it and how it must hurt, the knowledge that it was she who gave it to Luke. But what about the father or brother as a donor? Maybe Timmy is not the right blood type and the brother is probably too small. What about all those Christians out there, especially the ones who have come in contact with Luke? Wouldn't they just be lining up to do this, give him a lobe in the name of God? Is it Luke again—refusing to let anyone take even the smallest risk? It says that donors have a one percent chance of dying and a ten percent chance of complications, scarring, or a bile leak or some such unpleasant, sick-making thing that can linger, causing fatigue and weight loss and nausea. I bet it is that, Luke being noble, even though I realize I don't really know him yet. But I feel as if I do.

And then, of course, it hits me. This is my call. I can do this. I can be the donor. I can bring my nephew back to life. I rush to the bathroom to weigh myself. One hundred nineteen pounds. I bet that's close enough. Luke is tall but very thin. I don't have any disease that I know of, never have had anything serious (better cut back on the booze right away). The blood type is the vexing one. I knew mine at some point but am not sure. I know I'm not O, the universal donor. I'm either A or B, which means he has to be A or AB (if I'm A), or B or AB (if I'm B). I ransack my brain for where I might have a note about my blood type somewhere on some document in the apartment but cannot think what or where it would be. Have to wait until morning. And then I'll have to find Luke's. His doctor won't talk to me without parental approval and I cannot imagine how they will feel about all of this, given how we parted. Anyway, I don't want to talk to any of them until I have my plan in place. I'll cajole it out of somebody in the morning. I'm a journalist, after all, know how to wheedle information out of people. I am absolutely giddy. What a Christmas gift: a lobe for Luke Brown.

But if he won't let anyone else give him part of a liver, why me? He hardly knows me. And then there's Louise. He'll make me talk to her. That I am sure of. I saw him hold her there in the rain, folding her hard against his thin chest. Mother and son. I will find a way. I start the conversation in my head, about bygones being bygones, about just doing what needs to be done for her son. It's a little weak, disingenuous. I'll have to do better. I'll start with Timmy, though I clearly will have a little repair work there, too, a little peacemaking, a little repentant groveling. They have to let me do this. They will have to. I will have to make Luke understand and he will help me make them understand. This can be done. I should do it. The perfect person. No need to feel guilt if I have a rough time, which I can't imagine. I'm getting way ahead here. There are a lot of other tests I'd have to pass, even if our blood is compatible—my liver has to be accessible; they have to be able to get the right amount to put in him. But I am, standing now on my toilet perch, window open, the frigid New York night air bringing near-instant sobriety, wildly optimistic. It is my chance to do something good, something noble, my chance for—what was Luke's exact word?—redemption.

Michael and I are sitting at a pub in the Village. We are crammed in the corner on a hard, upholstered bench, sipping our tall pale ales and eating tough little brisket sandwiches on hard rolls. The sun has come out today. It is still cold and there is still snow on the ground, but everyone coming through the door seems to bring a little of the sun in with them, laughing, stamping their shoes to get the dirty snow off. Coats and mufflers are everywhere, over chairs, on the banquettes as if, in their haste and joy, people have simply flung off their heavy clothes in momentary exultation. There are gaudy gold and silver garlands around the bar, wrapped with little twinkly colored lights. The whole place is sweaty and Christmasy and good-natured. I am happy. I am on the way. Luke's blood type and mine are the same: A. An omen. For mine all I had to do was call my own doctor—needed to make an appointment anyway—and Luke's I managed to find out by tracking down a nurse in the hospital he had been in when he was sick. I stabbed at it, missed a couple of times, then found the hospital, then found a nurse who had known him and was sympathetic to the whole donor business and just coughed it right up. "Let me just check," she said and when she came back, I was holding my breath and had my fingers crossed like children do. "A," she said, and I said, "Yes," as in a cheer, and we laughed together. Michael is looking at me as I look around the bar.

"So," he says, nodding at my clothes, "pants for a change."

"It's freezing out," I say. And I feel my hands flutter up to my hair, which makes me laugh.

"What?" he says.

"Nothing," I say.

"What's going on?" he says. "You've been avoiding me."

I look now at his face. It is the face I have loved best on the earth, rumply and slightly misaligned, that sensual mismatched lip.

"I'm not sure yet," I say. "I'm going to spend more time in Florida with my sister and her family."

"You don't even get along. Last time we talked you were furious at her and before that you were making fun of her." He takes a sip of his drink. He looks sad. "Look," he finally says, "is there someone else?"

I burst out laughing and say, "Sort of," and then see he has taken it the wrong way. "No, not like that. My nephew is sick and I want to go down there and try to help."

"Clare, none of this makes sense. It's all out of the blue. You never even mentioned any of these people before."

"I'm just going to go down there for a little while and see what I can do."

"He has cancer or something?"

"No. He needs a liver transplant." I didn't want to say it. I don't want to talk about any of it yet, until I know what's possible. My doctor's appointment is this afternoon.

"So what are you going to do, go down there and wait with him? That can take months, you know."

"I know."

"So you're going to stay down there?"

"I don't know. No. I guess I'll come back and forth."

"What about work?" he says.

"I can do it from there."

"What about us?" he says and the pain flickers again across his eyes.

"It's Christmas," I say. "I never see you at Christmas."

"So this is payback time."

"No, it really is about my nephew."

"Bullshit," he says, not angry but plaintive, if "bullshit" can sound plaintive.

"Michael," I say, reaching to touch his thigh next to me, "I don't know yet what's going to happen."

"Do you want me to stop calling?"

Six years and then, from one day to the next, no calls, no courtship, no coupling. Is it possible that's what I want? I look around the pub, all the holiday jollity. These are the places I have loved, with Michael, tucking in beside him, lovers taking refuge from the city.

"Well?" he says.

"I don't know. I just think I have to do this thing."

"Go down there and sit?"

"At least that."

"I'm going to tell you what I think. I think you're using all this as an excuse and that if I hadn't had this prostate thing you wouldn't be running away. That's what I think."

"No, that's not it."

He says "bullshit" again, but this time it is angry.

I am on the street, in the cold, bright day, before I know it. Michael is gone. I have watched his departing back, sun picking out the remaining coppery hairs threaded through the gray. He has walked away, been reabsorbed by the city, disappeared into its energy and agendas and exigencies. The temptation to go after him is huge, but I don't. I turn and walk the other way, toward the doctor's office, threading a path through the post-lunchtime crowd. Who needs a gym when you've got the streets? Fragments of things he said float in and among and through the urban racket, the boom boxes and taxi screeches. You're beautiful. More than a mouthful is superfluous. Did we just break up?

I put my head down and think about livers. That's the order of the day. At least for the moment. The waiting room is full and not just overheated but stifling. Everybody is complaining. We are just below ground level on Park Avenue. Just as I've never quite gotten used to having my hair done on high, in a second or third story, I have also never quite gotten used to having a doctor at a slightly subterranean level. The things should be flipped: doctors up, colorists down, as befits the exalted status of the former and the rather mundane status of the latter. I am scrunched between two coughers, causing me to keep head and nose and mouth straight ahead, eyes buried in a magazine so no one will talk their germs at me. I am finally called. Dr. Meyers has been my internist for a few years. He is sixtysomething, calm and avuncular, generic doctor material, generic Park Avenue doctor material. I tell him, without getting ahead of myself, that I need a workup. I use the word workup, not checkup and I see he notes the difference. He cocks an eye, as much as a calm, avuncular Park Avenue doctor ever cocks an eye.

"What's this about? You haven't been feeling well?"

"No," I say. "I'm fine. It's just that . . . this may sound crazy, but I'm thinking of donating my liver, or rather part of it. I guess that's all you need to donate."

I've got him. A full eye-cock, even a tinny laugh. "Okay, what brought this on? Are you researching a piece, writing a book? This is pretty extreme lengths to . . ."

"No, actually, it's my nephew," I say and as I start I have actually cued some tears, genuine, Michael's back mixed up in them. I have to stop for a minute.

"He has chronic hepatitis."

"A, B, or C?" he says.

"B. And he's on the list, but he's getting sicker and he's not high enough up so I'm proposing myself as a donor."

He sits down on the little chair beside the scale. I am on the papered examining table, legs kicking a bit so that there's a constant low-decibel crackly sound. I can see his skepticism or maybe just concern. Everyone is going to be a hurdle, I realize. I am at the beginning. I have to pace myself, be reasonable but resolute. No more tears.

"So, the family has asked you to consider this?"

"No, not exactly. It's a little more complicated. We're not all that close, but I am to my nephew."

He adjusts his glasses. "You know this is complicated stuff. Even if you were a match, this is hardly a cakewalk. It's a major ordeal, the surgery, the recovery, the possible side effects."

"I know," I say, "I've done a lot of research. My nephew and I have the same blood type—A—and we're enough of a body match—he's seventeen, but tall and thin. I think I'll be perfect. I just need the full pre-transplant workup, blood tests, X-rays, scan of the liver."

"Where's he having this done?"

"I'm not sure yet. He's in Florida—outside of Orlando."

"We're a little ahead of ourselves, then," he says, standing, a slightly patronizing smile. "You should talk to your family first and to your nephew's doctor—or they should—and then you can be properly evaluated."

"It won't work that way. I've got to do it the other way. I've got to be evaluated first."

"Clare, this is highly . . ." His brow is wrinkling, his calmness is being challenged. I'm losing him.

"Dr. Meyers, my nephew is religious" (I don't say the word Christian, I'm playing ecumenical here, thinking or hoping that the doctor has some orthodoxy in his own tribe; doesn't everybody now?) "and he is skittery about using a live donor in case something happens. But I'm his aunt and I think if I'm a match, he'll let me do it."

He sits back down. He has made a little tent of his hands over his mouth.

"What about the boy's parents?"

"His mother gave him the hepatitis, or rather, he was born with it, and I don't know about the father. Maybe the wrong blood type."

He is looking hard at me, assessing, I think, my resolve. Finally he says, "Okay, I'll do some blood work and an EKG, standard stuff, and refer you to a hepatologist for further evaluation. But the way you're doing this, your insurance might not . . ."

"That's all right," I say. "Absolutely all right." I am beaming and I think he thinks I might be a little nuts.

"There is also a required psychiatric evaluation," he says.

"What," I say, a little cheeky now, "don't think I'll pass?"

I start making the medical rounds, being poked and prodded and examined and scanned. I am on autopilot. I do not notice the city at all, even at its time of greatest allure. Occasionally I see an over-the-top window, pawing and snorting stuffed reindeers, mechanical elves, or hear the ding-dong of the Salvation Army "soldiers" and I remember what season it is. Otherwise no. My blood is fine, my liver accessible, my lungs and heart tip-top. Dr. Meyers calls to report all this.

"All your tests are fine," he says.

"Great," I say.

"You are still intent on doing this, then?"

"I am," I say.

"Okay, then. Let me know what happens."

"Aren't you forgetting something?" I ask.

"I don't think so," he says.

"What about the psychiatric part?"

"You don't need to do that until this all gets put in place. Then you can see the social worker at the transplant center where this is going to be done."

"No, please, Dr. Meyers. I want it all done now."

I hear a big sigh and then he says, okay, he'll get me a name at the center where I had my scan. "I'll have the nurse call you back with it."

I have dressed down in recent days, jeans, a ponytail, and a big, old, heavy, dark coat. But now, for my meeting with the mental evaluator, I dress again, not as if for Michael—skirt and pumps and silky turtleneck—but good pants, long tweed jacket, delicate makeup. Dressing for the part of the attractive, well-adjusted liver donor who clearly isn't in this for the money. That, I have read, is one of the things they look out for, somebody scamming to get under-the-table money (you can't pay outright for a body part) out of the desperate recipient or the family. Not me. Just look. That's not why I am doing this.

"Why, then?" Ms. Jamison asks, in her clipped, hard-to-place accent. New Zealand? South Africa? She is tiny, looks to be about sixty, pixie haircut, no makeup, kindish eyes. No wedding ring.

"My nephew, Luke."

"Someone you've been close to, then?"

"Not exactly." I was thinking about trying to shave the truth, just hold it a little, but I see her watching me. I have been interviewing long enough to know when a skilled interviewer is on the other side of the desk. I see now that there is in her eyes, along with kindness, what Michael calls a "built-in shit detector." She doesn't say anything. She just lets me keep going.

"I mean, I love him."

"Your only nephew?"

"No, there are two. Luke has a younger brother . . ." (I hesitate, his name disappears for a minute as she stares at me) ". . . Matthew. Matt. They call him Matt."

"What do you call him?"

"I don't really know him."

"These are your brother's or sister's . . ."

"Sister's children."

"You are close to her, then."

"We were."

She registers that, almost invisibly, but she does.

"And now?"

"A work in progress," I say as cheerfully as possible, resorting to the cliché.

"So what does she think about this, about your being a liver donor for her son?"

"She doesn't know," I say.

She gives me an enigmatic smile. "So this is all your idea?"

"So far."

"Okay," she says. "What about your own family—what do they think about it?"

"I'm not married," I say, holding up my left hand.

"I am," she says, holding up her equally ringless one, as if to say, don't make assumptions.

I'm being bested, off-footed. Nothing left but the truth, which I just blurt into.

"I just really want to do this," I say. "He is an amazing boy and he won't—at least I think he won't—let a stranger take the risk of being a donor and I just think he'll let me."

"Ms. Layton," she says, "I am not here to judge you. Over many years of doing this, I have found that altruism is always a bit muddy."

She is shutting the manila folder in which she has jotted some notes as we've been talking. "Do you have children of your own?" she says casually, almost as an afterthought.

"No," I say.

"Well," she says, standing now and extending her hand, "I hope it works out for you and your nephew."

Michael finally calls late one night. It has been six days since we last spoke, since I last saw him. There is something different in his voice.

"Oh my God," I say, "you're dead sober."

"You sound pretty sober yourself," he says.

"I am," I say, and we both laugh, gingerly.

"So," he says, "you've given up men—at least me—and booze all in the same week?"

"I'm purifying my liver," I say.

"For science?"

"No, for donation."

"So," he says, "the plot thickens. You're not just going to sit by the little bastard's bed. You're going to give him your liver."

"Just some of it," I say. "It's not a big deal."

"Clare, who are you kidding? It is a big deal. Some guy just died giving his brother a piece of his liver."

"I know, but that was just a fluke."

"As you remind me, everything's a fluke. We're a fluke. Were a fluke."

I don't say anything.

"Don't you at least want me to come kiss your tummy before it has a nice scar on it?" he says.

"Oh, Michael," I say. I hear him breathing and I want to say, "Sure, come on over. I've missed you." But I just know I can't do that, can't see him, certainly that way. I am getting ready for Christians, for Luke and Louise. I need to give Michael back. I need to clean up my act so Louise can't use it against me. I try to tell Michael this but it sounds so spurious, so suspicious, so not me.

"So what—you've been born again?" he says.

"No, not that. Just for right now I need not to . . ."

"What—fuck me?"

"Don't, Michael. It sounds so ugly."

"Sorry," he says. "I don't mean to offend you."

"I know this is all weird, but it's just something I need to do."

"And you expect me to buy this religious stuff? I've never heard you utter anything but contempt for . . ."

"For what . . . your ready-made avenue of repentance? Let's go screw the mistress, pop by the confessional booth, and toddle on home to the wife and grandchildren with a cleansed conscience. Yeah, I've had some trouble with that."

"You might have said so sooner."

"Let's not do this, Michael. I'm sorry. I love you. I will always love you. I just . . ."

"Don't Hallmark card me, Clare. I'm too old for that."

He hangs up. I hold the phone a while longer because this time I know he won't call back. Not for a long time. Not till one night when he's somewhere again, a few drinks, Yeats kicking around in him, and he can't help himself. I might do it, too, down the road, whenever this is over. Call him. I put the phone down. I think about what the psychiatric social worker said, about altruism being muddy, and wonder if Michael is right on some level, that my motives are mixed and that I might just be pulling back, in part, because I just have no stomach for the sexual fiddling that will inevitably ensue now—Viagra, etc.—when it's all always been so sweet and easy and ribald, no prompts, no (extra)marital aids and stimulants necessary. He might be. That might be part of it. I feel bereft as I stand on the toilet and look out at the night, as if the city, now that I have turned away my lover, my companion, my garrulous guide to all its dens and pubs and nooks and crannies, itself has changed, turned cold and hard and daunting, as if it is no longer mine.

.23.

I am beaming. I have just, with a pleased flourish, dropped in front of Timmy my thick medical file certifying me to be ace donor material for his son. We are sitting in the coffee shop of my new home, the same Orlando Airport Motel I stayed in last time, picking over some coconut-crusted shrimp (actually very good and not too greasy; I have eaten them three nights running). I have had one white wine spritzer and Timmy has had a beer and we are being delicate, feeling each other out. I have apologized for my last expletive-studded send-off of him from my apartment in New York. Odd circumstances, I say with a smile, to say the least. He nods his head in seeming agreement but doesn't say anything. He is a quiet man, at least with me, but not aggressively so or passively-aggressively so. That's the way he feels so far. I may be projecting, but this seems to be who he is, a somewhat laconic, sentimental (and deeply religious? haven't gotten there yet), family man and provider. He agreed to see me after I called Luke and told him what I was proposing. I hadn't spoken to Luke since I left him cradling his rain-drenched mother outside that Chinese restaurant. I wanted to wait until I had all the goods and then, nervous as a cat, like a girl calling a boy she has a crush on, a few sips of wine under my belt (just a few; the rest of the bottle at the ready should he immediately spurn me and my liver—no need to be abstemious then) I dialed his cell phone. The first time I got only voice mail, but even that, the sound of his soft, young (disease-weakened?) voice riled my heart. I waited twenty minutes and called back and he answered.

"It's Clare," I said.

"Yes," he said, "I recognized your voice."

Now what do I say? There was silence and then I said, "Hey, did you win?"

"No," he said, "came in third."

"You were robbed," I said.

I heard a small chuckle. "Happens," he said. "I'm not to everyone's taste."

His laugh gave me courage; sounded like Daddy, no malice in it, no undertow.

"Luke," I said. "I have a proposition. You don't have to give me an answer now. I've been doing a lot of thinking about how I can help and I know there are things you don't want, no articles and stuff, and I respect that—more than you know—but there is another avenue here and I would really like you to think about it."

"Yes?" he said.

"You know, I'm sure, that someone living can give you a piece of their liver. Maybe your parents have proposed that, either doing it— your father or maybe your brother—or someone else, and I don't know what you think about all that, whether it's something you have considered or . . ."

"We've talked about it," he said.

"And?"

"It makes me uncomfortable."

"Because?"

"Because there are risks. A donor could have complications or even die."

"Those likelihoods are very small."

"I still have reservations. Why should I be able to get something from someone that so many others cannot get? It's like getting ahead of the line."

"Oh, Luke," I said, with a small chuckle of my own.

"I know," he said, "I'm a hard case. That's what they all say."

"Has anyone offered?"

"Dad's not a match. Obviously Mother can't and Matt's too young. That's it for family. Anybody else would be unacceptable because of the risk."

"That's not it . . . for family, I mean."

There was a pause and then Luke said, "You mean you."

"Yes," I said.

"Why?" he said.

"Because I want to. Because I'm a good match. Luke, I've checked, we have the right blood types and everything."

"That's not really an answer," he said.

I started to mount a case, internally, but he stopped me before I could speak again.

"Why don't you think about it and I'll think about it and then we'll meet and talk. But before we do, you need to talk to my parents. I wouldn't even consider it if they are not comfortable."

"Okay," I said, "bring them on," which I instantly regretted because it sounded tinny and lightweight and a little challenging. "Luke," I started . . . but he was gone, leaving me to wonder if indeed we were going to take the next step. He called a day later— me hovering over the phone as I had so long, so hard with Michael—and said his father would come see me the next evening. I had hoped for both of them at the same time, Louise and Timmy, but it was not to be that easy. One at a time, a serial audition, this would be: Timmy first, then Louise, then Luke, if I continued to make the cut.

———

AS IF LOVE WERE ENOUGH 291

T immy is now thumbing through the file. I am trying to read his
attentiveness, ascertain how much he knows of all this, the medical details, what's involved. I am trying to be quiet, not pushy, not
New York. I have actually done something corny, chameleon-like,
shameless. I have puffed up my hair, just a little, trying to look a
little less urban hip, and put on a soft, pink pullover sweater. I feel
like I'm dressing for the part, the kind, big-hearted aunt who wants
to give away part of her liver. For love, for family. Because it's the
right (the Christian) thing. I look around the room as he continues to
peruse the papers. It's almost Christmas and there are little spiky silver tinfoil trees everywhere. There is even, in one corner, a kind of
crèche scene with giant plastic mice as the Mary, Joseph, angels, and
Wise Men. Once out of New York, it seems to be everywhere, the
spillage of faith, coexisting with the cheeriest hard-sell commercial-
ism. I am desperate to ask Timmy about their faith, when it began,
who instigated it, how rigid it is (there is still a flicker of doubt in me
that says this kid is snowing me, that he's hard-core in a way I
couldn't stomach, can't deliver a liver to) but I haven't had an opening yet. The waiter comes by, asking if we'd like coffee or any
dessert, which brings Timmy's attention back up from the pages.

"You've certainly gone through a lot," he says.

"Well, I just wanted to do it ahead, rather than offer and see that
I wasn't suitable. It all makes sense, doesn't it—I mean, the file?"

"I guess so," he says. "Louise knows much more about all this
than I do."

"The bottom line is that I am a great match for Luke." I'm trying
to modulate, not be too enthusiastic.

"Yes," he says, but he's not looking at me. His lower lip is trembling. "If it were up to me . . . That's all I can think about, Luke being . . . but it's, it will be . . . it's Luke's decision, but he won't do
anything that his mother is not . . ."

"I understand," I say. "I will talk to her." When I say that I catch a smile on his face, just a teeny corner-lift on one side but I seize it gratefully.

"What?" I say.

"I don't envy you," he says.

"No," I say, and we smile together. I am grateful. He has finally given me an opening.

"Timmy," I say, "can you tell me about your faith? That's obviously a big part of your lives."

"That was all Luke's doing," he says and the smile is still playing around his mouth but the pain in his eyes—the same look that flits across Louise's face when she speaks of their son—takes precedence. "He just came out that way. We've been following his lead since he was born." And now the tears are pooling again. I want to reach and touch his hand but I don't know what the lines are yet. I have to be careful.

"I really want to help," I say, tapping the file folder that is lying there between us.

"That'll be between you and Louise," he says.

"I understand," I say. We sit for a little while longer. "How did she get it? Was she ever really sick the way Luke is?"

"She wasn't sick. It turns out she was a carrier but never got the full disease like he did."

"And she didn't know."

"They didn't test for hepatitis then when you got pregnant. That's what we were told, anyway."

He's almost chatty, for him, and he's looking me in the eye and I see whole pools more of unshed tears, beneath his semi–crew cut and square jaw.

"Timmy," I finally say, "how did she get it?" I'm thinking drugs, of course, even though I never saw her use a needle. Or unprotected sex with someone infected.

"They think it was probably that tattoo she got when she was . . ."

"Oh, my God," I say, putting my head in my hands. "Tommy." I see him, the two of them, that day, about to be separated, bouncing in, brandishing their brand-new tattoos. "Sixteen," I say, "when she was sixteen."

A tattoo, a little heart with a boy's name in it, a boy about to go off to Vietnam, bought for peanuts no doubt from some unsanitary little hole-in-the-wall tattoo parlor probably in Venice—that hippie girl had taken them; I've lost her name for a minute—manifesting years later in the body of another boy. Tommy's revenge: a liver for an eye. He wouldn't have wanted that, no matter what. It was all so intense so early. They were, and Daddy let them be. Maybe he felt he had no choice. Maybe he felt Tommy would protect her from every-thing and everyone else. I wonder if he knew how it had turned out.

"Did Daddy know about Luke?"

"No," Timmy says. "He died before Luke got sick. It was one of the things Louise was grateful for. Phil was crazy for his grandson."

"I can imagine," I say.

Timmy reaches for the folder and starts to back his chair up. "I'll take this to Louise," he says.

"I have only one request," I say. "I want this to be anonymous. I don't want anyone to know it's me. We'll all know obviously, and the doctors, but nobody else."

I've thought this through: I don't want to be PR fodder for some Christian machine and I still don't quite know what I'm dealing with here. I like to think, too, that there is something else: some hu-mility on my part, some sense that if this is done for public applause or accolades, the whole thing is diminished, made less pure. Luke would understand; he will understand. Of course, even humility can seem egocentric, can it not? I keep wondering if Luke is leading us all. Timmy said he was and I am inclined to agree with him. But where exactly are we being led?

"What will you tell Louise?" I ask Timmy as we say good-bye, "I mean, about what we talked about?"

"I tell my wife everything," he says and it feels like a rebuke whether it is or isn't.

D ays go by without a word—two, three, five. I am living in my little motel room as if it were home. I even went and bought a small, green Christmas tree, mostly for the smell, a little hot plate, a French press coffeemaker, a small bottle of Jameson's (can't help it), and a few other odds and ends to tuck into the little minibar refrigerator. I have reverted to my dinner of choice those final days in the house on the bluff, melted cheese, which I eat by gooey forkfuls from out of a small frying pan heated over the hot plate. I also bought a book of photographs of New York and I have cut them out and pasted them around, particularly over the framed pictures. Now I awake to black-and-white skyscrapers, construction workers eating sandwiches astraddle girders hundreds of feet above the ground, the ice rink in Central Park. Cold, urban pictures. I wonder how long I will be here. I wonder what it will feel like to go back there. I wonder how long it will take Louise to call. I am trying to be stalwart, optimistic, but the old irritations start up, the sense that she is toying with me. The weather turns very warm and I buy a bathing suit at the little gift store downstairs and start swimming laps, early before the Christmas tourists are awake and the pool is toddler-choked. Then, just as suddenly as the heat came, it gives way to strong winds and storm warnings which drive me back to my room and marathon sessions of old-movie-watching while the winds bang outside the motel. Are they waiting me out, the Browns, waiting to see if I will go away, if I am not made of stalwart stuff? Or maybe having my file scrutinized by their doctors and/or surgeons? That's what I hope. I lose track of the time and don't even realize it is Christmas Eve until the phone rings around ten. Michael, whiskey-lit, in some closet in his house.

"How can you bear life without me?" he says.

"Tough," I say.

"Do you have your scar yet?"

"No, no, this is just all preliminary stuff."

"Everyone getting along?"

"I guess so."

"You sound sad."

"I am," I say.

"That's what you get for breaking up with me."

"You weren't mine to break up with . . ."

I hear a pounding and then Michael whispers, "Gotta go, we're playing hide-and-seek."

When the phone rings a few minutes later, I hesitate. I don't want to talk to him again, don't want to hear myself talk to him. But I pick it up, hoping—as I have been—for Louise.

"It's Luke," a voice says, not a strong voice.

"Are you okay?"

"I've had a bad patch. I've been in the hospital, but I'm home now."

"For God sakes, Luke, can't we get this thing going? I'm prepared to stay. I mean, I've made a little home up here in the airport motel. You should see it."

"I know, Clare, I know you're there. Mother's going to call you tomorrow. Be gentle with her."

I am sitting across from my sister in the corner of "my" coffee shop. It is early afternoon so the place is nearly empty. A wan sunshine comes in through the window. I see us, as if from some spot on high, dressed—for once in our lives—remarkably similarly. We have split the sartorial difference, she edging in from the big hair–matron side, I from the sleek, fitted career gal side, which leaves us both in quiet lightweight pantsuits with collared shirts underneath. We look like sisters today. I can see it, though she still favors Mother, and I, I guess, Daddy. We have ordered wine.

"I'll only have one," I say, after ordering. "Have to protect my liver."

It clunks, but not too badly and she manages a small twinge of a smile. I had thought to let her do the talking, thought to follow her lead, but I'm not sure that's going to work. I try something else.

"I gather Luke has had a bad stretch again. I am so sorry."

Our wine comes, a thankful distraction, brought by a chatty, middle-aged waitress named Cheryl I'm now familiar with and who always asks about how I'm doing and how long I'm staying.

"Still not sure," I say.

"Getting a jump on the drinks today, I see," she says. "I have half a mind to sit down and join you."

Louise tries to smile at her, but can't quite manage, so I throw around a little more chipper banter and then, after Cheryl's gone, we sit again in silence. Finally Louise says, "Why are you doing this?"

"Doing what?"

"Why did you come here?"

"I came after you came to me. I wasn't the one who initiated this, Louise."

"I know that. But all this hard push stuff, the file, moving in on us down here."

"Louise, your son is sick. . . ."

"You don't have to tell me that."

I ignore her. "And I want to help. That's all. You asked me to and I think I found the best way."

"So you can be the hero again."

"When was I ever the hero?"

"When weren't you? Looking after Daddy, looking after all of us, making the meals, cleaning the house. You even did my home-work." At that she laughs, unexpectedly. "You did it all."

"And that was a bad thing?" I say, trying not to sound defensive.
"As I recall you did pretty well in school till you dropped out."

We sit for a long time without saying anything. "He's mine," she finally says.

"I know that, Louise, and he is remarkable, just like you said. I just . . ."

"You want a piece of him now. People always do. I watch them."

"That's a good thing, Louise. That's what he's supposed to do, let us be a part of . . ."

"How would you know? You don't even know him. And now you want to give him your liver." The way she says that makes us both laugh and I think, okay, maybe this is it, mutual ground. Oh, Louise, we did have fun, we did, in New York, yes, just like you said, but back then, too, sometimes. You remember Jesus and Marshmal-low, no, no, that was someone else's little white dog, Elephant, Ele-phant, how could I ever forget that? And Uncle Marty and those two girls. It was a zoo but we were okay and it was fun, even after Mother left. We were okay. And I was good at that, at making us okay. I was, admit it. You have to admit it, if you're being fair.

"My pork chops were sure better than hers," I say.

Louise looks blank. "Mrs. Palmer," I say. "She was the worst."

But I've lost her again, Louise. She is back with her son. I can see that.

"How bad is he?" I say.

"We need to do the transplant," she says. "I have no choice. They've looked at all the stuff and it seems, from what everyone can tell, you will make a good match."

I feel—no, I want to feel—some joy but I realize I don't. This is what I've been waiting for, pushing for, Louise's benediction, but it comes not with love or warmth or gratitude or any recognition of the largeness of what this is, of what I've offered, and I feel cheated, completely cheated, then I realize that's part of it. You do it because it's right, not because anyone will thank you, even your sister, especially your sister. It is a bitter sweetness, another of Luke's little eye-openers, I think. This is where he is leading us.

I could leave it here. I should leave it here. I should let Louise go. Now. Reach for the check, reach for her hand, say, "Just tell me what hospital to show up at and when and I'll be there." And maybe after it's over and Luke is pink and rosy again and in his element, we will be friends, or something. I can only assume that's part of his (Christian) master plan: family reconciliation. But looking at her suddenly, remembering all that she has said, remembering what Daddy said—"She's a survivor"—remembering what they said he said about me—"She's gotten a little hard"—I say what I will regret, shoving myself off again into exile, I say: "Whose baby was it, Louise?"

She glares at me, but in the glare are incipient tears. I wonder if she will bolt now, call the deal off, but she can't, can she? She's a mother. I'm a donor. She's stuck with me and she knows it. I have her over a moral barrel here and she knows it and has been kicking at it, at me, and now I've kicked back. I want to say, "I'm sorry, it's none of my business," but her glare is winning out over her sorrow and she says it. "It's none of your business, Clare."

Then for some reason I get it. I always thought it was that older guy's, the one in Topanga, because that was the timing, always figured him to be the father when I put things together and realized she was pregnant that night of her birthday, that sudden plumpness, her sudden disappearance. But now I see in her eyes that I was wrong.

"It was Tommy's, wasn't it?" I say.

"I loved him," she says, and it's almost inaudible.

"I'm so sorry," I say, meaning it. "It must have been awful."

"What—the abortion? Is that what you're driving at?"

"Louise, do we have to do this?"

"What does your married man think about all this, about you getting cut open for . . ."

"I am not seeing him."

"Cleaning up your act, huh? Luke has that effect on people."

I fight my own tart tongue, the "You should know" rejoinder, and reach for kindness again, some note we can end on. "He is remarkable, Louise. You must be very proud."

"You know," she says, with a faraway voice, "he's always reminded me of Tommy. He has that same deep sweetness." She isn't looking at me and seems to be talking to herself. By the time she turns back, she is recomposed, her wide mouth set. She takes the last sip of her wine and I can see she is getting ready to leave.

"Timmy will talk to you about all the details," she says. "He told me you want this to be anonymous. Does that mean for you, too?"

"What do you mean?" I say.

"I mean, are you going to keep your own anonymity?"

I see what she's driving at. She is stripping me of subject matter. "Yes, Louise," I say, standing myself.

"We are grateful, you know, all of us. We're all grateful."

L uke comes the next evening. He asks to come to my room and smiles as he looks around it.

"Wow," he says. "You're really living here."

He doesn't look well. This time he is yellowish and he looks even thinner. I offer him tea and while I go fill the pot, he slips a little present under my Christmas tree. A picture book of New York at Christmas.

"I figured you were homesick. Guess I was right," he says, nodding his head at my photos.

"That's so thoughtful," I say.

"In the circumstances, the least I can do," he says.

Side by side on the bed, we sip our tea and I tell him about New York as we turn the pages of the small book. "I'll show it all to you in person someday," I say. That's the dream, isn't it? Showing my nephew my world.

"Is there anything you want to ask me?" he says suddenly, his narrow face grave and direct.

"What do you see ahead?" I say. "College, your own church? Is that how it works?"

"How what works?"

"The religious life. Your life."

"I'm not going to fit in, Clare, take on the trappings. I want to travel, talk to people about Jesus . . ." He is looking closely at me. "It still scares you, doesn't it, the religious stuff?"

"It does, yes. You're young and I just don't know where it will all end up."

"If you knew I was pro-life, would you back out?"

"I'm being tested, aren't I?"

"We're all always being tested."

I start to laugh, but his face is still grave. "No, I wouldn't back out. I want it to be a fair fight. You well and me well. And if you're going to go that way—or are that way . . ."

"You're going to have to have faith, Aunt Clare. I told you I don't believe in mixing politics and religion."

"But it will become inevitable at some point, don't you think?"

"I hope not. I don't know."

I am looking at him, eyes even more direct than usual, more blue in his yellowed face, and wondering what's ahead and whether he could turn doctrinaire, reactionary, and I realize I have no way of knowing, that that's what it means to have a kid, help raise one—or help save one. An act of faith.

"Can I ask you something?" he says.

"Yes."

"Why are you doing this? This is a lot, the surgery and the recovery. You won't just bounce back even if things go perfectly."

I laugh. "I will bounce back. I'll have you know I've been swimming laps out there," I say, gesturing out the window.

"Tell me the truth," he says.

I take a deep breath. "I suppose I want to try to make things right, something right, though I don't think your mother and I . . . I don't know. There's something else. I want you to know carnal bliss. I want you to know that kind of joy. I want you to be well enough for that."

"A fair fight," he says.

"Yes," I say. "Then it'll be a fair fight."

"I have one favor to ask. I don't want to ask it now. But later, I want you to do one thing for me."

"You mean, one more thing, after I give you my liver?"

"One more thing." He smiles.

"How can I refuse?" I say. I get up and start rummaging in my suitcase, my back to him. I turn, a pair of white shoes in my hands, one in each, and he grins from ear to ear.

"Papa Phil's white shoes." He's up and taking one.

"You know about them, then?" I say.

"Sure, he always took us there for a laugh, whenever we were in Palm Springs."

"You were there a lot?"

"Oh, yeah," he says. I see them there, a family: Daddy and nut-brown Mignon with her smears of makeup, Timmy and Louise, hand in hand, in matching Hawaiian prints, Luke and Matt, gawky, ice cream dripping from their cones, all of them staring in the white shoe window, laughing.

"You liked him, your grandfather?" I say.

"He was a nice man."

"He was a weak man," I say, allowing myself to feel it and say it for the first time out loud. I look at Luke's uncomfortable face. "I'm sorry," I say, "I shouldn't have said that."

"He always told me he hoped we would know each other. He thought you were very special."

I have been rebuked—so deftly, without a trace—by my seventeen-year-old Jesus freak of a nephew who scares me and whom I love. I've known him a minute and a half and have upended everything, left a carefully constructed life—and a lover, for whom, yes, I ache; I've been stoic down here in my little New York–bedecked motel room, but the ache is palpable, even as I've pushed it away—to sit here, the ultimate middle-aged maiden aunt, importuning him and his parents to let me gift him with a body part. This is absolutely nuts, demeaning. I have, for a moment, a flash of anger, looking around at my silly surroundings, my nesting attempts, thinking about all of it, all of them. I've got the part; I've aced the audition. But I feel a lot more resignation and fatigue than pleasure.

"You all right, Aunt Clare?" Luke says, touching my arm.

"Yes, just fine," I say.

"Well, then," he says, standing—reminding me again of how frail he is—"see you in the hospital."

"Here," I say, standing and holding out the pair of shoes, "take these. I brought them down here for you."

"Let's each keep one," he says, "for good luck."

"Why do we need luck?" I say, trying to be chipper. "Isn't God on our side?"

"We're on his side."

"Oh, shit," I say.

"I wonder if I'm going to start swearing when I have some of your liver."

"I certainly hope so."

· 2 4 ·

We are finally here in our back-gaping hospital gowns in our respective rooms on the transplant floor of a big hospital in Miami, just waiting. I stayed. I never got back to New York because Luke took a turn for the worse. Timmy called with updates. He was sort of base-level warm, asked me if I needed anything. Never mentioned Louise, never invited me to their house. I let it be. I knew their hearts were with Luke anyway. I remained holed up, waiting for my summons to Miami—that's where they had decided to do it—eating my hunks of melted cheese (I couldn't look at any more coconut shrimp or fajitas or theme park–bound families), watching CNN and fiddling with my stories. I polished the pit bull one and thought maybe I should push it into a longer form, maybe a novella. I wasn't unhappy. I felt a bit numb, waiting for my turn at bat, my starring part. The reality of it was finally sinking in a bit. There was going to be no swelling string section, no bouquets from over-the-moon grateful parents of the liver recipient. (Oh, maybe a requisite little pot of daisies.) It was going to be odd, to say the least. And it was going to be grueling. They were all right about that. I had read more and been briefed by the surgical crew via phone that it was no small thing. Five hours of surgery for me, if all goes well, Luke prepped and ready for the hand-off in his operating room.

Then twenty-four hours in intensive care with various drainage tubes here and there and five to seven days in the hospital. Then very reduced activity for a month, with a crawl back to full life. Not to mention my little boomerang-shaped, abdominal scar, my self-inflicted stigmata, my welt of redemption. I hadn't thought all this through very well, just figured I would "bounce back," hang around for a few days after getting out of the hospital, then go back to New York. In the winter. Without Michael. He hasn't called again. Is it possible I have truly given him back, possible he will never kiss my scar, possible that I fell in love with him because he could never leave me because he was never really mine?

I drifted through the winter-warm days, making myself—even on the cooler, grayer ones—swim laps in the little rectangular pool, twice a day, without fail, amused at how quickly we long-term singletons hone our habits. I got a nice, muted tan—the better to show off my hospital gown—and took to tacking my lengthening hair up into a Katharine Hepburn knot. I was preparing, going ascetic, lean and clean, as befits a liver giver. And I waited, getting not more and more anxious, but, in fact, less, so that when Timmy finally called and said could I be here today I was calm. My stomach didn't kick at all as I packed and bid good-bye to my momentary home. I went down and thanked Cheryl for her good cheer and said I would probably never see her again and have a good life.

"You too, sugar," she said, hugging me, reminding me again that I was far from New York, in another region of the country, on another planet.

Timmy came and got me at the airport. His eyes were red from, I imagined, both crying and sleeplessness. Luke was having memory loss, couldn't count some days or remember simple things. The ammonia his damaged liver couldn't process was backed up in his brain. That's how Timmy described it. I reached to touch his arm, the first time I had touched him, and said, we will do this thing and it will be okay and he, for the first time, touched me back, a pat on the back of my hand. He brought me straight to the hospital and helped me get settled in my room, putting my suitcase in the closet, offering hangers, looking me somewhat in the eye, somewhat not. Once, as I was taking stuff from my carry-on bag and putting it out on the windowsill (hand cream, paperback, slippers), catching sight out the window of palm trees, jaunty and silly in the sun, their fronds tickling the afternoon sky (don't they know what's going on here? people are near death in here, not people, Luke Brown, my nephew), we bumped into each other and he let himself collapse, just a little, against me and I put my junk-filled arms around him and we stood for a minute saying nothing.

Then the medical whirlwind began: tests. I was wheeled hither and yon in my gown, poked and X-rayed again. Temperature and heart and lungs and another scan of the liver.

"Haven't touched a drop in weeks," I proudly told the young male Cuban technician—a diamond stud in one ear.

"That's what they all say," he said with a smile. "After all this, you'll want a nice Cuba Libre," rippling the words so prettily it made me want to get out and see Miami, which I had never done. Too late for that.

When I got back to the room, there it was: my little potted flowers, violets not daisies, and a little card. "For your bravery and generosity, Love from all the Browns." I smiled, the button-down sideways sentiment of it, and wondered where Louise was and how she was and how long it took her to compose that little card. I sent a sharp little arrow of leftover love to her through the hospital corridors, figuring it would find her there, sitting beside her son's bed. *Zing.*

I had not seen him yet, did not know whether they wanted me to. The nurse said he was having a hard time and that they would keep me posted as to just when the surgery would be. That was last night, after my chicken and black beans and rice supper (thank God they chose Miami and not Pittsburgh, the other possible transplant site). Timmy came and sat on the edge of the bed, eyes redder still, and then, while he was there, Louise stuck her red-eyed face into the room.

"You need anything?" she said to me.

"No, you?" I said.

She just shook her head. "I just want this to happen," she said.

"Sweetheart," Timmy said.

"It's okay," I said. "I'm beginning to feel exactly the same way."

"Really, just call if you want something," she said, coming in and leaving a little piece of paper on my rolling table. "That's our cell phone. We're just across the street in a motel."

"Why don't you both try to get some sleep," I said "I'm not going anywhere."

Timmy stood, but he gave my calf a slight brush with his hand. I was grateful, grateful, too, when they left. Their faces were hard to look at. When the night nurse came, I asked her for a favor: Couldn't I just go see him, Luke? She said he was sleeping, that he'd spiked a fever, which is why they hadn't scheduled the surgery yet, but that if I just wanted to go in for a minute, she would take me to his room. Odd being healthy, so healthy walking down a hospital corridor in a gown. This is the place for sick people. I had actually never been a hospital patient. I'd been there with Daddy on a few occasions, the heart mainly, and gotten my bearings a little in my New York rounds, but nothing quite prepares you for being an inmate. All so bright and purposeful, even at night, TVs flickering, and all those impatient patient feet—that's what you see as you go by the semi-open doors of the rooms—hopeful feet, feet wanting to get out of this bed and touch the earth again, skip, run, dance. You see them all as you go by, those feet, and then the beehive of the nurses' station, all so efficient, everything quantified, lives measured in charts and machine readings. At the door of Luke's room I hesitated for a moment. I knew he'd look less, smaller, and that he would probably scare my heart and make me worry that he might die before we even got to do our thing, our magical liver-swap. I leaned over him. He was seriously tethered to various machines and quite seriously yellow now. I leaned to kiss his jaundiced brow. First time. First kiss. Stolen in the bright hospital night.

"Come on, baby, come on. I'm ready. I'm right down the hall."

I heard the heavy door push open behind me and turning, saw Louise's head as she quickly ducked back. I let her go. There was nothing to say. She would go somewhere until I was back in my room and then come keep her own vigil, whisper her own exhortations, maybe prayers, probably prayers. I didn't know how deep her faith really was. In my unkind moments, I figured her to be a dabbler, a pious poseur. But maybe now, Luke-led, she was deep in. Certainly now, at a time like this, no doubt. I now knew that in New York, she—they—had stayed with church friends out there in Brooklyn, friends who must have known, mustn't they, about how she was playing me and harbored her nonetheless, which didn't seem very Christian to me, but a lot of things about all of this didn't. Except for Luke. He felt like the real, unnerving deal. I stole another fevered kiss and said night-night to all the feet, covered and uncovered, that I passed on the way back to my room.

Now I lie in my gown, he in his down the hall, waiting. I have been here three days. His fever went down and back up, his lucidity waxing and waning with it, Timmy stopping by occasionally with a Starbucks, tall wet capp for me, iced blended mocha for him (we now have our routines) and we chat or watch the Weather Channel, for which we have a mutual affection. He says he misses California, the nature of the air, so much lighter than Florida and that he loves the desert. I ask about Matthew, whom I still haven't met (he's home, staying with church friends, of course) and Timmy shakes his head and smiles.

"He's our goofy one," he says, "just a regular kid."

"Must be a little restful after this one," I say and we share a small laugh.

He stays as long as he can stand to be away from Luke and Louise, and I know he is trying to cover for her, for her not dropping by. I want to tell him it's fine, I get it, but I figure now it's best just to be quiet about anything and everything.

O n day four, at five in the morning, we get our go-ahead. It feels for a moment almost anticlimactic as I am rolled on my gurney past all the sleeping rooms and into the OR. I have been told every-thing and chosen to let most of it go, just figure I'll wake up achy, maybe a little nauseous, with a couple of tubes, one to drain the bladder, the other to drain the liver. For the pain, I'll have a little morphine machine that I control with a push button.

"Don't be shy about using it," they say.

Luke will be at least five more hours in surgery, as they remove his diseased liver and give him mine and then, with breathtaking ex-actitude, hook up all the veins and arteries. After, he will be in the ICU pretty snowed for a couple of days, followed by at least seven to ten more days in the hospital—the sort of death watch for organ re-jection, if it's going to happen. This I have pushed from my think-ing, that his body might reject my liver, on every level a devastating thought. But we're not going there. I have not allowed myself (isn't the mistress's practice of longtime denial helpful here?) to think of this, let alone contemplate that he might die on the operating table. He's young, they say, should do fine, they say, will regain all his physical strength and mental acuity, they say. This is what I hope for, pray for. But to whom does a secular humanist, being wheeled down a sleeping hospital corridor, toward major surgery, offer prayers? To the hands and minds of the scientists and surgeons who make a liver transplant even possible, the breathtaking reach of their skills and focus and dexterity, all of human history and human knowledge being brought to bear now, here on my body, on the extracting of part of it and placing it in another body. To Daddy, smiling somewhere, in his old cardigan. To the fates, the sense that Luke's time and my time aren't up yet, shouldn't be, won't be, can't be. Just at the doors to the OR, as they shoosh open, Timmy is beside me. He leans to kiss me on the forehead.

"I promised Luke," he says.

And then he's gone and I'm being moved off my gurney onto the operating table and it's very, very cold and there are masked faces everywhere, all hushed and kind with their eyes and I want to say, just once, "I'm scared," but I don't get the chance.

I have never awakened in a recovery room. Things swirl before I identify pain in my midsection, just a foretaste, before I hear, vaguely, a voice saying, "It's over, fine, you . . . did." I am shivering and suddenly there is a warm blanket on me, toasty, and I smile and drift back away, waking later when the pain is sharper. This time, coming to, I try to read the clock. Five hours it was supposed to be and we started around five and it's now two P.M. Luke, where's Luke? I try to ask, but I can't be heard and then someone is there with ice chips, spooning them into my mouth, and I say, when she stops, "Luke."

"He's still in surgery," she says. "Everything will be fine."

I don't like the way she says it, but I know I'm woozy and I want to go back under where it doesn't hurt so much, but I want to know. "Luke?"

"Your surgery went a little longer so his started later. Rest now."

I have no choice. The leftover anesthetic and the pain medication take me away again. When I next awaken, everything hurts. I realize I have my little push button in my hand and I use it. Maybe I've been using it all afternoon. I can see the clock and it is now seven forty P.M. Maybe I've had awake or lucid moments. I don't know. I have the urge to pee, now that I am more fully alert, and then remember I have a tube in me. And then, of course, after a brief body accounting, I reach for Luke again. I press another button and someone comes and she says, "He's still in surgery," and unbidden, unhinged by pain, I feel tears all over my face. "No," I say. "It's over."

"Not yet," she says. "It'll be a few more hours. Your brother and his wife were here"—I smile at that inversion, think I smile, but I still feel like I'm crying, too—"to check on you. They'll be back."

Now I can't go anywhere until Luke is back on the earth, back in one of these little ICU pods like mine, with all his tubes in place. The pain and I keep each other hard company until I get nauseous and throw up, but through the bouts of pain and vomiting I still keep an eye on the clock as the night moves on and he's not back. Timmy comes by, Louise just behind him. Their faces are strained, but they force smiles out, at least he does. It's too soon for thank yous. I see that. What if my lobe hasn't taken hold or is somehow defective? My eyes must look a little wild.

"Is the pain bad?" Timmy says.

"What about Luke?"

"It's taking longer than they thought . . ." Timmy clears his throat and Louise puts her hand on his arm.

I want to be up, part of the waiting room claque, instead of lying here, feeling sick and scared to death that things are going wrong.

Louise, to whom I have barely spoken since arriving at the hospital, leans around Timmy and says with a sad but assertive look, "Don't worry. God won't let anything happen to him."

I try to smile back, but a wave of queasiness doubles me over my little kidney-shaped plastic bowl, where I throw up again, which sends a trill of pain through my gut which causes me to moan. "No," is all I can say.

Morning takes forever to come and I go in and out of a drugged sleep, eyeing the clock whenever I come to. I think Timmy comes back again to check on me, maybe twice, and then finally he is there with a tentative smile, saying Luke is out and in recovery and so far everything is doing what it should do and I reach out, forgetting there's an IV in my hand, to touch his arm, wincing as I reach. I am able to rest now, cozy back up with the pain without fighting it. They've given me stuff to stop the nausea and I start to sleep hard on and off through the rest of that day. Timmy pops by, as does the surgeon (one of them; I know there were a number) and he looks as whipped as I do. I tell him that and he smiles, or at least I think I tell him that, remarking, in my morphine haze (to myself I hope, though this I also might have said out loud), that I'm glad to see him without a mask to make sure he doesn't have a weak chin. By the end of that day, they tell me Luke is resting comfortably. (Are they kidding? They're talking to me and I've been sliced up and he's been more sliced up and I am not resting comfortably. I just say great.) I start to drink fruit juice and broth and the pain finally eases, except when I move. One more day of roughly the same and I am back in my room, leaving Luke behind, though now I feel an umbilical tether to him and there is beneath my scar—which I have only just seen; it's quite decorous and looks, they say, perfect, unangry, should heal nicely—this huge, secret smile that is threatening to break out all over the place but is held back by a concomitant terror that we are, he is, still not out of the woods. The first time I see him after our surgeries, he is still in ICU and is still pretty out of it. I am alone for a

moment with him—his parents have gone down to the cafeteria—
and I see his sweet, calm eyes there shining out amid all the cumbersome, beeping equipment.

"Thank you, Luke," I say. "Thank you."

On day five, I check out of the hospital and into the little motel
across the street where Louise and Timmy are staying. All thoughts
of getting on a plane and going back to New York have fallen away.
I am staying until Luke is well on the mend, maybe not until he walks
out of the hospital, rather, is rolled out—as I was rolled over here—
but close enough. He is doing well, so we cannot, as we come and go
from the motel dining room or the hospital cafeteria or, most especially, from his room, help but grin at each other, even Louise and I.
Once she actually puts up her hand as we pass each other on the
street between motel and hospital, I coming, she going.

"Give me five," she says, something so girlishly ebullient and
un-Louise that I laugh and slap her palm.

"We did it," I say.

I tire easily and spend a lot of time sleeping and watching TV
and I realize, even for me, there will be no "bouncing back." Timmy
knocks softly every now and again and brings me a coffee or a special
pressed Cuban sandwich he gets at a nearby stand or an update on
Luke. Louise barely leaves her son's side. Other friends visit now,
church friends. I have come upon prayer circles, heads bowed, and I
back away down the corridor until they disband. I don't see the
weather, don't feel it on my skin as I cross the street back and forth to
the hospital, stepping gingerly, pain-folded, the way Michael was
that day we walked New York after his prostate surgery. Once, when
there is a wind-whipped rainstorm, I get drenched just going to see
Luke, oblivious as I leave the motel of what's going on, arriving
soaked, causing him to laugh. They check the rebounding of my
liver and it all looks fine, should be back to full size within a couple of

months. I say to that same technician that he will have to take me soon for my Cuba Libre.

Day nine brings questionable liver tests for Luke, something elevated that shouldn't be. Nobody's voicing major alarm, but new drugs are ordered, steroids and then, as concern grows, something stronger. And then the "R" word rears its head. Rejection. His body is attacking the new liver, my liver, our liver. It is Timmy who brings the news to me at the motel.

"Oh, shit," I say, in lieu of crying and then I am crying while apologizing for swearing.

"It's okay," Timmy says, "I wasn't always a Christian," which for some reason makes us both laugh and then we are crying together, holding each other as we sit on the bed.

"They say it's normal to have a rejection episode," he says. "So we just have to pray."

"You do that for the both of us," I say, holding his hand.

But I do pray, alone in my room and walking across the street and riding up in the hospital elevator. The act of prayer, I am clearly learning, does not belong only to the religious, those who think somebody is up there. It is a human howl into the universe. At least that's how, lying in my bed, doubled in grief-flecked fear, I am choosing to see it. I pray to Daddy and the fates and some planetary sense of Justice, with a capital "J," and to the piece of my liver in Luke's gut. And I fight my own fears of rejection. This can't happen. No, no, no. Please, please, please. They give Luke an infusion of some strong anti-rejection drugs, which make him fiercely ill with flu-like symptoms, aches and high fever. He becomes delusionary again. His mother goes deathly quiet, to a place now beyond tears. She and Timmy are hand-locked at the bedside hour after hour. I stay in my motel room. I am not needed. Not wanted. I would feel lonesome but for the fraying umbilical tether to Luke. I tug it. Stay with us, stay with me.

For twenty-four hours, I hear nothing. Timmy doesn't come. I call the nurse, Flora—I know them all by now—and she says he's having a hard go but that the numbers are improving. I pray harder. Timmy comes late that night. He looks run over, but he thinks the crisis has passed. He doesn't stay as he sometimes does. There is a new, exhausted formality. He has moved all of his allegiance back to Louise. I see it. And in the next couple of days, as Luke continues to improve, and the knot in all of us unknots, I see that we will not regain the bonhomie we had in our original post-transplant high. No grins or high fives. It is time for me to go.

I slip into Luke's room when I know that, for a rare moment, no one is there. I have, from a safe distance down the corridor, watched the comings and goings, enlisted Flora to help me. He is asleep, an IV still in his arm, which is thin and bruised. I cannot help but stare. He is, regardless of our surgical intimacy, still so new to me, such a surprise. It's a beautiful day, big soft clouds in a warm Florida morning. His curtains are open and there on the sill—maybe I noticed before, I don't remember—next to his display of get-well cards and his Bible, a family photograph: Daddy and Mignon with Luke and Matthew. Daddy was weak, but he was funny and he begat us both (to use a little Bible-speak), Luke and me, and I wish he were here. I had forbidden myself the missing of him forever, it seems, but now it comes rumbling up through my delicately scarred belly, full longing. He would have been so happy, wouldn't he, that Luke and I have found each other, though he would never have been able to imagine—despite our most inventive scenarios for *The Doctors*—the circumstances of our connection.

I am standing over by the window looking out when I hear Luke stirring behind me.

"Hey, donor," he says.

I turn. He sees the remnants of longing in my face.

"You okay?" he says.

"You know," I say, "if you licked any outside wall of the house it tasted like salt."

He smiles and I realize he doesn't have a clue what I'm talking about. Then he says, "You're leaving."

"I am."

"Going back to New York."

"Yes."

"But you'll stay in touch."

"That's my line," I say. "I expect postcards from everywhere as you run around the globe proselytizing. . . ."

"When I get stronger, I think I'll come up there and let you show me around."

"Will you?" I say, feeling a thump of joy in my chest. "That'll make it easier to go."

"Not yet," he says.

"What do you mean?"

"You promised me a favor, remember?"

"I hoped you'd forgotten in all your delirium."

"Not a chance. You're leaving when?"

"Early evening."

"Daddy driving you?"

"No, he's done enough. He's been very sweet to me."

"He would be," he says. "Here." He hands me a folded piece of paper with a little map. "Hand this to the cab driver. It's actually on your way to the airport. Leave a little time."

"Luke, I . . ." I shake my head against the enormity of feeling. "Take care of our liver," I say. "We don't want to have to do this again."

Halfway there, I know. I have been so full of leaving feelings that it's not until then, halfway, that I even think about it. I got in the cab in front of the motel—Timmy and Louise there to see me off, to hug me, to say thank you and stay in touch and we'll keep you updated, a string of pro forma send-offs that leave us all feeling a little unsatisfied and sticky, given all that we've been through—and just handed the driver the little map. I didn't look back as we pulled away, sure that they were already crossing the street to go back to the hospital to be with their son. I had no idea when I would see them again. We had all behaved well. We had gotten through. Maybe down the road, at Luke's wedding. Or maybe they'd bring Matt to New York; I realized I still hadn't even met him. Must be jealous, no? Maybe that's it. Maybe his older brother, sensing that, has sent me to meet and greet him somewhere before I fly home—a ball field, a church. Maybe they've brought him down here from Orlando now that Luke is out of the woods. But then I know, just as you know anything.

When we pull up in front of the place, I think about not going in, about going on my way. But I have promised. I ask the driver to wait, tell him I'm happy to pay and that I won't be long and then I walk up the little pathway and inside to the front desk and say, "I'm here to see Mrs. Layton." As I wait I look around, the normal cheerfully depressing convalescent feel, a room to the right where people are watching TV, a little sunlit courtyard where two gray-haired men in warm-up suits are playing cards and coming down the hall, an elderly woman with a walker. *Clank, clank, clank.* To me. Of course, to me. I've been watching her come with a mixture of incredulity and recognition, looking every way—at the TV watchers and card players—but straight at her.

"Shall we go outside?" she says. "This way. There's a pretty little lawn farther out back."

I follow her slow steps, to the side and slightly behind her, so talking isn't really possible, the men in the courtyard smiling at us as we shuffle past. It takes years for us to get outside, that's the way it feels, and then we're there, sitting on a bench next to each other. I feel perched for flight, rotated on my edge of the bench to see her. Now I cannot stop looking. It's some of Luke; mostly, as always, it's Louise.

"You're still very beautiful," I say, and she is, the blue eyes, the pale, sun-protected skin. She isn't plump the way she seemed to be the day I saw her picnicking with Daddy. But of course that was a long time ago. She must be now—what?—seventy-two, seventy-three? She sees me looking at the walker.

"I had a hip replacement," she says, and there is still a theatrical stir to the voice. "It was their idea to bring me here so I could be close during Luke's ordeal. I haven't been able to see him yet, but I can't wait."

"He's doing fine," I say. "I just saw him."

"And you?" she says. "Louise says you've been very brave."

"Comes with the territory," I say. I sound brisk. "I'm sorry," I say. "There's just been a lot of emotion."

"I know, dear," she says, "I know. For all of us."

Dear. She calls me dear. Is that what mothers call their adult daughters? I have no experience of this.

"So where have you been, I mean, where are you living?"

"In an apartment near Timmy and Louise. I've been there now about four years."

"Well then, you must be Christian too."

She laughs. "Well, you know, Luke has his way."

I start to stand. "I just don't know how to do this," I say, "not today, anyway. I'll come back, maybe to see Luke, and we can try this again . . ."

"It's all right," she says. "I understand how you feel."

"You do?" I say.

"Clare, I've worked a long time on forgiving myself. Louise and I have been able to be close again and I would . . ."

"Yes, Christianity's good for that, isn't it—forgiving oneself, I mean."

She ignores that remark. "Your father was very proud of you," she says. "He sent me all your pieces."

"You guys were cozy, I guess, or something."

"I always loved your father and he loved me."

"Like I said, cozy."

"Clare, you've lived long enough, I'm sure, to know that love is complicated."

"Is it?" I say, wondering if she knows about Michael, betting she does.

"You stayed with him a long time," she says. "I wondered if it was because you felt guilty for telling him about Joe. He would have found out anyway."

"Thanks," I say. "That makes me feel a lot better." I wonder if she'll bolt soon. She can't exactly bolt but get up and clack away, leaving me feeling sad and smug and—what?—vindicated. I want her to leave and I don't want her to, not before I have a chance to try to be at least a little kind, the new liver-donating Clare who prays in the dark of night (not their prayers, okay, but prayers) and whose nephew would be proud of her and get a good report on her.

"What happened to Joe?" I say.

"He went back to his wife," she says, and I see that all these years later his going back to his wife is a freshly remembered wound.

"Did I know he was married?"

"Probably not," she says.

I reach back in memory and find the night Louise came home from the hotel sobbing and Daddy took her up and put her to bed. Something had happened. And shortly after that, Mother—this woman sitting in front of me—disappeared for real.

"What happened, I mean, to you?" I say. Our voices are quiet now, hers stripped of actress, mine of acrimony. "That night that Louise came home so upset."

She takes a deep breath and looks away from me, then looks back and she is just so radiantly sad it is hard for me to look at her. "I had gotten pregnant. I honestly don't know if I did it deliberately or whether it was an accident. They say there are no accidents. I don't know. Maybe you know, Clare. You're very smart."

I leave that remark alone. I don't know if it's got a dart of malice in it or she just means it. I don't really know her. But whoever this is now, my heart is creeping out to her.

"But Joe couldn't leave, not for good, and there I was, having broken your father's heart, pregnant. So I had . . ."

I start to reach, hand toward an arm, not crepey like Mignon's, I can't help but notice, but there's still a hitch in me. I drop my hand back in my lap.

"It wasn't maybe what you think. It was all safe and I was fine physically, but I just couldn't stop crying. I scared Louise to death and then your father came and held me and told me it was all right and that I wasn't a bad person. But I felt like I was and I kind of fell apart after that; I'd done so much damage. I hoped your father would find a nice woman and get married again."

And then I see something, some eye shift, some body shift, some pulling of the self back up out of sorrow toward pride, just a glint of, "But, of course, I was irreplaceable," and it offends me and I'm relieved to see it. I can leave now. She's back together. This is a woman I know. This is a woman I can leave. Will I see her again? Maybe. Like the rest of them. At Luke's wedding or if Matthew does something astonishing, goes into space or something, I don't know. Or if—never if, never, never, never—Luke gets sick again.

We say good-bye. I thank her for seeing me, for being direct. She smiles broadly.

"Well," she says, "you gave us our Luke back."

"Our" Luke, she says. That's okay because I'm tucked in there in his gut and maybe that's as close as I'm going to get to this reconstituted family. I don't know. I didn't do it. I couldn't do it, put my hand out across the years—not to Louise, not to Mother—couldn't show my hand. How simple it would have been. What a bridge, what a show of female solidarity. Yes, I might have said to Louise, I know what it's like. Yes, I might have said to Mother, I've been there. In that antiseptic room, legs in those stirrups. I know. I had one too. I'm in a cab riding away from these women, out of the Southern sunshine and back into the frigid cold of New York and I can't help but remember the day, not that I had the abortion, not that, but the day I conceived. There are no accidents, are there, Clare? You're smart. Maybe you know. It was our very first time, Michael and I. He had picked a small hotel on the Upper East Side near the museum, quiet and elegant, all pinks and roses, lush urban-feminine I would have called the decor if I were writing about it. It was a cold snap—*snap, snap,* everything snapping and crackling underfoot, and the branches crisp with ice—as I walked up Lexington from my apartment to that hotel like a bride to an altar. He was there waiting, phone tucked between chin and shoulder, as he let me into the room, already barefoot, jacket and tie thrown over one of those stuffed chairs by the window, a few coppery hairs peeking out. I felt, for the first time in years, shy to the bone, could not remove even my gloves or hat or mufflers. Closing his phone, he sat down opposite me, grinning.

"I can't see if you're smiling back," he said, "with all that crap on."

I managed to take off my gloves and then my hat and two mufflers. Finally he said, "Look, nothing has to happen here."

"I'm scared," I said.

He didn't say anything. He just got up and took me by the hand and led me to the bed, pulling back the big comforter. He sat me down and reached down to take off my shoes and then swung my legs up and pulled the comforter over me. He went around and turned off all the lights, so the only light came from the window, and then he got under the comforter beside me and rolled me toward him so he could hold me. Neither of us said anything. He rubbed my back and tucked my head against his chest and those coppery hairs tickled my nose. I backed away to itch it and then moved right back against him. We lay like that for hours, it seemed. The room darkened. I felt him grow hard against me at one point and then slacken again. I drifted along and found myself smiling into his chest because of all the scenarios—X-rated and not—this was hardly the one I imagined, the two of us lying fully clothed, pressed together, through the waning winter day. I made an amused noise into his chest and only then did he lift my head up and kiss me.

He excused himself to go to the bathroom and I heard him in there on his cell phone. I got up and started undressing and then without a sound, it seemed, he was behind me, where I stood in front of the window, his hands on my breasts, the wool of his pants against my bare legs and I leaned back into him. He had that heft, thick torso, solid arms. I remember thinking, propped against him: animal, male. At some point he stopped and said, "Are you okay, we're okay to do this?" (code for protection, I assumed) and I, calculating— never been pregnant, period just a week past—simply said yes. I hadn't even thought about it because all the men now came with condoms, standard operating procedure in an age of AIDS. But Michael was of an older generation; birth control was a woman's thing. I got that, but I didn't think about it. He did. Next morning when he came back—we had the room overnight and I stayed and he hurried back for "breakfast"—he had condoms and was funny about it, buying them—again, at his age—and I realized that perhaps he wasn't the randy old pro I had suspected him of being.

That was it: that one sweet, lubricious night of unprotected sex. No better than amorous teenagers, were we? Three weeks later I found out I was pregnant. I thought, for a flicker, of telling Michael. What then, though? Keep it and lose him, keep it and get him—on what terms? None of it came out right. I had been seeing that nice man who had talked about marriage and children and I thought, for another flicker, of passing off the baby as his, marrying him. Or running away and raising the child on my own, while denying him or her the identity of the father. But none of that came out right, either. I made the appointment and it was over. I walked there and walked home, after lying there a while, eating my little crackers and juice, staring at the ceiling while the cramps subsided. I never told Michael, though on certain days when he was with me and being particularly funny and playful and mine, I grieved for what had not been. Sometimes I just grieved anyway, in the middle of a boring day, or at those dinner parties watching people like Gardner and what's-his-name ogle their toddler. Yes, then, a big wallop of politically incorrect grief would hit me. You weren't supposed to go grieving about your abortion in religiously reinflamed America. Oh, no, you couldn't let your grief out there because it would be snatched up by ideologues. You couldn't say it was (mostly) the right decision, but it left a hole, a space which you could sometimes crawl into, especially since the father was someone you were crazy for but could not have. Like Mother and Joe and Louise and Tommy. We're of a piece, after all, we Layton women, aren't we? I wonder, riding in my cab away from them, whether they are secretly—at least secretly to me—the den mothers of some group of abortion-repenters, women who go around making touchy-feely, grief-stricken confessions about their own abortions. But I'm going to give them the benefit of the doubt, as I gave Luke; I'm going to think they're real enough or something enough not to go flaunting in public this particular sadness to score brownie points. I think Luke might have told me if that were part of the familial package because I pressed him on the point. I like to think so. But the truth is, I don't know, deep down, who he is and who he will become. Not really. But I love him. And I gave him part of my liver and that feels like a kind of compensatory birth, and if he turns out to be a little zealot I'm still going to have to love him. Point to your side, Mom: Love is complicated. I hope, sitting there in the sun with those old duffers in their warm-up suits, you miss me. It's about time.

Spring is finally coming. Winter has been endless, sludgey, gray, sour-making. Everyone's been sour. But, just today, there is that first inkling of warmth, the first chance to take off a coat. Still need the lightweight sweater, but it's coming, the trees stirring, taking on some green. I want to feel, I try to feel, that old climatic excitement, the seasonal joy after all the cold. I feel a smidgen but only that. I have never quite nestled back in after Florida. The recovery has been longer and slower and part of my head and heart have been with Luke. Timmy has called once a week with updates. Luke is home. He's had a somewhat hard time with the immunosuppressant drugs, but they finally seem to be in balance. Louise sends her best. He always says that and I always say, send mine back. I picture, because I cannot help it, she and Mother kibitzing about me and sometimes it makes me smile—even smirk—and sometimes it makes me angry and sometimes it makes me sad. If I keep my focus on Luke, I'm okay. I came home, in fact, to find a bouquet from him, white roses and a sweet note: "Our liver is doing fine." There was another bouquet, delivered three days after I got home, from Michael. He must have been casing the place. This one came with—surprise, surprise—a poem, the rest, in fact, of that oddly starting poem he had quoted to me in Florida, the first time I was down there: "Do you not hear me calling, white deer with no horns." It's the title that's the killer, one of those heart-lancing, hold-nothing-back Yeats titles: "He Mourns for the Change that Has Come upon Him and His Beloved, and Longs for the End of the World."

Melodramatic to be sure, but lovely. I don't call to thank him. He doesn't call me. It will peter out on the occasional Irish stanza. I go to my various appointments now on a sort of automatic pilot: to Miriam's office—I have managed to crank out the obligatory makeup piece, one of my stock-in-trade, pseudo-deep essays on women making the decision not to have children (it's all seeming a little trivial after Florida, speaking of children)—to the doctors, for checkups, to the market or liquor store, though I am still not drinking much. I have tried to regain my cooking zeal, but fancy dinners for one seem silly now, pathetic. When there was a lover on the loose, a solo dinner was a kind of delight, something to be savored between visitations. I think about reconnecting with some old friends but the effort is too huge, the news-gap even bigger. I don't want to tell anybody about the liver transplant because it would sound inevitably self-congratulatory and also because I said I wouldn't—I made the rules which Louise was only too savvy-happy to take me up on—and because it's mine. I don't want to give it away to anybody.

As the spring comes on I start to walk, miles. My abdomen is scarcely twingeful anymore and my strength is back. I walk to the tip of Manhattan, down through Soho and Tribeca, putting my face into the wind off the water, saluting the Statue of Liberty out there. I walk through the park and up the West Side and then into Harlem. I walk over to Broadway, dense and noisy, and by all the theaters and then on to the water that way. Living here, inside of the place, all tied up and taken up with it, you forget it's just a little island, but when you touch its watery edges on foot you remember that. I go through the vaulted romance of Grand Central and down to the

Lower East Side, the old immigrant tenements. I don't stop to eat. I
don't stop to look in shops or galleries. I glance at them, walking by
at my steady pace, my sweater, after an hour or two, usually off and
tied around my waist. I take in the seasonal spill on the sidewalk:
people eating at outside tables, displays of books and records, the
zippy skaters in the park. And I smell everything: garlic and exhaust
and cigar smoke and, yes, those clumps of horse manure around the
Plaza. And it is only when Michael finally calls one day that I realize
what I've been doing.

It's May, full spring. We haven't talked since before Christmas. I
seem to know it's him before I hear his voice.

"Wanna have lunch?" he says. "It's a beautiful day."

I don't say anything. I don't know what to say. There's a long
pause and then he says, "I moved out."

I'm not sure I hear him right. I don't say anything.

"So, you wanna have lunch?" he says again.

I sit down on the bed, holding the phone. I'm looking out the
window. Michael has moved out. I think that's what he said.

"Michael?" I say.

"Don't want lunch," he says. "Then how about a ferry ride or a
picnic?"

"For good?" I say.

"Yep," he says.

"Why now?" I say. "It's late."

"Not getting any younger," he says. He's trying to be breezy.
He's scared.

"Michael," I say, "it never occurred to me I could, we could . . ."

He cuts me off. "Want me to call back at another time?"

"No, no," I say. "Michael, will this work—you leaving her?"

"I think we'll part friends," he says. "We haven't made each
other happy for a long time." After a long pause, he adds, "I'm tired
of not making someone happy."

I hear him breathing. He's waiting for an answer. "Michael," I finally say, "I'm going home," knowing when I say it, sitting there on the bed in my apartment, looking out the window, that it's true and that that's what I've been doing on my walks without realizing it: saying good-bye to the city.

"You're going back to Florida?"

"No, home, California," I say. "Will you come with me?"

We fly west with the sun. I had forgotten that sensation of chasing daylight, as if you could recapture time. I say something to Michael about it but he is a little nervous for my poetics, sipping red wine as we get farther from his coast and closer to mine. It already feels like that. I am a little giddy, babbling at him about what it will be like, what we'll do, hiding my own nerves in the babble. But when we finish crossing the flat center of the country and I look down and see the Rockies, the remembered bigness of the West, I fall silent for the rest of the trip, holding his hand until we touch down in Los Angeles.

I have booked a suite at the Beverly Hills Hotel. Behind the wheel of a car again in my native city, I am alternately cautious and incautious, a little lurchy with speed and memory as we take the noticeably more clogged freeway north from the airport.

"Jesus, Mary, and Joseph," Michael says.

I see his profile against the palm trees out the window, and I think, "Oh, my, my fish out of water."

But he's sweet and when we nestle into our pink room with a bottle of champagne, me prattling a bit about how we hung out here as children and about how it now seems sort of quaint, passé, and full of tourists, he says, with a tired, suggestive wink, "Do I get to see that scar now?"

"It'll keep," I say, leaning to kiss him gently. "It's been a long day. Let's just tuck in."

I'm up at daybreak. I put on my walking shoes and take to the streets, stopping first by the hotel pool, the still quiet Polo Lounge, then across Sunset and into the little park and down onto Rodeo and Beverly and I swear I pass—no doubt in a new incarnation—that hair salon where Mother had my hair "feathered." By the time I get back Michael has shaved and showered. He's propped up in bed, shirtless, drinking fresh orange juice and reading the *New York Times*.

"I think I'm going to like being a kept man," he says.

"Who said anything about that?" I say.

"Come in here," he says, throwing back the covers. He's had, I'm guessing, a Viagra along with his juice. I strip and get in beside him, reaching to tease the hairs on his chest. I can't do more just yet.

"I'm scared," I say.

"That's what you said the first time," he says. "And look where that got us."

We banter and snuggle and finally have sex. It feels strange, obligatory, and a little awkward. It's been a long time. If Michael notices, he doesn't say anything. Afterward he is happy, whistling his tunes and planting little kisses on my scar. He asks me about Luke and about the surgery and I start to tell him and once I start I cannot stop. Luke's face those days before, so yellow and scary, then the surgery, the morphine and nausea and terror because he kept not coming out of the OR, living in the motel, the rejection scare, cool Louise and sweet Timmy and the capper: Mother in her convalescent home. I tell him about the coconut shrimp and Cheryl and the nativity mice. It all comes tumbling out as I lie there in his arms. He doesn't interrupt. When I finally stop, a couple of hours later, he says, "Nap now, sweetheart. I'll be here when you wake up."

We begin a life together. I scour the hills for a place to live, above the Strip and in Hollywood. Michael likes the hills. I tell him New Yorkers always do because they're used to sleeping up above things. But there isn't much to rent. We want home offices, a nice kitchen—

no island. He laughs when I tell real estate agent after real estate agent, "No island," both because I am so emphatic and because the island problem is something he's never encountered in New York, where most kitchens are the size of closets. We're okay for money; I sold my apartment for a nice profit and Michael has a pension. He hasn't divorced and nobody's talking about that. I don't ask. But even so, we can't find something we like. Michael says it's me, that I'm too picky and one day, on my own, I drive the other way, away from town and toward the coast. I have been resisting. But once I turn onto the Coast Highway, the ocean on one side, the hills on the other, everything familiar, and put down the windows and smell the smells of my childhood, I know that I will have to try to talk Michael, urban to his core, into coming out here. We won't be able to afford the coast itself; that I know. It's all gone crazy, tiny seaside shacks hanging off the edge of the highway, renting for a small fortune. I keep driving and then at Topanga I turn off the highway and start up. It gets warmer within a half a mile, as I curve up through the canyon, the steep sides, the coast oaks, everything sunbaked. There it is: that same little market with a big bulletin board outside jammed with mostly hand-scrawled cards and notices. I scan them for a rental and there are some but they read funky. I figure I'd better use an agent out here. I go into the market and it smells exactly the same, grainy and fruity, a whiff of incense; it smells like the sixties. I smile and drive on farther, wondering if the little stream-side restaurant is still here and it is and now I wish I had Michael with me. He'll be enchanted, won't he?

He is game, though enchanted might be too strong a word. For him Topanga is like living in a counter-culture California theme park. He shakes his head a lot when, sitting by that trickly stream, we sip wine with our salads with tahini dressing and our seven-grain burgers ("Shit," he says, "I thought I got rid of all that vegan stuff with the daughter-in-law"), though the little yellow hillside house we rent has a comforting New England feel, wooden floors, a fire-place, a simple, sturdy little kitchen and off the living room, in front, a pitched patch of grass surrounded by a tangle of flowers and weeds. We settle in through the summer, buying outdoor furniture, assembling bookshelves, doors open to the outside late into the evening. Michael takes up gardening and spends part of his days, in a dirty sweatshirt, weeding and planting flowers, even putting in tomato vines, while Tony Bennett or Beethoven plays on the living room stereo and I sit in my little office finally finishing my stories with the anchoring novella "The Wimpy Pit Bull." I've gotten a small contract for them and at night sometimes I read them to Michael, who says I'm perverse but gifted. We sleep as spoons. The sex grows less and less frequent; sometimes we rouse to it, one or the other of us, and the effort is made, the Viagra taken. Michael came home one day with a porn video and we watched it, we tried to watch it, but if you have loved somebody chemically, their touch and taste and smell, this third party interjection, all this flagrant, faceless plunging, is obscene and hurtful. We never tried it again. But nights, waking behind him, that downy back, my arms around him, the doors open, the Topanga night-sounds—rustlings and animal calls, wind through the canyon tunnel—I have a surge of pure happiness, anchored always by the scar I finger, lying there, and the thought of the nephew who occasioned it.

I hear from him about every six weeks. A postcard from Florida. He got a batch as he left Miami and he sends me health updates on them. He says he is thinking about college now—a Christian college? He doesn't say. I just say, "Go for it" and "Have you considered anything on the West Coast?" He says why don't I come back there for the holidays and I say I'll have to see, trying to finish a book, keep a garden going, raise a puppy. Michael came home with one a week ago, picked up from the regular monthly pet adoption at the old general store at the bottom of the canyon. He appears to be everything: part shepherd, part Lab, part low-slung something or other. In short, he's short-legged, thick-chested, floppy-eared, and mostly golden and makes us both laugh. He came with the name Dennis and we wanted to rechristen him, but Michael says that might cause him canine bewilderment and that, given his polyglot genes, we'd better not confuse him any more. The dog with us at night in the bed, scrunching his warm body between us or around us, is a tender balm for our diminished lust.

I don't try to revisit that Topanga house up the long, steep driveway. I haven't taken Michael up to our bluff, either. I thought I would, almost right away after we got here, but I still haven't. It just seems superfluous, somehow. I know the houses, what happened in them. Seeing them now won't change that, won't make them any more mine or any less mine. I understand that. I do, however, delight in taking him to all the ultra-L.A. spots, Forest Lawn and Grauman's Chinese Theater and Venice Beach. Everywhere, he tut-tuts about the excesses, the vulgarity, the on-display flesh.

"Told you you were an old puritan," I say.

Everywhere, he buys souvenirs for his grandchildren. I ask if he wants them to visit or wants to visit them. Not yet, he says. He spends more time on the Internet. "I always wanted to be a surfer," he says, coming out at night, adrenaline up, with printouts of breaking news stories which, pacing and declaiming, he reads to me as he used to recite Yeats or Dylan Thomas. I think he's also e-mailing a lot, his kids, those grandkids. I try not to think too much of what kind of future we all might have together—us visiting them, them visiting us, a reconstituted family like that one of mine in Florida. They have asked me for Christmas, no doubt at Luke's behest, and I know Michael's children have asked him to come back, but we are both reluctant to go— this thing of ours, in this little house, Dennis, tomato plants, matching "Venice Beach" sweatshirts, so unexpected and sweet we want to savor it, without getting involved in any of those other cross-country entanglements.

We have Christmas by ourselves, our house echoing day and night with Michael's moody and, I admit, moving Gregorian chants. I picture monks in high, austere monasteries. Michael is stunned at the weather, seventy-eight degrees on Christmas Day. He mutters a lot, bemoaning the warmth, but we celebrate by barbecuing a turkey and drinking champagne all day, actually making love after, Viagra-less, on the living room sofa, Dennis snoring at our feet. It's different, not a hard hard-on, but we are tipsy and the softness is not bothering. We work with it, not in an arduous way, just gently, bringing pleasure to each other. We have both, during the day, wandered out into the yard with cell phones to call loved ones out of earshot of the other. I talked to Luke and Timmy and even said "Merry Christmas" to Mother. Luke came back on at the end, saying his mother had her hands in the stuffing and couldn't talk right now but sent season's greetings.

My book is turned in and accepted and Michael throws me a little party, inviting the one couple we have become moderately close to, an aging hippieish woman with long hair and a big laugh and her younger aspiring chef of a boyfriend. When Michael holds me in his arms that night he says, should we swap, we've got the ages all loused up here. I say, you've gone California awfully fast, haven't you, this talk of swapping. And he says, I was thinking of you. It's not too late. You could still have a family. And I say, I have my family right here. And I say, I'm happy.

We celebrate the anniversary of our first year here and on a fog-fuzzy spring day I finally drive him up the coast to see our house on the bluff, to see if it's still there in any form. Gone is our big, old gate, replaced by a mechanical grillwork thing that bespeaks major security. I park on the shoulder and peer down and see the bastardization of what once was—gables and turrets—and I can't be sure if it's our house transmogrified or a wholly new one. Michael says, taking my hand, "Let's go home."

Waiting for my book to come out I try to start another one, but find myself reading back through all my old books, even my college books, all of them heavily annotated and underlined. We spend the summer in the yard, I reading under a big hat while Michael, grousing about weeds and rapacious insects, works in the garden, music playing in the background. I come one afternoon upon a passage about forgiveness in one of my old Hannah Arendt books. It is underlined three times, a star by it. It must have gotten my attention way back then and, reading it again, I seem somehow to remember it. "The discoverer of the role of forgiveness in the realm of human affairs was Jesus of Nazareth. The fact that he made this discovery in a religious context and articulated it in religious language is no reason to take it any less seriously in a strict secular sense." Forgiveness, she says, "is the necessary corrective for the inevitable damages . . ." I read it over and over, as I must have done back then as a dogged student and a sassy, methodical fornicator. Here he is: Jesus made safe for a secular humanist, not just safe, essential even. I tap my scar through my cotton T-shirt. For good luck. For Luke. For Jesus. Can you imagine that.

It turns very hot. Michael and I sleep outside sometimes on an old mattress and I tell him about the night of the crying moon. In early September the hot winds blow and there is a fire warning and we spend a few days worrying and watering everything down—the brush on the hillside, the dried-out patch of grass that is our garden, the roof—and watching things burn down on television. Michael hates the winds. He says that they're creepy, that the malevolent weather he's used to is cold not hot. I tell him that's not true, what about those humid summer days when there are those terrible blackouts and people get trapped in elevators? I ask him if he misses New York and he says, sometimes.

It's early morning and I am in the garden watering his new flower bed, Dennis biting at the stream of hose water, as is his habit, Michael in the living room watching the morning news shows, as is his habit. I'm reaching to turn off the water when I hear the phone ring. Then Michael, alarmed. "When? Where?" I rush in. He is standing, phone still at his ear, morning-rumpled in T-shirt and boxer shorts. I know instinctively not to go to him. I want to say, "Just tell me it's not one of the kids," but I just stand inside the door and let him finish the call.

"It's my . . . wife," he says. "A heart attack. They're going to do surgery."

After that Michael is on the phone a lot of the day. He calls his kids and grandkids, they call back—a transcontinental telephone marathon. He talks to doctors, old friends, while I stay on the periphery, offering a sandwich, a glass of beer, a hand brush of the back. I get into bed early, Dennis next to me, leaving Michael in the living room still working the phone. He finally crawls in beside me in the early morning.

"I'm sorry," I say. "You go back. It's okay."

"Just a week," he says. "I don't want you getting used to life without me." I turn into his chest and put my arms around him.

Two days later I drive him to the airport. He is holding my right hand in his, I'm steering with the left. Down the canyon, past the little market and the general store at the bottom and onto the Coast Highway. We have the windows down to let the sea air in. It's early and the ocean is sparkly in the morning sun. New York seems very far away. But not. Michael will touch it for both of us and then come home. This is his home now, my pub-crawling, urban Irishman— with me, in Topanga Canyon. The days without him have some of that old voluptuous bittersweetness of those weekends in my apartment, the little solo meals, missing him, knowing he would come back with the week. When he comes back this time, he misses New York, sometimes fiercely, and I learn to leave him alone with it.

I am at work on a new book, thinking about calling it *Inevitable Damages*. She wouldn't mind, would she, our brilliant Hannah? Luke writes to say he's planning a June visit with "his friend." Was I right all along—my nephew is of that persuasion? Or am I being ridiculous and reading into things? We shall see. I start planning all our outings, the rounds that I took Michael on when we first got here. In his next postcard Luke gives me a heads-up: Louise has written a book that is about to be published: *A Mother's Love: The Story of a Son's Liver Transplant*. I have to assume that she honored my anonymity but am a little frantic until I am assured, by Luke—via next postcard—that she has. He offers an advance copy, but I say no thanks, I can wait. One cool, rainy day, a fire going, I am channel-surfing between bouts at the laptop while Michael snoozes on the sofa, and there she is, smack-dab front and center on *Oprah*. Beat me to it, didn't you? She looks—you know how she looks?—great, Midwestern Mom chic great via Oprah's makeover artists, not unlike she did that time in New York when we left Bloomingdale's. Hair quieter than normal, makeup quieter. I wonder if she's had some media coaching. She's camera direct, just the right amount of sentiment. Good tears. The audience loves her. They love her son, the one she describes. They love her faith. They love her commitment to the "Luke Foundation," her new organization for donor awareness. Listening to her, I can't help thinking about Tommy. What if he's watching with his one good eye, trying to shush the kids or grandkids bouncing around him while he watches, on television, the still lovely, middle-aged woman who once broke his heart and cost him half his sight. Inevitable damages. I remember something Michael said to me.

"I recognized you right off," he said. "You're just like me—tough on the outside and soft on the inside. Probably better to be the reverse, but that we don't get to choose."

Louise is that reverse. I guess she always was. I struggle with forgiving her (and Mother): the leavers. But Louise gave me Luke—I never forget that—and I gave him back repaired and now we are stuck in the animosity of mutual gratitude. But I always miss her, especially up here in the canyon or on a beautiful day along the water. Not as she is now but as she was then. Maybe I'll write about it, about her. After all, she got to write about my liver.

June is imminent. Luke is coming. I wonder what Michael will make of him—or vice versa. He says he'll leave us alone a lot, doesn't need to do the tourist rounds again.

"I'll stay here and keep the home fires burning," he says. He's being accurate. He's turned into a mean barbecuer. "Don't tell me he doesn't eat meat," he says.

"I didn't say that."

"I'll bet he doesn't. Those religious types are often vegetarian. You know—all God's creatures and that shit."

"I don't know about meat, but he doesn't like swearing."

"Damn," he says, winking. "Don't worry. I'll be good."

That's what we'll all try to be, in whatever fashion—good—under Luke's delicate stewardship. I hope he'll stay for a while; maybe he'll start a prayer group for the local surfers. I don't know, something. Maybe we'll go to Palm Springs. I hope he doesn't want to moon around and match livers and talk about redemption. I hope he wants to do everything. I think he will. I'm sure he will.

ACKNOWLEDGMENTS

There are those in a life without whom good things would not be possible. In mine, they are:

My husband, Karl Fleming, who has given me decades of love, conversation, and his brute passion for words.

My agent, Lynn Nesbit, who has given me years of guidance and friendship.

My forever friend and early reader, Judy Kessler, who encourages me daily to keep going.

My mother, Phyllis Avery; my sister, Avery Taylor Moore; and my niece, Martine Avery Moore, who are my solid ground.

All the friends who walk with me and talk with me during the months I rattle around in my fictional universe, including my pals at the Sun Valley Writer's Conference.

My personal tutor in the whys and ways of liver transplants, Dr. Vera Delaney, who deserves special mention.

And, of course, all the people at Hyperion, who have brought their enthusiasm and talents to this book and made my transition into fiction so happy.